Nothing Good
Gets Away

Once & Future Book 4

Meredith R. Stoddard

Fredericksburg, Virginia

Erkita Press
P.O. Box 293
Spotsylvania, VA 22553
www.meredithstoddard.com

Publisher's Note: This is a work of fiction. Names, characters, places, and incidents are a product of the author's imagination. Locales and public names are sometimes used for atmospheric purposes. Any resemblance to actual people, living or dead, or to businesses, companies, events, institutions, or locales is completely coincidental.

Book Layout © 2014 BookDesignTemplates.com

Nothing Good Gets Away/ Meredith R. Stoddard. -- 1st ed.
ISBN 978-1-7333933-5-5

For Eric, my careful steward

CHAPTER ONE

April

Edinburgh, Scotland
April 1996

Morning came too soon and not soon enough. In the blue-gray hour before dawn, Sarah drifted between sleep and self-doubt. Each time she opened her eyes in the unfamiliar hotel bed, the light filtering through the blinds grew brighter and the pressure in her chest mounted. For once the drowning feeling that had plagued her dreams since childhood now came to her when she woke. Then Dermot would shift in his sleep, pulling her closer. His embrace making her warm and languid, she would relax enough to drift off again. Her dreams in those brief bouts of sleep were filled with castles and car accidents, princes and prophecies, wizards and women lost in time.

Finally, she opened her eyes to see Dermot standing in front of the window. The rising sun struck his back sending shafts of light around him. His silhouette was rimmed with it like golden armor. Her knight, her champion. He was giving up everything to be with her, to live a life always looking over their shoulders and wondering what would happen to the friends and family they left behind. What would happen to his mother? She wondered once again how she could possibly be worthy of that sacrifice.

"Good, ye're awake." He offered her his hand. She took it, and he pulled her into a sitting position. Planting a kiss on her forehead. "We have time for a shower, but we've got to get going."

Sarah rubbed her eyes. As sleep ebbed away, the here and now came back into focus. Her legs were sore from trekking through the Highlands followed by hours in the car. Her elbow ached where it had been dislocated in the car accident two days ago. Her brother had warned her it would hurt for a few days when he had popped it back into place. Had that really only been two days ago?

Dermot started the shower in the bathroom. He returned to rummage around in a plastic bag on the dresser retrieving a bottle of antiseptic. "Come on, sleepyhead. We need to treat those cuts again. Gorse thorns can cause terrible infections."

Sarah looked down at the lattice of scratches that covered her arms and part of her legs. She had fallen out of their wrecked car directly into a gorse bush. Considering the recent turn her life had taken, it would be just her luck to escape the paparazzi, and the clutches of the Stuarts only to die of sepsis that she got from a gorse thorn covered in sheep poo. That thought got her out of bed and into the shower. Although it was definitely nice to find a naked and wet Dermot Sinclair waiting there to wash her back. All they had to do today was make it out of Scotland. Then they might just have a chance.

***

They stepped off the bus on Princes Street near North Bridge. Slinging his bag over his shoulder, Dermot surveyed the street hoping that the heavy foot traffic meant they could blend in. Sarah slipped her hand into his and their fingers laced together. The coiled tension that knotted the muscles in his shoulders eased a fraction. He marveled at the experience of actually holding her hand in a public place. After hiding his feelings for her for so long, to stand in the sun with her was indescribable. Soon they would be able to live together without any restrictions. As soon as they met up with Des, Sarah MacAlpin and Dermot Sinclair would disappear. They would start again with new identities.

He lifted their joined hands and kissed the back of hers. She rested her cheek on his arm. Turning, he found her eyes on him, crystalline green and brimming with love. Her hair was once again tucked up under a brown knit hat to hide her distinctive curls. He flashed back to the wee hours of the morning when she'd awakened him and they'd made love again, her hair brushing his chest soft and ephemeral. She squeezed his hand in reassurance.

Someone on the street bumped his other shoulder reminding him that they needed to be moving. They merged into the flow of pedestrians up North Bridge. To the High Street before turning down Cockburn. The cafe where he was to meet Des was a few doors past Fleshmarket Close. He walked Sarah to a tourist shop across the street. He didn't like leaving her there, but after Des's warning the day before, he wasn't entirely sure he could trust his old friend. She could watch from a safe distance here and her American accent wouldn't be noticeable among the tourists.

They spent a few moments browsing the souvenirs. The shop keeper fortunately seemed largely indifferent to the half dozen shopping tourists. After a few minutes, he picked a snow globe from a shelf and stepped closer to Sarah, who was combing through a rack of tartan ties.

"Amy would love this." He spoke loud enough for the middle-aged woman a few feet away to hear.

Sarah leaned in as if to look at the snow globe. "You're right. She would."

In a low voice. "I'm going. If anything, anything happens across the street, or if I'm not back in ten minutes…"

"Don't say it." She hissed.

"…Take yer papers and go. Start a life somewhere."

"I'm not leaving you." She was adamant.

He appreciated her tenacity, but he hoped that she would leave if it came to that. Behind her, another tourist walked within earshot. "I think that saltire tie would be great for yer da."

Sarah looked over her shoulder at the older man who was a few feet away looking at golf club covers. She turned back to him and lowered her voice to just above a whisper. "I wouldn't blame you if you changed your mind. But if that's what this is, just tell me now."

He smoothed a hand down her arm and caught her eyes with his. "My mum told me to take care of ye. That's what I mean to do. Nothing else matters."

"You're giving up so much."

"Ye're worth it. We are worth it. Never doubt that." He whispered. "Dinna be here in ten minutes whether I come back or not."

She handed him the snow globe before pressing herself against him with a devilish look in her eyes. "Have I mentioned how much I liked waking up next to you this morning?"

God, he loved her. "I mean it. Stay safe, no matter what." He planted a kiss at her temple and deposited the snow globe on the shelf beside them. He left making his way across the street.

***

Sarah left the ties and positioned herself by a rack of T-shirts where she could watch the cafe through the shop window. She saw Dermot cross the street and go inside. Naturally, the mysterious Des had not picked a table near a window for their meeting. Dermot disappeared behind the glare of the sun on the glass. Sarah forced herself to look at the shirts to keep up the pretense of souvenir shopping. She rolled her eyes at one that read 'Kilt Inspector' and flipped past a bright yellow one with the Stuart lion rampant. She couldn't help feeling as if they were being stalked by that lion. There she was hiding in the tall grass hoping that she and Dermot could get to a safe place before the Stuarts could devour them.

Out of the corner of her eye, she noticed a motion from across the street. A couple of women were coming out of the cafe laughing at something. They strode on down the street continuing their conversation. Sarah shifted her eyes back to the cafe. All she saw was a typical day on a street in the Old Town. Tourists strolled by pointing at the architecture of the stone buildings or pulling their suitcases down the steep, curving street to Waverley Station. Locals bustled by on their way to work. Nothing out of the ordinary. No stalking lions. She checked her watch. Five minutes.

Another shopper began flipping through the shirts on the opposite side of the rack, and Sarah's pulse leapt. She hoped that tourists would be too interested in their own travels to pay attention to the local news or tabloids. It was why she had stayed at the hotel yesterday while Dermot had run about town getting cash and if all went right across the street a new identity. It had been weeks since the tabloids had first published her picture and connected her to billionaire playboy James Stuart. Weeks of cramming her hair into a hat and wearing fake glasses. Weeks of living in fear of someone recognizing her. Now that she and Dermot had disappeared after getting run off the road by an assassin in the Highlands, James himself was flashing her picture all over television. If they stayed in Scotland much longer the hat and glasses were not going to be enough of a disguise. Sarah glanced up at the woman who gave her a cordial smile and moved on to the next rack that held rugby shirts.

She felt a second of relief before checking her watch again. Seven minutes. Dermot better come back soon, or she might have to go into the cafe to get him. She had no intention of leaving without him, even if that was what he'd told her. With all that he was willing to give up for her, she rather brave the lion than be without him. She picked a shirt with some clan badge on it and held it up in front of the window. Looking past the shirt she eyed the cafe and tried not to look like a ball of nerves.

CHAPTER TWO

Sarah turned her attention to a rack of hats on the wall near the window and selected a black one with the blue and white Scottish flag printed on the front. Maybe the brim would shield her face even more. She checked her watch again. Nine minutes. She took the hat to the counter and paid for it. The young man tending the shop was far more interested in the magazine he was reading than he was in the people in his shop. He barely looked at her as she paid for her hat with some of the cash that Dermot had given her. They had been afraid to touch her bank accounts, so were relying on the money that he had squirreled away for a rainy day.

She was putting her change back in her wallet when a hand slid around her waist and Dermot's voice rumbled in her ear. "Miss me?"

His face showed a hint of a smile quieting her nerves a fraction. "Every minute."

"Let's go." His hand on her back steered her toward the door. "Ye'd best wait to change yer hat."

"Did you get what you needed?" She asked when they reached the street.

"Aye, I did." He leaned down to her ear as they walked keeping his voice low. "I also got a warning. There are a lot of people of Des's ilk looking to collect James's reward."

"Great. That's going to make getting out of Dodge a lot harder." By 'Des's ilk' Dermot meant businesspeople operating in the wrong side of the law. Dermot's army buddy seemed to do a good business forging documents among other things. They walked up Cockburn to the Royal Mile. "Wouldn't it be faster if we cut through Fleshmarket Close?"

"I think we're safer on the busy street. More people to blend in with."

"Okay, but can we slow down a little." Sarah was struggling to keep up with him. "My legs aren't as long as yours."

He slowed the pace and they walked along the High Street trying to look like a couple enjoying the day. They had just crossed North Bridge in front of the old British Linen Bank building when Dermot leaned down again to say, "I think we're being followed."

Sarah's pulse leapt. Dermot took her hand and picked up the pace. They walked briskly down North Bridge before veering off the street into a hotel.

"Look like we belong." He whispered. She wasn't sure how they would manage that. The hotel was a posh one and they were dressed for utility in their jeans and jumpers. But as Duff always told her, confidence can be very convincing. So, she pulled her shoulders back and tipped her chin up striding through the lobby as if they knew exactly where they were going.

Without slowing his pace, Dermot pulled her down a hall that led to a lounge and restaurant. They ducked into an alcove that held a chair and a house phone on a small shelf. Dermot whispered to her. "Pretend to make a call. Dinna turn around whatever ye hear."

Sarah picked up the phone and pretended to be talking to someone about something completely inane. Sneaking a peek over her shoulder, she saw Dermot press himself to the wall near the opening of the alcove so that he couldn't be seen from the hallway behind her. She forced herself to say something like, 'You don't say,' or 'That's what I thought.' To make her pretend phone call sound convincing.

She didn't hear footsteps behind her as the man approached and resisted turning around when a voice with a vague Mediterranean accent said, "There you are."

In the next second, Sarah heard a sharp crunch followed quickly by a pained grunt. Before she had a chance to turn around, Dermot pulled her back into the hallway and deeper into the building.

Sarah glanced back to see a swarthy man on his knees in the alcove. He had one hand cupping his nose while the other was braced against the wall. The man's eyes locked with hers as Dermot pulled her around the corner. The pure malice in that look gave her chills.

Another turn and they were in the hotel's kitchen. That early in the day, the staff was sparse, but the few there were startled by their sudden entrance. With complete confidence, Dermot asked. "Where is the back door?"

A dumbstruck woman at a cutting board lifted a hand and pointed past an enormous walk-in refrigerator.

"Cheers." Dermot said as if it was perfectly normal for strange people to go streaking through their kitchen.

They hustled around the refrigerator, out a metal door, and into the close that ran behind the hotel. Closes were a network of narrow alleyways that ran between the main streets of Edinburgh's old town. They were usually too narrow or steep for cars, but some were wide enough that they supported businesses and residences. This one appeared to be mostly walls and stairs. Dermot stopped short and looked both ways before turning downhill. After a short span of stairs, they came to a door with a pointed arch. He muttered, "Please be open."

His shoulders sank with relief when the ancient iron latch gave way. He yanked Sarah into the dark room beyond and closed the door behind them.

They stood still for a moment listening for activity inside. A light came from down the hall and Sarah thought she caught a glimpse of stained glass. "Is this a church?"

"Aye, Old Saint Paul's." Dermot kept his voice low. "We'd best keep moving. I think I bought us a few minutes, but not much more."

"What did you do to that man?" She had known that he had killed one man who had been sent to kill her, but she hadn't been there for the actual deed. It was one thing to know that he was capable of that sort of violence, but another entirely to have it happen right behind her. She knew about his time in the army and his security work, but she had mostly seen him in an academic setting. This Dermot, coiled and ready to strike was new to her.

"Elbow to the nose, and a punch to the kidney." He led her down the hall. He was matter of fact about it as if he'd told her it would rain that afternoon. He stopped in the doorway to the sanctuary and looked back at her. Something of her alarm must have shown on her face because he stopped and lifted a hand to her cheek. "I had to slow him down. I've done far worse to keep ye safe, and I'd do it again."

Once again, Sarah wondered how this had become her life. "I know, you're right."

"The main door of the church is on Jeffrey Street. We should be able to get a taxi there." He took her hand again; his grip was gentler than it had been on their mad dash from the hotel.

They made their way quietly through the sanctuary. Sarah wished she'd visited the church before when she'd had time to admire it. As it was, she got the vague impression of polished wood, stained glass, and gothic arches. They came out onto Jeffrey Street, and tried in vain to hail a taxi. Every car that passed them seemed to have a passenger already.

"Damn!" Dermot swore after yet another car drove past.

"We're too close to the train station." Sarah observed. "They're all picking up fares there. They don't need to stop on the street."

"Ye're probably right. Train station it is. We can blend in with the travelers."

They crossed the street, Sarah looked back in time to see the man from the hotel coming out of the close beside the church. His face was bloody, but he seemed to be moving well enough. "Dermot."

He whipped his head around and caught sight of the man, who was already making his way across the street. His hand was in his pocket and there seemed to be something poking out of the corner. "Bollocks! I think he's got a gun."

Dermot broke into a run. If he hadn't kept a good grip on her hand, Sarah would never have kept up with him. "He wouldn't shoot us on the street. Would he?"

"I dinna mean to find out." They went through the gate leading to the station and hurtled down the stairs dodging around other passengers. Sarah's foot slipped on the bottom step nearly sending her tumbling across the floor. Dermot was there to catch her by the elbow and pull her back up. He took the opportunity to look behind them. "He's still with us, but not moving fast. That kidney shot must have been harder than I thought. We can lose him in the platforms."

Sarah found her feet, and soon they were making their way among the platforms. Dermot always kept a wary eye on the direction where he thought their would-be attacker was.

"Maybe we should get on a train." They stopped to catch their breath after a few minutes of weaving their way through the train platforms and travelers. They had lost sight of the man who was chasing them, but now he could be anywhere just waiting for a train to move out of his way or for them to come out into the open. "We need to get out of the city, and this would be a way to do it."

"It would." Dermot craned his neck trying to look through the windows of the train in front of them. "The alternative is up the steps to Princes Street, but we'd be in the open up there. We just have to find the right train."

"Or would any southbound train do?" They needed to get out of the U. K. But getting out of Edinburgh would be a step in the right direction.

Dermot grunted thoughtfully and turned to look at the large display of departing trains. "I had hoped to leave by ship. They'll be watching the airports and possibly here. But they can't watch every dock in Scotland. We can get a train to Berwick upon Tweed and catch a freighter from there."

"A freighter?"

"Aye, some will take a few passengers, or let us work our way across." He took her hand again and pulled her further down the platform still scanning for their pursuer.

"Across to where?"

"Anywhere that Alba Petroleum doesna have an office." He shot back, "But we can start with Calais."

"Okay, so when is the train to Berwick upon Tweed?"

***

Dermot wished he felt as confident about that plan as he sounded. She was trusting him to keep her safe from all enemies, but he wasn't sure who all the enemies were. So far, their big plan to run away together hadn't even made it outside of Edinburgh before the Invigilare were on their trail. They might be running from the Stuarts, but at least the Stuarts wanted them alive. The zealots that made up the Invigilare, an underground group of militant Catholics convinced that Sarah's child would be the Antichrist wanted her dead. Fortunately, they also wanted to stay in the shadows. That was something he could use.

He hoped that once they were out of the city, they would be less recognizable. Taking the train was a risk. The more people were traveling with them, the more chances for them to be recognized. But Sarah was right. The priority now was to get out of the city. Even if they were recognized on the train, no one could stop them until they got to the next station.

He skimmed the departures board until he saw what he was looking for. The next train south was leaving in ten minutes, two platforms away. They could go all the way to London or get off at any port in between. He pulled Sarah into a shadowed corner behind a rack of maps and timetables. "Wait here. I'll go get us tickets."

He could tell by her mutinous look that she didn't like splitting up, but she nodded. He pulled his jumper off in a small effort to change his appearance and kept his head down. The woman at the ticket counter smiled broadly and even flirted a little, but she didn't seem to recognize him. Tickets in hand he went back to the corner where he'd left Sarah. She was still there, looking anxious but beautiful. He couldn't resist kissing her. "Ready?"

"As I'll ever be." Now, they just had to get to the right platform.

"We've got to get across the footbridge to platform ten and avoid our friend for the next ten minutes. He tucked a stray curl under her hat.

"We can do that easy." Her face showed nothing but complete faith in him.

Once again, he lifted their joined hands and kissed the back of hers. They made their way up the stairs to the footbridge where they could cross over to the stairs to platform ten. Parts of the footbridge that spanned the station were railed with intricate ironwork that could offer them some cover. But the main part across the station had glass railings. They'd be sitting ducks. "Try to stay a meter or so in from the railing."

Dermot kept an eye on the concourse below, looking for their man. He didn't see him on the platform anymore. He supposed it would be too much to ask for the man to give up.

They were crossing over the concourse near the ticket office when he heard Sarah's sharp in-drawn breath. Following her gaze, he spotted the man near a kiosk on the level below them. Just as Dermot laid eyes on him, the man turned their way. Their eyes locked and the man sprinted toward the stairs to intercept them. "Damn!"

Dermot tightened his grip on Sarah's hand in anticipation of another chase when she gasped again. "Is that Calum?"

"What?" He turned to see Calum Ridland, the Alba Petroleum Security guard who had been one of Sarah's bodyguards until they had left for their research trip, coming up the stairs behind them. Dermot might have been able to handle Calum, but he came with reinforcements.

"Shit! Archie Sinclair." He bit out.

"Relative?" Sarah asked.

"Fleming's father." He whipped his head back to the Invigilare assassin in front of them. Calum and Archie were on their way up the stairs, effectively cutting off any exit they might have had. Short of jumping over the railing to the concourse below, they were trapped. Jesus, he'd promised to keep her safe last night, and had failed her on their first day out. Feeling one hundred different kinds of worthless he turned to her. "We're out of options. D'ye think we can get past the assassin or do we take our chances with the Stuarts?"

Sarah looked back and forth between their pursuers who had stopped at the tops of their respective staircases and stood poised waiting to see what they would do. She must have come to the same conclusion he had, because her face took on a look of resignation. "At least the Stuarts need us alive."

"Well, they need you alive." He grumbled.

Sarah turned to where Calum and Archie waited on the balls of their feet ready to pounce. She raised one arm and pointed at the assassin on the other side of them and shouted. "Invigilare!"

CHAPTER THREE

"And just where have ye been for the last two days?" Archie Sinclair sauntered toward where they stood on the footbridge. His salt and pepper hair was cut short. In spite of his age, he kept himself fit. His suit was cut to hide the radio and likely tactical baton that he doubtless carried. He approached them with the swagger of a man who'd been on Alba Petroleum's security staff for decades.

"Making our way back here, Arch." Dermot hoped Sarah would follow his lead on the story.

"For two days?" Archie looked skeptical.

"Aye. We were trying to stay under the radar." He looked over his shoulder in the direction Calum had chased their attacker. "For obvious reasons."

"Mmhmm…" Archie's mouth firmed as if he were thinking hard about whether to believe them. He scanned them, taking in their backpacks, clothes, and shoes. Dermot was glad he'd taken the time to pick up some new shoes and to drop his blood-soaked trainers in a dumpster outside Inverness. Archie looked past his shoulder at Sarah distaste evident on his face. "So, ye're the one that almost got my lad sacked."

"I didn't intend for that to reflect badly on Fleming." Sarah's tone was apologetic. "I did get him reinstated when I could."

Archie's face warned that he didn't think much of her efforts to help her bodyguard, Fleming, after she'd given him the slip in North Carolina. He'd had to return to Scotland with egg on his face, and it was only the combined efforts of Sarah and Dermot that had gotten him back into the Stuart good graces. It appeared that Archie still held a grudge over Sarah's earlier stunt. He turned to Dermot. "What's in the bag, lad?"

Dermot shrugged trying to look innocent. "Clothes, maybe some granola bars."

Archie looked doubtful. "Ye dinna mind if I have a look then?"

"Are ye confused, Arch?" Dermot narrowed his eyes at the older man and stepped closer, almost nose to nose. "We're on the same side here."

"Are we?" Archie lifted his chin and stared Dermot down. "Seems to me yer heart's never been in this work."

"I lost him." Calum jogged up, stopping beside them to catch his breath. He looked back and forth between the two men squared off in the middle of the footbridge. "What's going on?"

Dermot and Archie didn't take their eyes off each other. They stood for several seconds without answering Calum. "Grab his bag, Calum."

"Is this really the place to be getting into this?" Sarah spoke up, but none of the men seemed inclined to listen to her. Calum, who may have been shorter than Dermot, but was built like a heavy weight fighter gripped Dermot's bag, slid it from his shoulders and tossed it to Archie.

Archie unzipped the bag and looked inside. Dermot prayed silently that the man would be satisfied with what he saw on top. He had carefully tucked his portion of their cash reserves in the bottom of the bag under a spare jumper that should hide it from a casual look inside. But Archie Sinclair was nothing if not thorough. He plunged a hand down into the bag and came up with not only the cash, but a passport as well.

In the middle of the crowded train station, Dermot could do nothing but stand by. The last thing any of them needed was the attention of the police.

Archie cut his eyes to Calum and jerked his chin at Dermot. His mouth made a sneer of disgust. "Grab him."

Sarah slid lightning quick between Calum and Dermot. She focused her attention on Calum who until a few weeks ago had been her near constant shadow and upstairs neighbor. Their relationship hadn't been friendly, but she had always been nice to him. "Don't even think about it. Calum, you know Dermot."

"Aye, we do. And we know better than ye the oath we took to the Stuarts." Archie grabbed her arm to pull her from between the younger men.

Sarah wasn't having that. She turned on him, her eyes blazing. Keeping a protective hand on Dermot, she lowered her voice to address Archie. Her southern American accent thickened with fury. "Get your hand off me! If you took the same oath he did, then you must know who I am."

They all froze. Archie and Calum out of respect or fear of what her word in James Stuart's ear could do to their careers. Dermot gaped in astonishment. Sarah had never accepted that she was who or what the Stuarts thought she was. She had fought her birthright from the moment she learned of it. But here she was willing to trade on it to protect him.

Archie kept his face impassive but leaned slightly away from her. He released her arm. "Ma'am."

Sarah shot a look at Calum to make sure he was not moving to take Dermot. When she looked back at Archie, her voice was low and hard. "Y'all lay one hand on him and I will scream bloody murder in the middle of this train station. Then you can explain that gun in your jacket to every transit cop that comes running, and how you terrorized me in public to James."

Archie seethed. The muscled in his jaw jumped with tension, but when he spoke his tone was respectful. "Will ye join us in returning to the Alba Petroleum offices...ma'am?"

Sarah pulled her shoulders back and lifted her chin regally. She may have been raised on a farm in the mountains of North Carolina, but she was every inch a queen. "No. I'm not going anywhere with you, and I'm not leaving him. If James wants to talk to me, he'll have to come here."

Archie glared at her for several beats. Dermot thought he must be debating how far he could push her. "Calum, go and ask the police if there is a room that we can wait in for the Stuart."

***

"How did ye know he had a gun?" Dermot asked once they were alone. Archie and Calum had escorted them to the Transit Police office in the station. The police had agreed to let them wait in an interrogation room while Archie relayed Sarah's demand back to the Stuarts. The room was bare with nothing but a metal table and two chairs. Dermot nodded at the corner by the ceiling. Sarah followed his look and saw the security camera there.

"I didn't." He gaped at her and she shrugged. "I thought I saw a bulge and took a chance."

He looked to the ceiling as if searching for patience. "Well, we're well and truly trapped now. Short of ye escaping through the air vent, there'll be no getting out of here."

"Feeling a little claustrophobic?" She stayed on her feet, leaning against the wall furthest from the camera. "You should take a few deep breaths. I expect we'll be here a while."

He stopped pacing and gave her a sharp look. "Ye seem remarkably calm. I hope that means ye have a plan."

"I do. I don't know why I didn't think of it before." She waved him over to her. When he was close enough to hear a whisper, she told him. "Instead of trying to run away, we push through. We lay it all out, my parents, the mismatch, the trouble it caused, and the cauldron that everyone thought was dormant healing you. Everything we've seen suggests that you are my true match. When there was a mismatch before, it destroyed my people. Their whole community fell apart. If we can convince James that another mismatch could put everything he's working for in jeopardy, then he can't do anything else but let us go. We could be together without having to give up everything we've been working for."

He stared at her in disbelief. "That's yer plan? Tell them yer theory and expect everyone to play fair. D'ye really think that they're going to give up all their plans that easily?"

"Not all their plans. They can keep pursuing independence. They don't have to give that up. As for the heir, I think people will fall in behind James, and James is persuadable." At his incredulous look, she leaned closer to him. "James isn't entirely comfortable with his role in all of this. He feels as trapped as we do."

"That may be, but he also thinks he's in love with ye." His eyes told her his opinion of that. "And ye should never underestimate the influence of Walter on James's life. He's been pulling the strings for years."

Her green eyes sparked with determination. "Then I think it's time to cut those strings."

Doubt was clear on his face. "That's a verra big gamble."

"You said yourself. We're trapped." She pressed two fingers between her eyebrows trying to push back the start of a headache. "I'm just doing what Duff always taught me. Improvise, adapt and overcome."

"I just hope ye know what ye're doing. Walter Stuart is going to fight ye every step of the way. And I'm not so sure James is as ambivalent about his role as ye think."

"You just leave James to me." She hoped her hunch about James was right.

To Sarah's relief, Dermot eventually stopped pacing and leaned against the wall under the security camera. She took one of the chairs and rested her elbows on the table trying to think her way through her argument. She thought she had burned the bridge with James the last time they'd spoken. She told him that she didn't want a public life, and he couldn't help but have one. He was a tabloid darling; billionaire playboy with movie star good looks and more money than any one person had a right to.

At least that was what the world saw. Sarah knew him a little better. James Stuart was a young man trapped under the weight of his family's, his company's, and the world's expectations. He hadn't chosen the life of an oil executive.

He'd been born to it. Just like he'd been born the heir to a cabal of neo-Jacobites intent on putting him on the throne of an independent Scotland with her at his side. Those expectations were so ingrained in James, that he could barely conceive of a life lived on his own terms. Sarah hoped that the temptation of that kind of freedom would be enough to convince James to let them go.

She was still formulating her argument when the door opened and the man himself walked in. His double-breasted suit and perfect hair should have given the impression of the cool executive, but it was belied by the almost frantic look on his face. He made straight for Sarah, who rose to meet him. "It wasn't me. You must believe me. I did not give the tabloids your name."

"I know," She took the hand he extended toward her. The gesture a mix of soothing, but also keeping him at arm's length.

"No!" Dermot barked pushing away from his place in the corner. He was at the door in two strides. "Not you."

"I'm with my nephew." Walter Stuart's voice held all the authority of the international puppet master that he fancied himself. He was an imposing figure, tall and slim with the same chiseled features that seemed to run in the family. He might have been handsome if he didn't always wear a superior and calculating look on his face. As it was, he brought a chill to every room he entered.

"Not today, mate." Dermot moved to close the door in the older man's face. James watched this exchange with curiosity.

"James," Sarah sought his eyes with hers. "Can we have this conversation without your uncle?"

"It's alright." James told Walter. "I think I can handle this."

Walter pressed his thin lips together in obvious disapproval. "I would rather stay."

"And I would rather Sarah talk with me candidly. I doubt she will do that with an audience. Why don't you both wait in the hall?"

Dermot looked sharply at Sarah. It was clear he didn't want to leave, but it was a small concession. She was willing to give it in the hopes of convincing James. She gave Dermot a nod. He returned a look that said, 'I hope you know what you're doing.'

So did she. She also hoped Dermot and Walter could manage to wait in the hall without coming to blows. The two of them were like oil and water.

***

"You seem to have forgotten your place, Sinclair." Walter Stuart's nose wrinkled with disdain after Dermot closed the door to the holding room.

Dermot wasn't going to rise to the old man's bait. He folded his arms across his chest and stood in front of the door, his face impassive. If he couldn't be in there to help Sarah make their case, he would at least make sure they weren't interfered with.

Stuart glared at him, contempt coming off the man in waves. After a few seconds, Walter turned to the police captain who was standing nearby. The poor man didn't dare leave such illustrious personages as Lord Caledon and his uncle unattended.

"Is there a way that I can watch what's going on in there?" Walter asked the captain.

"No." Dermot cut the captain off before he could answer. "This is private between the two of them. I'm sure that James will tell ye whatever he thinks ye need to know when they're done."

Walter looked down his nose. "You should know by now that James has no secrets from me."

"D'ye follow him into his bedroom, then?" Dermot asked flatly. "Wipe his arse too?"

"I know your mother didn't teach you to be vulgar."

Dermot tightened his arms around his chest, fighting the urge to pummel Stuart. His voice was low but threatening. "Dinna mention my mother to me again."

Victory flashed in Stuart's eyes. He knew better than anyone how to get under Dermot's skin. Walter turned back to the captain with a questioning look.

"Right in here." The captain reached to open the door next to the holding room. Quick as lightning Dermot's hand covered the doorknob before the captain even touched it. He caught the captain's eye. "I said it's private. This isna a police matter. People have rights."

The police captain pulled his hand back and stepped away leaving the two of them to square off in the hallway. Walter Stuart watched Dermot; one gray eyebrow arched in derision. "You do realize, you work for us?"

Dermot leaned down into Walter's face. "Not anymore."

Red started creeping up from the old man's collar. "You swore an oath."

"Aye, I did." Dermot grinned back at him. "To her."

Walter swelled with fury. "You think you can defy us?"

"I think she's the most important person here; more important than James and certainly more important than the likes of ye."

"He is your king." Walter hissed through his teeth. It was a refrain Dermot had heard for as long as he could remember. He'd told Sarah the same thing months ago in Chapel Hill when he had tried to explain his relationship to James and why they couldn't be together. He had learned so much about the legend and himself since then.

He shook his head. "Ye forget that when I'm not guarding Sarah, I'm studying the legends that made ye believe that. I've got news for ye. That prophecy ye use to justify ruining that lass's life, might not mean what ye think it means."

CHAPTER FOUR

"What was that about?" James turned back to her once the door was closed.

"It's better if we have this conversation alone." Sarah returned to her seat.

"Alright, but since when does Dermot look to you for orders?" James came around the table with a glance at the door, as if he could see Dermot through it.

"Since you sent him to North Carolina to spy on me." Sarah hoped that the shock of revealing what she knew might give her the upper hand.

His head whipped from the door to her in obvious surprise. "How long have you known that?"

"A few months." She clasped her hands in front of her on the table. "Something Ryan Cumberland said while he was holding me at gunpoint made me ask questions. Dermot, bless his heart, answered honestly."

"You've known all the time you've been here, and you said nothing." James looked from her to the closed door his jaw clenched in anger. "So much for my most trusted friend."

"Your friend?" She emphasized the word 'friend'. "Dermot is your friend? When was the last time you asked your friend how he was doing, or how his mother was doing? You call him your friend, but you know nothing about his life, and I haven't seen you make any effort to know."

"He would tell me if he needed anything, and Walter usually asks about his mother when we're together." James's eyebrows knit and he looked confused about why they were talking about Dermot.

"Are you really that ignorant of what goes on in your name?" Sarah cocked her head to the side and gave him a sharp look. "I thought I only had one story to tell you. It seems we've got a couple of items to cover here."

His gaze sharpened on hers and he stepped closer to the table using his height in an attempt to intimidate her. Walter Stuart might be pulling the strings at Alba Petroleum, but James wasn't spineless. Sarah hoped she could get that to work in their favor. "Enlighten me."

Sarah looked up at him with a smile letting him know his intimidation tactic wasn't working. "If Dermot hadn't told me about the fun you had when you were children, I wouldn't know that there was any deeper connection between you two. He didn't ask for his role in all this anymore than you did, and because this is 1996 and not 1696, he tried to get out and make his own choices. That's why he joined the army."

"And he was injured during the Gulf War. I know this." James pulled back the chair across from her and sat down irritably.

"I don't think you know the whole story. He wasn't fighting when he was injured. He was attacked in camp." She sat forward in her chair, leaning over the table. "His attackers were sent by your uncle. Dermot heard them say they'd been paid to injure him after they smashed his leg. And Walter was right there with a job offer as soon as his knee was healed."

James leaned back, head shaking. "No. I don't believe it."

"Okay. A year or two into working for A. P. Security, Dermot tried to get out again. He went back to school to start a new career, while having to put his mother in a care home. Until last spring, when he came home from a research trip to find out that somehow your uncle had gained power of attorney over Seonag, moved her to a different care home and wouldn't tell Dermot where she was until he agreed to go to North Carolina to establish surveillance on me. Even now, Walter Stuart controls everything about Seonag's care. Her own son can't make decisions for her. All he can do is visit and hope that she remembers who he is. So, whenever you hear Walter ask Dermot about his mother, he's not expressing concern. He's issuing a threat."

James looked down at the table, head shaking. Sarah could almost see him searching his memory for clues to prove or disprove what she was saying.

She leaned down to catch his eye, her tone fierce. "Dermot is not your friend. He's not even your employee, or faithful retainer, or whatever ridiculous feudal relationship you seem to think you have. He's your hostage."

James lifted his head, his eyes steady on hers. At first, he looked guilty, but then something changed. Understanding swept over him. "He's the one you're in love with."

She nodded, silent. There was so much that could be said, maybe should be said. That stuff could wait for later. Now was the time for hard truths, not excuses and qualifications.

James was out of his chair like a shot. He turned his back to her and threaded his fingers through his hair. After several seconds he asked without turning around. "Were you lying to me a few weeks ago, when you said that he wasn't the man you thought he was?"

Sarah thought back to the months that she and Dermot had been at odds about their relationship and whether they had a chance to be together. "No, I wasn't. He was trying to protect his mother, and he pushed me away. He's done little but keep me at arm's length since all of this started. He's been very...professional about it."

"Until he wasn't." James bit out still facing the wall.

"The last few weeks have taught us a lot." Sarah spoke calmly. "I've learned that a life in the public eye is not for me. Dermot has learned that he's never going to earn his freedom from your uncle, he's going to have to take it. And we've both learned that we can't be without each other. We were miserable when we tried."

"And I'm left out in the cold." He faced her holding out a pleading hand. "I love you, Sarah."

Sarah let that hang in the air for a few heartbeats. She flattened her hands on the table in a gesture she hoped would be calming. "I think you believe that, and I won't argue with you about whether or not it's true. But I want you to think about the nature of that love."

He took a step toward the table and started to speak, but she held up a hand to stop him. "Hear me out. You don't really know me, James. You know what other people have told you about me, but we went on one date and even you can admit it didn't end well. How much of the love you say you feel is actually for me, and how much is for what you've been told I can do for you by Walter and the rest of your family?"

"I know my own heart." He pulled his chair back to the table and sat across from her reaching for her hand.

Sarah pulled her hands back a couple of inches and gave her head a quick shake. "I don't want the life you're offering."

James turned his palm up on the table. "But we're meant to be together. Your own people's prophecy says you are the mother of the king."

"Oh, James." She gave him a pitying look. "I of all people know how legends can get changed and muddled over time. I don't even know if I believe that. But if I did, the legend doesn't say who the father of the king is. You have all concluded that it will be the Stuart heir, but the legend doesn't say that. It's not specific at all."

That shocked him. She could tell from the waves of confusion and doubt washing over his face that James had never considered that he might not be the father of the legendary king. "Who else would it be?"

Sarah laid her hand in his. "Let me tell you a story. You know about my people, right?"

"I know they are what most people call the Auld Folk." He closed his fingers gently around her hand.

"That's close enough, although you can't believe everything you hear about the Auld Folk. According to our legends, we were founded by an ancient king, his queen and her two sisters. We have lived apart from the world, keeping our traditions and maintaining certain traits through careful selection of mates, at least for three lines coming from the original three sisters. The matching was done through some sort of divining ceremony. Some of us ventured into the world outside our hidden glen usually to bring new people to the community to prevent inbreeding. Sometimes people left for other reasons. My grandmother left before the war because they realized that the Germans were looking for them. But the descendants of the three sisters have returned each generation to be matched with the ideal partner to maintain the bloodline."

"I think I have heard this story before."

"Have you heard about the cauldron of plenty?" She asked.

James searched his memory. "It provided food, right? Some scholars think the legend of the Holy Grail was inspired by Celtic legends about the cauldron."

"You do know a bit." Sarah smiled. "It's how the Auld Folk were able to stay hidden for so long. They had no need to farm on a large scale. The cauldron also had healing properties."

"Had? Past tense?"

"That's what I'm getting to. When my mother returned to the village for her generation's matching, there was a..." She paused searching for the best word. "...mistake. Because of the war and the Clearances before that, the descendants of the three sisters were spread out for their own safety. That year, the two of the sisters were only able to send their daughters for the matching. There was only one of the previous generation there to oversee the ceremony, my great aunt Eilidh. The trouble started when Eilidh didn't like the match that she was shown for her daughter. So, she lied about what she saw. She put my mother with the match that was meant for her daughter and gave her daughter my mother's actual match."

She went on. "When that happened, the cauldron stopped giving food. If it weren't for the ingenuity of the few of them who had lived in the modern world our people would have starved. But my mother fell in love with the man who was her correct match in spite of Eilidh's efforts, and he fell in love with her. When they started to act on their feelings in secret, the cauldron started working again. When Eilidh realized that I had been conceived with the man she had matched with her daughter, she banished my mother from the village."

"And the cauldron stopped again." James supplied, understanding.

"It has done little more than hold water ever since." Sarah watched his face, keen to see his reaction to her next words. "Until two nights ago."

She thought back to the chills she'd felt when she saw water from the cauldron healing Dermot's wounds, and the realization that there was some truth to the legends she'd heard. "The village fell apart without the cauldron. My people scattered about the Highlands and elsewhere. The cauldron was moved to a secret location and stayed there, until we were led there. Dermot was injured fighting off the Invigilare assassin.

"Assassin!" His face showed his alarm, and his grip on her hand tightened.

She smiled slightly to reassure him. "We weren't run off the road by paparazzi. It was an assassin. He tried to finish us off at the car, but a good Samaritan stopped to help us. Then the assassin chased us on foot through the hills. Dermot..." She cleared her throat. "...Took care of him, but he was hurt in the struggle. Water from the cauldron healed him. According to those who keep the cauldron, it hasn't done that in decades."

"Wait, are you saying that Dermot is some sort of king?" He looked incredulous. Sarah tried not to be offended on Dermot's behalf.

"Not necessarily." She shifted from storyteller to advocate. "I'm saying that the cauldron works when the matches are done right. It didn't work until Dermot and I were there together. Just like it stopped and started and stopped again when my parents were separated."

James fell back in his chair. His hands rested limply as he stared at the top of the metal table stunned. Sarah decided to let him think in peace. She knew he was an intelligent man. He would put it together, and she would give him the space to do that. "And you believe that Dermot is your true match. Dermot Sinclair, the son of an academic rather than the actual descendant of a king, whose family has protected your people for countless generations?"

"I believe that the cauldron is an indicator. According to our tradition, it was given to us with the caveat that as long as we kept our people and traditions, it would continue to provide for us. It works when we're preserving our people. It stops when we're on the wrong track."

"And you believe that a bad match would make it stop again." She could see the wheels turning in his mind, gaming out different scenarios and trying to chart a course to the result that he wanted. "But your people don't depend on the cauldron anymore. Is it that important?"

"If you believe that gaining independence and restoring the Scottish throne is dependent on the prophecy of my people, I think the cauldron is our compass. It's going to tell us if we're moving in the right direction. And the last time it worked was when Dermot and I were together. I believe a mismatch like the one that happened to my parents, would derail all your plans for Scotland."

That was it. That was the key question. Was the Stuarts' pursuit of this match about gaining independence for Scotland, or more power for themselves? Was James patriotic or power hungry? She knew the answer for Walter, but what was it for James? Could he shift all his expectations given this new evidence? He pursed his lips and raised a skeptical eyebrow. "Was anyone else there? Is there anyone apart from you and Dermot who witnessed this miraculous event?"

"Yes." Sarah hoped like hell that the old wizard wouldn't mind her pulling him into this. He did say that it was his job to make sure events happened the way that they were supposed to happen. "Mr. Green. I believe he's on your board of directors."

"Lyall Green?" He asked in disbelief.

"Yep. That's him." She nodded. "He takes care of the cauldron."

James's gaze turned inward once again. Sarah thought he must be wracking his brain trying to find any indication that the mild-mannered solicitor he knew was somehow involved with Sarah's people. Good, she thought. The more we can up-end his perception of the situation, the more we can substitute our own. "I'm going to have to think about this some more. I need to talk to Green."

"Let's talk to him then." She hoped she sounded more confident than she felt.

James cast his eyes around the bare, dimly lit holding room. "I suggest we take this to somewhere more comfortable. Shall we have Green meet us at my house?"

That was a risk. Here in this tiny room, she was on neutral ground. If she went to his house, full of all the trappings of Stuart money and power, she might lose the ground she had gained. And it would be harder to keep Walter Stuart out of the conversation. She wouldn't put it past Walter to take her prisoner until she complied. "Why don't we go to Green's office?"

He thought about that for a few seconds. "Alright. I'll have my driver call ahead and tell them we're coming."

"Great." She was relieved at least for the moment. "And Dermot stays with me."

The muscles in his jaw jumped with his displeasure at that idea. "We'll all go there together."

CHAPTER FIVE

Dermot had to hand it to Lyall Green or Lailoken, or Merlin, or whatever name he used for this environment; he knew how to blend in. No one would ever guess that the birch and glass offices with the abstract art and modern leather furniture in the waiting room would house an ancient wizard, or whatever he was. His chambers could rival anything in ultra-modern London.

They were met at the door by his assistant who looked almost as old as the man himself. Her steel gray hair was slicked back into a French twist and her tailored suit was designed to instill confidence in even the most nervous client. If she was at all unnerved by their sudden insistence on a meeting, she didn't show it. "Lord Caledon, Mr. Stuart, Miss MacAlpin and Mr. Sinclair, I am Mrs. Jeffries. Please follow me."

The men waited for Sarah to follow. Dermot stuck close behind her. Mrs. Jeffries led them through a glass walled waiting room flooded with natural light, to an interior conference room. They arranged themselves around the long birch wood conference table. There was an awkward moment when James moved to pull out a chair for Sarah next to him at the head of the table, but Dermot also pulled one out further down. Dermot tried not to look too smug when she accepted the chair next to him, sending James an apologetic look.

"Can I get anyone anything? We have tea, coffee, water…" Mrs. Jeffries asked from the doorway.

Everyone shook their heads. Mrs. Jeffries gave them all a cordial smile. "Very well, then. Mr. Green will be with you in a few moments."

She left them to stew in the conference room. Walter Stuart seethed at being left in the dark about Sarah's conversation with James. Well, he wasn't the only one in the dark. Dermot only knew what she planned to tell James. He had no idea why they were suddenly in Lyall Green's office, nor could he tell how James was reacting to what Sarah had told him. Sitting at the head of the table, James appeared thoughtful rather than angry. He hoped that was a good sign. Dermot laid his hand over Sarah's on the table. She gave his fingers a squeeze that he thought was meant to reassure, but he could tell she was on edge.

"Does someone want to tell me what is going on here?" Walter's annoyed voice broke the silence.

James took a breath before answering. His fingers smoothed along the edge of the table. "We're here to verify some things that Sarah told me."

"With Green?" Walter looked at Sarah in confusion. "Do you even know Green?"

"We just met recently. But I'm told he knew my mother." Dermot enjoyed the alarm that flashed through Walter's eyes at that. Suddenly, Lyall Green, solicitor and Alba Petroleum board member was something more, and he could tell Walter didn't like not knowing exactly who Green was.

"What does that have to do with anything?" Walter sneered.

Sarah gave a quick laugh. "Everything."

Dermot eyed her wondering how she could manage to seem this confident when so much of their lives hung in the balance. She must see some sign of hope in James's reaction.

"While we're here, uncle. Sarah told me some things about you as well." James gave his uncle an assessing look. "Do you have power of attorney over Dermot's mother?"

A frisson of shock ran down Dermot's back, and his eyes flew to Walter. He hadn't expected his mother to come up in this conversation. Walter's pause was short but perceptible. "Yes, she gave it to me when Dermot was out of reach in the Western Isles. She was concerned that someone be able to make decisions for her on her less lucid days."

"The Western Isles are the other side of the country not the other side of the moon. Could her son not have been called?" James asked coolly.

Walter cleared his throat and cut his eyes down the table toward Dermot before looking back at James. "He wasn't available."

James met that with a thoughtful mmhmm. "Was one of those decisions to move her to a different care home without his knowledge?"

Dermot cocked his head to the side, biting his tongue. This was a confrontation that he hadn't expected today, but he was more than interested to see how it played out. "The other care home was inferior, and it lacked the memory care services that she needs." Walter fumbled for an acceptable answer where there was none. Dermot couldn't believe he would try to rationalize what he'd done. "I moved her somewhere better."

"And refused to tell me where until I agreed to go to America to spy on Sarah." He spat no longer able to remain silent. James turned his way and Dermot met his eyes for the first time. "My mother was in the best care facility I could find. The one he moved her to is no better than the last."

James turned to Walter, "And why, when he returned to town did you not give power of attorney to Dermot?"

"It simply slipped my mind." Walter tried to look affronted that anyone would suggest a nefarious reason.

"Though I'm certain is hasn't slipped his mind? Has it?" James looked down the table to Dermot.

"Not for a minute." Dermot ground out through his teeth.

James gave Walter a cold smile. "Then you won't mind giving it to him now. We can add that to the list of things Mr. Green can do for us today."

Walter looked like he'd just swallowed a hot coal. He looked at James for a moment before saying. "Of course."

Dermot had to hand it to James. He hadn't questioned Walter's motives or accused him of keeping his mother hostage. He had merely established the facts and suggested the next move. That approach left Walter with the choice of giving in to his suggestion or admitting that he had been extorting Dermot's cooperation and arguing that it needed to continue. It was a neat maneuver. Either way, Walter knew he was caught.

"I'm sorry to keep you waiting." A resonant voice sounded from the doorway. "Gentleman, Miss MacAlpin, I had not expected to see you again so soon."

Lyall Green looked every bit the topflight Edinburgh solicitor that he was in this incarnation. Dermot was sure they had only seen a couple of Green's many faces. It was amazing the difference the right clothes made. Two nights ago, they had met Green in a cave in the Highlands. He'd looked completely at home in hiking gear making tea over an open fire. Exchange cargo trousers, boots and jumper for a bespoke suit and tea kettle for a leather portfolio, and he looked like a totally different man. Dermot wasn't sure how, but he had known exactly who Green was when he'd gotten a good look at him in the cave. He'd called him Merlin, although today he doubted he would have made the connection.

Today, he was a polished and professional looking man just past middle age. He made his way around the table shaking hands and greeting each of them individually. He gave Dermot a hint of a smile. When he came to Sarah, she spoke. "I have just been catching Lord Caledon up on recent events. I believe he's hoping that you can corroborate what I've told him."

Green studied her as if searching for something. Eventually, he smiled and gave a slight nod before taking a seat between Sarah and James. "I can certainly try."

"Thank you." James continued in the business-like tone he had used to corner Walter moments ago. "Miss MacAlpin tells me that you have a relationship with her family in the Highlands."

"Of sorts." Green spoke carefully. "I have helped them with some legal and financial matters over the years."

"And is one of those matters a cauldron that is kept in a secret location?" James got straight to the point.

Green shot a concerned look at Sarah. "They have entrusted me with such an heirloom."

"And were you near that heirloom two nights ago?" Dermot was starting to think that James had missed his calling as a detective.

"I was." Green told him with a smile. "I enjoy hill walking, and I often combine that passion with the need to check on that particular heirloom periodically. I spent the weekend in the Highlands. It's where I met the lovely Miss MacAlpin."

"So she said." James looked thoughtful. "But you knew Miss MacAlpin before that night."

Green turned a fond smile on Sarah. "We had not been properly introduced, but I had taken an interest in Miss MacAlpin. You see, I met her mother just a few months before Miss MacAlpin was born."

"You were helping her family that long ago?" James asked.

"Oh yes. The MacAlpins have been clients since almost the beginning of my career."

"Did you disclose that relationship when you joined the AP board of directors?" Walter's question sounded almost like an accusation.

Green gave him a cool look. "I wasn't aware that that was a conflict of interest. It seems to me that we are all working toward the same purpose."

That shut Walter up. Again, he was in the position of agreeing or revealing too much about his own agenda.

"To your knowledge, what was special about the cauldron before two nights ago?" James asked.

"Ah." Green steepled his hands on the table in front of him. "I'm afraid there was nothing remarkable at all about the cauldron, apart from its age, until the other night. I am aware of the legend around it, and even saw for myself many years ago what it is capable of. That is, what it was capable of. It stopped giving food twenty-seven years ago."

"Before Miss MacAlpin was born." James looked significantly at Sarah.

"I believe that's right, yes." Green acknowledged. Dermot was sure he knew exactly when the cauldron had stopped working, but he wasn't likely to volunteer more information than was explicitly asked for.

James shifted more to face Green. "Do you know why the cauldron stopped giving food?"

Green appeared to weigh his words carefully. "There are different opinions among the people of Miss MacAlpin's clan. The cauldron's gifts had become unpredictable that year. Some believed that it was the result of members of the clan returning from the new world and questioning their way of life. Others believed that there was some mistake, some betrayal of their faith. The cauldron did stop, seemingly permanently when Molly MacAlpin left the village."

"And what do you believe?" James pressed him.

Green raised his eyebrows and pursed his lips as if thinking. "It is difficult to say. The cauldron first stopped after their matching ceremony that year. It began again some months later and stopped again when Miss MacAlpin left. To use a legal term, correlation is not necessarily causation, but I don't believe the timing is a coincidence."

James hummed in thought. Seconds later he switched his line of questioning. "When you encountered Mr. Sinclair the other night, was he injured?"

"He was, yes. And covered in blood." Green looked at Dermot his expression grave. "He had a large cut on his calf. It should have needed stitches."

James glanced up at Dermot, his brows creased in concern. "Should have?"

Green answered. "Yes, but when we began cleaning the wound with water from the cauldron, it began to close on its own."

James looked at Sarah who gave him a hint of an I-told-you-so look. He asked. "Had you ever seen something like that before?"

"Never." Green gave his head an emphatic shake. "I had heard that the cauldron could heal, but from all that I knew the clan had only used it for food."

James looked confounded. He leaned back in his chair and looked at each of them in turn. Dermot could see his mind working. Whatever Sarah had told him, it seemed that Green had confirmed it. "Miss MacAlpin has a theory about the stoppage being caused by a bad match made that year. And that when the two who were meant to be together found each other, the cauldron started again."

Green considered the theory. "That could be. I have long suspected that the matching ceremony that year was not conducted according to tradition."

"She also believes that the cauldron healed Mr. Sinclair because the two of them were together and he is her true match."

"What?" Walter exploded. It was the first time he'd heard Sarah's theory and he clearly wasn't pleased by the idea. He fixed his angry gaze on Dermot. "Why you jumped up-"

"Uncle." James interrupted. "I would like to hear Mr. Green's opinion on that theory. We can deal with Dermot later."

"But he ca-"

"Uncle!" James barked. Walter subsided glaring daggers at Dermot. James pointedly turned back to Green.

***

Sarah tried hard not to grin as the room went silent. It was rare that James asserted himself over his uncle, rarer still that he felt the need to raise his voice. Any disagreement between James and Walter could only work in their favor. This entire conversation was good for them. It was a risk telling James Stuart that he might not be the second coming of Uther Pendragon or whatever he thought he was, but she and Dermot were literally backed into a corner.

Thankfully, Green appeared to be supporting her so far. They all waited for the solicitor's answer to James's question. Green's enigmatic eyes caught hers looking thoughtful. "It's an interesting theory. When the cauldron was entrusted to me, it was inert, empty. It gave no food, nor water. I put it in a safe place, and it has done nothing but collect rainwater since. I have occasionally used that water for making tea on my trips to check on the cauldron." He gestured to himself sheepishly. "I am not a young man. You can imagine that hill walking is not a pain free experience for me. In many trips to visit the cauldron, it has never healed me."

Once again, Green had confirmed her narrative. James didn't show any reaction to this news. His blue eyes came to rest on Dermot. "Will you show me your leg where this supposed wound was?"

After a moment's hesitation, Dermot pushed away from the table, casting a wary look her way. He went to the head of the table where James sat, and pulled the leg of his pants up to show his calf. Sarah knew from inspecting it that morning that there was a slight scar, a faint pink line that curved across the muscle. She still couldn't believe it. Green was right that it should have needed stitches.

Walter leaned across the table to see and scoffed. "That could be an old scar or done with a razor. It proves nothing."

James looked up to meet Dermot's eyes. "How did it happen?"

Dermot pressed his lips together and took a breath. He obviously wasn't comfortable talking about it. "He tried to cut my Achilles tendon, but I moved, and he sliced my calf instead."

"How did you get away?" James didn't take his eyes from Dermot's studying every breath, every jerk of the muscle in his jaw, watching for every flinch.

Except there were none. Dermot didn't miss a beat, nor did he try to soften the truth. "I slit his throat."

Sarah closed her eyes. She could still see the stricken look on Dermot's face when he had stumbled into the cave two nights ago covered in the other man's blood. He hadn't told her the details of the fight and she hadn't asked. He had killed to save her. She would never forget that.

She didn't see James's reaction, but the room fell silent. In the end James murmured, "Thank you."

Dermot stalked back to his seat next to Sarah and took her hand in his. Sarah looked at him, but his eyes were shuttered giving away nothing. She squeezed his hand offering what silent comfort she could.

James cleared his throat drawing attention back to himself. His lips pressed into a firm line. He addressed Sarah. "All of this confirms what you have told me."

"I have never been anything but honest with you."

He bowed his head in acknowledgment. "And I appreciate that. It is one of the things that I admire most about you." He flattened his hands on the conference table in front of him as if to absorb its solid strength. "The difficulty that I have is that for hundreds of years, my family has operated under the belief that we are the line that will bring about the return of the once and future king. You're asking me to set all of that aside on a theory."

"Isn't Dermot part of your family too?" James had been introduced to her as Dermot's cousin when they met.

"The connection is of little consequence." Walter waved a hand as if waving away any link that Dermot had to the Stuarts.

Dermot's eyes narrowed at the older man. "It was of enough consequence when we were spending summers at Tweedholm, or when ye were visiting me at school, or every time ye refused to let me leave Alba Petroleum Security."

"That doesn't make you one of us." Walter looked down his nose at Dermot.

"Arguing like children will get us nowhere." James raised a hand to stop them before their bickering completely derailed the conversation. James turned to Sarah, his face apologetic. "I cannot simply change course after so long."

"I truly believe that if you don't, if there is another mismatch like there was with my parents, everything you've been working for will be lost." She edged forward in her chair, leaning into her argument. "Look, I'm still trying to wrap my brain around this whole situation. It's honestly too bizarre to even fathom. But if we accept that I'm some sort of magical princess from an ancient prophecy, and you're secretly descended from Jesus, then we have to follow whatever magical rules apply. We don't get to choose our own path because we like it better or it's more convenient. My great aunt tried that and it all but destroyed our people."

"But we don't know what the rules are." James shook his head.

"I think some know more than others." Sarah turned to address Green. "My great aunt is no friend of mine, but if you asked, I think she might share what she knows. I'm sure her daughter would be willing to help, and Isobel MacKenzie. There has to be a way to test the match. Generations before did it."

Green nodded thoughtfully. "Generations before had the pool for the matching ceremony. It's no more than a bog now."

"Can we add water? There has to be a way." Sarah pleaded.

"I don't think it's as simple as adding water." Green's eyebrows drew together as if his mind was already trying to solve the problem. "I will have to research ways to revive the pool."

"Could we not test it with the cauldron?" James asked. Sarah felt a surge of excitement that he might be following her logic.

Green thought a moment. "That is a possibility. As Miss MacAlpin said the cauldron does appear to be an indicator. The challenge is that we don't know exactly what it's indicating, or how to structure a test of it." He paused as if considering how it might be done. "It's also possible that Sarah's presence alone started the cauldron again. No, I think that a matching ceremony would be the best test. I will have to do some research to see if we can make that happen."

"We have plenty of chemists and geologists at Alba Petroleum who could help." James offered. Sarah imagined it wasn't easy for James to understand why a solicitor should be trusted with researching an ancient ceremony.

Green smiled at him the way a preschool teacher smiles at a child wanting to help. "I have made a career out of studying Miss MacAlpin's people. If there is anyone who can find the answer, I can."

"If Lord Caledon agrees to it." Walter interjected having regained some of his usual cold authority.

All eyes went to James, who was watching Sarah. It was hard to tell what he was thinking. Between boarding school, board rooms and paparazzi, James had developed a great poker face. Now that it was clear to him that Sarah wasn't available, he wasn't letting his guard down around her as he had before. She felt the loss. She may not want to marry James, but she did consider him a friend. He stood, buttoning his jacket. Everyone rose with him. He spoke to Green first. "Do your research. Find out how this can be tested. I will consider whether I am willing to test this theory." His gaze shifted to Sarah. "I would like you to stay in Edinburgh while we untangle this mess. I assume that you will keep your flat in Bernard Terrace."

"Sure." It wasn't as if she had much choice.

As an aside to his uncle. "We'll need to increase security at Bernard Terrace to keep the press away."

"I'll call Shaw." Walter agreed.

"I will expect you both at Polwarth Terrace at nine o'clock sharp tomorrow morning for a statement to the press. The sooner they know you've been found, the sooner the story will fade from the tabloids." James looked between Sarah and

Dermot and heaved a sigh. It was the only hint that he felt even slightly defeated. "I can't ask the two of you to stay apart. But for appearances sake, I would appreciate if you kept your relationship private, at least until this is settled."

It was Dermot who answered. "We can agree to that. We're not eager for attention any more that you are."

"Thank you." He turned to Green. "We need something drawn up giving Dermot power of attorney over his mother and revoking it from my uncle."

"Mrs. Jeffries will draw up the papers. I'll bring them to your office to sign when they are ready." Green replied without moving to follow James.

"Very well." James left. Walter followed on his heels, but not without casting a disdainful look toward Dermot and Sarah.

Lyall Green turned to Sarah and lowered his voice. "You are going to have to tread very carefully. This test you propose may not turn out the way you think it will."

"We'll see about that." She told him. "I have someone who can help with your research. He already knows about The Nine, even figured out that I was one on his own. His name is Jujhar Gurudat. He's better suited to this than my brother."

"I see." Green gave a short laugh. "You really are full of demands today."

"You people want me to be a queen." Sarah pulled her shoulders back looking downright imperious. "I'll be a damn queen."

CHAPTER SIX

The heavy front door slammed shut behind them. Calum and Archie Sinclair had checked the building at Bernard Terrace, and declared it clear. Calum took a position near the back door while Archie stood with his back to the front door. Unlike his earlier disdain, he had been carefully polite and efficient since they left Green's office.

Fortunately, Sarah was used to being surrounded by people who viewed her with suspicion or dislike. That's the way it had always been back in Kettle Holler. If they weren't mad at her for her Granny's still, they were scared she was 'tetched' like her mother. Sarah could almost forgive Archie. She had gotten his son into a lot of trouble, but she wasn't about to let his dislike bother her.

Dermot took her hand and pulled her up the stairs. "Night, Arch."

Sarah shot a smile over her shoulder for the older man. Her flat looked just as she'd left it. Clean lines of modern furniture contrasted with the antique molding and fixtures of the old row house that was divided into three flats. Sarah dropped her backpack on the chair near the door and sank down on the couch. It was only mid-afternoon, but she felt exhausted.

Over the last few days, she had been chased by paparazzi, survived a car accident, been shot at, hiked for miles, and attempted to flee the country. And now she was back in the flat that she thought she'd never see again. She liked her flat. She'd been delighted when Dermot showed it to her on her first day in Edinburgh. Now, it only looked like defeat. "I think I'm going to sleep for a week."

"Not before we talk about what's going on." Dermot's tone was serious, but not angry.

She lifted her eyes to his. "I bought us time."

"Time for what?"

"I don't know. All I know is that I'm tired of getting swept along as if I don't have any choice in all this. So, I'm going to stand up on my surfboard and ride the wave, or at least find a way to get out of the water."

"And ye think this test is it?" He sank onto the couch beside her. "Do ye even believe what ye told James?"

"I don't know. I don't know if I believe any of this." Sarah scooted closer to him, throwing her legs over his lap. "But a legendary wizard made me tea the other night and showed me events that happened before my mother was born, and I watched your leg heal in minutes with nothing but water. None of it makes any sense."

He made one of his speaking grunts that she thought was agreement and wrapped his arm around her. She laid her head on his shoulder, and he rested his cheek on top of it. His voice rumbled against her ear. "Do ye really think I'm yer match?"

"I think I love you, and I tried pretty hard not to." She rested her hand over his heart. "I don't know if we're some kind of magical prophesied match, but I do know that we fit. I don't want anyone else."

He brought his hand up to rest on hers above his heart. "So, what do we do now, *a bhanrigh a t-shighean?*"

She scoffed. "Fairy queen, my ass."

"That's my girl." He patted her hand.

"Now, I guess we wait for James to make a decision and in the meantime, we look for another chance to get away."

"A sound plan, except that Arch took my passport." Dermot told her.

"Right." Sarah closed her eyes in defeat. "And I take it you won't be able to get another one from Des."

"Not anytime soon. I spent a fair bit of my reserves on that one." Dermot kissed the top of her head before letting his fall back to rest on the back of the couch.

Sarah yawned and murmured. "We'll figure something out."

"We'll have to." Dermot sat up. "Come on. Ye need sleep."

He pulled her up from the couch and wrapped an arm around her. They began walking toward the bedroom. She leaned on him. "Stay with me?"

"Always."

***

A chill wind brushed Sarah's cheek bringing her out of her sleep. The rustle of grass and leaves was preternaturally loud. She opened her eyes and looked around. Moonlight trimmed the edges of trees and the kudzu that climbed to the treetops in silver. Sarah recognized the forest on Grandfather Mountain from the summer before. The wind swept up behind her blowing her hair in her face. She pushed it back and a flash of white caught in the corner of her eye.

A woman in white stepped behind a great tree, her skirt blowing out behind her. Mama. Sarah stepped forward, the grass brushing her ankles. She paused at the tree line where the moonlight barely penetrated the canopy. Lightning bugs blinked in and out showing a path through the trees. Sarah glimpsed her mother further along the trail. She stepped onto the carpet of fallen leaves.

"Mama." She called out, but Molly kept going. Her long skirt trailed behind her through the underbrush.

Sarah followed her mother, just as she had the summer before. This time, she saw the stones that marked the boundary of the clearing. They weren't great monoliths like Stonehenge or Callanish, but they were too evenly spaced to be accidental. Mama stopped in the center of the circle.

"I think I get it now, Mama." Sara stepped into the circle. Molly shook her head slowly. A tear ran down her cheek. Unlike Sarah's vision from last July, there was no anger in Molly's eyes, only sadness. She lifted a finger and pointed to the space between two of the stones.

Sarah looked to where Molly indicated, and a white light filled her vision. When it faded, Sarah was once again in the upstairs hallway of her childhood home. The usual leaping panic that she felt at the memory of finding her mother coursed briefly through her blood. Its power was blunted now, by time and understanding. Now, as the door opened Sarah only felt sadness. She didn't run into the room as she had when she was six years old. She stood in the doorway and watched as her mother fell to the bed, her blood-soaked fingers having finished the last letter of the message scrawled on the wall. *Ruith.* (Run.)

"I tried, Mama." Sarah whispered tears pricking her eyes.

Another bright flash of light to her left, and she saw another scene from her encounter with her mother last summer. This was the one of the hard-eyed old woman singing "The River Maiden". Now, she recognized the woman as her Aunt Eilidh, and wondered why she hadn't seen it when she met the old woman in person. Molly had been trying to warn her in the forest last year.

Light flashed again, and she turned to see the couple making love on the stone. Last summer she had been shocked to see herself in that vision. This time she tried to see who the dark-haired man was. She walked closer, but the man in his passion kept his face pressed to his partner's neck. Sarah suddenly became desperate to see him.

If the other visions were true, was this one? She circled the couple making love on the square stone, feeling both awkward and fascinated. He was tall. His hair was dark and his body leanly muscled. What was Molly trying to tell her with this vision? The Sarah on the stone leaned her head back in ecstasy, but the man frustratingly did not. Their love making intensified, the man's grunting came fast and loud. A groan seemed to bubble up from him, and he began to lift his head. Suddenly, everything went white.

***

Sarah sat up with a gasp. The room around her was dark, and for a second she didn't know where she was. Her heart was racing near panic. A warm heavy arm tightened around her waist. She turned and caught the lines of Dermot's face in the faint light from the window. At the sight of him, she remembered she was in her flat in Edinburgh. She let him pull her back down into his arms.

She settled into his warmth and he sleepily mumbled. *"Trom-laighe?"* (Nightmare?)

"Seadh." (Yeah.) She nestled her nose into her favorite spot just between his earlobe and jaw.

He grunted and settled curled himself protectively around her. Sarah tried to go back to sleep. She was tired enough, but as the images from her dream drifted back to her, she found her mind's eye continually circling the couple on the stone trying to see the man's face.

CHAPTER SEVEN

"Thank goodness you're safe." Felicia Banks came rushing over to Dermot on too high heels. Dermot and Sarah had dutifully presented themselves at James's house on Polwarth Terrace at exactly nine o'clock. The door was answered by the ever-efficient Audra Lennox, James's executive assistant, who had immediately ushered them into the study where Felicia and her public relations team waited.

Dermot and Felicia kissed hello, not unusual for friends in the UK, but Sarah had to resist the urge to squeeze herself between them. Dermot had told her that Felicia was only a friend, but Sarah still wasn't sure that Felicia was aware of that. Dermot turned to her. "Felicia, I don't think you've properly met Sarah MacAlpin."

Felicia grinned, her wine-red lipstick a stark contrast to bright white teeth. She held out a tastefully manicured hand. "Miss MacAlpin, of course I've heard so much about you I feel like we're already friends."

Sarah gave her a doubtful look but shook her hand. "Nice to meet you."

Felicia laughed low and sexy. "Oh, I doubt that. Most people only notice me when there is a mess like this to be cleaned up. But I really am here to help."

Her honesty disarmed some of Sarah's lingering suspicion. She could see why Dermot liked Felicia. They would still do well to remember that the woman worked for James and

Walter. "Thanks. Whatever we need to do to get my name out of the papers."

Sarah pulled back an inch when Felicia surprised her by tapping a finger under one of Sarah's eyes. "You look tired, but that might work in our favor." Felicia hooked an arm through Sarah's and pulled her toward a chair near the window. A thin man in a ruffled pink shirt and peg leg pants stood beside an enormous makeup case.

Felicia stopped Sarah in front of the chair and pushed down slightly on her shoulder. Sarah sat. "This is Tony." She jerked her head toward the man who smiled. Sarah noted his incredibly smooth skin and perfectly shaped eyebrows. To Tony, Felicia instructed. "I want her to look innocent and aggrieved. We want the public to turn on the press for what they've done to this poor woman."

Tony tilted his head, examining Sarah. "And the hair? Ingenue or librarian?"

Felicia gave Sarah a similar perusal. "Ingenue." She patted Sarah's shoulder before walking away. "Now, Dermot. I'd tell you to look concerned and protective, but that seem to be your default." To another of her minions. "The wardrobe trunks are in the ballroom. Check them for a jacket that'll make him look more academic?"

The young woman she'd spoken to jumped to do Felicia's bidding and hustled out the door. Sarah caught Dermot's eye over Tony's shoulder while he began to sponge something onto her face. Felicia was right about concerned and protective. He had that look down.

Minutes later as Tony was using a clip to secure some of Sarah's hair back from her face, James walked in. His gaze went straight to Sarah, and she thought she saw his shoulders relax a little. He came around the table to her ignoring Dermot as he walked past him. "You look lovely."

"Uh-oh, Tony." Sarah joked. "I think the order was to make me look innocent and aggrieved."

"Even aggrieved, you're beautiful." Sarah was sure she blushed as James took her hand and bussed her cheek. She would tolerate James's flirting if it helped bring him over to their way of thinking. She couldn't afford to antagonize him.

"Flatterer." She teased.

James grinned that spotlight grin of his. "Whatever works."

Dermot cleared his throat behind James who shot a baleful look over his shoulder at his one-time friend.

"So, tell me what's going to happen." Sarah drew James's attention away from Dermot. No need to let those two keep staring daggers at each other.

"I'm sure Miss Banks can tell you better than I can." But Felicia had rushed off to prepare the area around the doors where they would be talking to the press. He gave her a reassuring look. "We'll be doing this on the front steps. Miss Banks thinks that appearing like regular citizens will gain us some sympathy. You don't need to say anything, just look like the injured party."

"That shouldn't be too hard." Sarah rubbed her still-sore elbow.

James hummed in agreement. "I will do the talking."

Sarah was on the verge of asking what he planned to say when the young woman who had gone off in search of an 'academic jacket' bustled in carrying a tweed number with suede patches on the sleeves. Sarah wondered if Felicia Banks traveled with her own costume department as well as a makeup artist. Dermot slipped on the jacket and the young woman handed him a pair of glasses to go with it.

He put them on and looked at Sarah, who stifled a laugh. Dermot lifted an eyebrow showing that he didn't find any of this humorous, but it only added to the harried professor look.

Felicia breezed in as if she were running a fashion show and not a press conference. "Everything is ready."

"What about Jujhar? He was in the crash too." Sarah asked.

James waved a dismissive hand. "He declined to appear. I think he would prefer to maintain what privacy he can."

"Can't say I blame him there." Dermot grumbled tugging uncomfortably at one tweed sleeve.

"Alright." Felicia clapped her hands in the doorway. "Last pass. Let's make sure everyone looks their part."

Sarah, Dermot, and James stood side by side for inspection. Felicia gave each of them a once over, straightening this and rumpling that to create just the effect she wanted. When she was done, she stood back and admired their handiwork. "James will give a statement, then you'll take a few questions, because if we don't take any they'll think we're hiding something. Then, you'll be done. Shouldn't take more than a few minutes."

She led them to the front door. Sarah noticed Walter Stuart and some men wearing A. P. Security shirts in the front hall. Calum and another enormous security guard took positions in front of and behind them. Felicia went straight to the door.

"Put your righteous indignation faces on." With that she opened the door, and the world erupted into chaos.

***

Even in the daylight, the camera flashes were nearly blinding, and seemed to be coming from every direction. Once they were on the front steps, Felicia closed the door behind them. Dermot knew they could go back inside if they needed to, but it didn't help the feeling of being trapped. James took the lead. He was flanked by Dermot on the right and Sarah on his left. A bodyguard stood on either side of the trio.

Sarah must have felt as trapped as he did. She took a half-step behind James and might have gone for the door if James hadn't stopped her by taking her hand. The flash bulbs went wild.

James cleared his throat. "I am pleased to say that my friends have returned to us. Thankfully, they survived the car accident in the Highlands without serious injury and are looking forward to returning to their normal lives." James emphasized the word 'normal'. "As I said yesterday, these people are not public figures. They are not politicians or celebrities. They did nothing to seek the media attention that they have received in recent weeks, and they want nothing more than for it to go away. Your behavior toward Miss MacAlpin has caused great difficulty for her both personally and professionally. She would like to get back to her own life and her studies, which is the reason why she came to Scotland."

"We request that you," He looked pointedly at a few photographers who were in the crowd. "And the editors who buy your photos think long and hard about the damage that your aggressive pursuit of innocent citizens can do. These people could have been killed in that car accident. Please stop this before someone is killed."

He finished by saying, "We will answer a few questions, and then we will not comment on this incident again."

Then the questions began to fly. The first to filter through the noise was, "Where have you been the last two days?"

James glanced between them. Dermot answered. "A good Samaritan stopped to help us and brought us back to the city."

The next question they could understand was, "What about the ten thousand pound reward?"

James leaned toward the nearest microphone. "As they have returned on their own there will be no reward. However, we will do our best to make sure the Samaritan who helped them is compensated for his trouble."

"Is there any word on who the driver of the other car was?" A woman near the front of the crush of reporters asked.

James looked at her. "We believe we may know and will be pursuing that privately."

That prompted another fusillade of questions. "Miss MacAlpin, will you be returning to your research trip?"

Sarah eyed the questioner, a man with glasses that were slightly crooked. She blinked several times and tried to speak but the words caught in her throat. In the end she only shook her head and mumbled, "I don't see how I can now."

She caught Dermot's eye behind James's head. He knew she would have bolted back inside if she could. Only the dread of making a further spectacle was keeping her there. James must have sensed it too. He turned half away from the crowd. "I think that's enough. We'll not be commenting further on this matter. Thank you."

"Can you confirm that you are in a relationship?" A woman shouted from somewhere in the gaggle.

James stopped and turned back toward the reporters regarding them with flinty eyes. They waited silently for his answer. "Whether we are or not is immaterial. People have a right to privacy. Please respect ours."

The three of them turned to find the door to the house open. They went back inside pursued by flashbulbs and more shouted questions.

"That was spot on!" Felicia gushed. "You all handled that well and looked perfect. Sarah, your answer to the question about work was handled incredibly well."

"Thanks." Sarah muttered before turning to James. "Let's hope I never have to do that again."

Dermot noticed James studying her. He knew that look; he'd worn it plenty of times himself. It was the look of a man who truly cared for her but couldn't get too close. He expected a surge of jealousy like he'd felt before when he'd seen them at the Burns Supper, or hiking on Arthur's Seat, or the first time he'd seen the photos of them in a tabloid.

This time he only felt pity. He'd been in that position; loving Sarah, but not being able to do anything about it. This time he knew she was his in her heart, whether they got away from the Stuarts or not. He wasn't going to lose her heart to James. Now, they just had to make sure he didn't lose the rest of her.

CHAPTER EIGHT

"I'm just saying that I've been in his shoes." Dermot told her as they walked to the university campus the next day.

"Mmhmm, would that be the Gucci sneakers or the Ferragamo loafers?" Sarah shot a look at his shoes. "I had no idea you were the same size."

"Ye know what I mean." Sarah had been in a mood since they'd left Polwarth Terrace after that press conference without an answer about her proposed test. "I know what it's like to care for someone ye canna have."

"I just want all of this settled." She looked both ways at the corner. Traffic was busy at that hour.

"At least that press conference or whatever it was seems to have done the trick." Dermot noted. They hadn't had any photographers outside their house since.

"I would feel a lot better about that if James had firmly said that we aren't in a relationship. That was a dodge, and one that they're not going to swallow for long." They reached the curb and turned toward the building that housed their research team's office.

"Sorry, love. He's going to keep that door open as long as he can." They were passing a chrome and glass building when the door opened in front of them showing them a reflection of the street behind them. Something caught Dermot's eye. At the next corner while they were waiting to cross, Dermot surveyed the street behind them.

Fleming Sinclair was roughly ten feet back. They had agreed on that arrangement early that morning. They could both protect Sarah, without making her feel like a prisoner. Of course, Dermot also noted that they couldn't leave their building without an A. P. Security guard with them. At least Sarah liked Fleming, and he was easy to work with.

But about twenty feet behind Fleming was the swarthy man that chased them through the Old Town. "Bollocks!"

"What is it?" Sarah whirled around concern on her face.

"Our mate from the train station has found us." Dermot took her arm as the light changed and they crossed the street. She started to look behind them, but he hustled her on. "Dinna look back. It'll be fine. Fleming is there. He willna let anything happen to ye."

"Should we call the police?" She had to step quickly to keep up with his long strides.

"He hasna done anything illegal, so there's little they can do." They reached their building and went inside. I'll catch up with ye in a minute. I just want to tell Fleming about our friend."

"I'll stay. I don't want to leave you." She gripped his arm nervously.

He decided to ignore her protest. "Use the phone on my desk. The second speed dial button. Ask for Mark Shaw and tell him what's happening." She gave him a mulish look as the elevator doors opened. "Ye've left me before in worse circumstances than this and that turned out alright."

"I didn't like it then either." Her eyes sparked with temper.

He kissed her and stepped forward, backing her onto the elevator. He hit the button for their floor as he backed out. "Go on. I'll be there in a tic."

"You'd better." The doors closed.

Dermot turned to see Fleming coming in the door behind him. "We've got a tail. Probably not far behind ye."

"Right. What's the plan?" Fleming didn't miss a beat.

"Get behind that desk. I'll be over here. We can take him as soon as he gets in the door." Dermot moved to stand behind the door, while Fleming hid behind the desk.

Seconds later the glass door opened, and the man entered. He stopped a couple of feet inside and looked to the left. Dermot used that second to move closer. When the man turned to look to his right, the bridge of his nose collided with Dermot's elbow. That sent his head flying back and unbalanced him. Dermot hooked his knee with a foot and had him on the ground before Fleming came out from behind the desk.

Fleming reached down and flipped the man onto his stomach. He pulled a zip tie out of his jacket wrenching the man's wrists together. "Is there a closet we can use to wait for Shaw?"

Dermot took a left and walked down a hallway looking for a room. "Here."

Fleming yanked the man to his feet and walked him back to the closet Dermot had found. There was room enough for the three of them. They emptied the man's pockets finding a passport, cash, and the gun that Dermot had seen him with a few days ago. They checked him over for any other weapons. "Well, Felipe if that is yer real name, ye should really work on this tailing thing. That's twice I got ye with the same elbow. Are ye with the Invigilare?"

The man simply shook his head and shrugged unwilling to answer.

Dermot glared at him. "Well, yer the second Invigilare I've bested in the last week. I'm going to turn ye over to my friends and let them deal with ye. Ye'll most likely be deported." He leaned closer. "Yer friend didna fare so well."

The man's eyes shot daggers at him, but he said nothing. That wasn't surprising. Secret organizations didn't stay secret for long if their henchmen went around talking about them. Dermot glanced at Fleming. "Can ye handle this while ye wait for someone from the office?"

"Aye, mate. I've got him." Fleming unfolded a chair and pushed it into the back of the man's knees. The assassin dropped into the chair. After making sure it was loaded, Fleming pointed the gun at the man, and settled in to wait.

"Cheers." Dermot clapped Fleming on the shoulder as he opened the door. "I'll tell the office to send a car."

CHAPTER NINE

If he hadn't given her a job to do, she would have come right back down on that elevator. As the doors closed between them, she felt like she was back in the cave in the Highlands leaving him to deal with the assassin who had been taking shots at them. This time she didn't have her brother to drag her away and the temptation was almost more than she could resist. But he had given her a job to do. No doubt they would need A. P. Security's help once they did whatever they were going to do with the man. At least Fleming would be with him.

The elevator dinged and the doors opened. Sarah poked her head out into the hallway worried there might be someone lying in wait up here. What she found was Isla Reid, who instantly pulled Sarah out of the elevator and into a hug. "Thank God you're safe."

Sarah returned the hug, wishing she had time to catch up with her friend and colleague. "I've got to get to the phone. Dermot's dealing with a man who was following us."

"Right," They hustled down the hall toward the team's office. "Let's call the police."

"It's better to call Alba Petroleum Security. James has loaned them to us until this dies down." Sarah explained. They sped through the main room where the desks and worktables were, and down the hallway to Dermot's office.

She had a faint impression of Ewan and Jujhar sitting at their desks but couldn't stop to talk.

In Dermot's office, Sarah grabbed the phone and hit the speed dial button. The phone rang twice before a woman answered. "Alba Petroleum Security offices."

"I need Mark Shaw right away." Sarah didn't have for pleasantries.

"Mr. Shaw is in a meeting just now. May I tell him-"

"This is Sarah MacAlpin."

"I'll get Mr. Shaw right away." The woman's tone was clipped.

"Miss MacAlpin." An authoritative male voice came on the line. "This is Shaw."

"I'm at University Square offices. Dermot and Fleming Sinclair are downstairs dealing with a man who was following us as we walked to work." She hoped that was enough detail for him to work with.

It sounded like Shaw snapped his fingers a couple of times. "Is that person familiar to you?"

"He's the man who was following us at the train station two days ago." Sarah didn't want to mention the Invigilare with Isla standing beside her.

"I see." Shaw must have put his hand over the phone. Sarah heard muffled voices but couldn't make out what was said. "A car will be there soon. Tell the Sinclairs to be ready."

"Will do." She heard the click of him hanging up on the other end and let the hand that held the receiver drop. She heaved a quick sigh before putting it back in the cradle. Sarah rounded the desk and headed for the elevator with Isla hot on her heels. Now that she'd done her job, she needed to know that Dermot was okay.

They were halfway down the hall when the elevator doors opened, and Dermot stepped out. Sarah broke into a run and threw herself at him wrapping her arms around his neck.

He caught her lifting her a few inches off the floor. When he put her down, he found her mouth with his in a fierce kiss.

"Finally." Isla whispered behind them.

Dermot chuckled as he released her. "I told ye not to fret."

"Okay. Next time, I'll send you away while I stay to fight. See how relaxed you are about it."

"Fair enough." They walked toward the office. "Did ye talk to Shaw?"

"He said he's sending a car." Sarah wondered not for the first time about the size and scope of A. P. Security. It seemed like James operated his own personal police force, which Sarah found thoroughly chilling. That was going to make getting away from them much harder.

"Good. Fleming is waiting downstairs with our friend." In the offices, Ewan and Jujhar were now standing near the door eager to learn what was going on. "Morning, lads. I'll just be a minute."

To Sarah. "I'm going to call Shaw and tell him where to find them."

She gave him a thumbs up and tried to stay positive despite her jangling nerves. She turned to the rest of the group. Ewan stood dumbfounded by the sudden bustle around them. Jujhar gave her a tentative look. She hugged them both in turn and invited them to sit down at the table again. "I'm so glad to see y'all."

"Aye, we're that glad to see ye too." Ewan sat next to Isla.

"I see you're still being followed." Jujhar's dark eyes showed concern.

Sarah tried to wave it off. "Probably just another photographer looking for a new score. We hoped that statement yesterday would put an end to it, but they seem insatiable."

"But ye're not stepping out with James Stuart, are ye?" Ewan asked.

"Of course, she's not." Isla swatted his arm. "She's with Dermot."

At that Ewan's eyes went wide. "How did I not know that?"

"Because ye've got yer face stuck behind a camera most of the time." Isla teased him. "Go back and watch the footage. Ye'll see it."

Sarah hoped they hadn't been that obvious. "It's okay. Ewan. We kept it on the down low while we were working together."

"Wait." Isla leaned forward in her chair. "Were working together? Are ye leaving us?"

Sarah tried not to let the news she and Dermot had come to deliver upset her. "That's one of the things we're going to talk about in today's meeting."

"It is." Dermot came back into the room and took his place at the head of the folding table. "Sarah and I are both taking a step back. None of us wants this business with the media to distract from the real goal of the team."

"Who's going to lead us?" Asked Isla.

"I was hoping ye would." He pinned her with a look before grinning.

Isla opened her mouth to say something and then closed it and looked thoughtful for a second. "Aye, alright."

"That means ye'll have to plan the next swing of field work up the north coast. Might be good to pick up around Drumbeg or Lairg since we came home before getting to them."

"I can handle that." Isla was nothing if not confident. A traditional musician, Isla had been a good friend and a tireless worker in the field. Sarah was sure she would do a great job. "I reckon we'll need to find a couple more fellows to pick up for the two of ye and Kirstie."

Dermot answered with an affirmative grunt. "Where is Kirstie, anyway?"

They all gave him a look that said he shouldn't have been surprised not to see her. It had been Kirstie who had called the tabloids to identify Sarah as the mystery woman with James Stuart. Ewan was the first to speak up. "She was shaken after the drive out of Lochinver, and then when we heard ye were missing…"

"I think she got spooked." Isla finished after Ewan trailed off. "We found a letter for ye slid under the door when we got here. I expect it's her resignation. I put it on yer desk."

"I see." Dermot sighed. "Well. I canna say I'm surprised. She put us all in danger over petty jealousy."

The group around the table nodded in agreement. Sarah spoke up. "Dermot and I can still help with transcribing what we collected on the trip and the things that need to be done around the office. We just think we should take a step back from the public eye where the team is concerned."

"We can use the help." Isla sounded relieved. "We've got a lot of recording to go through."

"Isla, will you take the step of contacting Kirstie to find out if she has any notes about her recordings that can help us with that?"

"Yeah. I'll take care of that." She made a note in her organizer.

Dermot turned to Ewan. "Will ye get together any footage ye have of the photographers following or chasing us, and send it over to Felicia Banks at Alba Petroleum? She runs their public relations arm. It may be helpful for them to show how dangerous this mess really was."

Ewan who had been filming their team's work for a documentary slid a video cassette in a case across the table. "I thought ye might say that, so I cut some of that footage together yesterday."

"Cheers, mate." Dermot spread his hands out over the table. "That's all I had. I think we'd best get to transcribing and cataloging what we've got."

"Right." Isla jumped into the role of organizing. "The tapes are in those boxes. Grab a box and get to it. I'd leave Kirstie's recordings until we get her notes."

The meeting broke up with everyone picking a box of recordings from their research trip through the Highlands and Western Isles. Sarah was sliding a box of cassette tapes onto her desk when she felt eyes on her. She looked up to find Jujhar watching her warily. "Can we talk?"

"We do need to talk." She hadn't spoken much to Jujhar since he'd revealed that he had been working side by side with her and befriending her while secretly suspecting that she was part of The Nine.

To Jujhar The Nine was a mysterious group of people with supernatural powers who held some secret knowledge about the world and its workings. Sarah still wasn't one hundred percent sure she knew what The Nine was, but she knew that too many people thought she was part of it. She had felt betrayed that one of the few people she'd come to trust in Scotland had secretly been poking around in her life. He claimed that his interest in The Nine was out of academic and spiritual curiosity. She was further convinced of his good intentions by the endorsement of her brother, Ruaraidh, whose manifestation of the family gifts made him a sort of human lie detector.

If Jujhar wanted to learn more about The Nine, she had just the resource for him. Although he might come to regret looking for those answers. She stood and motioned for him to follow. "Maybe Dermot will let us borrow his office."

Jujhar nodded and followed her down the hall.

Dermot was on the phone with someone, but waved them in. Speaking into the phone before he hung up. "Aye. Let me know what ye find out."

"Is that about the other thing?" Sarah asked.

"Just making sure the package got picked up." They were getting good at talking in vague shorthand. "What can I do for ye?"

"Actually, Jujhar and I were hoping to have a private conversation." Sarah sat down in the chair that stood in front of Dermot's desk.

"Want me to leave?" Dermot offered.

"I don't have any secrets from you." Sarah looked at Jujhar in question.

Jujhar looked between them. Sarah thought she noticed a touch of disappointment on his face. "That's just as well."

"There's a folding chair behind the door." Dermot jerked his chin in that direction. "Have a seat."

Jujhar closed the door and unfolded the chair for himself. He sat down and crossed his legs folding his hands in his lap. The action seemed to restore some of his usual calm. When he spoke, he leveled his warm brown eyes on Sarah. "Once again, I would like to apologize for deceiving you about my motives for joining the research team. I'm also sorry that you found out the way you did."

Jujhar had revealed his activities in her Aunt Eilidh's kitchen after they had been run off the road and taken refuge there. Considering the series of life-altering revelations on that trip, Jujhar's was minor. Still, it had hit Sarah hard. She had grown close to the team's linguist, appreciating his insights and relaxed demeanor. "Did you join the team to get close to me?"

"No." His eyes never left hers. "I joined the team to collect folklore hoping that some of it would help in my search. The fact that you were on the team, was pure chance, or fate, if you believe in that sort of thing."

"I'd rather believe in free will, but that's a whole other conversation." If one more person told her about her fate, she was not going to be responsible for her actions. "Let's say that my great aunt was telling the truth." Sarah watched him closely. "What do you plan to do with that knowledge?"

"As I told you before, I believe The Nine should be kept secret. I have no interest in interfering with your purpose." Jujhar's voice was even and measured, something that Sarah used to find soothing. Like everything now, she wondered if that was a way of hiding what he was really thinking.

"And you still believe in this mystical Nine with their powers?" Sarah cocked her head. "Even though one of them is a neurotic graduate student, and another is a cranky old hag living in a run-down croft house?"

He smiled. "Actually, I think it makes it more believable. You're hiding in plain sight." He leaned closer. "I saw you use your gift."

"You saw me meditate and give an answer." Sarah arched an eyebrow at him. "You didn't see what my gift can do."

"True enough." Jujhar inclined his head to acknowledge the point. "I chose to believe you. Will you choose to believe me?"

Sarah held out a hand in question. "And if not, you're just going to what; walk away satisfied that you're right?"

"I would like to stay and help you." He told her, his eyes full of hope.

"Help me what?"

"Bring about whatever comes next." His face was straight. "Your aunt seemed to think that there is something great coming, something that you will be involved in."

She studied him, wishing that her brother was there to tell her if he was genuine. They would find out soon enough. "A man named Lyall Green will be calling you. He has some work for you to do."

***

That evening at her flat, Sarah massaged the back of her neck with one hand. It had been a while since she'd spent that many hours bent over a keyboard transcribing. At least here they had computers to use rather than handwriting on paper as they had in the library at Carolina. That certainly sped things up, but it didn't help her neck any.

"Come on." Dermot nodded to the space in front of him on the floor. They were relaxing after a dinner of take-out Thai food.

Sarah sat cross-legged on the floor between his knees. Dermot took over massaging her neck. She groaned. Her muscles were sore, and the pressure hurt, but the relaxation that followed it was such a relief. "Do you think he's made a decision yet?"

"Don't know." He did know exactly who she was talking about. His hands were warm on her shoulders, as his thumbs circled on either side of her spine.

Sarah leaned into his hands and closed her eyes. "Do you regret the loss of his friendship?"

Dermot kissed the back of her head. "It's hard to regret anything that brought us together. But aye. We were great friends when we were younger. But we started drifting apart years ago, long before we ever knew yer name."

Sarah remembered James's face when he'd realized that she was in love with Dermot. He had called Dermot his 'most trusted friend'. "I'm not sure he sees it that way."

Dermot's thumbs had worked their way up the back of her neck. They rubbed gentle circles near the base of her skull. Muscles all along her spine relaxed in a wave. "How did I not know you were so good at this?"

"Probably because I've spent most of the time I've known ye, trying my best to keep my hands off of ye."

She sighed and tilted her head so that he could get at a particular knot. "Thank goodness you gave up on that."

He grunted in agreement. His thumb pressed through the knot where her neck and shoulder met. When he had worked that knot out, he bent down and kissed the spot. "This is my favorite part."

"The part where you kiss me?"

"No, this part right here." He gently bit the spot that he'd just kissed.

She let out a sound somewhere between a groan and a whimper. His teeth on her sensitive skin sent tendrils of desire snaking through the muscles he'd just massaged.

She could hear the wolfish grin in his voice. "I love that sound."

I thought you were supposed to be getting the knots out of my neck." Her tone was half teasing. "This is not going to help me relax."

He kissed his way across the back of her neck. "I could if we do it right."

***

Later when Dermot lay beside her snoring softly, and Sarah enjoyed the boneless aftermath of lovemaking she had to admit that it was indeed relaxing. But even her post-orgasmic stupor wasn't enough to keep her worries at bay. Her thoughts drifted again to James, and she decided to put this boneless feeling to good use. Since their failed escape, she hadn't even thought of using her gift. With the frustration of still being in the grip of the Stuarts and waiting for James's decision, she doubted she'd have been able to relax enough to cast out. Now, it was worth a try.

She inhaled deep and slow, and exhaled relaxing further. On the next breath she cleared her mind. The next breath turned her focus to James Stuart. In a few more breaths she was in the dimly lit study at Polwarth Terrace. James stood with his arm propped on the mantle looking into the fire, a snifter in one hand. The tense planes of his face were a mask of shadow and firelight.

"I cannot understand why you are so troubled by this." James closed his eyes at the sound of his uncle's voice, and Sarah got the impression he was heartily sick of hearing his uncle's opinions on the matter.

She turned to see the older man sitting on the couch cradling his own drink. It was probably the most unguarded she had ever seen him. He had unbuttoned his jacket, though he hadn't loosened his tie. He leaned against the back of the leather couch; legs crossed. Even in this informal setting, he still looked every bit the urbane puppet master that she knew him to be. It was a great contrast to the angry bluster he had shown in Lyall Green's office. "There is no possible way that they can argue that you are not the heir. You have the money. You wield the power. You have the where-with-all to become a king. What can that errand boy have that compares with what you can offer?"

"It seems that Sarah is not that mercenary. She cares about more than money and security and cares precious little about the prophecy." James didn't take his eyes off the fire.

Walter held his brandy up to the firelight swirling it around in his glass watching the color. "I'll wager she cares about her safety. There are enough factions who do believe in the prophecy and want her dead. We are the only ones who can protect her from the Invigilare, the Circle and anyone else."

James took a sip of brandy, his lips pulling back for a second as it burned his throat. "I'm not so sure of that. I sign checks for bodyguards, many of whom neither know nor care about the prophecy." He huffed out a sharp laugh. "What is an army of mercenaries she doesn't know to a man she cares about, a man who has killed for her?"

"All you have to do is snap your fingers and you can have any woman in this country." Walter sipped his brandy and shook his head. "You can win this one. Snap your fingers, sign a check, send the Sinclair boy away, and marry her. I don't see why you are so bent on wooing her. We are going to shape history."

James turned around at that. He looked at his uncle with disbelief. "Is that how my father won my mother, by offering her the power to shape history?"

"We didn't know enough back then. They were from the right families and had the right connections to ensure financial success. But you know that love was never a factor." Walter shifted on the couch to face him more fully stretching an arm across the back.

James took another swig of brandy. "Yes, well, Sarah isn't my mother."

"More's the pity." Walter muttered. "You could do a great amount of history shaping with a woman like your mother at your side."

"And I'd be miserable through every minute of it, just like my father was." James set his glass on a side table and turned back to the fire bracing his hands on his hips. "I don't want a marriage like my parents have; in name only, living separately in the same house. My father didn't want that either. That's why he left the business as soon as I was old enough."

"Henry is weak. He always was." Walter set his brandy on the table. "It's why he needed a wife like your mother, someone who could take him in hand. And you've just described most of the marriages of people in our class."

"That doesn't make it right for me." James shook his head. He looked over his shoulder and caught his uncle's eye. "And if this king you think Sarah and I are supposed to produce is going to be a good leader, I think he'll need parents who love him and each other. It's terrible to grow up in the middle of all that animosity."

Sarah could see on James's face what those years of living with his parents' loveless marriage had done to him. She started to understand a little why he was so insistent that he loved her. He genuinely wanted to.

"You're not going to go through with this ridiculous test, are you?" Walter's tone dripped with derision.

James looked back into the fire. "I don't know. I can't imagine that we've all been wrong all this time. But if Sarah is right, there is a real risk in not doing the test."

"And if she's wrong?" Walter hissed. "If you are the heir, and you are her match, do you think she'll honor the result?"

She couldn't be wrong, Sarah thought. She just couldn't. James shrugged. "I don't know. Would you give up someone you loved that easily?"

Walter picked up his brandy again and looked down into the amber liquid. His shoulders sagged. "I made that choice long ago. We all have to at one time or another."

James turned to study him; his eyebrows drawn together as if he was trying to puzzle out what Walter meant by that. He seemed on the point of asking about the choice that Walter had made that seemed to weigh on him still, but Walter spoke again. "You don't have to do this test. You are the heir. You are her match. Assert that. Then you can shape whatever relationship you want with the woman once you have her."

"But I won't have her if she's forced into it." James snapped.

Walter made a tactical retreat. He turned to look out the window at the traffic driving by on the street and sipped his brandy. After giving James a few minutes to cool off. "You could eliminate the competition."

"No. We've had more than enough of those tactics." James gave him a horrified look. "Not to mention, she would never forgive me."

"She wouldn't have to know." Walter waved his snifter in James's direction. "Accidents can be arranged."

"Absolutely not!" James took a step toward his uncle. "I will not have it. Do you understand me?"

Walter regarded him with disappointment. "How on Earth did your mother raise someone so naive?"

James shook his head in exasperation. "She didn't. She shipped me off to a boarding school where they taught things like philosophy and ethics. Thank goodness."

"What good will those ethics do you when Sarah MacAlpin and everything that comes with her slips through your fingers."

Sarah felt something pulling at her. It was like a thousand threads pulling her backward. In seconds she was back in her bed staring up at the ceiling. Dermot was nuzzling her neck, his stubble scraping the sensitive skin. His arm tightened around her waist. She turned into him, snuggling closer. His warmth drawing her deeper toward sleep, but her mind kept drifting back to the conversation she'd just seen. She'd learned at least two things from that. First, that James was truly considering her proposed test, and second that Dermot was in danger from Walter Stuart.

CHAPTER TEN

Sarah came out of the bedroom still half asleep. Her neck felt better, but her concerns about what she'd seen when she had used her gift had kept her from sleeping deeply. At the end of the short hallway, she stopped dead. There was someone in the living room. Her heart raced and her blood felt electric. Silently, she flattened herself against the hallway wall where she was partially shielded from the room.

Leaning forward she peeked into the living room. The silhouette of a tall man stood in front of the window. The early morning light coming in made it hard to see anything but his shape. He had a straight back and broad shoulders. She might have mistaken him for Dermot, but she knew he'd gone for a run. He'd awakened her ten minutes before to tell her where he was going and kiss her goodbye.

The man turned and the light glinted off his gold watch. "James?"

He whirled around. "You're awake."

"Yeah." Shocked to see him so soon after her spying expedition last night, she wondered if her guilt about using her gift showed on her face. She went into the kitchen putting the island between them.

"I hope you don't mind." James came to stand on the other side of the island. "I waited until Dermot left. I would like for us to talk."

"Well, scaring me half to death is not an ideal conversation starter. You of all people know how many times I've been stalked." She turned the faucet on to fill the coffee pot effectively drowning out his apology. She watched the water level rise in the coffee pot and tried to keep her temper from rising with it. "And I know you own this building, but you don't own me. You don't just get to appear in my apartment. If you tell me I'm not a prisoner, then you can't treat me like one."

"I'm trying to keep you safe." He pleaded, his voice rising to be heard over the running water. "As you pointed out, someone is trying to kill you."

She turned the faucet off, and gave him a look that said, 'And whose fault is that?'. She resisted the temptation to say it out loud, and instead asked. "Would you like a cup of coffee?"

He took a breath and looked as if he might respond to what her face said rather than her words. In the end, he chose conciliation. "That would be nice."

Sarah turned away from him to pour the water into the incredibly fancy coffee maker he had given her a few months ago as a housewarming gift. The coffee maker had been followed by a cashmere shawl, and she'd had to put her foot down telling him that expensive gifts made her uncomfortable. "I don't want to argue with you, James."

"I don't want to argue with you either." His smooth patrician voice came from behind her. "I hoped we could talk without other influences chiming in."

Sarah set the carafe back in its place in the coffee maker and opened the cabinet in front of her to retrieve the coffee. She was relieved that she had something to do with her hands, something that would hide their shaking both from the scare he'd given her by appearing in her living room and from the knowledge that James Stuart held her future in his hands. She scooped coffee into the filter basket. "I have said everything that I have to say about this situation."

"I haven't." His voice was closer this time. Sarah tried to ignore his nearness busying herself with preparing cups. "I wanted to talk about us."

"There is no us, James." She didn't want to be rude, just unequivocal.

"I have to disagree." Like hers, his voice was soft but sure. "I don't care about your people or my people or the cauldron. I want to talk about Sarah and James. We've talked that way before." He paused and Sarah looked over her shoulder. He smiled at her in a way that reminded her of the morning he'd dragged her up Arthur's Seat. She'd been hungover, but he'd shown her that she was stronger than she thought. "We were friends once, not that long ago."

It was true. It was difficult for them to forget all the different agendas that were pulling at them, but they had formed a friendship in the weeks that she and Dermot had been at odds. When he wasn't being the CEO of Alba Petroleum or the Stuart heir, and he was just being James. She thought of the alias, Alan Young, that he used when traveling to avoid the press. "Sarah and Alan, then."

A hint of a smile teased at the corner of his too perfect mouth. "If you like."

"I can do that." She'd been able to reach him on a personal level before by shutting out everyone else's expectations. Maybe this would be the avenue to convince him to let her go. "Let's get our coffee and go sit down."

They poured two cups and took them to the living room. Sarah was careful to sit in the chair, so that James couldn't sit too close.

James took a seat on the couch near her. He sipped his coffee and set it down on the end table between them. "I want to start by telling you that I am not your enemy. I feel as though this whole business with the press and my uncle and Dermot has given you the impression that their concerns are mine. They are not. I want you to be happy, and you cannot deny that Dermot hurt you before."

"That was because of all the things we said we don't want to talk about. Dermot has been trapped between his feelings for me and his desire to take care of his mother. We've both tried to resist whatever it is between us, but we're miserable when we do, like a part of us is missing." Sarah reached across the space between them and put her hand on his arm. "Please don't be angry with him. He misses the friendship you used to have."

James pulled away picking up his cup again. He braced his elbows on his knees and held the cup between them. "I won't lie and tell you that I don't feel betrayed by him. He knew what our expectations were when he met you. And he knew that I was falling in love with you when you left for your trip."

"And he feels terrible about that." Sarah watched him as he studied the steam rising from his cup. "He never wanted to hurt you. But you also have to remember what his association with your family has taken from him. He lost you, his best friend. He lost the first career that he chose for himself. And when he started building a new career, even that was invaded by Walter's machinations. When you add in the situation with his mother, you have to see why he just wants to get away."

"Just as you do." Bitterly. He didn't take his eyes off his coffee cup.

"I want to live a life that I choose with the man that I love." It was that simple. James's life was so full of complications. She hoped he could understand. "Where I grew up, people always viewed me with suspicion or derision. They thought my mother was crazy, and even though they bought my grandmother's liquor, they despised her for being a woman who made money off their vice. I know what it's like to live under the weight of things you didn't choose for yourself. I also know what it's like to walk away from that and build a life. I don't want to give up that freedom."

"But you were about to give up your whole career to get away from my family's expectations." He lifted his head. She watched the muscles in his jaw flex with tension.

Sarah knew she had to choose her words carefully. She and Dermot had been desperate to get away from the Stuarts and all the intrigue that came with them. They had been ready to leave their lives behind them and start over. But she couldn't put that on James. It wasn't all his fault. "When you were going off to boarding school in Switzerland, I was foraging for our dinner and hoping we'd sold enough moonshine for me to buy some new winter shoes. When I was barely an adult, I lost the only family I had. I sold the farm and rolled out of Kettle Holler with the money from that sale, a trunk full of memories, and nothing else." She hated the way her voice cracked as she remembered driving away from the home where all her memories were made. "I know what it's like to build a life out of nothing. I can do it again if I have to."

"You were running away from me." His voice faltered and his face reflected his pain.

James was such an imposing, larger-than-life figure that it was difficult to imagine his heart being broken. For the first time, Sarah believed that she had the power to hurt James. "I wasn't running from you, specifically. I was running from everything; the press, your family, my family, the prophecy…all of it."

"Doesn't it matter that I love you?" His voice was soft. He remained in his position, but he turned toward her, his impossibly blue eyes pleading.

"Of course, it does. I don't want to hurt you. I don't want to hurt anyone." Sarah was almost sure that James was in love with the idea of what she was, or what Walter had told him she could do for him. She didn't believe that he was really in love with her but telling him that wouldn't help their case any. She had to convince him that what he thought he felt for her wasn't the kind of love that either of them wanted. She remembered something she'd read years ago. 'Are you familiar with John Steinbeck?"

"What does that have to do with anything?" He looked annoyed and confused at her change of tack.

"He was a Nobel Prize winning American author. Anyway, he was a prolific letter writer as well. There's a letter that he wrote to his son, about his first love. I'm paraphrasing here. He talks about two kinds of love. One is possessive and clinging, self-important. It drags us down. The other is," She looked for the right words. "Giving, and kind, respectful. It builds us up." Here was where she needed to be careful. His eyes had returned to his coffee, so she slid out of her chair to kneel at his knee. She put a hand on his arm, and when he looked up at her. "With your family, and my family and the prophecy all weighing on us, when you say you love me, I have to wonder which of those loves it is."

His eyes closed, as if he wasn't ready to examine that himself. When he spoke, his tone was resigned. "And you know which it is with Dermot."

"I do." Dermot had been ready to give up everything for her. Whenever Dermot's actions had been questionable, it had been at the behest of Walter or James. Left to his own devices, Dermot built her up.

"I see." He bowed his head and covered her hand on his arm with his own. After a moment, he lifted her hand from his arm, and cupped her face. "I don't want to lose you, either of you."

"Don't let the fear of losing us stop you from making the right choice, the generous, respectful, uplifting choice." She looked up into his eyes and hoped that what she saw there was understanding. "It's so cliché to say, 'If you love someone, set them free.' But it's a cliché for a reason. That was also in Steinbeck's letter, but in much more eloquent words than I have. He said, 'Nothing good gets away.'"

James slid his hand back into her hair, and for a second Sarah was afraid that he was going to kiss her. He brought his forehead to rest against hers and closed his eyes. He held her there for a moment before kissing her forehead softly.

"You've given me a lot to think about." He set his cup on the coffee table and stood. His voice was subdued but had returned to his usual polite formality. "I appreciate you sharing your perspective with me."

He stopped to give her a lingering look before opening the door. In the hall, his bodyguard fell into step behind him.

Sarah watched him go, hoping she'd convinced him to go through with the test.

CHAPTER ELEVEN

Sarah tried not to be intimidated by the mahogany paneled walls of the Alba Petroleum executive suite. She sat at the conference table with Dermot waiting for James.

They had been drinking their morning coffee and tea when Fleming had knocked on the door of her flat. "Lord Caledon has asked me to bring ye to his office." He looked sternly back and forth between the two of them who were dressed for a quiet morning in. "I would recommend dressing for the occasion."

She and Dermot looked at each other. This had to be it. They would hear James's answer. Panic surged in Sarah and her breath came short.

Dermot gripped her arms. "It's alright. Dinna worry about this. We'll see what he says and figure things out from there."

She gave him a hesitant nod.

"I've got to get dressed, but I'll meet ye downstairs shortly." He kissed her, not caring that Fleming was there to witness it. It was a hard, possessing kiss. When he let her go, she felt the lack of him. She opened her eyes to see Fleming closing the door as they both went out.

Sarah had put on her only casual dress, a conservatively cut green one, and pinned her hair up. She looked like an ingenue taking a page from Felicia's playbook, hoping that it would put James in a kind mood.

The conference room door opened and Lyall Green strolled in. He took a seat across from them. Nothing about his face or demeanor gave any indication that he knew what was about to happen. It reminded Sarah of what he'd told her about his role. He was an observer and only in rare circumstances, a guiding hand to steer this ship back to the right current.

A moment later Walter Stuart stalked into the room, seating himself to the right of the head of the table. His eyes scanned over each of them. After another minute, Sarah noticed Walter tapping his fourth and fifth fingers on the arm of his chair. Was he nervous?

It had been three days since she'd talked to James in her flat, six days since she and Dermot had tried to escape. Six days of being constantly watched by A. P. Security. She had hoped for a quick decision, but now that they were about to hear it, it seemed like such a short time. The door opened again and Audra Lennox looking prim and put together breezed in and placed a portfolio and pen at the head of the table. She left without a word.

Exactly thirty seconds later, James strode in. He took his place at the head of the table but didn't sit down. "Thank you for coming, everyone. I know the short notice may have been inconvenient for some of you."

Everyone bowed their heads to acknowledge his greeting, but no one said anything waiting for James to go on. "I'm sure I don't need to remind anyone of the seriousness of the decision we're facing." He scanned the people at the table. "We are making choices now that will affect the course of history not just of Scotland, but potentially the world. We must be careful. And we must do everything in our power to ensure that the choices we make are the right ones."

His eyes settled on Sarah before shifting to his uncle. "With that said, I have decided that we must go through with the test that Sarah has proposed. We have to be sure that we are on the correct path."

Walter Stuart did not speak but blinked rapidly and clenched his jaw as if fighting back angry words that wanted to burst out. Sarah thought she saw a hint of red rising from his starched collar.

James continued. "Mr. Green, perhaps you can fill everyone in on what your research has found about our ability to conduct this matching ceremony."

Green's face gave away nothing. If he had an opinion about this turn of events, he was keeping it to himself for now. When he spoke, it was all about logistics. "I believe that we can bring together enough of The Nine to ensure a fair result untainted by any one party's agenda. Although it will take some time. Some of the parties involved live outside of Scotland and we will have to bring them here. I also believe that to get an accurate result, we will need to perform the ceremony on the summer solstice as is tradition. That will give all of the involved parties time to assemble."

"Who are these other parties?" Walter's tone was indignant, as if the introduction of anyone else was an affront.

Green turned calm eyes to him. "The Nine are three generations of the daughters of the old ways. So, the elder Misses MacKenzie and MacLeod, and their daughters. In this new generation we have Miss MacAlpin here and her half-sister, Miss Ballantyne."

Sarah's heart sank. She didn't want to drag anyone else into this and hated that the half-sister she still hadn't met would have to return to Scotland to resolve her problem. Still, she couldn't really complain. She'd set this ball rolling.

"That's only six." Walter pointed out.

Green smiled at him like you would a child who thought he'd found a loophole in an adult's rule. "Seven actually. My mother was a child of the old ways. I can take the place of Miss MacAlpin's late grandmother. I have other ideas to solve for the missing sisters of the other generations, but they will take some additional research."

"And the test?" Dermot asked. Sarah could feel the tension rolling off of him. "How can it be conducted when the pool is dried up?"

"That is something I am still working on." Green nodded at Dermot. "You are right that the pool has dried up. I am getting a sample of the remaining silt to analyze what may have been in the pool to give it its unique properties. If we can determine what those properties are, then we may be able to chemically replicate the process that reveals the matches. There are some other possibilities that I am researching in case that doesn't pan out. Worst case scenario, we can use the cauldron itself and test Sarah's theory that its behavior is some sort of compass for the prophecy."

Walter shook his head looking skeptical. "That's not an accurate enough indicator. Who even knows why that does what it does and who judges whether it's working or not?"

"Either you believe in this fairy tale or you don't." Sarah pointed out. "Because if you don't, I can walk out that door right now and go back to my simple, obscure, happy life. If you're in for a penny, you're in for a pound."

Walter's lip curled back in a sneer, and Sarah thought if he were a cat, he'd be hissing. "That same can be said for you. You proposed this ridiculous test. If we're going to the trouble to do it, you had better abide by the results."

"Uncle." James laid a hand on Walter's shoulder. "There is no need for that tone. We are all working toward the same goals here."

"I'm not so sure of that." Walter stared daggers across the table at Sarah.

"Well, that's neither here nor there." James opened the portfolio at the head of the table. His fingers plucked up two paper clipped documents. "I have taken the liberty of drawing up contracts for Miss MacAlpin and Mr. Sinclair." He walked around in front of them. "These simply state that you will agree to abide by the results of the matching ceremony whatever they may be."

Sarah eyed the paper in front of her like it was a spider that might bite. Dermot's face twisted with bitterness. He didn't lose his temper often, but when he did, diplomacy was not his strong suit. She laid a staying hand on his arm and looked up at James. "And you? Is there a contract that says you and the rest of your family will abide by the results whatever they may be?"

A corner of James's mouth ticked up in a smile. "Of course." He went to the head of the table and pulled out another sheaf of papers which he slid across the table to her. "Whenever you are ready, we can call Miss Lennox in here to witness the signing of these."

Sarah laid Dermot's contract on top of hers and slid them across the table to Green. "I'd like our solicitor to read through these before either of us signs."

Green took the contracts and began reading them silently. Sarah did the same with the one that James had given her. After several paragraphs of standard contract language, it got to the point. The undersigned agreed to abide by the results of a matchmaking ceremony as prescribed by the tradition of Làrachd an Fhamhair.

"This states that a match with Mr. Sinclair absolves the Stuarts from providing protection for Miss MacAlpin and her heirs." Green looked up from the contract he was reading, concern written on his face. "Your family has always protected the people of Làrachd an Fhamhair."

"Until said test is completed, Miss MacAlpin will refrain from sexual relations with anyone?" Dermot read out loud, his volume rising with every word.

"As this is a question of heirs and succession, you can understand why that matters." Walter had regained some of his cool, as the rest of them had lost theirs.

"That's really not a concern." Sarah held up her left arm and pointed to the spot where her contraceptive implant was just under the skin. "I have an implant. I got it a couple of years ago, because what grad student wants her career derailed by an unplanned pregnancy." She cringed at the irony of that statement.

"We should amend the contract to demand that gets removed once the ceremony is done." Walter pointed to the contract in Green's hand.

Sarah looked at him as if he were a dinosaur who just appeared at the table. "I can't imagine why you're still single."

"I think that's a bridge that we can cross when we come to it." James waved off his uncle's suggestion.

"This security provision." Green drew them back to his original question. "How are we to guarantee the safety of the heir if you withdraw security aide. You know as well as I do that the factions who are against this child will not stop."

"If Mr. Sinclair is the heir, then that is no longer our problem." Walter answered before James could.

Sarah looked to James for his answer. He let his uncle's statement stand. She shook her head at him. "I can't disagree with a contract to abide by the results. I proposed that. It's only fair. But the security withdrawal? That proves that this was never about the prophecy, or your so-called future king. It's about solidifying power for you." She cut her eyes to Walter then back to James. "And you. That is small and spiteful. I thought you were better than this."

For the first time since walking in the door, James's confidence slipped. He looked at her with wounded eyes. Sarah leaned forward looking directly at him. She spoke to him as if they were alone. "I appreciate the needle you're trying to thread here, but this was badly done."

"They've won, mate." Dermot stood beside her and addressed James. "As long as I've known ye, I've been fighting to keep ye from the grasping forces that wanted to pull ye into their mercenary web. When we were lads we used to talk about honor. Do ye remember? I saw then that all yer mother and Walter cared about was power, but we..." He stopped overcome with emotion. "...We had bigger plans, better plans. But this?" He waved his hand at the contracts, his face twisted with disdain. "There's no honor in this."

He stalked up to James contract in hand. To James's credit, he didn't flinch at Dermot's fury. Dermot sneered and dropped the contract on the table in front of James. "We used to be like brothers, but ye're their creature now. At least I can stop feeling guilty about loving her."

He left the conference room, the door slamming behind him. James blinked rapidly, his throat working as he swallowed. Whether he was suppressing hurt or fury, Sarah couldn't quite tell. After a moment, he collected himself and took his seat.

Green cleared his throat. Breaking the tense silence in the wake of Dermot's outburst. "Of course, there is one problem that you have overlooked with these contracts."

"And that is?" James leveled blue eyes on him. His face wore a 'what now?' look.

"They're completely unenforceable." Green dropped the contract he was holding on the table. "The matching ceremony, the prophecy, even the existence of Làrachd an Fhamhair are all secrets so fantastic that no reasonable person who hadn't seen the truth for themselves would believe them. Dragging this out in a court of law would make you and Alba Petroleum a laughingstock. You would be the Lord of Fairy Tales in a modern world."

James picked up his pen and tapped it impatiently on the table. His eyes were focused on the portfolio in front of him. He had the look of a serious chess player whose gambit was just thwarted by his opponent. "Of course, you are right. They are more a symbol of our mutual agreement than an enforceable document." His eyes lifted to Sarah's and he motioned for her to pass the contract that she still held back to him.

She slid it down the table. James reached for the contracts that Green still held. He very deliberately stacked the three contracts together, then tore them in half. "I agree to abide by the results of the ceremony. I will not put you in danger before or after whether you are with me or Dermot. You have my word."

Sarah stood, looking him in the eye. "And you have mine that I will abide by the ceremony whatever the results."

She nodded to Mr. Green on her way out the door. "Gentlemen."

"Sarah," James called as she stepped out of the conference room. She stopped and looked back at him. Gone was the businessman who had just tried to pin them down with mean-spirited contracts. He was once again the man who had asked to be trusted with her happiness. "I found a copy of that letter, the Steinbeck letter. It gave me a lot to think about."

Sarah cut her eyes to the contracts on the table in front of him. "I think maybe you should read it again."

***

"Bloody James and his stupid bloody contracts." Dermot muttered as they arrived back at Sarah's flat. His blood was still boiling.

"I wouldn't worry about that." Sarah tried to soothe him. "Green pointed out that those contracts aren't enforceable. James just wanted a symbolic agreement."

"But that bit about the security." He poked the air with a finger as if pointing to the contract again. He could still see the offending lines, an open threat to Sarah's safety. "It amounts to extortion. He as much as said ye dinna matter if ye're not his. I thought better of him, or at least I wanted to."

"I know." She took his hand and drew him toward the couch. He could feel the thin bones of her fingers laced with his, reminding him of the imperative to protect her. "But we got what we asked for in the matching ceremony. You made your point. He tore them up and gave me his word that he would abide by the ceremony. I gave him mine."

"Do ye think he's telling the truth?" he didn't know any more if James could be trusted. They'd grown apart as their lives had pulled them in different directions. But when they'd been boys, they had been inseparable.

Sarah thought for a moment. "I think he will. I can't speak for Walter, or Walter's influence on James."

"Aye, ye have to watch that one." The very thought of Walter Stuart put Dermot's teeth on edge. The Machiavelli of the Mound was not to be trusted, and his influence on his nephew was on full display in that meeting. "James didna used to be so…transactional. I'm afraid that Walter holds too much sway over him."

"Yeah." Sarah agreed. "Still, he seems to care what we think, and we might be able to influence him to a better path. But we're definitely paddling upstream."

He made one of his speaking grunts. Sarah leaned her head on his shoulder. "Do ye really think we're the right match?"

She sat up and looked at him, her face full of determination. "I'm sure of it."

"It just makes me wonder. If this is about genetics, what does that mean for me?"

She studied him, her green eyes reading more in his expression than he could put into words. "You mean about your father?"

He nodded but couldn't quite voice the question that was running between them.

"Do you have any ideas who your father might be?" Her voice was hushed. She didn't want the guard that might be standing outside the door to hear.

"My mother never said anything to me." He matched her volume. "I always wondered why we spent summers and holidays with the Stuarts, but she only said that we were distant relatives and that James's father was a friend from university."

"Do you think they..." She trailed off, her eyes finishing the question.

"I have wondered."

"Does James's father have blue eyes like the two of you do?"

"He does. But if Henry and my mother..." He let his statement trail off as Sarah had the question. As if saying that might make it so. Why had he never made the connection with James and his eyes before? "Why would Anne allow us to stay around?"

"Who knows?" Sarah shrugged. "I don't think she married Henry for love. Maybe she was okay as long as it was kept secret."

Dermot looked incredulous. "How secret is it to invite us to Christmas and summer holidays?"

Sarah settled beside him. They sat in silence, each deep in their own thoughts. "Of course, it might not be about genetics at all. If a magic cauldron can supply endless food, and a tribe of people can stay hidden in the Highlands for thousands of years, what's to say the matching isn't about emotional or intellectual compatibility, or just fate? I mean the idea that I'm the genetic model for anything is just bizarre. I'm short, stubborn and I have problematic hair."

He slid an arm around her shoulders and pulled her close planting a kiss on the top of her head. "Ye're absolutely perfect, and dinna let me hear ye say otherwise."

"Clearly your judgment is impaired. She settled her ear against his chest. "I'm starting to wonder about this whole prophecy thing. They must have the wrong couple entirely."

A laugh rumbled up from his chest. God, he loved her. "That's wishful thinking."

CHAPTER TWELVE

June 1982
Scottish Borders

"Dermot!" James shouted as he came barreling out of the front door of the stone manor house. Dermot barely had time to step onto the gravel drive before he was tackled by his friend and cousin. They fell to the gravel, but neither of them took much notice. Dermot had been in the car so long he was ready to run, and it seemed so was James.

"I'm so glad you're here!" James chattered before Dermot could get a word in edgewise. "I've been here a week already and I'm bored witless. Where've you been?"

Dermot picked himself up and brushed himself off. "My school didna get out until Friday."

"Well, mine got out two weeks ago." James reached into the car to get Dermot's satchel. He hung it on his shoulder. "Mum's been driving me mad, and we had to go to Switzerland for a stupid school thing. Hello, Mrs. Sinclair."

"Hello, James." Dermot's mother smiled indulgently at him from across the roof of her Austin Metro. "How tall ye're getting!"

James pulled his shoulders back and lifted his chin looking pleased. "Dad says I'm going to be taller than him one day."

"I've no doubt." She assured him. "Where are yer parents?"

He jerked a thumb back at the house. "Dad's in the study with Uncle Walter and Mum's worrying Mrs. Miller about the linens."

"I'll just go and find them." She told them leaving the car in the drive. One of the staff would come back for their bags and move the car.

Dermot watched his mother walk up the front steps and into the gray stone facade of the enormous house. She paused at the top of the stairs and pulled her shoulders back taking a breath. He never quite understood the connection that they had with the Stuarts and why he and his mother spent their summers with them at Tweedholm House. All he knew was that they were somehow related, and Mum had attended St. Andrews with James's father.

"Anyway, it rained for days after we got back." James chattered on following Mum toward the steps.

Dermot finally registered what James had said. "Did ye say Switzerland?"

"Aye, Mum says all the right families send their children to this school. I don't know why I can't go to a public school here in Scotland, but you know how she is."

Indeed, he did. Dermot wasn't sure he knew who the 'right families' were, but he was fairly certain that he and his mother didn't qualify. If she was anything, Anne Stuart was consistent in her snobbery. It was another mystery about their friendship with the Stuarts. Dermot's mother was just as comfortable with crofters as she was with titled lords.

James went on. "Let's put this inside and go to the ruins."

"Aye, alright. Race ye." Dermot crouched into a starting position.

"You're on." James grinned. They both took off up the steps into the hall and up the winding staircase to the bedroom that they would share. Even hampered by the satchel, James kept pace with him, and they arrived in the room they would share laughing and out of breath.

James tossed the satchel on Dermot's bed. They had shared this room every summer for as long as he could remember. It was cleverly separated from the other bedrooms by a bathroom and the servant's stairs enabling them to talk late into the night without disturbing any of the adults. At twelve, they would likely be left to their own devices for most of the summer break, and that suited Dermot fine.

"Let's go to the ruins. We can play kings and knights." James hopped from foot to foot as they made their way back out into the hallway.

"Aren't we getting a bit old for that?" They were twelve now, after all.

"Psht." James waved that idea off. "You sound like Mum. It's summer we're supposed to play."

"Alright, but I get to be the king this time." James usually got to play the role of king.

"I need the practice." James teased. It was a running joke between them. James was descended from Bonnie Prince Charlie, something his mother rarely let him forget as if being the heir to a growing oil empire wasn't enough.

"Psht." Dermot mimicked his previous reaction and slapped him on the back as they headed down the stairs. "Maybe ye need me to show ye how it's done."

"Your accent sounds funny. Where've you been?" James asked.

"Dublin. Mum was at Trinity College this year." They rounded the landing and started down toward the front hall. "Next year we'll be in Edinburgh, but I suppose it won't matter as ye'll be in Switzerland."

"Bollocks." James muttered just as they reached the bottom of the stairs. "I would leave just as you're back in town."

"I wouldn't let your mother hear you talk like that." Dermot looked up to find Henry Stuart, Lord Caledon, standing there a rakish grin on his too handsome face. Henry was larger than life to Dermot. He was everything that Dermot thought a man should be; classically handsome, fun to be around, and successful. Despite all of that, he always seemed to have time for his son and oddly enough for the fatherless child of his old university chum. "Hello Dermot. I trust you've had a good school year."

"Yes, sir." Dermot bowed slightly.

"Dermot got the headmaster's award for excellence." His mother stood behind Henry, her face glowing with pride.

Henry looked back at her, eyebrows raised, before turning back to the boys. Lord Caledon's striking blue eyes met his. "I'm not at all surprised. You've always been a good student."

Dermot's chest swelled. Lord Caledon always asked about his schooling when they gathered at Tweedholm. Most of the time the only people who cared about Dermot's marks were his mother and his teachers. It was nice to imagine that Henry cared. "Thank you, sir."

Henry strolled up to them laying a hand on James's shoulder. "Where are you lads off to?"

James glanced back toward the kitchen where his mother was no doubt still harrying the housekeeper. When he turned back, he answered his father in a hushed tone as if he didn't want anyone else to hear. "We're going to the ruins to play."

Henry leaned down to James and motioned for Dermot to come closer. "You can play around the ruins, but don't climb on them. Mrs. Miller says some of the stones at the top of the walls are loose. And don't go too close to the river, the water is still high from the rain."

"Alright, Dad."

"Yes, sir." The boys said at the same time.

Henry gave Dermot a pat on the back. "Now go on before Lady Anne comes up with something else for you boys to do."

James and Dermot went for the back door, careful to skirt past the kitchen quietly. They were almost out the back door when Dermot heard Lord Caledon say, "You've done a wonderful job with him, Seonag."

"He's a good boy." His mother matched Henry's tone. It seemed so soft and personal. Dermot looked back to see Lord Caledon ushering his mother back into the study with his arm around her waist, his mother looked up at him fondly.

"Come on, Dermot." James called from the end of the stone patio that led down to the manicured lawn sweeping away from the house to the river Tweed.

Tweedholm House was situated on a bend in the river that marked the border between Scotland and England. The southward curve meant that they were surrounded on three sides by England on the other side of the Tweed, making Tweedholm a strategic point that had been used for centuries before the Victorian era mansion had been built on the land. In a copse of trees to the east of the house were the ruins of a tower. Dermot had no idea how long ago it had been used to watch the English on the other side, but now it was not much more than a few walls and fallen stones. Although, the boys imagined that at one time the tower had offered a view across the river all the way to Norham.

It was the perfect spot to fire the imaginations of young boys and fill their heads with border clashes and the adventures of knights errant. James picked up a stout stick and swung it as a test. Satisfied with its weight he knelt a few feet in front of Dermot and bowed his head. "I pledge my fealty to you, King Robert the Bruce."

Dermot quickly found his own stick and tapped James's shoulders. "Arise, Sir James Douglas. Help me drive these English hordes out of Scotland and I'll return your ancestral lands to you."

James rose and they proceeded to defend the ruins from invading Englishmen with great abandon. They did not climb the walls, heeding Lord Caledon's warning. But they were not so careful on the stones that had already tumbled on the ground. James was standing on one of those stones when he swung his sword high and overbalanced. He fell backward against the stone wall behind him. His back slammed into the wall knocking the wind out of him.

Dermot heard the thump and whipped around. James was lying half on the ground with his back against the wall. He heaved in a breath filling his lungs again and started to roll to his hands and knees.

"Are ye alright?" Dermot started toward James to help him up. The wall he had hit wasn't one of the taller ones, only about twelve feet high. As Dermot approached, he glanced up to see one of the large stones on the top of the wall wobbling. It was right above James. Dermot didn't have much time to think or plan. He just acted on instinct. He surged forward and covered James's head and shoulders with his own body making sure to keep his own head out of the way.

The stone caught him a glancing blow on the meaty part of his shoulder and rolled off. Dermot cried out as the stone scraped through his shirt. It hurt like the devil, but he didn't think anything was broken. Still, better he had a bruised shoulder than James taking a blow to the head.

James looked over his shoulder at Dermot with wide frightened eyes. "Are you alright?"

"Aye, right enough." Dermot still braced against the wall.

James slid out from under him and grabbed his arm to pull him away from the wall before any more stones fell.

Dermot winced at the pull on his arm. James let go, but they both scooted away. They eyed the stones at the top warily. When they were satisfied that no more were going to fall, James turned to Dermot. "Let me look at your back. Where did it hit you?"

"My shoulder." Dermot grunted, the mere mention of it seemed to make it hurt worse.

That wasn't helped when James went behind him to look at it and winced. "It's scraped up and red. It's already starting to bruise."

"I'll survive." Dermot pulled his right arm close to his side. It seemed to hurt less if he kept it still.

James kicked at the offending stone, which was the size of a football, and didn't budge. His voice was hushed. "That would have killed me if it had hit my head."

"That's why I jumped on top of ye."

James looked at him in awe. "You saved my life."

"Dinna be daft. Ye'd have done the same for me." Dermot was sure of it.

"I think this might be the last time we play in the ruins."
James looked around at the ruined tower as if it had betrayed
them.

"Eh. We're getting too old for that kind of game anyway."

They made their way slowly back to the house. Dermot
held his arm and James looked at him like he was seeing him
for the first time. They went straight to the kitchen where Mrs.
Miller kept the first aid supplies. When the matronly
housekeeper saw them, she sprang into action. She sat Dermot
on a bench in the kitchen and sent a maid to tell the family
what had happened.

By the time his mother came rushing in, Mrs. Miller was
cleaning the scrape on his back with alcohol. Seonag ran
around to look at the damage to his shoulder. "What
happened?"

"Dermot saved my life!" James exclaimed as his parents
came in. His uncle Walter trailed behind them.

"Are you hurt?" Lady Caledon's hands fluttered over
James checking for injuries.

"I fell against a wall, but I'm fine." James explained
enthusiastically. "Dermot saw that a stone was going to fall on
my head, and he jumped on top of me and took it on the
shoulder."

The adults all looked at Dermot with expressions that
varied from pride to calculation. He hissed as Mrs. Miller
dabbed his scraped shoulder again with the alcohol. All he
could think to do was shrug his uninjured shoulder. "It's no
bother."

His mother put her hand on his good shoulder. "I'll take it
from here, Mrs. Miller."

"Of course, dearie." Mrs. Miller handed her the cotton ball and alcohol and moved aside.

Lord Caledon knelt in front of him, his expression serious. "We can't thank you enough, Dermot. You'll tell me if there is anything we can do for you."

"Thank you, sir."

"What have I told you about playing in those ruins?" Lady Anne gripped James's arm.

"We weren't climbing on them. I swear." James exclaimed as she pulled him out of the kitchen. "We weren't, Dad. We listened to what you said."

"It's true. James tripped on a rock and fell against the wall. We weren't climbing on them." Dermot added between winces.

"I believe you." Lord Caledon told them. "But I think we may have to keep our distance from the ruins from now on."

The three Stuarts left, James recounting the events again as his mother admonished him to get cleaned up for dinner.

Dermot looked over his shoulder at his mother. "We really weren't climbing.'

But his mother wasn't listening. She was looking at Walter Stuart who stood next to the door, his eyes on Dermot. His mother shifted her eyes back to Dermot. "Ye did exactly right, love. I'm proud of ye."

CHAPTER THIRTEEN

May

"You did not tell me who Lyall Green is." Jujhar admonished Sarah, as they sat down on her couch with two cups of tea. He seemed almost bubbly, a change from his usual calm.

"Would you have believed me if I had?" Sarah blew across the top of her cup to cool the tea that Jujhar had brought with him. "This smells lovely, what's in it?"

"Chamomile and lemon balm. I thought you could probably use something to help you relax." He drank from his own cup.

"And there's nothing else in here?" She arched an eyebrow still wary of him after his previous deception. "Green didn't give you some special brew to make me have visions or sleep until you guys figure things out?"

He gave her a look of censure but didn't argue at her suspicion. "Nothing else. I promise."

Sarah hoped that Jujhar's days of hiding his motives were done. She had taken a chance putting him in contact with Green. Hopefully, having a friend working with Mr. Green could give Sarah some insights that the mysterious watcher would have kept secret. "So, tell me all about it."

"I don't even know where to begin. That was one of the strangest most intimidating meetings of my life." His eyebrows drew together at the memory. "He approached me in the library. After talking with you the other day, I was expecting a phone call. Instead, I went to the stacks to get a book and when I came back to my table, your Mr. Green was sitting in my chair flipping through my notes."

Sarah remembered Green as the homeless person she had given money to on the street, and the formally kilted A. P. board member who had attended their Burns Night fundraiser. "He has a way of turning up places you don't expect."

"Well, he certainly surprised me." Jujhar took a sip of tea, his mind clearly on the memory of that first meeting.

"What did he say?" How did a wizard or whatever he was go about hiring an apprentice?

"For starters, he commented on my note taking skills. Apparently, my notes are very disorganized." He arched one dark eyebrow at her indicating disagreement with that opinion. "He also noted that I didn't have anything about my...how did he put it...'particular fascination' in that notebook. I told him that I didn't carry that sort of thing around with me every day."

"Probably wise." Sarah agreed.

Jujhar tipped his head in agreement. "Exactly. He asked if I knew who he was, and I guessed that he was the Mr. Green you had mentioned." He took a quick sip of his tea. "Then he asked if I knew who he was again, as if his name and association with you was only the half of it."

Sarah gave a short sharp laugh. "It's not even half."

"Yes, well I know that now." Jujhar gave her a you-could-have-warned-me look. "He didn't say it there in the library. He held that bit of information until the next day."

"What happened at the library?" Sarah pulled her feet up onto the couch to sit cross-legged.

Jujhar looked off to the side as if remembering. "It was strange. He invited me to sit down and talk. He asked me some simple questions about what I have been studying and my background. He changed languages several times during the conversation: Gaelic, Welsh, Latin, Hindi…He spoke about my family as if he knew them already. He asked me why I had resisted my parents' efforts to arrange a marriage for me. He seemed to be vetting me, like a job interview but far more personal. And it seemed that he already knew many of the answers to the questions he asked but wanted to hear my answers."

"Well, apparently he liked your answers if he told you his big secret." Sarah gestured with her coffee cup before taking a sip.

"Yes. After a battery of questions about everything from my time in India to which football team I support, he stood up, buttoned his jacket, and handed me a card with his address on it. 'Be here tomorrow no later than four o'clock.'" Jujhar took a thoughtful sip. "It's an unassuming house tucked away in a wooded corner of Dean Village. It's not even terribly well-kept. But inside he's got a library to rival the Bodleian and a still room or laboratory…I don't even know what to call it, but it's chockablock with jars of who knows what and glass vessels for almost any sort of process you could imagine. It's like an alchemist's lair."

"Do you think he's turning base metals into gold, or looking for the elixir of life?" Sarah asked half-joking.

"I think he's Nicholas Flamel, the Comte de Saint Germain, and Victor Frankenstein all rolled into one."

"And a super spy, and a puppet master..." Sarah held up a finger for each point.

"I guess you develop a lot of useful skills when you live as long as he has." Jujhar looked skeptical. "Do you really think he's a hundred and forty-seven?"

Sarah took a sip of tea and thought about it. "It seems crazy, right? I honestly don't know if he's telling the truth or building myth when it comes to his age. But he's not the one who told me who he was. Dermot guessed it. And I saw him when we were in the cave. I saw him before he did whatever glamour he does to put himself together. He looked ancient and bent. He hobbled off into the mist and came back a few minutes later, every bit the fit, fifty-something that you saw. If we could bottle whatever he uses to do that, we'd make a killing."

Jujhar put his cup on the table and scooted closer to her. "He says that he needs a successor. That he is from a long line of...what was the word he used?"

"Facilitator?" Sarah offered.

"Yes, that's it. He told me it's a bit like the priesthood. He explained I would have to forgo personal attachments and professional goals in favor of ensuring that The Nine is protected and the prophecy is fulfilled." He looked down at the table for several seconds. "It's a grave responsibility."

"If you believe in all of this, then yes, it is." Sarah acknowledged.

"Do you not believe?" His dark eyes were serious when they met hers.

"I don't know what to believe. There are certainly a lot of powerful people who believe it enough to kill for it, enough to entrap me into whatever scheme they are trying to promote." She shook her head thinking about Walter Stuart's hunger for control. "I have seen amazing things. Things that I could not possibly have imagined. I have people that I trust, and some that I don't telling me the same things. But to believe in it, all of it, means I have to give up so much of myself. I have to turn my agency over to what these other people intend for me, or what they think some ancient prophecy says about me. I don't think I can do that."

Jujhar studied her. "It seems we're facing a similar dilemma. We're each being asked to give up some of ourselves for the greater good."

"But is it for the greater good?" Sarah questioned. "We don't even know where this is all leading. The Stuarts think it's a restoration of their monarchy. The zealots think it's the anti-Christ. I don't think either of those things is even possible, and even if restoring the monarchy is possible, is it worth thousands of years of guarding and guiding? What is this king supposed to do that's so great?"

He let her go on until she ran out of steam. Then he reached over and took her hand where it rested in her lap. "I believe that The Nine is about far more than some silly monarchy. I think the gifts you have will lead us to something that will change the world for the better. The union with the Stuarts, if that's even needed, is not the end result. But it may put your child in a place where they can affect that change. It's entirely possible that the monarchy is an incentive to move the baser concerns of people like Walter Stuart. In the grand scheme of things, I'm not convinced that it is relevant."

Sarah gave him a surprised look. "Don't let James hear you say that. Or maybe do."

"We'll keep it between us." His eyes sparkled with the warm smile that Sarah had become accustomed to.

"Have you told Green that theory?" She asked while he took a sip of his tea.

"I have actually." He put his cup back on the coffee table. "He didn't agree or disagree. He just looked at me for several seconds and then assigned me a task."

"What task?"

"I am to research how to revive the pool for the matching ceremony." He met her gaze. "Actually, you might have a resource that can help with that."

"Really?" Her brows drew together in confusion.

"Yes, the sources of information about the matching ceremony are sparse and are accounts of facilitators like Green. Your mother's account of the ceremony and the pool might prove useful in seeing the problem from a different angle. Could I see it?"

It made sense, but she wasn't about to give up Molly's journal. "Sure, although I would rather the journal stayed with me. Can I make you copies of those pages?"

"Of course." He nodded. "And I will keep them private. We don't need those getting in the wrong hands."

"Mmm." She agreed. "So, does that mean you're going to be Green's apprentice?"

He blew out a long breath. "That's going to take a lot of thought. I'm not sure I'm ready to give that much of my life over to the cause. But I can still try to help with this test."

"Thank you. There's a lot riding on it." Like her whole future.

CHAPTER FOURTEEN

"Give me the low down on the Stuarts." Sarah and Dermot settled into the back of the car that would take them to the Stuart's house. She shifted uncomfortably in the dress and tights that she had put on.

Dermot thought for a second brushing a hand down his tie. "Anne runs the show. She's the one with the ambition and the drive. Henry is nice enough; a sort of bon vivant. He softens her sharp edges, and she hardens his spine."

"Sounds like a pretty good partnership." Sarah looked out the window as they neared the Old Town. She never tired of looking at the oldest part of Edinburgh.

"It would be if I thought for a second that they cared about each other." His tone was laced with bitterness. "Anne only cares about restoring the Stuarts, specifically James, and keeping up the appearance of an aristocratic life."

She turned back at his tone and watched his profile. He was so handsome, but the set of his jaw suggested he was resigned to the battle to come. "What does Henry care about?"

He gave a half-shrug. "Ten years ago, I would have said he cared about Alba Petroleum and building the company and their wealth. He was a gifted businessman. Then when James got old enough, and they deemed him ready, Henry decided he was going to retire. He buggered off to the continent and after a while Anne followed him. I think he meant for James to stand on his own, without his parents to guide him."

"Except that ceded the ground to Walter." Sarah could see how they would want James to establish himself, albeit from a lofty starting place. But that gave a lot of influence to his uncle.

He looked over at her and reached across the back seat to take her hand. "Aye. I think that Walter and Anne work together. I dinna think Lady Anne ever intended to give up her influence in her son's life."

"Then why follow Henry to the continent?" She rubbed her thumb over his knuckles.

He smiled. "Because appearances matter a lot to Anne. She canna have the upper reaches of society gossiping that there's a rift in the house of Stuart. That wouldna do at all."

"Right." She gave him a mischievous smile and deepened her accent. "So, if I turn my hillbilly way up when I'm talking to her, she might give up on this whole marriage thing and send me packing."

That got a chuckle out of him. "Well, there is that whole prophecy thing. She might be willing to overlook the accent to regain the throne."

"Mmm…maybe I should show up barefoot in some cut-offs and flannel, eating corn on the cob, and carrying a jar of stump water." She held out an arm as if she were holding a jar of moonshine. This time he laughed outright, and she was relieved. "Good. I got a laugh. You've been so serious the last couple of days."

He sighed. "This is serious business, love."

"I know." She squeezed his hand. "But we have to find joy wherever and whenever we can, right?"

"Is that how ye do it?" He lifted her hand to his lips and kissed the back of it.

"Keep eating. Keep sleeping. Keep breathing, right?" She recalled what she'd told him the morning after Ryan Cumberland had tried to kill her the previous December. "We have to keep going, we might as well try to have a little fun along the way. Besides, I think I can face anything as long as you're with me."

The car pulled up in front of the grand house on Polwarth Terrace, and a security guard opened Dermot's door. He offered Sarah his hand to help her out of the car. She stood and checked his tie. He pulled her shawl up onto her shoulder where it had slipped off.

She took his arm as they climbed the steps to the house, thankful for his help. She didn't think she would ever get used to wearing heels.

The front door was opened by the butler, who took Sarah's shawl and ushered them toward the room where everyone was gathered for drinks. As they were approaching Sarah could hear some of the conversation that preceded them.

"I wish it had been the maiden in London. At least she has some talent." A woman's voice spoke with rounded vowels and soft consonants.

"Mother, I can assure you Sarah is very talented." She heard James say in a low voice.

"At what, talking to old people?" The woman's voice was sharp sharply.

They rounded the corner and stopped in the doorway as the butler announced. "Miss Sarah MacAlpin and Mr. Dermot Sinclair."

James jumped out of his chair and came toward them. "Good evening. Sarah, you look lovely."

"Thank you." She allowed him to take her free hand and pull her toward the woman in the burgundy dress who was drinking a glass of white wine.

"Sarah, allow me to introduce you to my mother, Lady Anne Stuart." James poured on the politeness. Sarah had no doubt he was hoping to distract from whatever she might have heard before she came into the room.

"James has told me so much about you. It is nice to finally meet." Anne Stuart lifted her chin and examined Sarah with a haughty air. Everything about her was perfect. Her dress tailored to fit her rail thin frame. Her bobbed hair curled under exactly at the midpoint between her chin and shoulders. Even her pearls rested in exactly the right spot on her chest to attract attention without being vulgar.

"It's nice to meet you too." Sarah didn't go full hillbilly, but she did allow a little more Western North Carolina to creep into her speech than usual.

"And this is my father, Henry Stuart." James waved a hand behind his mother to a man standing near the window. When he turned to them Sarah saw an extremely handsome man on the back side of middle age. He came toward them with his hand outstretched. She could see where James got his looks. When he spoke his voice and expression held a warmth that was disarming. "Wonderful to meet you, my dear."

"It's a pleasure to meet you." Sarah shook his hand and gave him her most beguiling smile. He returned her smile before shifting his gaze above her shoulder.

He offered his hand to Dermot in genuine pleasure. "Dermot. It's wonderful to see you again."

Dermot shook Henry's hand and cleared his throat. "Likewise, sir."

"How is your mother?" Henry gave Dermot a look of sincere concern.

Dermot cleared his throat again. Sarah could sense the tension that leapt whenever the Stuarts mentioned his mother. Who could blame him? Sarah wondered if Henry knew about Walter's use of his old friend as a hostage. "Her physical health is good, but her mind is locked in the past. She remembers me as a boy and doesn't recognize me anymore."

Henry pressed his lips together and nodded solemnly. "You'll let us know if there is anything we can do to help."

"I think this family has done quite enough on that front, sir." Dermot replied. Sarah noted the hint of bitterness in this tone and put a hand on his arm to calm him. They had talked earlier about being civil, but Henry had zeroed in on the one subject guaranteed to get Dermot's back up. Although, from the look on Henry's face, Sarah didn't think he knew just how fraught a topic that was. He seemed taken aback by Dermot's statement.

"Mr. Walter Stuart." The butler announced.

"Walter, darling." Anne met Walter as he crossed the room with both hands extended. He took her hands and kissed her cheeks in a formal way that was a contrast to her seemingly warm greeting.

Henry walked around the younger people to greet his brother and offer him a drink. Walter nodded politely. "A whisky would be nice. Thank you, Henry."

Henry poured a whisky from a crystal decanter. "Sarah, Dermot, can I offer you a drink?"

"I'm fine. Thank you." Sarah had a feeling she needed to stay on her toes around the Stuarts.

"I'll have a whisky." Dermot answered. Seconds later Henry returned to hand Dermot his drink. Sarah watched as he appreciated the first sip of what was no doubt a fine single malt. She hoped he wouldn't overdo it. Walter and Anne joined them where they stood.

"Miss MacAlpin, Dermot, James." Walter addressed them each with a polite nod. Sarah was puzzled by the change in Walter. He was usually polite, but before he had used his impeccable good manners to show his superiority. That night it seemed conciliatory, as if he actually cared about being polite to the likes of Dermot and Sarah.

Sarah wondered why the change until she glanced at James. He watched his uncle intently with an assessing look. Maybe James had once again put Walter in his place.

They all fell into an awkward silence. Sarah hoped this wasn't a sign of the evening to come with everyone standing around looking at each other and no one willing to take the chance of saying something that might set someone else off. When she was young, Sarah had often wished for a bigger family. If this tension was what came with that maybe she had been better off.

"Dinner is served." The butler said from the doorway saving them from the embarrassment of prolonging that awkward silence.

"Thank you, Conley." The relief in James's voice was obvious. He offered his arm and led his mother to the dining room. Henry offered his arm to Sarah. "Allow me, my dear."

Sarah glanced over her shoulder at Dermot. He jerked his chin Henry's way indicating that she should go. No doubt there was some ridiculous order to who escorted who to diner. Sarah suddenly felt like a hillbilly who had wandered into a palace. She smiled at Henry and took his arm leaving Dermot and Walter to trail after them.

That fish-out-of-water feeling wasn't helped when they arrived in the dining room. Worthy of any grand estate, the dining room sported dark wood wainscoting contrasting bottle green walls. The mahogany table had been shortened for the six of them, but there was clearly room for it to be expanded to accommodate much larger parties. It was set with the finest china Sarah had seen outside of a museum, crystal glasses and a confusing amount of flatware.

***

"I'm so glad that you could make dinner tonight. I wanted us all to get to know each other better." Anne broke the ice once the first course had been served. She looked directly at Dermot. "I know that there has been some tension and I hope that we can all work together to find a resolution to the situation we find ourselves in."

'As long as it's the resolution you want.' Dermot thought. Anne might be prettier than Walter Stuart and she might have a nicer way of going about things, but Dermot had no illusions that she would be open to any kind of compromise.

Anne went on shifting her gaze to Sarah. "I understand that there have been some missteps on our part and for those we are sorry. I hope we can all agree to move forward in good faith."

Sarah looked up from her plate to meet Anne's eyes. Sarah cleared her throat and glanced at Walter. "If we are indeed moving forward in good faith, then I'm all for that."

"I can assure you that we are." James's eyes rested on Sarah, and the hope that Dermot saw there set his teeth on edge.

"Good." Henry looked around the table with patriarchal authority. "Then I say we move on to something more pleasant. "Sarah, James tells me that you had a very interesting childhood."

Sarah cocked her head to the side. "I suppose that's a word you could use for it. I was raised by my grandmother in the mountains of North Carolina. She was a moonshiner and subsistence farmer. We grew or hunted everything we ate and sold liquor to pay for anything we couldn't make ourselves."

"Fascinating." Henry looked at her with wonder. "But you clearly went to school."

Dermot debated stepping in. He knew how little Sarah enjoyed talking about her upbringing. But she answered Henry without the usual bristling. "Yes, I went to the public school in our county. Then I got an academic scholarship to a university. After my grandmother passed away, I used the proceeds from selling our farm to fund my graduate school."

His look changed to one of sympathy. "And I understand your mother died when you were very young."

Sarah cleared her throat. "Yes, she was killed in an accident when I was six years old."

Henry laid his hand on top of Sarah's on the table. "And you knew nothing of your extended family until recently. Is that correct?"

Sarah's eyebrows lifted in surprise and she cut her eyes to James. "Yes, I met a great aunt when I was doing fieldwork in the Highlands, and another previously when I was in Nova Scotia, although I wasn't aware of it at the time."

Henry nodded thoughtfully, and Dermot wondered just how much the Stuarts knew about Sarah's family. He supposed they would find out soon enough if they were to conduct a matching ceremony, but he knew that Sarah wanted to limit the amount of intrusion into the lives of her father and brother.

"Did you not know that you had family in Scotland?" Anne asked.

"Only in the most general sense. My grandmother didn't tell me much about the specifics of her family. I know she missed the village where she grew up and I think she found it painful to talk about it." Sarah replied being noticeably careful not to give too much away.

"I would think she could have prepared you better for this situation by telling you more." Walter put in.

Dermot shot him a warning look. Anne went further by saying. "Let's not question the decisions of people who aren't here to defend themselves."

"It's alright." Sarah gave Walter Stuart more generosity than he deserved. "I have often wondered the same thing. But you don't know what it's like to be a foreigner in a rural and devout community like ours. My grandmother was viewed by many of our neighbors with suspicion because of her accent and how she made her money. Sometimes that tension could become violent. Some of the customs that she brought with her from Scotland made her a target for people who didn't understand them. The less attention we attracted, the safer we were. And children are terrible at keeping secrets. She died right around the time I would have been old enough to understand."

"That must have been terrifying." Anne's tone resembled sympathy.

"For my grandmother, I'm sure it was." Sarah agreed. "She didn't really explain those fears to me. I felt the community's judgment in other ways. Not having a father and my mother's death brought their own social repercussions."

"I can imagine." Anne looked distinctly uncomfortable when it came to the idea of Sarah's upbringing. No doubt she would have preferred Sarah came from the ranks of James's boarding school classmates. Dermot took a little perverse pleasure in Anne pinning so many hopes for James's restoration on someone she would normally consider far beneath her.

"Sarah is also a very talented singer." James chimed in probably hoping to turn the subject to something lighter. Henry turned back to her in surprise. "Ah. Perhaps after dinner you could give us a song or two."

Sarah gave him a ghost of a smile clearly uncomfortable being called on to perform in this setting. "Maybe."

"And how did you come to choose to study folklore?" Anne asked from her place at the end of the table.

"My grandmother raised me with stories of auld ways, and fairies. Those stories have always interested me, and I see them being supplanted by modern life. I wanted to preserve her stories and those of the mountain people who lived around us. And I saw a lot of crossover between the stories that my grandmother brought from Scotland and the American stories and songs that I heard. That confluence is fascinating. That's why I chose to research it for my dissertation."

Henry caught Dermot's eye, with a look of nostalgia. "I think Sarah reminds me a bit of your mother, Dermot, dedicated to studying the old ways."

Dermot looked at Sarah, his eyes full of love. "Aye. They have that in common."

"Yes." Henry looked down at his plate pensively.

CHAPTER FIFTEEN

July 1982
Scottish Borders

"I warned ye that would happen." His mother raised an eyebrow at Lord Caledon. They were seated around the small round table in the informal dining room for lunch. Dermot always liked these meals when they all sat around the table, even Walter. If it had been dinner, he and James would probably have taken theirs in the kitchen. But for lunch, they all sat together. It felt like he had a whole family.

Henry laughed shaking his head. "And you're usually right about those things. I wish I had your talent for reading people. It would be so useful in the board room."

"Ye're welcome to yer board rooms. I much prefer classrooms." Seonag took a sip of her wine and shot Dermot a smile.

"I'll wager your students never get an excuse past you." Henry grinned at her fondly.

"Rarely." She gave him a saucy smile. No one seemed to make his mother laugh the way that Lord Caledon did. Dermot reckoned it was their friendship that brought them back to Tweedholm every year.

"Seonag." Lady Anne spoke from across the table. "I thought we could go to Norham this afternoon for a bit of shopping. There's a new boutique that I think you might like."

"That sounds lovely." No, it didn't. His mother hated shopping. Dermot would never understand why his mother went to such effort to get along with Lady Anne. Lord Caledon's wife always looked down her nose at them, but his mother pretended not to notice. He had asked her once why she made the effort. His mother had explained that Henry cared for Lady Anne, and he was their friend. So, she should try to be friends with Anne too to make things easier for Henry. Dermot supposed he understood.

"Dad, can we go fishing in the river this afternoon?" James asked eagerly.

Lord Caledon turned his smile on the boys. "I think that can be arranged. Walter will you join us?"

"I think not." Walter looked up from his plate where he was cutting his fish into small pieces. "I need to pack this afternoon. I have a meeting in the city tomorrow."

Dermot was not disappointed by this news. A few minutes later, Lord Caledon asked his mother. "Where will you be teaching this fall?"

"I'll be back in Edinburgh this year." Dermot was happy about that. Ireland had been alright, but he had more friends in Edinburgh including James. Although James would be going to boarding school at the end of the summer holiday.

"Where will you be sending Dermot to school?" Walter asked. Since the incident at the ruins, it seemed that Walter had taken a greater interest in him. Dermot could have done without that. He'd never liked Walter Stuart, always lurking on the fringes of things watching everyone else move around him like a trap door spider waiting to strike.

His mother looked at Walter for a few seconds. Dermot recognized that look. It was the one that she gave him when he was too fractious in church, or when he went to the cookie jar one too many times. He wondered what James's uncle had done to earn that look. "He'll return to Heriot's. We liked it alright, and it's close to the university."

"At his age, I would think you would want him to go to a boarding school." Anne commented.

"I have a friend on the board of Gordonstoun." Walter offered. Dermot's eyes shot to his mother. He'd heard horror stories about Gordonstoun and its austere practices. He couldn't imagine why anyone would want to send children there, but he knew the upper echelon of British society did.

Seonag gave Walter that look again, the one that warned he was treading on thin ice. Dermot was relieved when she said. "I prefer to keep my son with me."

"It would toughen him up. Truly prepare him for the future." Walter added. "It did wonders for Henry and I."

"Speak for yourself, brother." Henry put in. "I hated every minute of it. And I'm not sure Dermot needs that kind of toughening up."

"But it taught you discipline." Walter gave his brother a baleful look.

"There's discipline, and there are cold showers and running laps in the winter. And don't get me started on the corporal punishment." Henry gave a dramatic shudder. "That's why James isn't going there."

"I'm still not sure that's the right decision either." Walter leaned back in his chair.

"Fortunately for James, it's not your decision to make." Henry's eyes were steely. This seemed to be a conversation that the two of them had had before.

"I'm only thinking in the best interests of both of the boys." Walter bristled at his brother's censure in front of others.

"I think I'll decide what is in my son's best interest." His mother's tone was just on the polite side of sharp. It wouldn't do to upset their hosts, but she was clearly done with discussing schools. "In my experience a student's performance depends more on the student and the support of their family than it does on where they go to school."

"Here, here." Henry seconded. Lady Anne for her part seemed focused on her salad, but he saw her sneak a conspiratorial look at Walter.

***

May 1995
Edinburgh

"Thank you for talking with me." Henry closed the door to the study after dinner. When they had left the dining room, Henry had pulled him aside and asked to talk privately. Dermot had watched Sarah follow Anne toward the drawing room. She had looked over her shoulder and shrugged at him.

Dinner had been an awkward affair of the Stuarts politely interrogating Sarah about her life before coming to Scotland as if she were an object of study at their own private geographical society. Even if he hadn't loved her, he would have felt sorry for her for fielding their questions patiently while simultaneously trying to remember which fork and spoon and wine glass went with which course. She was a bloody champion for running that gauntlet and he was loath to leave her. Still, he could hardly refuse their host.

"Of course." He told Henry.

"Whisky?" Henry went to the decanter on the cart near the fire.

"Aye, cheers." Dermot accepted a glass and the seat on the couch that Henry waved him to.

"James informed me of the situation with Walter and your mother." Henry took a chair beside him with a sigh. "I would like to apologize to you for my brother's behavior. I wish he had gone about things differently."

"Aye, well." Dermot took a sip, and the highland malt burned a path down his throat. "There's not much to be done about it now."

"I hope that's not true." Henry looked at him, his eyes full of concern. "You know that I've always considered you and your mother to be like family."

Dermot let his next sip of whisky sit in his mouth for a few seconds savoring the sweetness. "Like family, but not family."

Henry looked down into his own glass as if he could find the right words in the swirling golden liquor. "Sometimes, the family we choose is a stronger bond than the one we're born into."

"I can agree with that." Dermot watched his mother's friend. If he could have chosen a father for himself, it might have been Henry not because of the privilege that Henry enjoyed or his money, but because he was a good father. He enjoyed being with James and cared more for James as a person than Anne ever had. She only cared about the status and maybe the power that came with being the mother of the future CEO and possible king. "And I've chosen Sarah. More importantly, she's chosen me."

"Just as your mother chose us many years ago." Henry looked up at him, his blue eyes so like James's were serious. "You and your mother have always been welcome with us."

"Is this where ye tell me that I won't be welcome if I take what James thinks is his?" Dermot cocked his head to the side. It wouldn't be the first time. James had always gotten first choice when they were growing up. As the poor relation, Dermot had often been given James's cast-offs.

Henry looked genuinely hurt. "Nothing of the sort. I hate seeing you boys at odds. You are both stronger when you are working together."

"Aye, well there's not much room on his pedestal these days, and I've grown rather tired of hanging on. My mother and I are different that way."

"Your mother was never a hanger on." Henry's brows drew together. "She was my dearest friend."

"Who was used as a hostage." Dermot set his whisky on the table with a crystalline clink. He stood to return to the party. Sarah had been left alone with the vipers long enough. "That's not something a simple apology and a dram can wash from my memory. I may not have gone to a posh boarding school, but I learn well enough from experience."

"And what does your experience tell you of me?" Henry asked pointedly before Dermot turned for the door.

Dermot couldn't hold Walter's behavior against Henry. He wasn't a bad man. "That much like James, ye're a good man caught up in a web of power grabbing spiders. And much like James, it leads ye to do things that ye think are justified by the ends. They're not. I dinna want to be caught in this web anymore, and neither does she."

"You have agreed to the matching ceremony." Henry pointed out.

"What choice do we have? Sarah is trying to reason with James in terms that he can understand and can justify. But the truth is, she just wants him to be a decent human being and let her go."

"You know he can't do that." Henry kept his eyes on his whisky.

"I know he won't, because you and Anne and Walter have spun him some fairy tale all his life that he's destined to be a king."

"We didn't do that alone, you know." Temper flashed across Henry's face as he rose to his feet. "Your mother was there too."

"What are ye saying?" Dermot asked in confusion.

"Who do you think brought us that fairy tale?" Henry gave him a fatherly look. "Who but a scholar of Celtic antiquities could have found that prophecy and told us about Sarah's people? We could never have come this far without your mother's help."

"But the Stuarts have been protecting Sarah's people for ages." Dermot was confused.

"They did, yes." Henry explained. "But after the Rising most of our family was exiled to the continent. I'm told that my grandparents may have known about it when they returned from France. Maybe our parents knew, but they were killed when Walter and I were so young. We had no idea until your mother showed up on my doorstep."

146 · MEREDITH R. STODDARD

Dermot thought back to when he had introduced Sarah to his mother. She'd called Sarah princess, and had known her right away. He sank back down to the sofa, dumbstruck. What had his mother told Sarah? 'I dreamed that ye loved my Dermot. I know it's silly to think of it.' And before they'd left. 'Take care of her. She's more important than me.' Of course, his mother knew all about it.

Questions spun through his mind, but he couldn't seem to decide what was most important. Most of his life he had wondered who his father was. Now, he was starting to wonder who his mother was.

"Did you never wonder why you didn't know your grandparents?" Henry put a gentle hand on his knee.

"She never talked about them. I always assumed they shunned her because I was a bastard." He was still confused.

"I don't like that term." Henry bristled.

Dermot looked up, Henry's thunderous face breaking through his fog of confusion. The older man leaned down to him. His tone was vehement. "It implies that you have no family that cares for you. This family has cared for you and your mother since before you were born. You have never been a bastard."

"Aye, but I've never been a son." The words were out of his mouth before he considered them. He hadn't meant to say that. He blew out a breath in frustration. "At least not to anyone but her. I've watched ye and James and other fathers and sons all my life and wished that I could have that. Mum always did her best, but it wasna enough."

"And summers at Tweedholm weren't enough either." Henry wasn't asking a question so much as stating a realization. He sat down again.

"They were just another taste of what I didna have." Dermot muttered. "A father and brother but only on summer holidays."

"I'm so sorry, son." Henry's voice was sincere.

"Unless ye have something to tell me." Bitterness seeped into Dermot's tone as he stood and tossed back the rest of his drink. His voice was whisky-rough. "Dinna call me son again."

As he shut the study door behind him, he thought he heard Henry say, "I wish I could, lad."

Dermot stalked down the hall. He'd had all of the Stuarts that he could take for one night, maybe for a lifetime. The whisky and rich food in his stomach turned sour. He was sick of people telling him what James needed, telling him to step aside for James, to back James up. All his life even his mother had shown deference to the Stuarts and James. He was just bloody done with it. He needed to find Sarah, needed to get out of that house.

CHAPTER SIXTEEN

"Would you join me in a walk through the garden?" James asked Sarah as they walked to the drawing room after dinner.

Dermot had already gone off to chat with Henry. She turned back to James to whisper. "And escape spending the next half an hour under your mother's microscope? Yes, please."

"I thought you might say that." He offered her his arm and they turned toward the back of the house.

They didn't say much until they reached the patio. Sarah briefly remembered when James had enticed her onto the patio last January and stolen a kiss. She took a step away from him. "Hands to yourself this time."

He held his hands up in surrender. "I'll behave. I just thought you could use a break from my mother. She can be overwhelming at times."

"She definitely has her eyes on the prize." Sarah decided understatement was best. They stepped off the patio and began to walk down the path toward the canal.

"And by prize you mean you?" James linked his hands behind his back, strolling beside her.

Sarah laughed. She waved the thought away. "I'm irrelevant. The prize is you on the throne."

"With your help." He added.

"You don't need my help, and I've told you before that I think the throne is a pipe dream. Who's to say that an independent Scotland would even want a king?" She still didn't understand wrangling for a throne that didn't exist anymore and would probably never exist again.

"Oh, there are thrones and then there's power." James strolled on, his tone matter of fact. "Whether Scotland wins independence or not, whether they want a king or not, a large part of the economy depends on oil, and A. P. controls a large portion of Scottish oil."

"So, in effect, you're already a king." She reasoned. "And you still don't need me."

"I do need you." His tone went soft, intimate. He paused at a break in the hedge. They had reached the steps down to the next level of the terraced lawn.

Sarah was afraid to look at him. She really didn't want to keep having this conversation. "James,"

"I owe you an apology." He didn't let her finish what she was about to say. He must have sensed that she was going to tell him again that she didn't love him. "That contract was insulting and a mistake. I should have known better."

"I can't disagree with that." She accepted the hand that he offered her and walked down the steps.

He continued along the path. "I am afraid I let my uncle convince me that it was the only way to get you and Dermot to keep your words. He means well. He just doesn't trust people."

"That strategy might be helpful in the board room, but it's no way to treat people you care about." They came to the end of the path where the garden met the canal. There was a small shed and cleats for tying up boats. "In my experience, if you go around expecting the worst in people, you are almost guaranteed to draw it out of them."

James looked down at his feet and then up at the canal. "I can't disagree. I believe I gave my uncle undue influence over my personal life."

Sarah wasn't going to hammer that nail anymore. She had made her point. She stood beside James and watched bicyclists on the path across the canal.

After a minute James spoke. "My uncle has been a valuable adviser to me in the business, but I think that maybe he is not the best romantic adviser."

"Has he ever been married?" Sarah tried to imagine a woman who would marry Walter Stuart, even if it was just for his money.

James looked up, thinking. "No, I don't recall him ever being involved with anyone."

"Yeah, maybe not the best person to consult on those matters." After another moment's thought. "You know, most of the leaders I've known became leaders by leading. You may have inherited your position before you were able to build some of the experience that happens when you have to work your way up, but that doesn't mean that you can't be a worthy leader." She turned to him. "But to do that, you have to lead. You might have advisers who give their perspective, but you have to be the one to decide whether to follow it. And you have to own those decisions."

He took her hand and focused those blue eyes on her. "You are right. The responsibility is mine, and I am truly sorry."

Sarah gave his hand a reassuring squeeze. "If you want the best out of people, you have to set that expectation. Give people a chance to rise to it."

He sighed. "This is why I need you."

"Sarah!?" Dermot shouted from the back of the house. Sarah looked up the path to see him striding through the upper garden. The hedges must have obscured his view of them. He seemed to be searching. "Sarah?"

"We're here." She let go of James's hand and started up the path. James was on her heels.

She met Dermot at the bottom of the steps. "What's going on?"

"We're leaving.' His tone was clipped and brooked no argument, not that she intended to offer one. He gripped her arm and pulled her back toward the house.

"Wait? What's happened?" James called from behind her on the path. His concern sounded genuine.

Dermot shot him a look over her shoulder. "Yer father's distracted me with talk of my mother so ye could pull her out here for…whatever ye had in mind."

"We were just talking." Frustration was evident in James's tone.

"Aye, right." Dermot snapped dragging Sarah up the path.

"Hey! Give me some credit." Sarah groused. Dermot stopped dead in the path.

He turned to her and brought his hand up to her cheek resting his forehead against hers. "Ye're right. I'm sorry." His grip on her upper arm softened and his hand slid down to take hers. He looked over her head at James, his eyes blazing. He looked like he wanted to say something more but, in the end, he just shook his head in frustration. Turning he led Sarah up the path.

In seconds, they were in the car. They hadn't taken leave of anyone. Sarah thought she had glimpsed a sad, resigned looking Henry coming out of the study door as they strode through the hall. Dermot spent the ride home fuming. After a couple of failed attempts to get him to tell her what had happened, Sarah decided that he would talk to her when he was ready.

Talking was not on his agenda that evening. When they arrived home, he helped her out of the car and did not release her hand until they were inside her flat. The door was barely closed behind them before Dermot had her in his arms. His lips came crashing down on hers with bruising force. His fingers threaded through her hair and he gripped tight, pulling just enough that sensation bloomed across her scalp. He walked forward backing her toward the hallway to the bedroom in a sort of hungry dance.

Sarah was completely overwhelmed by him. He blocked out everything else. All she could see, and feel was Dermot, and he needed her. He used every inch where their bodies connected to bend her to his desire. Everywhere she moved, he was there pushing her backward and pulling her close at the same time.

He didn't break his kiss until they reached the bedroom. He pulled back and growled. "Take that dress off."

In a fog of desire, she must not have moved fast enough for him. Before she could find the zipper in the back, he made a feral noise in his throat and spun her around. He unzipped her and had the dress falling to the floor faster than she thought possible.

"Get the rest off." He ordered but didn't back away from her. His lips found the back of her neck while she could feel his fingers working on the buttons of his shirt. Sarah unfastened her bra and before she had a chance to slide the straps off her shoulders, his hands slid up under it. They both groaned in approval.

He spun her around and kissed her again. His tongue sweeping into her mouth, and his teeth scraping along her bottom lip. Sarah felt drunk with desire. She pushed his shirt back from his shoulders and ran her hands down his chest. He hissed when her fingernails grazed his nipple. Then he pushed her back on the bed.

She looked up to see him in all his glory. His muscled chest in the moonlight from the window was a beautiful blend of shadow and skin. Good god, she loved this man. He came down to her on the bed and kissed his way up her stomach and chest. When his face was close to hers, his whisper was desperate. "I need ye."

"You have me." She assured him.

He took her mouth and slid inside her. He stopped. His heat seemed to scorch every inch of her skin. Resting his forehead against hers he inhaled deeply. Sarah held her breath waiting for whatever he intended next. She didn't know what had prompted this. He was passionate, but he'd never been this aggressive and dominant before. His voice was a low and urgent rumble. "Mine."

Yours. She would have said it, but he took her mouth again stopping all speech, all thought. He drove into her relentlessly, barely giving her a chance to breathe. Sarah relished every thrust, every kiss, every groan. She welcomed them all. When he had spent himself, he lay beside her and pulled her close. Sarah drifted off into blissful boneless sleep.

Sometime in the wee hours, she opened her eyes to find Dermot on his side with his head propped on a hand watching her. She wrapped her arm around his waist curling into his heat. He kissed her head. "I'm sorry."

"For what?"

He brushed a finger over a red love bite just above her collarbone. "I was too rough."

Sarah covered his hand pressing it to the bite. "I'm tougher than you think I am."

"I know yer tough." He brushed his lips over her temple. "Are ye sore?"

She took a quick inventory of sensations. She had nothing to complain about. In fact, she felt awfully good. "Only in the best possible way."

A soft laugh rumbled through his chest. "Ye never fail to surprise me."

"Do you want to tell me what that was about? I'm pretty sure it wasn't just finding me in the garden with James."

"Ugh. It's petty." He scoffed.

"Doesn't seem so petty. It was clearly bothering you."

"Aye it is petty." He sounded sheepish. "Jealousy. Pure simple jealousy."

"Not over me. You have me."

"No, and yes." He rolled onto his back propping his free arm behind his head. "Fear that I'll lose ye to him. Jealousy that it feels like everyone we know is working to make that happen. It's always been that way. Of course, ye know James had all the best things growing up including a father. But it was more than that. He was always the focus of attention." He spoke into the darkness of the room. "Something Henry said about my mother has me questioning things I thought I knew."

"Things about your father?" She looked up to see his profile limned in the moonlight.

"Things about my mother." His expression was inscrutable in the darkness. He hummed thoughtfully. "I think I was around twelve when Walter started grooming me to be a steward. He came to my school and told me that James was going to 'need intelligent, brave men around him' and they hoped he could count on me to protect and defend James, even when we were grown. He used to visit me at school periodically to inquire about my studies. I never talked about it much with my mother. I was sort of happy to have some man take an interest even if it was Walter. But she must have known. She must have approved of it or the school wouldn't have allowed it."

"You think your mother really took the whole steward of the king thing seriously."

"At least she wanted me to, although she never talked to me about it directly" His hand skimmed up and down her back absently. "She told me the Stuarts were our family. I never stopped to wonder about where she came from or why we never talked to her family. The Sinclairs were her stepfamily, ye see. And now, I can't even ask her, or expect a meaningful answer."

"Did Henry say something about your grandparents?"

"Only to illustrate a point." He paused seeming to think about whether he should elaborate. When he went on his voice was quiet, thoughtful. "He said that my mother was the one that brought the story of the prophecy to them. They had lost contact with yer people. They knew nothing about it until she came along."

"Wait!" She sat up to look at him. "They didn't know? I thought they had been working with my people for centuries."

"Henry and Walter's parents may have. But they were killed in a car accident. They must have died before anyone could tell the boys."

"I bet Green would know about it." She resettled herself in the crook of his arm. "It won't get solved tonight. You should try to get some sleep."

He grunted his agreement and went back to stroking her back. As soon as she was back in the warm cocoon of his arms, Sarah's muscles relaxed, and sleep pulled at her. She drifted off as Dermot continued to ruminate, his hand absently rubbing her back.

CHAPTER SEVENTEEN

In the months that she had lived in Edinburgh, Sarah hadn't yet managed to visit Dean Village, and that was probably a good thing. She was sure that if she had, she'd never have left it. Edinburgh's Old Town was breathtaking in its scale and age. The idea of a city being built on top of a city every few generations was fascinating, especially for a student of history. But it had nothing on Dean Village. With its blend of stone and half-timbered houses and sprinkled with gardens all crowded along the Water of Leith, the village was the epitome of old-world charm.

It didn't get more old-world than Lyall Green's house. It was tucked away down a side street, hidden from the main thoroughfare by trees and other houses. The mortar was crumbling, and the roof tiles were green with lichen. It looked like that house in every neighborhood that people walked by shaking their heads and wondering why the owner didn't take better care or wondering if anyone even lived there. It was the perfect home for a custodian of ancient traditions and left her wondering if Green had inherited it from his predecessor, and him from his. As she stood there with Jujhar, she tried to imagine him inheriting it from this green man one day.

Without Jujhar's help she would never have found Green's house. They had been going over their various transcripts and plans at a team meeting at the university that morning. Isla was proving to be a very efficient leader and was already planning their next research trip up the north coast picking up where they'd left off in Lochinver. Ewan had produced a documentary short film that they would be using to drum up donations. And they were planning another fundraiser that James would host.

As the meeting broke up, Jujhar had pulled her aside. His eyes were bright with excitement. "I think I've found it."

"Found what?" She asked absently rearranging her notes.

He leaned closer. "A way to revive the pool."

Her gaze snapped up to meet his. "Really?"

He nodded. "It was something your brother said that tipped me off. I asked him about the story of Eimhir, the mermaid in the loch."

"Yeah, I know the story."

"It was your recording that made me ask, actually." He noted. "But Ruaraidh told me that the rise and fall of the water level in the loch is sometimes affected by the water in that runs down from the mountains. So much of that runoff comes through the caves that are under the hills that it seems mysterious. Hence the legend to explain the rise when the runoff isn't visible above ground."

"You think we can harness some of that runoff to fill the pool?"

"Not exactly." He looked around at the rest of the team working on their projects. "But I can't really talk about the rest here. Why don't we go to Green's house this afternoon and we can talk with him?"

That suited Sarah. She had a couple of things to talk to Green about too. So, there they were standing in front of Lyall Green's unassuming cottage in its cozy little street.

Jujhar smiled at her in excitement as he knocked on the ancient looking front door.

"I'm afraid you'll have to wait here." Sarah told Fleming Sinclair, her bodyguard for the day.

Fleming raised a cynical eyebrow at her. "And have ye sneak out the back?"

Sarah deserved that. She had escaped his watch before, and he had nearly lost his job for it. She gave him a sweet smile. "Would I do that to you again?"

The look he gave her in answer said that he suspected she would at the first opportunity.

Sarah shook her head. "I thought we were past this. I will not do that to you again. I promise. Now, this man is very private and won't like unexpected company. Plus, the only thing out the back door is the water, and it's too shallow for a boat. There will be no getting past you."

Fleming cracked a half-smile. "I see ye've already considered yer escape route."

She gave him a resigned look. "In light of recent events, I'm starting to make it a habit. But I'm not looking to escape from you."

After another round of knocking and waiting, the old wizard opened the door. He looked more like the man she'd met hiking in the Highlands than he did the top Edinburgh solicitor. In his own home he wore a comfortable sweater, casual trousers, and soft soled shoes.

They had to duck their heads and step down to go in the door. Sarah imagined that at one time it had been street level but was overcome as the streets were paved and built up over centuries. The front room was little more than a dark stone-floored hallway. It was lined with pegs for coats and a bench for taking off boots. An oil lamp burned atop a narrow table, creating an air of stepping back in time.

Green stood in the shadows. "To what do I owe this pleasure, a nighean?"

"Jujhar told me that he has made some progress with the task you gave him, and I was hoping to hear what he's come up with." She told him.

Green shifted his eyes to Jujhar and waited. "I have an idea I would like to run by you."

Green studied Jujhar before waving them toward a doorway to his right and the narrow stairs behind him. "Library or still room?"

"Library for starters." Jujhar nodded toward the doorway.

Green ushered them through the low door. They came into a two-story room lined with bookshelves on three walls. Light spilled in through windows set in the thick stone wall, and shone on a round library table, and a rack of scrolls, quartos, and unbound manuscripts. A spiral staircase in the corner led up to a second-floor catwalk which was also lined with books. Sarah's innate curiosity was piqued. "I could spend years in here."

Green's low laugh was like wind through dry leaves. "I'm sure if you were to add up the time I've spent in here, it would come to decades."

"I can imagine." She scanned some of the shelves beside her. The volumes on it looked easily as old as the house around them.

Green set the lamp on the table and invited them to sit down with another wave of his hand.

"Do you not have electricity?" Sarah asked looking at the lamp.

"I do." Green lowered himself carefully into a chair before turning the wick down on the lamp. "But my old eyes prefer natural light and the softer lamplight. Tell me what you have found young man."

Jujhar reached into his backpack and pulled out his notes. "As I was telling Sarah earlier, I have an idea for bringing water back to the pool using the underground caves that run through the glen. But simply filling the pool doesn't seem to be enough." He flipped to a page in his notes. "I had some testing done on the soil within the boundary of where the pool used to be and the ground around it. Fortunately, I have a discreet friend who is a chemist and got the results to me quickly. I told him it was soil from two parts of my garden, and I wanted to know why plants were growing in one part and not in another."

As he spoke, he flipped through the pages in his notebook, until he found the right page. He spun the notebook around so that Sarah and Green could read it. "The ground under the pool contains a combination of salts that when diluted with water creates a solution that breaks down the cells of biological matter to a molecular level. It creates what a chemist would call a lysis buffer."

"You're getting a bit in the weeds for me when you start throwing around chemical terms." Sarah interrupted. Jujhar's notes were full of chemical formulas. The only one she recognized was the formula for salt.

"Sorry. For our terms, a lysis buffer is the first step in most molecular biology experiments including DNA sequencing." She looked up from his notes to find his eyes on her.

"So, we were right?" She glanced at Green. "The pool is some sort of primitive DNA tester."

Jujhar's brows knit together in thought. "With DNA sequencing there are additional steps after lysis. You must separate the DNA from what's left of the cell it came from and purify it from any other unwanted material. In normal DNA sequencing, those steps are completed in a sterile environment with alcohol."

"And the matching ceremony involves two different kinds of samples with the blood and burnt hair." Sarah had read through her mother's account of the ceremony at least a dozen times since copying those pages for Jujhar.

"Exactly. I don't know how those mixed samples combine into some sort of decipherable result." He flipped back a few pages. "Your great aunt said something about reading runes in the water, but she wouldn't explain much more than that."

Sarah rolled her eyes. "I'm not surprised. Eilidh will protect her own importance to the last."

Jujhar made a soft hmm. "Or it has something to do with her gift. She's the truth-seer. Maybe the ability to read the runes comes with that."

Sarah thought for a minute. "Her daughter was able to see it too. That's how she knew that Eilidh had lied about what she saw."

They both looked to Green. "Are you able to read the pool?"

Green looked unsure. "I understand the basics of reading it, but the MacLeods have their gift which has made their reading the most trusted over the generations."

"Not very smart putting all their trust in one branch of the family." Sarah muttered.

Green hummed in agreement. "The first of the three sisters were actually sisters and trusted each other. I'm afraid they did not expect one sister to betray that for their own self-interest when the tradition was established."

"So, you can act as a disinterested third party this time."

Green gave another soft laugh. "I wouldn't call myself disinterested, but my interest is in accuracy rather than power or status."

Sarah turned back to Jujhar. "I'll take accuracy. You said that you thought you had a solution for reviving the pool."

"Yes, thank you." Jujhar closed his notebook and folded his hands on top of it. "I believe that the original pool was generated by the water coming up through the salts in the ground."

"From the caves." Sarah clarified.

"Exactly. If we can draw water up through that ground into the pool, we should be able to recreate the solution." Jujhar seemed pleased with this deductive reasoning.

Sarah blinked at him. She looked over at Green who seemed lost in thought. Jujhar was still smiling when she looked back at him. "How do we do that?"

Jujhar's face fell. "That I don't know."

"But it does give us something to search for." Green rose from his chair and walked to a shelf on the other side of the rack of manuscripts. He ran a hand across the spines of a series of books and hummed thoughtfully. Moving to another shelf, he slid one book halfway out and looked at the cover, before putting it back in. He turned to a different bookcase near the stairs.

"Any idea what he's looking for?" Sarah whispered to Jujhar.

"Not a clue." He leaned closer so she could hear him. "If there is an organization to these shelves, I have yet to puzzle it out. His card catalog seems to be in his head."

"Ah! Here it is." Green's voice sounded, but she couldn't see where he was. He emerged from the shadows behind the staircase carrying a large volume bound in worn leather with a strap buckled around it. He set it down with a thunk on a book stand on top of a rack of manuscripts.

Sarah and Jujhar got up to look at the book. It was impossible to tell which color the book had once been. The cover was mottled with stains in various tones of brown, black, red, and green. The old wizard's fingers worked at the buckle. It appeared that it had been fastened very tightly and had been closed for a long time impressing itself into the leather. He stood back and motioned to Jujhar. "Would you mind, lad?"

"Certainly." Jujhar tried the buckle and after several attempts, was able to loosen it. As soon as the buckle came open, the pages expanded to reveal that many of them were warped and wrinkled. It was as if he had taken a corset off and the book could suddenly breathe again. Breathe it did. Old book smell mixed with the scent of dried herbs, resin of some kind and disturbingly some kind of biological decay.

"Is this a grimoire?" Jujhar stepped back allowing Green access to the book.

"It is indeed." Green pulled a set of reading glasses out of his pocket and perched them on his nose. "It belonged to one of my predecessors."

The old man pushed the front cover back until the book lay open. Several pages in the middle stood up stiffly. Green pressed them down with a crackle, and Sarah worried that the paper might disintegrate in front of their eyes. "Should we be wearing gloves or something? You don't want to damage it."

"Don't worry." Green blithely turned the pages ignoring the pops and cracks coming from them. "They're not paper, but vellum. They should last at least another few hundred years."

Looking at the stained and wrinkled pages, Sarah wasn't so sure. Green continued to search through the book muttering to himself as he went. After a few minutes of reading and searching, Green thumped the book in front of him with a finger. "This should do the trick."

Sarah leaned forward to look, but what she saw on the page looked like chicken scratch. "You can read that?"

Green tutted as if she should have been able to read the scribbles on the page. He turned to Jujhar. "Can you read it?"

Jujhar leaned forward examining the page. "It's a cipher."

Green grunted his approval, and Jujhar looked closer. "The numerals are Arabic. Can I have something to write on?"

Sarah returned to her bag and got a notebook and pencil. She turned to a blank page and handed them to Jujhar. He set the notebook beside the grimoire and began translating the numbers. After he had written out a few lines, he drew a grid on the paper and started writing letters in the grid. "Mr. Green, you can correct me if I'm wrong, but I think this is a Polybius Cipher."

Green didn't answer, he simply watched as Jujhar used his grid of letters and numbers to translate the lines. Jujhar glanced at Sarah who obviously must have looked confused. "Polybius was a Greek historian who created a cipher to communicate long distances with fire signals. It was especially useful in military campaigns. In part because it was easy for soldiers to memorize preset messages."

"Like Morse code before Morse code." She supplied.

"Something like that, yes. Unlike dots and dashes, the numbers are coordinates on the grid. If you know the grid, you can solve the cipher."

"It was a very effective tool at the time our friend was using it." Green put in. "Few people were literate, and only the most learned and traveled would be able to crack the code."

"But once memorized the person who used it could probably write it as easily as we write English or Latin." Jujhar's eyes glowed at being able to solve the puzzle.

"So, what does it say?" Sarah looked eagerly at his notebook.

Jujhar wrote a few more letters. "To restore a well that has run dry."

They looked up at Green who nodded in satisfaction. "Well done. I will have to test your skills with some more difficult ciphers in the future. Why don't you continue working on that while I give Miss MacAlpin something? If you'll follow me, my dear."

Sarah let him lead the way back to the small hallway and up the narrow stairs to his still room. At the top of the stairs, the room opened up into a bright sunlit space that was part kitchen, part greenhouse. One wall and half of the high roof were made of glass, which Green was taking advantage of to grow an indoor herb garden and light his worktables. One such table sported glass vials, tubes and vessels of various shapes and sizes. Some contained liquids in different colors.

One contained a black oily-looking sludge. "Working on the elixir of life?"

"Pish." He scoffed walking to a rack of jars with handwritten labels containing what looked mostly like herbs. "Elixir of life, philosopher's stone," He wagged a finger at her. "That garbage is the real fairy tale. Only simpletons would imagine that all of this was a get rich quick effort to turn base metals into gold or have eternal youth."

"Your motives are more worthwhile, are they?" Sarah was still skeptical. Although she had to admit, if she was going to design a magician's lair his library and still room weren't too far off the mark.

He shook his head at her question. "I would not do what I do if I believed it was for anything less than the survival of the human race."

"The survival of the human race depends on the Scottish Monarchy? That seems a bit overblown."

"Survival of the human race depends on The Nine." He explained flatly as if it were an indisputable fact before turning his back to her and scanning the rack of jars along the stone wall. "And most of you are here."

"So, alchemy is a sham?" Sarah asked with a smirk as she perused a plant stand lush with growth. She recognized a couple of kinds of mint, sage, and thyme. There were coneflowers of different types including chamomile in pots that lined the window. "Says the magician."

"Magic and alchemy are science before we called it science. Much like the pool your people used for matching ceremonies. There is an explanation for it all. People just didn't know it at the time." He pulled several jars from the rack and arranged them around a bowl on the worktable.

"That doesn't sound too different from my view of religion." Sarah rubbed the leaves of a plant that she didn't recognize with her fingers and sniffed. It smelled peppery, like the pepper weed that she used to chew as a child.

"They go hand in hand." Green glanced up from the herbs he was mixing in the bowl.

Sarah looked back at him as he reached for another jar of herbs and opened it. He sniffed and tipped some of the contents into his cupped hand. "So, what's the difference between them?"

Green looked up and studied her for a moment. "It is wise that you would think to ask that." He went back to mixing his herbs. "Religion is how most people explain things that they can't understand. How did we get here and why? Where do we go when we die? Magic is for a different class of people."

"A different class?" That sounded pretty elitist.

"I don't mean it that way." Green understood her meaning. "A category if you will, like your people as opposed to the rest of the world."

"So, my people are magic?" She raised a cynical eyebrow at him around a small potted tree that appeared to be hosting mistletoe.

"Your people have magic, more than most people." Green poured the contents of the bowl into a pint jar. He began writing on a label. He continued to talk as he wrote. "Most people, most humans resist admitting that they don't understand things. They like the confidence of knowing even if their sense of certainty is an illusion. Religion provides that certainty for many people. What people once would have called magic, is the ability to access knowledge that was lost to most people."

"Like the pyramid builders, or Mayan astronomers." Sarah thought back to the conversation she'd had with some anthropologists the previous fall about lost knowledge. She wondered if something in her subconscious had made her argue this very point.

Green fixed the label on the jar and carried it around the table to her. "Once humans knew far more than we do now. Far more. The memory of those things is locked in here." He tapped her forehead with a finger. "For everyone. For most people, it is locked away in some portion of their brain that they don't access. For others, the daily noise of modern life drowns it out and whatever additional knowledge might bubble up is labeled as ESP or deja vu. But some of us whether through genetic predisposition or mutation have more access to those memories than others. Sometimes it shows in larger ways; in people of great intelligence who bring about revolutions in our ways of thinking about the world."

"So, people like Isaac Newton, Darwin, Einstein, or Steven Hawking are more in touch with those collective memories of a past when we knew more than we do now."

"Yes, although they may not be aware of it in those terms. The consciousness of that aspect of human evolution or devolution as you might call it is reserved for only a few." He looked at her significantly.

"The Nine." Sarah supplied.

"The Nine. There may be some others, but they are outliers. The Nine are the only group that has consistently maintained the skills that allow them to access that knowledge." Now, the careful breeding made a bit more sense. They weren't just preserving special talents. There was a reason for preserving those talents.

"But do we?" Sarah thought of her Aunt Eilidh and the religious rigidity of the people of Làrachd an Fhamhair that her mother had encountered. "I might be smarter than average, but I'm certainly no genius. Given the way the Auld Folk treated my mother, I don't think they were particularly enlightened."

"They weren't, and most still aren't. The Children of the Footprint are people much like the rest of society. They may live with The Nine, and protect them, but they are not of The Nine. The only additional access that most of them have to the memories is an instinct for secrecy."

"Okay, but The Nine aren't exactly perfect. Eilidh still used her knowledge to try to manipulate things to her advantage."

"Ah, yes. I would caution against equating knowledge with wisdom." He gave her a fatherly look. "Eilidh may have the knowledge, but she is as human as the rest of us with her own foibles and weaknesses."

Sarah picked up the bottle of herbs that he had put on the table. She opened the top and sniffed. It smelled of mint and lemon and something else she couldn't quite place. "If The Nine can access this knowledge, why aren't they sharing it? Why keep it to themselves. They could be saving the human race as we speak, could have done it a long time ago."

Green rocked back on his heels and clasped his hands behind him. "It's a reasonable question. But you must imagine the sheer volume of knowledge to which The Nine have access. Much like our own working memories, we access what we need when we need it. To bring forth all of the knowledge that is available to The Nine would flood the brain with so much information it could at best cause enormous confusion and at worst cause it to break irreparably."

"Is that what happened to Willie Cross?" Sarah was starting to connect the dots here. But Green's answers were only prompting more questions.

He looked sad at the mention of his former apprentice. "No. It took far less than enlightenment to crack that young man's mind. After the loss of his parents, Willie clung to the religion of the people of Làrachd an Fhamhair. Just the knowledge that Eilidh had perverted what he thought of as a sacred ceremony was enough. I thought at one time that he might make a good apprentice, but he did not have the gift."

"What gift?"

Green took a breath and sat on a stool at the end of the table. "I do not have the same access to the lost knowledge that The Nine do. If I did, I wouldn't need that enormous library." He chuckled. "My gift is that I can help others access lost knowledge. It is how I helped you see your grandmother's memories from before your mother was ever born. Those memories are imprinted with you. I simply helped draw them out."

"Is that how I knew the words to that verse in the song? I didn't know what they meant until I heard Eilidh sing them." Sarah remembered the sickening rush of understanding that had swept over her when she finally heard the meaning of the words to the last verse of 'The River Maiden'.

He gave her a gentle smile. "The knowledge came to you when the time was right. If you had heard those lines before, you would not have believed it. Likewise, the knowledge that The Nine has that people need will come out at a time when the world is ready to hear it. To come out before then might mean that it will be ignored or mocked and lost again."

"Like the knowledge that James Stuart is descended from Jesus?" Sarah asked.

That got another laugh from Green. "It may be a long time before the world is prepared for that. Much like Willie Cross, that sort of realization could cause great upheaval."

"I'm not so sure. I think it might not cause any at all." Sarah picked up the jar again. "You may find that the modern view of a chaste Jesus is unshakable."

"It could be. Rumors and theories of his survival, marriage and progeny have circulated as long as stories of his divinity without making a dent in the accepted story." Green conceded.

Sarah held up the jar. "What is this?"

"A contraceptive tea." When she opened her mouth to protest, he raised a hand. "If you're going to continue having relations with Mr. Sinclair, you should make sure that nothing unfortunate comes of it before the matching ceremony. James Stuart may not be your true match. But if you were to conceive before that is proven, you would be making a powerful enemy."

"Okay, but I do have the implant. It's worked well enough so far." He had a point. Although she didn't think James would be vindictive about it, she was absolutely certain that Walter Stuart would be.

"Then an extra layer of protection shouldn't hurt." He nodded to the jar in her hand and rose to usher her out. "The brewing instructions are on the label."

"Okay." Sarah started for the stairs, before something occurred to her. "One more question. Is Seonag Sinclair from Làrachd an Fhamhair? Is she one of my people?"

His initial reaction to the question was physical. His shoulders slumped and he briefly reminded Sarah of the ancient figure she had seen in the cave. It was as if whatever glamour he used to make himself appear to be a third of his avowed age slipped. Just as quickly he recovered it, but his face was still grim. "No, she's one of mine. But that is a story for another day."

Before she had a chance to ask him anything else, Jujhar came bounding up the darkened stairs. "I've got the translation. We should be able to do this, but we're going need some dowsing rods."

CHAPTER EIGHTEEN

A couple of weeks later Dermot and Sarah found themselves dressed in their finest attending the fundraiser for the team's next trip. It went much like the Burns Night fundraiser that they'd held in January minus the auction, but with the addition of Lady Anne introducing Sarah to all her society friends as if she was a new member of the family. Sarah only managed to extricate herself when James came along.

"I have to hand it to y'all. You're smooth." She told James quietly when they had turned away from Lady Anne's coterie of socialites and walked toward the doors to the garden snagging two flutes of champagne on their way.

"I don't know what you mean." His tone was innocent enough, but he wouldn't meet her eyes as they stepped through the doors to the patio.

"Come on," She wasn't buying the act. "I tried to get away from your mother a few times, but she clung to me like a limpet until you showed up. Now tongues will be wagging about Lord Caledon and his American confirming everything the tabloids were saying. Did y'all plan how long I would have to run the socialite gauntlet before you appeared like Prince Charming, or was that improvised?"

They stopped at the edge of the patio and looked out over the people milling about in the garden. In the twilight, she could see frustration written in every line of his face. "It's not like that Sarah."

"Really?" She cocked her head at him. "If I weren't one of the sisters, your mother wouldn't even spare a second glance for an orphaned hillbilly from Kettle Holler."

"Perhaps not, but she would for an academic professional who cared about preserving our culture." He told her keeping his tone even. "As would many of the people here."

"Only for as long as it takes to write a check and notify anyone they want to impress of their generosity." She muttered taking a sip of her champagne.

"Cynicism doesn't suit you." His voice went incredibly quiet.

"And yet, I am given so many reasons to embrace it." She scanned the garden wondering if her entire evening was going to be spent trying to politely extricate herself from one of the Stuarts. With her luck, any moment Henry might come up and ask her to dance.

"Perhaps I should have left you to my mother and her friends." James grumbled.

Sarah closed her eyes and breathed, trying to calm her irritation. She turned and sat on the concrete railing of the patio. "No, I'm sorry. I shouldn't snap at you. I just don't like being shown off like an exhibit, and I hate being manipulated."

He stepped closer to where she sat, his blue eyes finding hers. "I am sorry. I will have a chat with my mother about that."

She bowed her head. "Thank you. I'm not sure I could have taken much more of that."

"You should be meeting those women." James warned after a moment of peace. "They could be of use to you someday."

"For fundraising?"

"And other things. They can help deflect media attention. They can usually be relied on to be quiet about things that you want kept out of the public eye. It's good to cultivate those friendships."

"Maybe in your world."

"Which may well be your world soon." He raised an eyebrow at her.

Sarah looked through the doors at the ballroom full of people in designer clothes drinking their whisky and champagne without a care in the world. "God, I hope not."

James looked in the opposite directions to where the canal slid by at the end of the garden. His voice was quiet, but full of emotion. "It's all I hope for."

She looked up at him. "You have to see that I don't fit here."

"I have more faith in you than that." James leaned down toward her, his blue eyes piercing hers. "You are more capable and adaptable than anyone I know. You can do anything you put your mind to."

She met his eyes with an equally pointed look. "But I should be able to choose what I put my mind to."

Sadness flashed across his features and he pressed his lips together. "We all have less choice than we would like. Sometimes we just have to play the cards we're dealt."

***

After the party, Sarah was seated beside Dermot on the love seat in James's mahogany paneled study. She'd chosen that seat to show that she and Dermot were together, an island to themselves among a room full of Stuarts. Green had summoned the interested parties to the study as the party was breaking up. Jujhar had found Dermot and Sarah while they were waiting for a car to take them home. He told them that Green would like to see all of the 'stakeholders'.

She and Dermot exchanged a look that said, 'Guess this is it'. They made their way to the study. Dermot asked in a low voice. "What d'ye think he's going to say?"

She matched his tone. "I don't think he'd be calling everyone together if he hadn't found a solution to holding the matching ceremony."

"Or that he's still searching." Dermot added.

"I doubt that. He's not really one for giving updates."

They were the first to arrive, and Sarah made note to thank Jujhar for telling them before the others. They settled themselves on the love seat and waited. Henry was the next to arrive. Sarah noted the tense nods he and Dermot exchanged before Henry made his way to the bar cart that had been positioned behind the imposing desk. He poured himself a tumbler of something and went to stand by the window, without saying a word.

He was followed shortly by Anne and Walter. Anne breezed in as if she hadn't a care in the world, but Sarah could sense a brittle energy under her cheerful veneer. Walter by contrast stalked in like a caged tiger and followed Henry's example by pouring himself a drink. He took the large wing-backed chair by the fireplace. There were several minutes of uncomfortable silence before James arrived, followed immediately by Jujhar and Lyall Green. Not to be boxed out of sitting next to Sarah, James perched on the arm of the love seat and draped his arm across the back. Dermot shot him a disgruntled look, but Sarah put her hand on Dermot's knee. There was no sense in starting this meeting with an argument.

Green took the other chair that faced the love seat in the small seating area in front of the fire. He looked at each of the parties arranged around the room. "I trust everyone has had a pleasant evening." When no one responded with anything more than a nod, he went on. "I'll be brief, as I'm sure you are all tired."

"With the help of Mr. Gurudat." He waved a hand toward Jujhar who stood near the door. "I believe I have found a way for us to conduct a matching ceremony that will be as close as possible to the traditions of Ms. MacAlpin's people."

"I still do not understand why all of this is necessary." Anne muttered from where she leaned on the desk.

"Mother, I explained this." From James's tone it sounded like this was a conversation he'd had with her more than once. "There was some question about how the ceremony was done with Sarah's parents, and the results were disastrous for her people. We want to ensure that we do not make the same mistakes."

"Well, we couldn't, could we." Anne countered, shrillness creeping into her voice. "Now that we are involved, it's not the same thing. You are the heir. She is the heir. There's nothing more to discuss."

"Anne." Henry tried to step in from his place by the window to quiet her.

"Oh, what do you care?" She snapped at her husband.

"Actually, my lady," Green tried to mollify her by addressing her with her title. "If we do indeed step onto the wrong path, the results could be ruinous for your family. Perhaps even for the country." He gave her a level look and held her gaze for an uncomfortable moment. "There is some question as to who is the correct match for Ms. MacAlpin."

Anne's eyes went wide for a second in surprise before she recovered herself. Sarah was sure there was some unspoken conversation going on between James's mother and the wizard. She wished she could know what was going on there. Lady Anne's temper subsided, allowing Green to proceed.

"What about the pool?" Dermot took her hand as he spoke. "We saw it. It's just mud now."

Green nodded to him as if granting a concession. "That is our one big variable, I'm afraid. Mr. Gurudat and I have tested a method for restoring the pool several times here, with good results. However, we cannot know for sure if that will work on the pool itself until we are there. I do have a contingency plan if we are unable to restore the pool for any reason."

"The cauldron." Dermot supplied.

"Just so." Green agreed. "We would like to conduct the ceremony on the same day that it has been traditionally done."

"And what about The Nine? Three of them are dead?" Sarah asked.

Green gave her a sympathetic look. Sarah wasn't sure if that was because The Nine were her family, or because she would have to see her Aunt Eilidh again. "There are the six who are living. Then we will need someone from each generation to make up Nine. I have a plan for that."

"Are we to summon ghosts now?" Walter Stuart scoffed.

Green turned to look at him for the first time with a look that would have chilled Walter if he wasn't already so cold. "You let me worry about that."

Walter looked as though he might protest the ceremony again, but Anne's misgivings had already been shut down. After a similar wordless exchange with Walter, Green went on. "As we are trying to replicate the ceremony as closely as possible, the summer solstice will be the best time. That gives us time to bring together all of the required parties."

"Do you think they will all come?" Sarah hadn't spoken to Isobel MacKenzie since her visit to Cape Breton, but she wasn't sure that Isobel nor her daughter, Rona would want to come after Bridget's death.

"I have faith." Green gave her a fatherly smile.

"The solstice is in four weeks." James sounded like he could be wrapping up a business meeting. "I'll have Miss Lennox take charge of the logistics."

"That would be helpful, especially for our Canadian friends. I shall take care of our accommodations." Green stood straightening his jacket.

James rested a hand on her shoulder and gave her a smile, his eyes alight with excitement and challenge. "Looks as though you'll get your wish. This uncertainty will be over soon."

Sarah gulped and tried to reflect his excitement. She had started this ball rolling but hadn't counted on the Stuarts calling her bluff. Now, she hoped her hunch about Dermot being her true match was right. She gave James a ghost of a smile. Dermot laid a comforting hand on the small of her back. "Looks like it."

"This is a waste of time, but I suppose there's no avoiding it now." Walter said into his crystal tumbler before taking a sip of whisky.

"Is your ambition so great, brother, that you would rather choose wrongly?" Henry had been quiet up to this point observing from his place by the window. Now he stepped closer to the rest of them. "Miss MacAlpin is right. We must make sure that we are on the correct path. If Green can't tell the answer to that, then we have to test all theories before we move forward."

"Now, you're interested in correctness?" Walter countered taking a step toward his brother. "Now, after abandoning the cause to me for the last ten years, you swoop back in to make sure everything is happening the way you want it to."

Henry took another step toward Walter. "Not the way I want it to. The way it should happen."

"Have I taken us down the wrong path, brother? Have I not done everything that I could to keep this on track? I found her when no one else could." He jabbed a finger in Sarah's direction without taking his eyes off Henry's. "I brought her here. I turned your feckless son into the most powerful CEO in Britain, and I have made sure that we are in the position to take the next steps. What did you do?"

"I fathered that boy and raised him to be a better person than either of us." Henry pointed to James, his face getting red with anger. "It's my son who will be leading us."

While they argued, Green and Jujhar slipped quietly from the room. James stood and pulled Sarah and Dermot with him out into the hall. Anne quietly went to the drink cart and poured herself a glass of something.

"Oh, will the two of you just stop?" Sarah heard Anne say as they left.

James pulled the door closed behind them, leaving his parents and uncle to their own devices. He ushered Sarah and Dermot down the hall toward the front door. "They're covering old ground. They'll tire themselves out in a bit."

"Are you going to be alright?" Sarah may not have had parents who argued, but she knew what it was like living in a house where there was tension.

"Thank you. I will be fine." He assured her before shifting his gaze to Dermot. The two of them had barely spoken since James became aware of her relationship with Dermot. Sarah didn't like that she had come between them, but the look they shared now was full of connection, the kind of shared understanding that must only come from growing up together. "Just like old times, eh?"

Dermot grunted in assent. "I dinna recall them being quite so direct before."

"Ah yes, well with age comes a dislike of wasting time, and they feel as though they have gotten so close to their goals only to have a new roadblock thrown in front of them. It has unsettled things."

"I'm sorry, James." Sarah told him. "I never wanted any of this."

James gave her arm a friendly squeeze. "In any case, we'll at least have one question settled soon."

Dermot offered his hand to James. "I'm sorry, mate." James huffed in agreement or resignation. It was as if they both were unable to hang on to their anger at each other after seeing the result of decades of tension back in the study.

James took Dermot's hand and clapped him on the shoulder. "Me too."

CHAPTER NINETEEN

"Have Walter and Henry always been at each other's throats like that?" Sarah asked from the bathroom as she patted her face dry after washing the evening's makeup off. She'd been so beautiful in her green dress. That row of little bows down the back made his fingers itch to untie them and slide it off her and he knew every man who saw her that evening had thought the same thing. Still, he'd take this Sarah, scrubbed clean and comfortable in her knickers and T-shirt over the smartly dressed, made-up Sarah any day. This was the Sarah that only he got to see, the Sarah that read the news while brushing her teeth in the morning and pinned her hair up with a pencil when she was working. He loved the Sarah who snored just a little and cracked her knuckles before bed. She didn't show that person to just anyone, and she chose him.

He folded his tuxedo trousers along the crease and hung them in the closet. "Not exactly. There's always been a sort of push and pull. I think tonight was a release of a lot of built-up tension."

"I hope Lady Anne was able to break it up." Sarah leaned in the doorway watching him.

"She's as likely to escalate things as she is to play peacemaker, and more likely to agree with Walter." He pulled on a pair of sweatpants. "Were you just looking at my arse?"

She batted her eyelashes and pursed her lips in mock innocence. "Maybe."

He brushed past her to get to the bathroom. On his way past he paused to look down the front of her old and stretched T-shirt eying her cleavage. He grunted and moved on to brush his teeth.

"Were you just looking at my breasts?" She turned to follow him.

He paused, toothbrush in hand and gave her a heated look. "Definitely."

"It must have been awful for James growing up with that three-way tension between his parents and Walter." She leaned against the wall just outside the bathroom door.

He finished brushing his teeth and rinsed his mouth out. "It wasna always three ways. Once upon a time, my mother was right in the mix with them."

"Please tell me she took Henry's side in the disputes, and it wasn't the three of them ganging up on him."

"It was never that simple." He ushered her into the bedroom with a firm hand on the small of her back. "They all shifted back and forth. Mum and Henry have always been thick as thieves, but they've had their share of disagreements as well. They used to argue politics all the time. Mum was always more labor. Ye can imagine Walter was more conservative. Henry usually agreed with Mum, and Anne doesna care as long as she's kept in Chanel and pearls."

"I'm not sure Anne is that shallow." Sarah rubbed lotion into her hands. "She's worked awfully hard to only care about material things. I think she wants status that comes with being the wife and now mother of someone so powerful."

"That's likely true." He pulled back the duvet and settled into bed. "She's not one to be trifled with, but she and my mum rarely saw eye to eye."

"I can see how your mother might have presented a unique challenge for someone like Anne." Sarah slid under the duvet and cuddled up to his side. "Smart and independent women tend to unsettle traditionalists."

"Speaking from experience?" He kissed the top of her head before settling back into his pillow.

She yawned. "You know it."

In the space of a few breaths, he felt her breathing slow and even and her muscles go slack.

***

Tweedholm
December 1982

"Thank you, Mrs. Miller." His mother relinquished her coat to the housekeeper. "The house is so quiet."

"It's just his lordship at the moment. Lady Anne has gone to fetch the young master from school." Mrs. Miller took Dermot's coat as well.

Mum shot him a sly smile. "That explains why James didn't tackle you the minute we pulled into the drive.

"Aye." He wondered if James would even do that anymore. How much would his friend have changed after his first term at boarding school? Dermot felt like he had certainly changed. After returning to his old school in Edinburgh, he'd felt like a different person from the boy he'd been last summer. He was taller now than most of the lads he went to school with. And then there were the lasses, or one lass in particular, Allison Palmer.

His mother leaned down to him. "Why don't you go with Mrs. Miller to inspect the Christmas biscuits while I say hello to Henry?"

Clearly his mother hadn't noticed the changes he'd been going through. She still often treated him like a child. Mrs. Miller did make wonderful biscuits. The housekeeper smiled warmly and jerked her head in the direction of the kitchen. "Come on, lad. I have a few that need tasting."

His mother walked past him to the study, and Dermot followed Mrs. Miller. He heard Lord Caledon's voice greeting his mother and glanced back over his shoulder to see them hugging. He turned and followed Mrs. Miller to the kitchen.

The biscuits were delicious, and naturally he ate too many. By the time he sat down for dinner with his mother and Lord Caledon, he really wasn't hungry. His things had been sent to the room he would share with James and he had unpacked, but without James there the room felt empty and Dermot was bored.

"What time do you think James will be here tomorrow?" Dermot interrupted the political conversation going on between his mother and Lord Caledon.

Henry gave him a half smile. "Not until the afternoon I'm afraid."

His shoulders sank. "Oh."

"Bored already are you?"

"He'll be fine for one day, Henry. A little boredom never hurt anyone." His mother arched an eyebrow at him.

"No," Henry shook his head smiling. "I have an idea. Why don't we all go to Norham tomorrow. We can see the castle ruins and finish our Christmas shopping. We'll make a day of it. What do you say, Dermot?"

That sounded a far sight better than wandering Tweedholm or being stuck at the library. His mother looked like she didn't think it was a good idea. "Can we, mum? I havena been to the castle before."

Her eyebrows drew together like they always did when she was about to say something she knew he wouldn't want to hear. "I don't think—"

"Seonag," Lord Caledon interrupted her. "Come on. It'll be fine."

They looked at each other and seemed to be having a conversation without speaking. He hated when adults tried to talk around him or over him when he was right there, but he tried to be patient. Henry was more likely to change his mother's mind that he was.

Eventually, Lord Caledon smiled, and his mother agreed, "Alright. I suppose it won't hurt anything?"

"Yes!" Dermot celebrated as much as he dared in the formal dining room. Henry gave him a conspiratorial grin and a wink.

***

"The most dangerous place in England!" Henry read the placard at the front of the castle in a dramatic voice. As an aside to Dermot, he added. "And not just because it's across the river from our tower, eh?"

Dermot grinned up at him. "James and I used to pretend we were attacking Norham from the tower. Well, when it wasna falling in."

"I did too when I was a boy." Henry laughed before turning serious. "I think we'd better leave our ruins alone now."

"Aye." He could hear the disappointment in his own voice. They'd been sad to lose the place that had fired their imaginations so much. Dermot turned to his mother. "Can I explore?"

"No climbing where there's not a path." She warned.

Dermot took off running across the bridge to the Inner Ward. He stopped when he reached the lawned area inside the inner wall. There was so much to explore. Jagged stone foundations hinted at where buildings once crowded the inner bailey. He looked down a grate covered hole that led to nothing but blackness. It was probably a well, but he liked to think it was an oubliette. The surviving walls of the Great Tower rose several stories above the Inner Ward. The upper floors would have commanded a wide view of the Tweed that rolled by. Dermot imagined long ago soldiers scrambling to defend those crumbled walls from a bombardment of Scots.

Under the dark arch of the crumbling great hall were stone steps to the next level. He stopped at every window to look over the river and the Outer Ward. It was just before the top of the passage that opened onto the other level that he caught sight of them.

His mother and Henry were below, under the arch. They stood close together and seemed to be talking. Henry's arm was around his mother's waist, and Mum's hand was on his chest. There was something about the way that Henry was looking at his mother, something that reminded him of the way he felt when he looked at Allison. Did Lord Caledon love his mother? They'd been friends for ages, but suddenly

Dermot wondered if they were more than friends. Dermot looked at Henry with new eyes. Could Henry be his father?

His mother and Henry disappeared into the darkness. Dermot turned away from the break in the wall pressing his back to the cold stone as his mind buzzed. He combed his memory for any clues or hints that Henry might be more than the family friend that Dermot had always believed he was. They spent so much of their vacations at Tweedholm House, they all felt like family. But then Dermot didn't really know what an extended family was like. He'd only seen that sort of thing in movies and on the telly.

Their voices echoed off the stone walls as they came up the stairs from below. Dermot tried to compose himself before they came into view. He hoped he looked calm enough when his mother rounded the corner. She smiled at him and walked past. Henry followed behind her. His blue eyes met Dermot's and he smiled warmly. "Standing guard, are you?"

He tried to think of something witty to say, but his mind was so full of confusion that he just managed to sound like a numpty. "Uh."

Henry didn't seem to notice. He ruffled Dermot's hair. "There's a good lad."

Dermot watched Henry step out onto the catwalk that skirted the remnants of the great hall. The sun shone bright on them as they wandered the upper level. His mother pointed out something or other in the ward below. Henry stood behind her and looked over her shoulder. He said something in her ear, and she laughed. They looked happy, but then they often laughed when they were together. They definitely cared for each other, but how much?

When they left the castle, they followed Henry's plan to shop for Christmas gifts and have lunch. Throughout the day Dermot watched them, wondering what it would be like if they were a proper family. They would have meals like this where they laughed and talked and were comfortable with each other every night. He and Henry would kick the football around the garden. Henry would teach him how to shave.

It was a magical day, feeling like they could be family. But then they pulled into the drive back at Tweedholm House and James came barreling out to meet them as he usually did. "Ah! Dermot I've so much to tell you about school, and girls, and how've you been?"

And just like that, the happy bubble that he'd been living in all day burst. Even if Henry loved his mother, they would never be a proper family. Henry was James's father, not his. His mood turned sour and once again he felt jealous of James. Why did James get to have a father when he didn't? What was wrong with him or his mother that his father wasn't around? What made James so bloody special?

He tried not to sound angry. "I'm well enough as long as ye dinna break my arm."

***

Dermot pushed away from the wall and stepped out of the elevator. The sharp tang of hospital grade antiseptic filled his nose. Residents and nurses made their way around from the lounge to the rooms beyond. The nurses desk stood sentinel in the corner of two halls that branched away from the lounge. The staff did what they could to balance a homey and comfortable environment with the hospital level cleanliness.

The building's wide glass windows that let the residents see much of the city outside. But still, it seemed a miserable place to live, a prison of infirmity and dementia.

He hadn't been here since he and Sarah had said goodbye to his mother two months ago. He'd never expected to see her again, and his mother in one of her increasingly rare lucid moments had told him that it was more important to protect Sarah. Not, he realized now, that his happiness was more important.

He hadn't returned to his regular visiting schedule for a few reasons. At first, he was so disappointed over his failure to escape the Stuarts that he didn't think he could take the emotional toll that a visit to his mother would have caused. If he caught her on a bad day, it would be more loss, one more day of her not recognizing him and wondering if he would ever speak to his mother again.

Losing someone to Alzheimer's isn't like losing someone to a heart attack or a stroke. It's not one death It's a thousand small deaths that build up over years. Every time they forget your name, every time they don't recognize you when you come to visit, every time they forget you mid-conversation, the person you love dies a little more. He hadn't been able to face that after the last time. She had told him goodbye. She had absolved him of the need to care for her any longer, and in his dark moments a small part of him had to admit that he was relieved.

If he came to see her on a good day, it was a risk that she might remember their goodbye. Then he would have to explain why he was back or risk upsetting her. He had learned over the last few years that anything unexpected could cause a lot of anxiety spiraling out of control. And he hadn't wanted to leave Sarah. Who knew how much time they had left together? He'd been determined to enjoy what he could.

Now that he was walking down the seemingly miles-long hallway to his mother's room carrying a bouquet of spring flowers and a bag of yarn, all those reasons just felt like excuses. Once again he started wondering what kind of son he was that he had let those seemingly small things keep him from her, from understanding her. He paused just before her doorway for a breath, and to prepare himself.

"Och. Look there Seonag. It's your Dermot come to visit." The nurse, Liz's voice was bright and cheerful as she tucked his mother into her chair by the window.

His mother's face peeked around the back of the chair. Her eyes were bright and happy, but some of the light went when she saw him. "Surely not."

"It's me, Mum." He allowed Liz to pass by before walking around the bed and kneeling beside his mother's chair.

She didn't argue, today. In her mind Dermot was still young, not the grown man who visited her in the care home. Her eyes raked over his face as if searching for the boy she remembered. She raised a hand to his cheek. "You look so old."

He closed his eyes. "I feel old."

She held her hand up in front of her face, tracing the veins across the back of it. "Am I old?"

He swallowed back the tears that clogged his throat. She wasn't that old, only in her fifties. She wasn't old enough to be living in a care home. If it weren't for her illness, she'd be giving a lecture at the university right now or writing another book. "No, ye're not."

He needed to change the subject before she asked more questions about why she was there, and why he was so old. "I've brought ye some flowers, and some new yarn."

"How lovely!" She clapped her hands together and her eyes lit up at the sight of the flowers. She took them from him, holding them under her nose and inhaling deeply. "Oh, that reminds me of Princes Street Gardens in the summertime."

"Me too. Here let me put those in water while ye have a keek at this yarn." He handed her the skein of yarn. He took the empty vase that rested on her dresser and filled it with water from the sink on the other side of the room. He slid the flowers into the vase and returned it to the dresser. "There ye are. Right where ye can see them."

"That's verra nice." Her eyes had gone slightly foggy as if she was distracted by some memory. She returned her gaze to the window. The yarn was in her lap. She'd slid a couple of fingers under a layer of yarn and was stroking her thumb across it.

"Will that yarn do for yer scarf?" Dermot tried to draw her back.

She glanced down at her lap, as if she'd forgotten the yarn was there. "Oh, aye. That'll do."

"The weather is turning warm." The care home had a courtyard garden in the center of the building that the residents could walk in. Dermot wasn't sure how often his mother made it outside. She had always liked to spend time outside before she got ill. "Maybe ye'd like to walk in the garden?"

"Och, I dinna thinks so. It's not a proper garden, all bricked in like that." She pushed with her foot to start her chair rocking slightly. "Not like Princes Street, or Tweedholm. D'ye remember the gardens at Tweedholm?"

"I do." He debated asking her some questions about their visits to Tweedholm. Asking his mother about their past was tricky. If her memory worked, he might bring up something hurtful. If it wasn't working well that day, he might start her on another cycle of confusion and anxiety. "I've been thinking a lot about Tweedholm lately."

"It was a good place to be a boy wasn't it?" Her eyes sought his. It seemed an important question to her.

"Aye, it was." He assured her. "James and I had a grand time there when we were boys."

His mother nodded approval before turning back to the window. Her thumb stroked faster on the yarn in her hand. In a soft voice, almost to herself. "I hope we did right by you boys."

"By James and me? We've turned out alright." He pulled a guest chair next to hers, watching her face as he asked. "Who do ye mean by we?"

She rocked for a moment, looking out the window. When she spoke, her voice had a dreamy quality. "All of us."

He waited for her to elaborate. When she didn't, he asked. "Who else did ye mean?"

"Me...Henry, Anne...and Walter." She spoke haltingly. "We were a team then."

"Then? What happened?" He decided to follow her lead and let her tell whatever came to mind. He had to treat this conversation like field work rather than interrogation.

She stopped rocking and turned her eyes to him confusion evident on her face. "I don't remember."

He placed a comforting hand on hers. "It's alright, Mum."

"No," She shook her head and looked deep in thought. "No, I dinna think it is. It's not finished."

He wondered if it was a good idea to continue asking questions. Still, he was closer to an explanation than he'd ever been before. "What's not finished?"

She shook her head. "We didna finish it." Her eyes darted back and forth as if she was searching her memory for something. She rocked faster in her chair and Dermot almost changed the subject rather than upset her. But then she stopped rocking and her eyes shot to his. "Where's Henry?"

"He's here, in the city." He kept his voice calm.

"He has to keep going. We didna finish it." She leaned toward him in urgency and gripped his arm. "Henry has to finish it."

"It's alright. Mum. Let's relax." He reassured her. When she had taken a couple of deep breaths, he asked. "What does Henry have to finish?"

She pressed back into the chair and looked at him with suspicion. "Mustn't talk about it. It's a secret."

He sighed frustrated. "A secret that ye'll only talk to Henry about."

"I canna tell ye." Her eyebrows drew together in alarm. "I don't know ye."

And there it was, the end to any information that he was going to get from her that day. Talking with his mother was like walking through a minefield of shifting sand. If he wasn't avoiding emotional land mines, he was sliding down dunes of ever-changing cognitive function. In frustration he asked. "Is Henry Dermot's father? Is that what he needs to finish?"

His mother made a sour face, and practically spat. "Dermot's father. What do ye know of my boy?"

'I am your boy.' He screamed inside his mind. "Nothing. It's alright Seonag. Let me get ye a glass of water."

He stood and walked behind her chair, taking a moment to get a grip on his own frustration and the pain of this latest taste of death. By the time he returned with a glass of water, she had calmed down. She was again fingering the yarn in her lap. "It's so soft. I think I'll make a scarf for my son. Have ye met my Dermot?"

CHAPTER TWENTY

June

June 19th, 1996

Sarah ticked the villages between Ullapool and Inchnadamph off in her head as the limousine passed through each of them. After spending the last two months transcribing the hours of recordings they'd made in Ullapool and Lochinver, her memory was full of legends and traditions from this area. She knew a story, song, or tradition for every hill and lochan they rolled past. And reviewing them all was far better than ruminating on the days ahead. They were at the decision point. It was time to prove her theory about Dermot being her true match right, or wrong. God, she hoped she wasn't wrong.

She thought that she was prepared for this trip. She should be looking forward to getting an answer, but she was more anxious than she expected. She'd packed carefully and cleaned her flat from top to bottom. She had checked her suitcase and locks twice and remembered to bring a book to read on the train and drive.

What she hadn't mentally prepared for was the awkwardness of sharing a car with James's parents for the two-hour drive from Inverness. They'd all been in the same first-class train car, but then she had been able to sit with Dermot enjoying her book and the scenery for the entire ride. But when they had changed to the cars in Inverness, James had been called to join the security team in the lead car and had asked Dermot to join him so that the two of them and Mark Shaw could discuss any concerns about site security at their destination. That left Sarah in the middle of their little caravan sitting almost knee to knee with Lady Anne and Henry making stilted conversation. Anne had attempted to tell some funny stories about James. Sarah guessed that was an attempt to endear him to her. Wasn't he a cute little boy, or an incorrigible adolescent? Sarah tried to deal with the Stuarts politely, but she was honestly too tense for small talk. Eventually, they gave up trying to engage.

They passed through Elphin and turned onto the A837. Sarah sat up straighter in her seat. They were almost there. In the distance she could see the ridges of the Moine Thrust rise above the hills. She craned her neck for a glimpse of the cobalt blue waters of Loch Assynt. As they drew closer, she caught sight of the little historic kirk on the shore of the loch dwarfed by the hills around it.

Finally, just past Inchnadamph they turned off onto a gravel drive. The drive skirted around the curve of a hill before sweeping up and away from the river that ran nearby. Around the next hill was an enormous white castle-like building, but Sarah was willing to bet it had been built in the last twenty years. Her mother hadn't mentioned a house that grand in her journal, and she surely would have seen it. It was hidden from the A837 by the hills but within walking distance of Làrachd an Fhamhair.

The car stopped near the huge arched front door. They waited for the security staff to check the area. After a few minutes, Fleming opened the door, and Sarah eagerly climbed out. She stepped away from the car to let the others out and looked around for Dermot. Instead, James was striding toward her. "I hope the drive wasn't too awful."

"Well, I think I bored your mother about folklore as much as she bored me about fashion. Oh, and you. She likes to sing your praises at every opportunity."

He shrugged. "Isn't that part of a mother's job?"

"Hmm..." She muttered turning back to the house. "I wouldn't know."

Before James could respond, the front door opened, and Lyall Green came out followed by Jujhar. He raised his arms in a welcoming gesture. *"Fàilte gu Taigh na Damh."* (Welcome to House of the Stags)

A grunt behind her alerted Sarah to Dermot's presence. "House of the Stags. Seems fitting."

Through the corner of her eye, she caught Dermot sending a sour look at James. He pushed between them, and Sarah followed him to meet Green leaving James by the car.

Lyall Green was greeting Henry and Anne near the front door and inviting them inside. Sarah took Green's offered hand saying, "This is your house."

His smile widened and he looked around them. Sarah followed his eyes taking in the view of the loch, Ardvreck Castle, and the land all around for what seemed like miles. "I bought it and much of the land around it after Làrachd an Fhamhair fell. My land borders your great aunt's. Between us, we can protect the village, pool, and cauldron from discovery."

"I should have known." Sarah turned back to him. "Well. Thank you for having us."

He gave her a fatherly smile. "I expect your family will be arriving this evening."

"And by my family, you mean?"

"The Ballantynes, and your great aunt. The MacKenzies should arrive tomorrow." He waved toward the door where a uniformed maid waited quietly for them to enter. "Cora and Jujhar will show you to your rooms. Then we can all gather for tea."

They stepped inside a front hall that was comparable to any country estate. Where Green's house in Dean Village was compact and unassuming, Taigh na Damh was the opposite. It was fashioned and decorated like a castle complete with a decorative armory installed on the walls, but with all the modern conveniences of indoor plumbing and electricity that was stealthily hidden so as not to ruin the illusion of a historic house. Sarah thought the wood paneling in the front hall must have been reclaimed, because it was covered in nicks and worn to a satin smoothness in some places.

The building was composed of two wings extending from the back of the house with a courtyard in between. At the back of the great hall, Cora led Sarah to the North wing, while Dermot and Jujhar went to the south wing. Sarah hadn't thought that they would be able to share a room, but she wasn't crazy about being in separate parts of the house. She asked Jujhar about it when he indicated for Dermot to follow him. "Boys and girls wings?"

He laughed. "Mr. Green thought it would be best if The Nine stayed in one wing and the Stuarts stayed in the other."

She looked at Dermot who was watching her as if waiting for her to determine whether he should make a stink about them being so far apart. She tried to reassure him. Cooperation was in their best interests right now. "I guess I'll see you later."

He stepped closer and kissed her. It was quick but possessive. "Ye'll call if ye need me."

"I'll give you a holler." She put on her best western North Carolina accent.

"I'll be there in a tic." His smile calmed her nerves enough to watch him walk away.

She followed Cora, who had been introduced as the housekeeper, to a neatly appointed room at the far end of the north wing. The view from the windows swept from Suilven to Ben Mor Assynt. Tucked between some of those hills were the remnants of Làrachd an Fhamhair and the divining pool. After a few minutes studying the landscape, Sarah decided to unpack. Most of her clothes went into a drawer in the dresser. She hung the one casual dress that she'd brought in the closet. She discovered that she was sharing a bathroom with the room next door when she put her toiletries on the counter. She wondered who Green would put on the other side.

***

A short while later, Sarah made her way back downstairs for tea in the drawing room, which had large south facing windows that captured loads of afternoon light. This room was decorated much the way the rest of the house was, although the colors in the drawing room were lighter and very soothing. When she arrived Walter and Anne were sitting close together talking in hushed tones. Walter must have arrived shortly after they did. He hadn't ridden up with them on the train or in the car. They stopped talking as soon as Sarah entered the room.

She arched an eyebrow at them. "Don't let me interrupt."

She made herself a cup of tea which she took to the window seat. There wasn't a window in the place that didn't have a breathtaking view, and Sarah settled in to enjoy it. A few minutes later Dermot and James joined them. Both of them brought their cups to the window where Sarah was sitting.

"The views are stunning." James leaned against the wall on the other side of the window.

Sarah hummed in agreement, her eyes following a stone wall that climbed the side of a mountain across the river. "It's beautiful."

"I'd hate to have been the poor crofter who had to build that wall." Dermot came up with his own cup of tea nodding to the stone wall that she'd been looking at. He wedged his way between Sarah and James to sit beside her on the window seat.

Sarah shot him a look that said, 'I see what you did there.'

He responded with a look that said, 'What would you expect?'

Sarah hoped the next couple of days weren't going to be spent watching the two of them jockey for position. James for his part looked annoyed. "How far are we from the coast?"

"Not too far. Lochinver is just over ten miles that way." Sarah nodded toward the northeast.

"I don't believe I've been to Lochinver." James took a sip of his tea.

"It's a lovely fishing village. Nice pub with views of the sea." Sarah had been charmed by the village when she visited a couple of months before, that was until the paparazzi chased them out.

"Perhaps we could go tomorrow. We could make a day of it. We have some time to kill."

"That sounds like fun. Maybe Ruaraidh could show us some of the sights." Dermot suggested.

James seemed to bite back a retort, and Sarah thought he must have meant for the two of them to spend the day in Lochinver without Dermot or a chaperone. "Who is Ruaraidh?"

As if they had conjured him up just by speaking his name, Ruaraidh Ballantyne's ancient Range Rover rattled into view and stopped in front of the house.

"Speak of the devil." Sarah patted Dermot's knee excitedly as the man in question climbed out. The late day sun glinted off the gold highlights in his red hair. She might have even squealed; she was so grateful to have another friendly face to balance out the Stuarts. She quickly set her tea on the window seat and ran from the room to greet her brother.

Without waiting for their host, Sarah threw open the front door and, in a few steps, flung herself into her brother's arms. Ruaraidh caught her up and squeezed her affectionately. In her ear he said, "That bad, eh?"

"You have no idea." She whispered back.

Ruaraidh set her on her feet and stood back. "Ye look tense. He brushed a thumb under her eye, and maybe a little tired."

Sarah half-shrugged. "It's been a long day. Really a long few months."

A throat cleared behind Ruaraidh. He stepped back to reveal a petite young woman with bluntly cut black hair. She wore paint spattered jeans and a leather jacket. It wasn't until Sarah met her heavily lined eyes and saw the light green reflecting her own that she realized who this was.

Oona Ballantyne looked so different now from the photographs Sarah had seen in their father's house. That fresh-faced girl with the strawberry blond hair who proudly held up a prize-winning painting had developed a definite edge since leaving for art school in London.

Ruaraidh came over to elbow the woman. "See. That is how ye greet a beloved brother."

Oona leveled her green eyes on him. "She's only known ye a minute. Give her time."

"Sarah, this hellion is our little sister, Oona." Ruaraidh hooked an arm around Oona's shoulders in brotherly playfulness. "Ye'll have to forgive her attitude. She's just fractious because she took the overnight train."

Sarah offered her hand to her half-sister. Sarah was the child of their father's indiscretion while he was supposed to be handfast to their mother. Rab had never gotten over the loss of Sarah and her mother, and Oona and Ruaraidh's childhoods had been affected by that. They could easily have viewed her with hostility. Sarah was still amazed at how quickly Ruaraidh had embraced her as a sister. But as he had pointed out, he'd had most of his life to get used to the idea of her. Who knew if his little sister would feel the same? "I appreciate you coming all the way up here. I hope it doesn't prove too disruptive."

Oona gave her hand a cursory shake. "I reckon we'll see about that."

"Sarah." Their mother, Sheila, came around the back of the car with her arms out in anticipation of a hug. There were only a few people in the world who could sympathize with her position, but Sheila MacLeod was one of them. Sheila and Sarah's mother had an understandably contentious relationship, but maturity had turned the once entitled princess of Làrachd an Fhamhair into a motherly figure who had been sweet enough to call Sarah family. "It's good to see you again."

"Thank you. I'm so glad you're here." Sarah returned her hug.

Sheila pulled back, "Let's make sure we get this one right."

Sarah nodded thankful for Sheila's encouragement.

An angry tapping sound came from the back seat of the car. They all turned. Eilidh MacLeod sat, rapping her aluminum cane on the window.

"Och, Granny." Ruaraidh jumped around Sarah and his mother to help his grandmother out of the car.

"Is Rab not coming?" Sarah asked Sheila.

Sheila gave her a warm smile. "Rab is in rehab."

"Really? That's wonderful." Sarah's father had been plagued by a drinking problem for decades. He'd been drunk when Sarah met him but had told her in April that he was going to try to stop. Sarah hoped his efforts would be successful.

"Leave a woman waiting in the car all day, ye would." Eilidh groused as her scarred feet met with the gravel drive.

"Hello, Aunt Eilidh." Sarah called from her spot.

"Feh!" Eilidh waved a hand in dismissal as she set her cane in position for the walk to the house. "Waste of time, this. Ye should just accept it, but I shouldna expect better from yer mother's daughter."

"Lovely to see you too." Sarah chirped. She had heard her great aunt's slurs against her mother before and knew them to be nothing but bluster. Eilidh was the one who'd betrayed their people, not her mother.

Ruaraidh supported her as she made her way slowly and painfully toward the house. Eilidh's feet had been burned badly in a fire set by Willie Cross when he learned of her perfidy in the matching ceremony decades before. She had never walked easily since.

James, Dermot, and Mr. Green waited for them near the front door. Sarah, Sheila, and Oona reached them first while Ruaraidh helped Eilidh shuffle along. Sheila greeted Dermot first. "Hello, Dermot. It's good to see ye again."

"Hello, Sheila." Dermot kissed her cheeks in greeting. "Sheila MacLeod, may I introduce James Stuart, and I believe you know Lyall Green."

"I do." She nodded to Green with a smile before turning appraising eyes to James. "My lord."

James offered her his hand. "Please, we're not so formal. It's lovely to meet you Mrs. MacLeod."

Sheila shook his hand her tone reserved. "It's lovely to meet ye as well."

"And this, gentlemen, is my sister, Oona Ballantyne." Sarah turned to her sister. "Oona, these are Dermot Sinclair, and James Stuart. And I believe you also know Mr. Green."

Oona gave them each a cursory look before offering a hand to shake that had paint stains around the cuticles. "Lads, Mr. Green."

The gravel crunched behind them, and Sheila stepped aside to let her mother and Ruaraidh join the group. "These are my mother, Eilidh MacLeod, and my son, Ruaraidh Ballantyne."

If Aunt Eilidh's feet hadn't been giving her trouble, she probably would have curtsied at the sight of James Stuart. As it was, she bowed her head. "My lord."

"Please, ma'am, there is really no need for that." James reached out and gave her a comforting pat on the shoulder.

"It's only yer due." Eilidh looked up at him with approval before turning a dirty look toward Dermot. "Upstart. I kent ye were trouble the first time I clapped eyes on ye."

"Alright, Mum. Let's see where Mr. Green has us sleeping. I think maybe ye need some rest." Sheila intervened.

"This way ladies.' Green waved them ahead through the front door.

"Always a joy to see ye, Mrs. MacLeod." Dermot called after them in a saccharine sweet tone as the newcomers followed Green into the house. He turned back to James and lowered his voice. "Dinna leave Sarah alone with that woman. She's pure poison."

James smirked. "She seemed fine to me."

"She would. She craves power and she sees you as a way to regain some."

Sarah joined them on the stoop. "She's the one responsible for the mismatch with my parents, not that she'll ever admit it."

"You seemed very happy to see your brother. I thought you said all of your family was gone." James gave her a penetrating look. "How long have you known them?"

"Not long at all." Sarah shook her head. "And Ruaraidh is special. He took to me as soon as he realized who I was, and he's been nothing but helpful since."

"He saved us from the assassin that ran us off the road back in April." Dermot added. "He's a good man."

"And the sister?" From the look on his face Sarah thought James was both curious and a little repulsed by her edgy-looking little sister.

"I'm meeting her just now too. I don't know anything about her except that she's an artist."

"And your father?" James asked.

"Apparently," Sarah shifted her gaze to Dermot. "He's in rehab."

Dermot's eyes lit up. "Oh, that's wonderful."

James looked alarmed. "Interesting family you have."

Sarah laughed. "You believe that they are from an ancient tribe of 'auld folk', but you're surprised when they turn out to be artists or alcoholics? Are we not allowed to have normal people problems?"

Dermot screwed his face up to look like a grumpy old person and mimicked Aunt Eilidh's voice. "Feh! We'll have none of yer *sluagh ùr* nonsense."

Sarah laughed even harder. "I shouldn't be laughing." She tried to choke it back. "You should be better than that, making fun of a wise woman."

"Oh, aye, wise woman." He rolled his eyes. He and Sarah elbowed each other over the joke and turned to go back inside. They left James puzzled and out of the loop on the doorstep.

CHAPTER TWENTY-ONE

They woke to rain the next day and everyone was relieved
that it wasn't the day that they would be having the ceremony.
Jujhar told them over breakfast that the rain might even help
them by giving them more water both above and below
ground to work with. After breakfast, they split off to pass the
day. Dermot, Sarah, and James decided to brave the rain.
They talked Ruaraidh into giving them a tour of Lochinver
and the surrounding area. Anne invited Sheila to a day spa in
Ullapool. Henry joined them for the trip saying that he would
find something to occupy himself. Walter stayed behind at the
house claiming that he had work to do. Mr. Green and Jujhar
had preparations to complete, and Oona wanted to stay at the
house and draw.

The rain cleared up by mid-morning and the tour of
Lochinver ended up being a pleasant way to spend the day.
That was if she didn't mind James and Dermot vying for her
attention all the time. They were surprisingly competitive,
even though Sarah had already made her preference clear.
Ruaraidh proved to be a good guide, but then that was how he
made a living.

They returned to Taigh na Damh late that afternoon. Sarah
was walking past on her way to the 'magic' wing to freshen
up when she noticed Isobel MacKenzie sitting alone in the
parlor. The old woman was sitting in front of the window, her
face raised to the sun. Sarah paused on the threshold, but

Isobel's keen ears must have heard her. *"Sin thu, a nighean."* (There you are, lass.)

Sarah came into the room and around the side of Isobel's chair to sit on a stool next to her. *"Feasgar math, a' antaidh. Ciamar a tha sibh?"* (Good afternoon, auntie. How are you?)

"Tha mi sgith, a' leanan. Tha mi uabhasach sgith." (I am tired, sweetheart. I am ever so tired.) Isobel lifted her hand toward Sarah, who took it in her own and put it to her face. Isobel's hands flitted over Sarah's features. *"Tha thu an-fhoiseil."* (You are troubled.)

"Gu dearbh." (Indeed.) Sarah tried to smile. She remembered the first time that she had met Isobel in her tiny home in Cape Breton. The old woman of her grandmother's generation had been able to sense that Sarah was alone in the world and that she needed her family. Isobel had also been the one to call Eilidh and tell her that Sarah was the one. But that hadn't been in time to save her granddaughter, Bridget, from the same assassin who had been sent to kill the sisters of her generation. Sarah went on in Gaelic. "I'm so sorry about Bridget."

"Thank you. She was a good girl." Isobel's voice went softer with the memory of the pretty, athletic, intelligent Bridget MacKenzie.

"Did she know?" Sarah asked quietly. The MacKenzie's gift was seeing the future. Each of the three sisters had a gift. Eilidh and her descendants saw the truth. Sarah's line saw the present, any part of it that they chose to look at.

"I hope not." Isobel's sightless eyes blinked back tears. "Like all of us, we only see with our gifts when we choose to. If she chose to look, she didn't say anything to me."

"Me neither." A voice came from the doorway. Sarah turned to find a woman in her late forties. Her thick brown hair was peppered with silver strands, and crow's feet were just barely visible at the corners of her eyes which reflected the still-fresh pain of losing her daughter. "I'm Rona MacKenzie."

Sarah stood and shook Rona's hand as she joined them by the window. "I'm Sarah. I feel like I know you already. My mother remembered you fondly."

Rona's expression softened. "I liked your mother. I wish she'd had an easier time of it."

Sarah hummed in agreement. "Have you spoken with Sheila?"

Rona nodded. "She's changed quite a lot in twenty-six years. She told me what really happened when we were matched."

"I can't help thinking my mother would still be here if things had been different."

Rona gave her hand a comforting squeeze. "She is here. She'll always be with you."

Sarah's throat felt suddenly tight, and she cleared it not able to meet Rona's eyes. "My grandmother too. I wonder what she would think of all this."

"She would want us to find the truth." Isobel nodded in approval.

"If she'd wanted the truth, she'd have taught yer mother more about our people." Eilidh growled as she stump-shuffled her way into the room.

Sarah drew in a breath, trying to summon the patience to be nice to the old woman. She reminded herself that she and Dermot needed all the allies they could get. She didn't expect to change Eilidh's mind but arguing with her might alienate the others.

In the end she didn't have to say anything. Isobel beat her to it. "You saw to it that we weren't there for our own daughters, sister. Just like you kept Maighread from coming home when the war ended."

Eilidh sat down on the sofa with a heavy sigh. "This is not my fault. I didna question the rights of the Stuart heir." She pointed a knobby finger at Sarah. "She did."

"No, you only destroyed our village and scattered our people." Isobel's hands gripped the arm of her chair until her knuckles were white. "You taught us the consequences of a bad match. The lass just wants to be sure of it."

"What would ye know of it? Ye've not been here since ye came for yer own matching?" Eilidh grumbled.

"I know that your grandmother and mine read the matches true and the cauldron continued to feed you after I went back to Cape Breton." Isobel snapped with more animation than Sarah had seen from her before.

"It's no use arguing about it now." Rona stepped between them both trying to calm them. "We have to deal with the situation as it is. And there's no need to make a show of our family conflicts for the *sluagh ùr*."

"Those *sluagh ùr* are royalty, and our joining with them is going to change the world." Eilidh whisper-yelled at them in answer to Rona's admonition.

"I think it's my branch that sees the future." Isobel reminded her.

"I see true." Eilidh barked.

"But you don't speak true." Rona kept her tone respectful despite her sharp words. "As we've all learned."

That seemed to shut Eilidh up. She humphed and sagged back onto the couch. Sarah was glad to be out of the line of fire for once. Isobel and Rona's attitudes toward Eilidh gave her some hope that they may be willing to be less dogmatic about the prophecy, and open to a different match. If she was superstitious, she'd be keeping her fingers crossed. "I think the key here is to remember that we are trying to find the best match. Much like my mother and Rab, every instinct I have is telling me that Dermot is my true match. We've tried to stay away from each other, but we keep getting pulled back together. Nothing feels right if we're not."

Eilidh made a sour face and opened her mouth to speak, but Sarah went on. "I know. It's easy to dismiss that as youth or infatuation, but I'm older now than my mother and Rab were. This isn't my first time out of the holler. I trust my instincts."

Rona studied her for several seconds. She seemed to come to a decision before saying, "Sit down over here."

Sarah went to sit next to the window where Rona had indicated. She took the stool next to Isobel. Rona pulled over a chair and sat it on Sarah's other side. She took Sarah's hand and looked at her. "Take my mother's hand."

Sarah slid her hand under Isobel's where it rested on the arm of the chair. Isobel closed her eyes and tilted her head back drawing in a long breath. Rona also inhaled and watched Sarah closely.

Sarah met Rona's eyes, but didn't say a word. She got the sense that they were looking into her future, and she didn't want to interrupt them. For all she knew, this could solve the question without having to do the matching ceremony. But after a few minutes their shoulders sagged from the effort. Isobel whispered. "I can't see it."

"Me neither." Rona's voice was filled with confusion and disappointment. "I can see you and a baby, but I can't see a father."

"And Dermot and James look enough alike that the baby's features probably wouldn't give away any clues." Sarah was disappointed.

"Exactly." Rona agreed. "I can try to look at their future's the next time I see them. Maybe I can see something."

"Ye'll see an independent Scotland and James Stuart, king of it." Eilidh grumbled from across the room. "This is all a waste of time."

Sarah sighed. She was never going to convince Eilidh, but Rona and Isobel might be helpful. Maybe they could see something in James and Dermot's futures that they couldn't see in hers. She wasn't sure how she felt about what they did see. She honestly hadn't given any thought to having children before this whole prophecy business. She'd been focused on her academic career, and it wasn't like she'd had an example of what a happy family life could be.

***

It was near two in the morning when he stole through the house to the wing where The Nine were. He'd had to wait for everyone to go to bed. Then he waited an hour longer to make sure that everyone was settled in their rooms. The moonlight shining through the windows in the entry hall limned everything in an ethereal blue light. He didn't know why he felt the need to sneak, everyone knew he and Sarah had been practically living together for weeks. Still, he didn't want to attract the attention of the rest of the house and have to deal with the recriminations and complaints.

He had to see her, needed some reassurance that she was his. He hadn't been alone with her since leaving Edinburgh two days before. James had been right beside them all day trying to impress her, trying to prove that he could enjoy the things she enjoyed. Sarah hadn't wanted to upset James by showing too much affection for Dermot. That distance was letting the self-doubt creep around him like a fog reminding him of every time James had gotten preferential treatment when they were lads. He needed to feel the rightness of being with her. He wished he was as sure as she was about the matching ceremony.

Her room was at the end of the hall in the north wing. He scratched at the door, a soft warning before he tried the knob. It turned and he pushed the door open. Sarah was standing by the window in a pool of moonlight. She glanced over her shoulder, and relaxed when she saw that it was him.

He closed the door behind him and joined her. His arm slipped around her waist and she rested against him, still looking out into the night. "The night before my mother's matching ceremony, there was a feast and a ceilidh. They celebrated all night like a fairy host eating from their magic cauldron and dancing until dawn."

"And here we are trying to sleep and pretending the uncertainty isna killing all of us." He huffed out a laugh.

"Do you really think anyone can sleep?" Her voice betrayed her skepticism.

"Probably not, but they were all quiet in their rooms when I walked over here."

"I'm a little surprised that Eilidh didn't insist that we do things the old way. But then I guess there isn't enough left of the auld folk to mount a feast."

"Likely not." He rubbed his cheek on the top of her head, loving the way her curls tickled his skin. "Then again, I dinna think anyone feels much like celebrating."

"Hopefully in a few hours, we'll feel like celebrating." He could tell it took an effort for her to sound hopeful.

"Tell me that ye're sure it will work out." He spoke quietly enough, but there was an urgency in his voice.

She pulled away and turned to him, taking his face in her hands. Her green eyes met his. "I don't know what is going to happen in the morning, but I do know that we are meant to be together. I can't tell you how. It's just a feeling I have, a feeling I've never had with anyone else. I'm yours, and you're mine. That's what matters."

She was so sure of them, and he was sure of her. It was himself that he had doubts about. Doubts that felt like a weight on his chest. "I canna shake this feeling of dread. I dinna want to lose ye."

"You are never going to lose me." She couldn't have said it more plainly. "You made an oath to me. I'll make one to you. Whatever happens tomorrow, whatever we have to do in the future, I pledged my life to the protection of yours and the lives of your children. Isn't that what you said?"

"I dinna need ye to protect me." Tears stung his eyes. "I only need ye to love me."

Her eyes sparkled like peridot behind a sheen of her own tears. "You know I do. I always will."

They met in the space between those promises. Their mouths hungry to prove their devotion. When their kiss broke, he whispered. "I'm terrified."

Her breath skimmed over his lips. "Me too, but we can handle anything together."

She pulled him toward the bed, and he let her. Their lovemaking was slow and consuming. They gave themselves to each other and then each took a little more. He demanded that she lose herself in his arms as he knew he would lose himself in her.

For all her confidence, he still felt the weight of the question that the morning would answer. He made love to her as if it might be the last time. He made note of every inch of her, just in case. He licked that spot on her neck that he liked noting the taste of her skin. He memorized every wrinkle of her puckered nipple. He etched the scent of her in his memory. He took mental photographs of her skin in the moonlight, made mental recordings of every hitched breath and whimper and what caused her to make it. He tattooed her touch on every part of his skin. And when she finally came apart in his arms, he told himself that he was the only one who got to see that part of her, with her defenses down and her heart laid open.

He had to pull himself away from her in the wee hours. They needed to be at the pool at dawn. He dressed quietly, watching her face at peace. Imprinting it on his memory, just as he had everything else. He picked up his shoes and opened the door. On the floor in the hall were a pair of wellies, and a saffron colored dress folded on top. A quick look down the hall showed that the rest of The Nine had the same in varying shades of yellow and orange. He took the boots and dress back into the room. He found Sarah's notebook on the desk and wrote her a note. He put the boots next to the bed and the dress on the night table laying the note on top of it. Then he kissed Sarah on the temple and made his way quietly back to his room.

CHAPTER TWENTY-TWO

Mist clung to the tops of the hills as they gathered behind the house. The sky was just starting to lighten. Two all-terrain vehicles were parked near the back door. They would ferry Eilidh and Isobel to the pool. Sarah was glad to see that they wouldn't have to walk. Their individual disabilities would have made an already difficult walk near impossible.

Sarah noted that the rest of the women who made up The Nine were wearing simple dresses like hers. Each generation's dresses deepened in color from a light gold to a burnt sienna. Then Ruaraidh stepped outside in a tunic the same color as her dress. "I guess you're standing in for Bridget then."

He glanced from her dress to his shirt. "Seems like it."

Sheila and Rona helped their mothers down the step from the courtyard to the lawn. They were followed by James and Dermot who were dressed for an early morning walk in the Highlands with boots and windbreakers. They both approached her and mumbled their greetings into the morning quiet.

Within a couple of minutes, Jujhar and Mr. Green came out of the house. Jujhar was wearing a white tunic, but Green wore and orange one in the same shade that Eilidh and Isobel wore.

Mr. Green addressed the group. "Good Morning. Ruaraidh and Jujhar, will you assist Mrs. MacKenzie and Mrs. MacLeod to the site? The rest of us will walk.

Ruaraidh wove through the group to take his grandmother's arm and help her to the four-wheeler. Jujhar did the same, bowing and introducing himself to Isobel. The blind woman reached up and ran her fingers down his face for a moment. When she was satisfied, she let him lead her to the other four-wheeler. When the grandmothers had donned their helmets and were securely on the backs of the ATV's, they took off at a slow pace.

"Shall we?" Green chimed with a wave toward the hills behind the Taigh na Damh.

No one seemed to want to go first, until Sarah decided to take the lead. She had asked for this after all. She stepped forward to follow Green. Dermot and James flanked her their flashlights trained on the path. The rest of the women followed. The walk was long and hilly. Some of the ground was spongy from the rain and made Sarah grateful for the wellies she'd been given, even if they looked a bit odd with the dresses.

When they arrived at the pool, the four-wheelers were already there and waiting for them at the bottom of the last hill. When the group came up to them, Isobel was still with her face turned to the sky. Eilidh was fractious. Ruaraidh was attempting to help her up the trail, but she was refusing his arm. He went to take her elbow and she swatted at him. "Feh! Go on wi' ye."

"Granny, the path is rocky." Ruaraidh pleaded.

"And I've been walking it since long before ye were a glint in Rab Ballantyne's eye. I ken it well enough." She started up the hill with her cane.

"Mrs. MacKenzie, can I offer you my arm?" Jujhar spoke politely to Isobel, ignoring the argument that was going on nearby.

The rest of the group followed them slowly up the hill. Green appeared to be watching the light in the sky judging how long they had left until dawn, but he didn't seem impatient.

When they reached the top of the hill, the light was starting to shift from twilight blue to predawn gold. Green stepped up onto the tree stump that used to serve as an altar at the edge of the pool. Now, it was several feet from the edge of the muddy depression that the well had become. Also laid on the stump were a staff and a sort of head dress. The crown was covered in fur, a leather chin strap hung from the cap, and an enormous set of antlers extended from the sides. Confirming what Sarah had suspected, that Molly's antlered man from all those years ago must have been Mr. Green. Sarah wasn't sure what that meant for them today. He had intervened before when things were going wrong. She hoped that meant he would steer them in the right direction today.

From his perch on the stump Lyall Green arranged them around the pool. "Sarah, I would like you to stand to my left, but I'll need you to leave space for another person to stand between us. Isobel, you should stand to Sarah's left, followed by Rona and Ruaraidh. Next Eilidh, Sheila and Oona. Each branch of the family stood together in order of veneration."

He turned to James, Dermot, and Jujhar. "Gentlemen, you should stand back behind the altar." When they had followed his instructions, Green turned back to the pool and looked around the circle. "Now then, we need to make up nine."

Sarah wasn't sure if anyone else caught his Shakespeare reference, but Green seemed slightly amused by it. He fastened the headdress to his head and drew in a deep breath as if he was preparing to begin yoga practice. When he had released the breath, he turned to Sarah. "Hold your right hand out, my dear, as if you are taking the hand of the person next to you."

Sarah lifted her open hand out to her side. Green spoke in a quiet, even tone. "Close your eyes. Breathe deeply. In through your nose and out through your mouth." Sarah breathed. "Concentrate on that hand. Imagine that you can feel another hand in it, a familiar hand, one you've held many times, one that you still see in your dreams. Breathe in. Breathe out. Now look at your hand."

Sarah opened her eyes and looked at her open hand. There was a hand in hers. Her eyes traveled up the arm to meet the dark eyes of her mother. She was there, but not there. It was as if the morning mist was thicker in that spot and her mother's image was projected onto it. Sarah squeezed her hand to be sure that it was real. She didn't feel flesh and bone, but something kept her from closing her hand. A tentative smile flitted across Molly's face, as if she weren't sure of the reception she would get.

"How?" Sarah whispered.

Green answered. "We all have a spiritual duplicate that walks with us through life. The Gaels call it a *co-coisiche*, a co-walker. Your gift exists because you are able to send yours out to observe things, but it is linked back to you by a sort of spiritual tether. When your mother took her own life, she cast out her co-walker. It attached itself to you."

Suddenly, things clicked into place. "That's why she tells me things in my dreams."

"Yes," Green agreed enthusiastically. "In a dream state you can see her, and in places of power like this one."

"And stone circles." Sarah thought of the circle in North Carolina where she had seen Molly. She knew she hadn't been sleepwalking that night.

"They are very good conduits for communication, yes."

Sarah glanced around the circle to see if the others saw the same thing she did. Sheila's eyes were brimming with unshed tears while Eilidh sneered. Ruaraidh and Oona looked on in wonder.

"Now that we are nine again. Let's begin to set things right." Green turned to the rest of the group. "Everyone, join hands."

It took some stretching, but The Nine joined hands around the pool. "Focus your eyes on the center of the pool."

The center was covered in a sickly looking greenish brown sludge. "I want you to feel the ground beneath your feet."

Sarah wiggled her toes inside her wellies, feeling the moss under them spring back.

"Feel the rock under the grass and soil. Within that rock are caves. They run all through these mountains. Imagine those caves filling with water the way that they do after rain like yesterday or in the spring when the snow caps melt. Picture those waters filling the caves and pushing up through the rocks, and ground. Hold that image in your minds."

Then he began to recite an incantation. Sarah didn't recognize the language. She had no idea what he was saying, but she tried to focus her eyes on the center of the pool and her mind on the image he had evoked rather than on his words. Soon the sludge at the center of the pool started to bubble as if something was under it moving. One of the men behind Green gasped, but Sarah kept her focus on the pool.

He repeated the incantation and then repeated it again. The bubbling became a steady flow, not like a fountain, but like water spilling over the sides of a cup. It was coming up from other points in the pool as well. Green kept repeating the words like a chant, and the streams coming up from the ground converged in the pool. With each repetition, his voice grew louder and the water level in the pool rose. He ended on a shout when the water line reached almost to the toes of The Nine standing around the pool. Green picked up the staff and stirred the water, achieving the murky greenish appearance that Molly had described in her memoir.

Sarah couldn't believe her eyes. They had called up water from the ground. She looked around to see if anyone else was as amazed as she was. They only looked half-surprised and half-satisfied, as if they felt vindicated by the restoration. She glanced over at her mother, who looked almost as shocked as Sarah felt.

***

Dermot stared at the pool trying to process what he had just seen. It was one thing to be forced into the Stuart's web of intrigue when it was all about power or money. He could scoff at the idea of restoring the crown. Madness about prophecies and bloodlines seemed like pipe dreams. He'd been half-dazed with fatigue and shock when the cauldron healed his leg, so he could write that off as illusion or say the cut hadn't been as bad as he thought. He could view this all with a cynical eye that needed proof. But he had no such excuse now. He had just watched Sarah's mother appear beside her out of thin air, and water bubble up from the ground on command.

Green looked across the glen to the eastern ridge where the sky was growing brighter. "Come, gentlemen. We haven't any time to waste."

James stepped forward with all the confidence of a man who'd been told he was the chosen one all his life. He was only somewhat subdued by the miracle they'd just witnessed.

"Bow your head." Green told him. James obeyed bowing to the magician. James seemed shocked when Green reached up with his left hand and plucked several hairs from the top of his head. James straightened up looking irritated. Green paid him no mind. He placed the hairs in his open right hand. He mumbled some words, and the hairs were consumed by a flame that appeared to come from nowhere. The flame died in seconds and Green tilted the minuscule bit of ash from his hand into the pool.

"Dermot?" Green turned to him. James stepped down from the altar, and Dermot stepped up. He looked at Sarah as he bowed his head so that Green could take some of his hair.

When it was done, Green repeated the process of burning the hair and dropping the ash into the pool.

With a glance at the ridge where dawn was breaking, Green turned to Sarah, "Princess."

She didn't object to being called princess, although Dermot knew she hated it. Sarah met his eyes as she took the step up onto the altar. He tried to look encouraging. This was what they wanted, right? She'd been sure that this would go their way.

Green produced a knife from under his tunic and looked at Sarah. His love stuck out her chin and stepped closer to the edge of the altar. She held out her open hand to him ready for the next part. She kept her eyes on the magician, and barely flinched when his blade sliced across her palm.

He went to take her hand to squeeze her blood out into the pool, but Sarah beat him to it. She stretched her arm over the water and squeezed it herself. She held it there until Green nodded that he thought she had shed enough blood. Then she let her hand fall to her side. She didn't attempt to stop the bleeding. She was focused on the surface of the pool.

Green picked up the staff and stirred the water. Everyone craned their necks to watch what would happen. The blood dropped below the surface and spread, swirling crimson through the greenish brown water. Dermot supposed that was what The Nine read in the pool, the swirling designs of the red blood. He thought it must be akin to reading tea leaves or entrails. He had no idea what meaning they were seeing in the pattern of the blood in the pool, but the three MacLeod women gasped and Ruaraidh's eyebrows drew together in confusion.

Green stared hard at the water. He swiped his staff through the designs in a sharp movement that sent the blood swirling again. Everyone leaned forward and watched as the pattern resolved just as it had been before. Green looked back at him and at James, then returned his gaze to the pool confounded. He tried stirring again, but the pattern returned.

"Will someone tell me what that means?" Sarah's voice was shrill as she looked from person to person.

Green looked again at Dermot and James as if examining them with new eyes. He turned to Sarah. "It means that they are both your matches. There is no difference between them."

Dermot felt like his blood had turned to ice and his mind buzzed with the implications. If the pool worked on genetics, then that would mean that he and James were closely related, or at least that they shared the same traits that would make them good matches for Sarah. What did that mean about his parents? Could Henry really be his father as he had suspected? Most of all how was he going to keep Sarah when James had as strong a claim to her as far as the prophecy was concerned?

"How is that possible?" Sarah's voice cut through the noise in his head.

"I don't know." Green shook his head in confusion. "I don't think this has ever happened before."

Sarah held her hand over the water, but the bleeding had stopped. "Do it again."

"I've looked three times." Green assured her. "The result was always the same."

Sarah was busy flexing and squeezing her hand trying to open the cut again. When that didn't work, she snatched the knife from Green's hand and cut her hand again before anyone could stop her.

Dermot jumped up onto the altar. He grabbed her wrist and took the knife from her holding it out toward Green so that he could take it. Sarah held her bleeding hand out over the water squeezing hard in desperation.

"Sguir." He tried to turn her toward him. *"Sguir, a ghaol."* (Stop. Stop, love.)

Her voice was shrill her eyes darting back and forth between him and the water. "Maybe it wasn't enough blood or hair."

Without even stirring, the red of her blood rose to the surface in the same swirling pattern as it had before. She stared at the surface, her face solidifying into a mask of fury. "It's not right. It's not right, Dermot. It's not!"

He pulled her to him crushing her face into his chest. He whispered for her ears alone. "It's alright. We'll figure something out. It's alright."

While he was soothing her a cackling sound came from the other side of the pool. They looked up to find Eilidh MacLeod doubled over laughing.

CHAPTER TWENTY-THREE

They made their way slowly back from the pool as the sun climbed over the hills, each person lost in thought developing their own interpretations of what just happened. Dermot kept an arm firmly around Sarah. James led the group, his back straight and head high. He didn't say anything or even look back at them.

Sarah lost track of time and everything else during the walk. Her vision narrowed to just what was in front of her. She was only conscious of Dermot's arm around her shoulders and the need to put one foot in front of the other. She felt the ground under them, but her mind could only see blood swirling and shifting into shapes in the murky water of the pool. She'd been right. Dermot was her true match. But somehow so was James. That possibility hadn't even crossed her mind.

Before she knew it, she was sitting down in the library at Taigh na Damh. Dermot squatted in front of her. "We'll figure this out."

He kissed her forehead and disappeared. The next thing she heard was Sheila voicing the exact question that was running through her mind. "What now?"

Sarah looked up to find the rest of The Nine seated around the coffee table. Someone had thrown a blanket over her shoulders, and she realized that she was shivering. She pulled the blanket tighter around herself.

"An excellent question." From across the room, Green pulled books from the shelves. "We can test the cauldron with James and see how it behaves."

"We have the cauldron?" Rona seemed surprised.

Green looked up from a leatherbound book with frayed pages. "I brought it here for this event. It will be hidden again when we are done here."

"It's here?" Sarah asked. Everyone turned their eyes to her. "Well, let's go. Let's test it."

Green held up a hand. "Let's not rush into this. We've already had one spanner thrown into the works today. We should decide what to do if the cauldron is also inconclusive."

Jujhar handed Sarah a cup of coffee. "You're having an adrenaline crash. This will help. We have some chocolate as well. The extra sugar will be good for you."

He sat down next to her and Sarah was grateful for his presence. The coffee cup was warm and solid, giving her shaking hands something to hold onto. Jujhar had been generous with the sugar and cream. He was right, it helped.

"My mother and I can try to see their futures. It didn't work for Sarah, but maybe we can see for the lads."

"And we're sure that Sarah is the one?" Jujhar asked.

"She's the one." Eilidh and Isobel said at once in a rare agreement.

"My mother and I have both seen it." Rona assured them.

"And she understood the key in the song when she heard it from all of us." Eilidh added. "Not that Oona or Bridget had the chance to hear the song from all of you." Sarah pointed out.

"That ship has sailed, sister." Oona put in.

Sarah couldn't blame Oona if she didn't want to be the one. Her supposed destiny was a life destroyer, at least as far as Sarah was concerned.

Ruaraidh who had been leaning against a bookcase near the door spoke up. "So, we can test James with the cauldron. We already know it heals Dermot. Green and I both witnessed that. The MacKenzies can look into their futures."

Green put down his book and went to a rack of scrolls. He was searching for something. "I have been looking at this situation for months with every method of divination I know, and I have not been able to see an answer. Today's results only make things more challenging."

"What do we do if the cauldron and the MacKenzies can't give us a clear answer?" Ruaraidh seemed to be taking charge of keeping the proceedings on track.

"We vote?" Rona suggested. "There are nine of us. We should be able to come to some agreement."

"Eight of you." Green slid a scroll out of the rack and carried it to a book stand. "I am merely an observer and facilitator. I cannot be part of the decision."

"Ye mean the fetch gets a vote?" Eilidh croaked.

"Co-walker, Mrs. MacLeod." Green sent her a withering look over the top of his reading glasses. "And yes, she does."

At least there was that. Molly was sure to be on Sarah's side.

"Right." Ruaraidh pushed away from the wall. "Do we all agree with that plan?"

He scanned the room. His jaw set firm, almost daring anyone to disagree. "I'll tell the others."

***

Dermot quietly closed the door to the library. He would have to trust that her family would take care of her for the moment. They had made it clear that the conversation going on in that room was only for The Nine and Green and his apprentice. He hated to leave her, but Dermot had questions of his own now that needed resolving. He stood there for several seconds staring at the door calculating what to do next.

"Is she alright?" James asked from a few feet down the hall.

Dermot turned his head to see his one-time friend and maybe brother looking like a kicked dog. "Did ye know?"

James pressed his lips together trying to marshal his emotions. "If I knew, do you think I would have agreed to this test?"

"I don't know what ye would do." Dermot muttered as he walked toward James. He needed to talk to Henry. "I havena understood yer motives for years."

James stepped in front of him. "I don't want to fight you."

Dermot's blue eyes met James's and he was struck by how similar they were. Why had he never noticed before? "But ye want to take the most important thing in the world to me." A childhood memory flashed in his mind of Mrs. Miller asking him to give up one of his toys because James was asking for it. "D'ye think I'll just give her up to ye? Is she like a toy that I got for Christmas that ye want? And I'm just supposed to give it up to 'young master James', eh?"

"That wasn't me. They told you that."

"Aye, but ye still got what ye wanted." Dermot pushed past him. "Ye had everything; the best home, the best schools, a father."

James froze realization dawned on him. "I never knew you felt that way."

"Of course not." Dermot snapped. "What good would telling ye that have done? It wouldna have changed anything. It would only make ye feel as bad as I did. It wouldna have made my father suddenly appear."

"I think a conversation with my parents is in order." James fell into step behind him.

"At least we can agree on that." Dermot muttered.

They found the Stuarts in the dining room having breakfast. Henry, Anne, and Walter were sitting around the table. They stood when the door opened.

"Well?" Anne asked urgently. "Where are the others?"

James put a hand on Dermot's arm to quiet him. Dermot was fine letting James do the talking. No doubt James could be more diplomatic than he could at the moment. "There's been a complication."

"What sort of complication?" Walter took a seat. "Didn't you do the ceremony?"

"We did." James went on. "Apparently, Dermot and I are both ideal matches for Sarah."

"That's impossible." Anne's fair skin started to turn mottled red around the neckline of her blouse.

"I can assure you, mother. We checked multiple times." James's tone was unequivocal.

"Henry?" Anne looked to her husband in question.

Henry sank into the chair at the head of the table, his eyes unfocused on the table in front of him.

"This next bit is rather sensitive." James kept his eyes on his father. "We believe that the pool uses some sort of primitive genetic analysis to determine the matches. A result like the one we got today could only happen if Dermot and I were genetically similar."

"That's preposterous." Anne sputtered; red creeping up her neck.

"I don't think so." Dermot watched Henry, who continued staring at the table. The room fell silent, waiting.

After a tense moment, Henry lifted his eyes to Dermot's. Tears swam in front of the same blue that Dermot saw when he looked at James. "I have cared for you all of your life, Dermot. Your mother was my best friend, and I'm so proud of the man she raised. You must believe me. If I thought for a moment that you were my son, I would have claimed you years ago."

Dermot closed his eyes, blocking out the words that he didn't want to hear. He didn't understand how that could be the case. He knew. He just knew that Henry loved his mother. He thought his mother loved Henry. And if it wasn't Henry, then who could his father be?

"I might have had something to say about that." Anne's voice was shrill.

"This is not the time, mother." James cut in.

"This is not the time for any of this." Walter spoke from his seat further down the table. "We're here for one reason, and one reason only. Dermot Sinclair's paternity doesn't matter, any more than the girl's preference does. James will be king. If the ceremony didn't rule him out, then he is the one chosen."

"It's not that simple." James's harsh tone caught Dermot's attention. He looked over to see James strung tight as a bowstring. "We need her to be cooperative."

"Why?" Walter asked as if it was the simplest question in the world.

A sharp response was on the tip of Dermot's tongue, but James put a hand on his arm. He pinned his uncle with a glare. "Because I am not a rapist."

Walter shook his head and blew out a long breath. When he spoke his voice was calm, but firm. "We are trying to secure something far more important than one woman's cooperation. Once the choice is taken away from her, she will come around to make the best of it."

"Ye fucking monster!" It only took Dermot two strides to round the table. In a blink he had yanked the old man from his chair and had him by the throat against the wall. He spat the words in Walter's face. "That's not going to happen."

Walter's upper lip curled into a sneer, despite his face growing red. "It's how this was done for generations. Why should now be different?"

"Because it should." James stood behind Dermot.

Walter looked like he would say something else, but Dermot tightened his grip on his throat.

"James, Dermot, we need ye." Ruaraidh's voice came from the doorway. "And I dinna think Green fancies disposing of a body. It's already been a busy day, aye?"

Dermot didn't look back. His eyes bored into Walter's. "Wouldna be the first time Green disposed of someone I killed for her."

He squeezed a touch tighter watching the color in Walter's red face deepen another shade. When he finally caught a flash of fear in the man's eyes, he let him go. He turned to the door where Sarah's brother looked stoically. "Ye're wanted in the library."

CHAPTER TWENTY-FOUR

Sarah cleaned and bandaged the cuts on her hand with a first aid kit that some thoughtful person had put in her room. She hadn't even thought to heal herself with the cauldron when they had tested its properties on James. The cauldron had told them nothing. After trekking through the basement into a chamber carved into the bedrock where Green had hidden it, James had been healed by water from the cauldron. In fact, they had tested its healing properties on Ruaraidh and Green with the same result. If the cauldron was an indicator as Sarah thought, they couldn't be sure what exactly it was indicating.

After changing out of the ceremonial dress, and into some comfortable old jeans and a Carolina sweatshirt, Sarah returned to the library. The Nine were waiting for her.

Rona looked as disappointed as Sarah felt. "We sat with both of them, the three of us. She waved a hand between herself, Isobel and Sheila. "We see you in both their futures. We see a child in both their futures. That's as far as we can tell."

"I can only add that they both care for you, and neither of them has done anything to try to change the result of the ceremony today." Sheila's lips pressed together in a frown.

Sarah sank down onto a couch beside Isobel. "We're right back to where we were this morning."

"And that means we vote." Oona had also changed, and was standing behind the couch where her mother, grandmother, and Rona sat.

"What do we do? Secret ballot, like a jury?" Sarah suggested.

"We can certainly start that way." With a nod to Jujhar. "Shall Mr. Gurudat collect and count the votes?"

"He's her friend. He canna be trusted." Eilidh rapped her cane on the floor for emphasis.

Sarah could see the effort it took for Green not to roll his eyes. "He has sworn to be impartial, but if it will make you feel better, Mrs. MacKenzie, then I will do it."

Everyone looked to Eilidh for further objection, but she merely rested her hands on top of her cane looking mildly satisfied if still sour.

"Paper, Mr. Gurudat." He picked up a pen box from the desk and dumped its contents on the blotter.

Jujhar grabbed a small pad of paper and a handful of pens. He began passing them out to each of the seven voters present. Everyone wrote their votes on their papers and folded them. It was all Sarah could do not to crane her neck to try to see everyone's votes as they wrote them down.

A thought occurred to Sarah after folding her ballot. "How can we collect Mama's vote?"

"Is there a chance she might not vote with you?" Ruaraidh asked.

"I don't think so, but she has been unpredictable before." She cut her eyes to Eilidh. "And we don't want to risk someone saying that this wasn't entirely fair."

Green looked thoughtful for a moment. "I think I can scry to find her vote. We can all do it together so that everyone can see her answer. Mr. Gurudat, can you fetch my bowl?"

Jujhar retrieved a ceramic bowl from a shelf in the corner. It reminded Sarah of the bowl that Green had used to show her the vision of her grandmother in the cave. While Jujhar went to get water for the bowl, Green carried the pencil box around the room collecting everyone's votes.

When Jujhar returned, they put the filled bowl on the coffee table, and everyone crowded around it. Jujhar went to close the curtains and darken the room, while Green lit a candle. "Everyone, focus on the bowl, and remember how Molly looked this morning when we saw her at the pool."

Sarah sat opposite Sheila who smiled at her before they all turned their attention to the bowl. Sarah watched the reflected candle flame flicker on the surface of the water and took in a deep breath. After a few breaths, the whole group around the bowl seemed synchronized. Inhaling and exhaling, focused on the bowl. Images of her mother flickered through her mind; Molly laughing while they played together, singing to her when she was younger, Molly crying quietly when she thought no one was looking, Molly looming over her as she held her down in the bathtub.

"Focus, Sarah." Green's voice was quiet, but insistent. "Molly from this morning."

This morning. This morning, Molly had smiled with tears shining in her eyes. She had been sad that Sarah was there in the same situation she'd been in all those years ago. But they could fix it. Molly could help her fix it. That was the Molly she focused on. She felt a sense of calm wash over her, and her mother appeared in the bowl.

"Molly," Her name came softly from Green. "We need..."

He didn't have to finish the question. Molly's face was replaced in the bowl with that of Dermot. It stayed that way for several seconds before Molly's image returned. With a nod, she confirmed her vote.

"I'd say that's pretty clear." Ruaraidh knelt at the end of the table.

"Indeed. Thank you, my dear.' Green addressed the image in the bowl before blowing out the candle.

Jujhar opened the curtains and everyone blinked as the afternoon sun flooded the room.

"Now, we count." Green picked up the pen box that contained their votes and carried it to the desk. He read the votes out as he opened each of them. "James, Dermot, James, James, Dermot, Dermot, James. With Molly's vote that makes four for Dermot and four for James. We are tied."

Sarah fell back on the couch. Not even voting could go easily. She was starting to wonder if she was wrong about the whole thing. Why was it proving so difficult to get an answer?

Sarah looked at each of the people in the room wondering who the James voters were. Eilidh she was sure of. Maybe Isobel. Her age might make her less likely to question the expected match, but then she'd been removed from Làrachd an Fhamhair since her own matching and there was no love lost between her and Eilidh. She was almost sure Sheila would have voted for Dermot, Ruaraidh too seemed to be on her side. That left Rona, Oona, and Isobel as the unknown quantities.

"Right." Ruaraidh stood by the mantle. "We're going to have to talk about the pros and cons, the reasons for James or Dermot."

"I might as well get the ball rolling." Sarah stood so that she could look at everyone while she spoke. "I love Dermot. You all have seen that. I have never felt drawn to a person the way I'm drawn to him. I trust him. We had our moments when we first met, but I trust him completely now. And if we are worried about the next generation, I can't think of anyone who would be a better father than Dermot."

She turned her attention to where Rona and Isobel sat next to each other. "James, I do not trust. He or people around him have deceived me and Dermot to their own ends. They have threatened people that I know. They have practically been keeping us prisoner for the last two months." She shifted her attention to Eilidh. "If you worry about *sluagh ùr* ways? The Stuarts are the poster children for deceit, greed, and a disturbing hunger for power. Now, James might be the best of them, but he can't help but be influenced by that. I've seen it. He has told me himself that he struggles under the weight of his family's influence. I don't believe that he is a strong enough leader to be the father of the future king."

"That's good enough for me." Ruaraidh stood and looked around the group. His eyes came to rest on his mother. "I've seen what one-sided marriage does to a family. I watched ye and Rab struggle for years while he had Molly MacAlpin in his heart. I wouldna put Sarah through the years of regret that Da went through. And what ye went through? I wouldna wish that on anyone. I don't know James Stuart, but he deserves to be happy too. If either man gets the same result, then it should be the man she loves, not just for her, but for the child."

"Ah, love." Sheila stood and went to her son, her eyes brimming with tears. "I'm so sorry."

"It's alright, Mum. It's spilt milk for us." He let his mother wrap an arm around his waist. "But we can save Sarah and her child that pain."

"Feh! James Stuart is already halfway to being king." Eilidh leaned forward in her seat, her rheumy eyes narrowed at her daughter. "Choosing the bastard would force us to start all over again."

"I think halfway is a bit generous." Sarah put in diplomatically. She could not afford to let Eilidh push her buttons in this conversation, and the old woman was guaranteed to try. "The Stuarts' business empire isn't going anywhere. If Dermot's father is a Stuart, they could claim him at any time. It's not like Alba Petroleum will just disappear if they acknowledge him."

"More pity that." Ruaraidh muttered.

"That may be, but is Dermot going to start running it? Does he have political aspirations? Is he for independence?" Eilidh fired the questions at her.

"Are those requirements?" Sarah cut her off. "James could just as easily continue doing all of those things but make Dermot or his child the heir. I don't recall anything in the prophecy saying that the heir has to be a politician or run an oil company."

"Then what happens when James produces his own heir and doesn't want to give it all up to Dermot's child?" Eilidh countered.

Rona spoke up for the first time. "I'm not unsympathetic to your feelings, Sarah. But Eilidh has a point. James Stuart is best positioned to produce the heir to the throne. Even if they are brothers, or cousins or something, James is the one with the training, experience, and most importantly the means to protect the future king until it is time to ascend."

"He's also got the weight of the Stuart name and considerable political backing to move the country toward independence." Oona rubbed at a spot of paint on her hand.

Sarah tamped down the feeling of betrayal that one of her own generation seemed to be arguing against her. "So, we're supposed to be from a mystery tribe of people fed by a magic cauldron who believe in and follow an ancient prophecy, but suddenly we're all political pragmatists."

"It's that pragmatism that has kept our people safe and secret for all this time." Rona pointed out.

"Not secret enough." Sarah heard her voice rising and took a breath before going on more calmly. "The Nazis, the Invigilare, the Circle and probably MI-6 seem to know about us. Jujhar pieced it together and found us all on his own."

"I'm painfully aware of that." Rona said quietly. "There's a reason my branch of the family has been living in Canada for generations. Your grandmother went to America for a similar reason. My daughter died because someone found out about the prophecy." Her brown eyes found Sarah's. They held all the pain of losing her daughter. "I can't let Bridget's death be in vain. I have to vote for the man in the best position to make this prophecy a reality."

Sarah wondered if Bridget would have felt the same way. Sarah hadn't known her long and hadn't known about the prophecy at the time. In hindsight, she thought Bridget had seemed relieved after meeting her, as if she or her grandmother had seen that Sarah was the one. That meant Bridget could get on with the rest of her life. Until she had met Ryan Cumberland who had murdered her and dumped her body in the ocean.

She couldn't argue with Rona's grief or her reason for voting for James. Isobel had been listening to the debate silently, her head cocked to the side, her eyes half-closed. Sarah expected she might feel the same as her daughter. Isobel cleared her throat and spoke in a halting voice. "There is something to be said for tradition. It has sustained us and our powers for thousands of years. It teaches us still. You know that it does *a'Mhorag* or you would not do the work that you do. It gives us a foundation. It gives us strength. It points us in the direction we must go. Changing course now would be a repudiation of all the generations before us from the moment the giants made us until now. It would be to say that none of the traditions that you have spent your life studying matter. I am surprised that you would do that."

Sarah sank to the couch deflated and defeated. She didn't see this as changing course, but she couldn't prove it. None of this had worked out the way that she had hoped.

She listened as the two sides argued themselves in circles. Ruaraidh and Sheila did an admirable job making the points that she would have made from the dangers of a mismatch to the importance of a loving home for child development. They held their own against the traditionalists while they all debated for what felt like an eternity. The only one who didn't join in was Oona, who seemed deep in thought. Sarah supposed she had made her point and didn't feel the need to add her voice any further.

When they had been at it for hours, Mr. Green who had been quietly observing the debate came around the desk to stand behind the couch. "I think that we have all made some good points and given ourselves a lot to think about. I suggest that we take the rest of the evening to consider our positions. We can come together in the morning and vote again."

Relief spread around the room. They were at a stalemate and continuing to rehash the same arguments wasn't going to change any minds. Oona was the first one to the door, but she stopped when Mr. Green spoke again. "I think it would be best if we did not discuss our debate with the others. Adding their voices is not likely to change any minds and will only muddy the waters. We can simply say that we are considering our options."

CHAPTER TWENTY-FIVE

Dinner was a tense affair. A few of them had tried to make small talk while they all eyed each other across the table wondering who the deciding vote would be, how the others would react, and who The Nine would ultimately choose. Dermot's concerns about his relationship to the Stuarts seemed secondary to the decision they were making.

He tried to show his support for Sarah in whatever small ways he could. Sarah did the same for him. They were a team and they wanted to make sure everyone saw it. James kept his own counsel. He was no longer vying for Sarah's attention, but seemed distracted.

When dinner was over, no one lingered to socialize as they had done the night before. Sarah claimed to be exhausted and decided to go to bed. Dermot didn't like to leave her alone, but when he had walked her to her room, she stopped him at the door. She told him that she needed to think and rest. After thoroughly kissing her goodnight, he walked away from her door saying a silent prayer that it would not be their last kiss.

He'd been up most of the night before, but with everything still up in the air, he couldn't even think of sleeping. He had to find something to occupy himself, then he remembered what Sarah told him Green had shared about his mother. He called her 'one of his'.

He found Lyall Green in the conservatory watering an array of herbs and other plants. Dermot spoke without preamble. He was too tired and tense for niceties. "Sarah said ye knew my mother."

The magician's shoulders settled back as if he were preparing for an unpleasant task. When he turned his face was grim. He motioned toward a small table with two chairs under a pair of lemon trees in giant pots. "Why don't we sit down?"

Dermot took a seat at the table and waited. Green made his way slowly. He sat on the chair as if he was feeling every one of the one hundred and forty-seven years he claimed to have lived. "It's a long story, but one that you should hear."

Green paused gathering his thoughts. "I wasn't always what I am now. I was young once, like you. With all the follies and peccadilloes that entails. I was a man, sometimes given to passions. When I took on my current role, I gave most of that up. Naturally, I still have hobbies and passions apart from my role with The Nine. If I didn't my life would be maddening. But a role like mine requires that you sever ties to the people of your old life, the loves that might pull you away from your mission. And I did that. I was twenty-eight, and Queen Victoria was on her way to becoming the grandmother of every royal house in Europe. I didn't miss it, living as a normal man. I never knew love the way that some of my friends had, and I didn't see much point in pursuing marriage and a family. Learning all the secrets of the world and how it works was so much more interesting."

Dermot had only asked about his mother. Listening to Lyall Green's life story might put him to sleep after all. He shifted in his chair as the old man went on. "It was the war that drew me out of my own studies and experiments. During the first World War, I had simply kept my head down and let them fight it out. There was no threat to The Nine with that miserable conflict. But the second World War? That was different."

"The Nazis had found out about Sarah's people and the cauldron. I suspect one of my colleagues was loose lipped."

That grabbed Dermot's attention. "One of yer colleagues? I didn't know ye had any."

"Oh, yes. There are more like me. At least one on every continent. We are scholars who study magic." Dermot tried to imagine more of Green, and what that would look like. "In any case, someone told them about the cauldron. You are aware I assume that the Nazis went about collecting objects that they thought were sacred, not just German or Christian sacred objects, but any they could find. They were collecting them and taking them to Wewelsburg."

"The SS Academy?" Dermot recalled reading about the occult underpinnings of the SS.

"Exactly. They were using folklore, especially from Northern Europe to support their ideological ends. After an Ahnenerbe researcher found his way to Làrachd an Fhamhair in the late thirties, I decided to take a more active approach to protecting the cauldron. I went to Germany and set myself up as an academic specializing in antiquities. I infiltrated the Ahnenerbe and spent much of the war planting red herrings and rumors to distract them from finding the cauldron."

"That's why Sarah's grandmother sent away. Because they thought the sisters would be safer away from the fighting." Dermot remembered something that he had heard in a history class years ago. "Is that why Hess flew to Scotland on his so-called peace mission?"

Green shook his head. "I don't know. I had more dealings with Himmler than Hess." He paused for a moment and seemed to consider that connection before shaking his head. "In any case, after the war I was exhausted from the charade, drunk on its success, high on survival...I came back to Scotland and attempted to settle back into my old role as observer." His face took on a softer look and he sighed. "I met her in the park behind my house in Dean Village. She was foraging for food. So was I. Everyone was hungry after the war, and if you didn't have land for a garden, you had to find extra food where you could. We made a trade, her sorrel for my mushrooms. And we struck up a friendship. She had lovely golden hair and deep brown eyes that a man could just fall into."

"Perhaps it was a case of post-war life affirmation, or plain old-fashioned male weakness. The life of an observer doesn't lend itself to relationships. But I forgot myself and behaved like many men just returning from war."

He looked regretful, disappointed in himself. "When she told me that she was pregnant, I fought with myself over what to do. I had made this promise to live apart from society. I had sworn to protect a whole tribe and I couldn't simply abandon my charge. There was no one who could take on the role, so many men died in the war. I offered to help her abort the child, but she wouldn't hear of it. She was in love and couldn't understand why I couldn't give up my vocation."

"What are ye saying?" Dermot thought he understood the point of the story, but he needed to hear the man say it. The magician's usual hints and euphemisms weren't enough for this.

Green leaned toward him, looking at him directly. "I am saying, dear lad, that I am your grandfather."

Dermot fell back in his chair stunned. He didn't know what to make of that revelation. "Did my mother know ye?"

Green looked pained, and Dermot thought he might have seen tears sparkling in his eyes. "I provided for them as well as I could. I observed them the same way that I do the people of Làrachd an Fhamhair, with reverence and care. Your grandmother eventually married a good man, Hector Sinclair, who raised your mother as his own. But he was killed in a lorry accident when your mother was twelve."

"I watched them in their grief, and I watched them survive. I wanted to go to them, but I couldn't." He paused; his eyes focused inwardly as if once again examining his dilemma from all those years ago. "Your mother came to me a few years later. Your grandmother was ill, dying actually. She brought your mother to me to care for her. I reluctantly agreed to take her in when her mother died. I was reluctant, not because I didn't want her or care but because I was sure that I would do something wrong, make some colossal mistake that would only make the trauma of losing her parents worse."

Green closed his eyes tight and pressed his lips together in pain. "I wasn't wrong. Seonag was a willful and extremely intelligent young woman. I tried to keep my role as observer secret from her, but she quickly deduced that I was hiding something. I think that her efforts to catch me out distracted her from her grief. When I realized that I couldn't hide who I was, I decided to train her. I thought that she could be my successor. She was inherently curious and a quick learner."

"I insisted that she continue her formal education, because she would need to be able to make a living even when she took over the role of observer. I'm afraid there isn't much money in being a magical witness." One corner of his mouth hitched up before he grew serious again. "It was at St. Andrews that your mother met Henry Stuart. I don't know if she sought him out or met him by chance, but that was the beginning of the end of her training as an observer. She began researching on her own, and eventually connected the prophecy with her friend. I warned her that she was getting too close to be the observer that we were supposed to be, but she wouldn't listen."

He took a deep breath before going on. "I think she felt that so much of her life had been out of her control after losing her parents that she wanted to use the knowledge she had gained to play a more active role. I realized that I had begun training her too young, and too soon after losing her mother. We had an awful row the summer after she graduated from St. Andrews, and that was the last time she willingly saw me."

"I continued to observe her when I could." His eyes found Dermot's and his affection showed in them. "I watched you grow up. I even helped make sure that she got a couple of fellowships early in her career so that the two of you would be provided for."

"And ye watched her get sick and watched me deal with that all alone." Dermot couldn't keep the bitterness from his voice.

"Would you have accepted the help of a stranger or a long-lost grandfather?" Green looked doubtful.

Dermot had longed for a family all his life. And here was the man that could have given it to him but hadn't. Dermot thought about his own willful youth and his struggle to deal with his mother's illness. "I don't honestly know. But I might have liked the chance."

"I'm sorry that you've had to deal with that on your own." Green's guilt was written in the lines of his face. "Your mother's earlier rebellion made me believe that my help wouldn't be welcome. If I had the skill, some spell or elixir that would help her, I would use it without hesitation."

Dermot felt the sting of tears in his own eyes at the mention of his mother's illness. "Do you..." He had to clear his throat. "Do you think that the knowledge of all of this affected her mind?"

"Oh, lad." Green looked on him with pity. "It might be reassuring to think that there is a rhyme or reason to what is happening to your mother, but life is rarely that tidy. Some things there are simply no explanation for."

Wasn't that the worst of it? He was surrounded by conspiracies and secrets, plans, and schemes, but this one thing had no explanation, no reason. His mother's memory had turned to swiss cheese and there was no understanding why. If he was a religious man, he might have been able to comfort himself with the idea that it was part of God's plan. But what kind of god plans for that sort of misery?"

Green pushed himself out of his chair with great effort. "I am going to spend the evening trying once again to divine an answer that will break this stalemate. I suggest you get some rest. No matter the result, tomorrow will be a full day."

"Aye." Dermot's mind was obviously still busy absorbing everything that Green, his grandfather, had told him. "Do you know who he is, my father?"

Green shook his head with obvious regret. "If I did, there would be no need for this ritual. We could answer the question easily and be done. I used to believe that it was Henry, but the more time that I have spent with him, the less sure I am."

Dermot looked around significantly at the magician's plants around them. "Do you have any method for testing paternity?"

Green let out a little laugh." None that I think they would accept. Science has managed that answer for us rather effectively."

"Aye, well. I dinna think it likely that Henry will submit to a blood test." Dermot remembered Henry's face earlier, and his claim that he would have accepted Dermot as his son gladly. It didn't bring Dermot any closer to having an answer, but he believed that Henry didn't know.

The events of the day seemed to weigh on the old man as he trudged across the conservatory to return the watering can to the workbench. He turned and was nearly out the door when Dermot thought of something. "Sir?"

Green stopped, bracing his hand against the door frame he turned around, eyebrows raised in question.

"What was her name? My grandmother?" Dermot asked wanting to make her a person rather than a misty figure in the memory of an old man.

A smile crept across Green's mouth and caused the corners of his eyes to crinkle. "Niamh." His attention seemed to turn inward, as if the name had conjured the woman's face in his memory. "Her name was Niamh."

With a quiet nod, the old man went back into the house leaving Dermot alone with the plants and a tale that answered some of his questions about his mother. Of course, it raised as many, if not more questions than it answered. Unfortunately, it called his mother's motives into question. Was she as mad about this dynasty and the prophecy as the Stuarts were? Is that why their families were so close?

CHAPTER TWENTY-SIX

Sarah had told Dermot that she was exhausted, but as soon as her head hit the pillow, her mind spun out with seemingly never-ending questions about the vote, the ceremony, and what the results meant for all of them. The ritual she had proposed had only generated more questions, and now she found herself at the mercy of a cabal of people she barely knew. She had no way of knowing if any of The Nine might change their votes, or what the Stuarts might do if the vote didn't go their way. There were too many variables.

She did have a way to identify some possible swing votes. Unlike the others, she had the ability to see what they were doing. It wouldn't tell her the outcome in the morning, but she might be able to see some of their intentions by spying on them tonight. The trick in this case would be getting herself to relax enough to cast out. She thought about what Green had said at the ceremony that morning. She wasn't projecting herself but sending her co-walker out to show her what others were doing.

Sarah laid flat on her back and folded her hands on her stomach. She began the breathing exercises that were starting to become familiar. Every exhale was another wave of relaxation, another deepening of the state that allowed her to see what her co-walker saw. When she felt weightless, she focused her attention on Dermot.

He was in the conservatory with Green talking about Green's activities during the war. That seemed odd, but she trusted that Dermot would explain later. So, she moved on to the voting members of The Nine. With a deep breath she saw the MacLeod's. Sheila was helping Eilidh into bed while the old woman complained about having to go traipsing all over the hills with her scarred feet for a ceremony that solved nothing. Sheila admirably tolerated her complaints, even when Eilidh's sharp tongue was directed her way. Sarah didn't know how she had the patience for it. Once she got her mother into bed, Sheila went to her own room deep in thought. Sarah felt sure that neither of them was about to change their vote. Nor would Ruaraidh, her steadfast defender. He was exercising furiously in his room, no doubt restless after spending so much of the day locked in the library.

Isobel sat in her room quietly singing to herself. Sarah paused to listen. She sang "The River Maiden". Sarah wondered if that helped Isobel understand the situation better. Maybe there was an answer to be found in the song that none of them had seen yet. She listened as the old woman sang and remembered the first time she had heard Isobel sing the song in the woman's little cottage in Cape Breton. She'd learned from Isobel, the same way that she'd learned it from her grandmother, knee to knee, the old way. The way that her people had been transmitting the song for generations.

Sarah wondered how many ways it might have changed in the many transmissions from one person to another, one place to another. She'd heard this song so many times, she wouldn't be surprised if Dermot told her she sang it in her sleep. But she'd only understood the lines in the last verse once. Only when she had heard it from all three of the sisters, did she understand those words. "Arise maiden of the river. You are the mother of the high king." This time they were clear as day. Their meaning was no different. The first time Sarah had understood the words, she'd been sick literally running out the back of Eilidh MacLeod's croft house and hurling her breakfast over the drystane wall at the back of her garden. She didn't dread those words any less now than she had the first time, but it was a more settled sort of dread, like an undercurrent in the flow of her life.

Sarah didn't bother spying on Rona. She wouldn't even attempt to change her mind. Her position was bolstered by a grief that Sarah couldn't imagine. Bridget had been taken from them far too soon. Sarah wasn't about to tell Rona that she was wrong in wanting Bridget's death to mean something. That left Oona, the little sister she'd just met. Oona hadn't given a reason of her own for voting for James. She had simply agreed with the reasons given by others. Sarah wondered if she could be the swing vote here. Oona was sitting in a window seat in the lounge, drawing by moonlight. She was drawing a woman who was laughing. Tight curls clung to the woman's head and her mouth was open wide, a light danced in her eyes. Oona was a truly gifted artist.

Sarah considered going to talk with her. Surely someone as young as Oona, with her whole future ahead of her could understand the desire to want to control her own destiny. Her sister seemed like someone who found her own path and wouldn't begrudge anyone else that opportunity. Sarah pulled awareness back to her body with a few breaths. She slipped on her shoes and went to find Oona.

When she got to the lounge her sister was gone. Sarah found her in the kitchen. Unlike the rest of the house, the kitchen was all modern. Sleek stainless-steel appliances and granite counter tops made it look like it was straight out of a magazine. Oona was standing in front of the pantry scanning the shelves. She had put two mugs on the counter next to the hob where a kettle sat on a burner.

"I didn't think you saw the future." Sarah nodded to the mugs.

Oona shrugged. "I felt a tickle when ye were looking over my shoulder."

"Good to know." Sarah wasn't aware that it was possible for someone to feel her when she was casting out. "I'll keep that in mind."

"I dinna think everyone can feel it, but we're special, aye?" Oona took a couple of boxes from the pantry. "Chamomile or orange pekoe?"

"Chamomile. I have enough to keep me awake. I don't need to add caffeine." Sarah went to get the kettle which was boiling. "I'm surprised to find tea bags in his pantry. I would think Mr. Green would have his own special blends. He usually sends me loose teas."

"I think these are Cora's. I'll leave her a couple of pounds and a note." Oona brought the boxes to the counter where Sarah was pouring the water into the mugs. "I'm not sure I'd trust any of Green's special blends."

"I have thought about that." She acknowledged. "And I've approached his teas with caution. I haven't had any ill effects yet."

"Still, I'd keep an eye on that." Oona dropped tea bags into the mugs. "Green is a great help as long as yer goals align with his. He might not be as helpful when they don't."

Sarah carried her tea to the bar on the kitchen island and sat down on a stool. "Do you think that's likely to happen?"

Oona took the stool next to her. "I think our situation is something that some powerful people care a lot about, and that includes Lyall Green. It's a difficult position to be in, and ye have to look out for yerself."

She wasn't saying anything that Sarah hadn't thought, but it seemed a cynical thing to hear from someone so young. "Is that why you went to London instead of staying in Scotland?"

Oona arched a sharp black eyebrow at her. "I went to London because that's where the art school was. I stay in London because that's where the art business is. The fact that it keeps me out of Scotland is an added bonus, although it doesna put me past their reach. I've got a steward just like yours. Her eyes twinkled with mischief. "Well, maybe not just like yours."

"Given what happened to Bridget, it might be a good thing to have a bodyguard."

Oona sighed. "Aye. Since that happened Alex has been right beside me all the time. He's not a bad bloke, but I feel like I have a nanny."

"I can see how that would feel intrusive." Sarah blew across the top of her mug to cool her tea. "Didn't that let up when they verified that I was the one?"

Oona laughed softly. "God no. What if something happens to ye? I'm the spare. I might not be 'the one', but I'm a close second."

"I don't think it works that way."

"Me neither, but I dinna think the Stuarts care." Her eyes drifted to the open sketchbook. "It's been made clear to me that one of us will be marrying James Stuart."

Sarah closed her eyes and groaned. "I hate that they think they can treat people like chess pieces."

"Ah, but they can." Oona took a sip of her tea. "Enough money and enough connections, and ye can do almost anything. Your lad, James, is proof of it. How many kids in their twenties become CEO's of oil companies right out of business school?"

There was no denying that, but then James was more of a figurehead. Sarah understood that Walter did most of the actual running of the company. Sarah's eyes followed Oona's to the sketchbook. "May I?"

Oona waved at the sketchbook and nodded. Sarah slid it closer and began flipping through the drawings. Her sister was incredibly talented. There were images of everyone from richly dressed women lunching in cafes to homeless people. All of the sketches showed more than the person though. The mood and tenor of the sketches changed based on the subjects, and other images showed around them like dreams, or double exposures hinting at the person beneath the surface of the image they presented. "You use your gift."

Oona's cheeks turned pink. "Most people think it's what I imagine about my subjects. Only a few catch on that I paint or draw their truth."

"These are amazing." Sarah flipped through some more. She noticed there were several of the same woman Oona had been drawing earlier. These were different from the others; the lines were sweeping and smooth. The mood was softer.

She was a beautiful woman, and Oona drew all her beauty both inside and out. "She's why you voted for James."

Oona went still. She set her mug on the counter carefully. "Her name is Rachel. She's from Cornwall. She fixes computers for a living. She drinks far too much coffee, chews the ends of pens, and is a terrible cook. I can't imagine spending my life without her."

Sarah couldn't help but smile at Oona talking about her love. "And the idea of marrying a man is anathema."

Oona gave a smirk that reminded Sarah of one she'd seen on their brother. "I have been known to enjoy my time with a lad or two, but I generally prefer lasses." She nodded at the sketchbook where Rachel reclined nude on the page. "That one in particular."

"I know just how you feel." There wasn't much that Sarah could say to that. Her hopes of convincing Oona to change her vote sank.

"I imagine ye're the only person who knows just how I feel. I know ye love him, and he loves ye." Oona looked at the sketch with longing. "If there was any other way, I'd do everything I could to help ye. But I canna give her up."

Sarah felt tears for the loss of hope clog her throat. She covered Oona's hand with hers. "I can't blame you for that."

Oona turned her hand over, and gripped Sarah's. "I'm sorry."

"Don't be. We didn't choose this any more than our parents did." Sarah sighed.

They talked on into the night getting to know each other, feeling their way through the awkwardness of their unusual relationship. Eventually, Sarah found her way back to her room, tired enough that she thought she might finally get some sleep. As soon as her head hit the pillow, she was out. She woke once during the night to find Dermot cuddled up with his arms around her. She settled against him and went back to sleep, but in the morning, he was gone.

CHAPTER TWENTY-SEVEN

Sarah wandered into the library while waiting for the others to finish breakfast. She had no interest in repeating the dinner experience from the previous night with everyone sneaking glances at her as if they were waiting to see when she would fall apart, explode, or just get up and run out the door into the hills. Also, her stomach was so tied into knots that the very thought of eating made her feel sick. She was ready to get this awful business over with. She had no idea how they would break the tie if no one changed their vote.

She strolled through the room looking at Green's books and knickknacks. She stopped at the scrying bowl, still filled with water from yesterday. Maybe her mother would have some insight. In the last six months, Sarah's feelings about her mother had changed. Where Molly had once inspired fear and bitter feelings, Sarah was starting to see her mother as a protector, a sort of supernatural warning system.

She looked into the bowl and thought about Molly. Within seconds, she could see her mother in the water, just as they had yesterday. She looked sad, but then her mother had often looked sad when she was alive. "I don't know what to do, Mama."

Molly gave her a look that said she didn't know either.

"I've boxed myself in here pretty good."

Molly nodded and one side of her mouth ticked up in a smirk. Then her expression changed to worry. Molly leaned her head to the side as if she were looking around Sarah. She looked back at Sarah with her eyebrows drawn together in alarm.

Sarah turned around to find Walter Stuart in the doorway. He held a large yellow envelope and eyed her with a predatory gleam. She had barely seen him except for meals since they had arrived. Unneeded for any of their magical proceedings, he had slunk around the fringe of their bizarre group. Sarah had a feeling that had been strategic. "I was hoping to catch you, Miss MacAlpin."

"And here I was hoping you wouldn't." She tried to keep her voice light. It was a bad idea to let Walter see any weakness.

His smile was more a baring of teeth than a sign of humor. He silently closed the door. The soft snick of the latch sounded like the spring of a trap. "I hoped to have a quiet word, just the two of us."

"I'm not sure there is much to say." Sarah didn't come around from behind Green's desk.

"Oh, but I have much to say, or to show you." He lifted the envelope as he came around the desk to stand beside her. "I understand that you are at an impasse on selecting a partner to fulfill the prophecy."

"I've already selected a partner. Y'all just refuse to accept that." Sarah took a step back from him.

"Mmm." He seemed to bite back a retort. "I think I have something that will help you with your decision."

"Somehow I doubt that."

He raised an eyebrow at her and reached his fingers into the top of the envelope. "I think you'll change your mind when you see what I have here."

He pulled out a stack of papers, keeping them faced away from her. He laid one down on the blotter. It was an eight by ten-inch photograph of Dermot walking out of their building on Bernard Terrace. Beside that he laid a photo of Seonag in her room at the care home. Next was a photo of Ruaraidh standing beside his ancient Land Rover. Then one of her father, Rab, sitting by the shore in Lochinver. Sarah looked up to find him watching her reaction to these photos. "They're creepy, but I'm not sure I get your point."

"Maybe these will clarify things." He laid down a photo of Grant MacDuff in his police uniform in front of the station in Chapel Hill. Sarah went still, her blood turning to ice in her veins and goose bumps pricked along her arms. The closest thing to a father that Sarah had had growing up, Grant MacDuff had been her mother's steward and like Dermot, had fallen in love with his charge. He had disappeared from her life after her grandmother had died but had saved her from Ryan Cumberland with a single shot. Duff had been pretty good at hiding from the Stuarts and their cabal of supporters for years. He'd even stayed hidden from her, while still looking out for her. That photo was a signal that he was once again on the Stuart radar.

Next Walter laid down a photo of Sarah's best friends Amy and Barrett carrying groceries into an apartment building. Amy had her head tossed back laughing and Barrett was grinning at her with that devilish look of his. "There is no one you care about that I cannot touch."

Sarah's chest hurt. She hadn't seen her friends in months, but clearly Walter Stuart had eyes on them. She blinked rapidly, trying to get control of her feelings. "You wouldn't dare."

"Oh, there is very little that I wouldn't dare to see my nephew on the throne." Walter's voice was full of quiet menace.

"He can have it." Sarah bit out. She waved at the pictures on the desk. "As you're so careful to point out money and influence make you practically invincible. He doesn't need me."

"He might gain the throne without you." Walter tended his fingers on the desktop just below the photos and leaned closer to her. His breath smelled of egg, black pudding and whatever was rotten inside him. "But we mean to start a new dynasty, and for that we need you."

"Do you honestly believe some ancient superstition is going to help you stay in power?" She looked at him still mystified that they would go to such lengths.

"I believe that my family will do anything to ensure that we are the tip of the spear for what comes next. The world is going to change, and your child will be the agent of that. We mean to have a hand in it." He cut his eyes down to the series of photos on the blotter. "Or the people you care about most will suffer the consequences."

"What kind of consequences?" Her voice was barely above a whisper.

"If you are not with us, then you will have no one." His eyes pinned her to the spot. He was deadly serious. "I will wipe them out."

Sarah leaned away from him. "You can't just massacre a bunch of people."

"They are spread out enough that their deaths would attract little notice." He made a negligent wave of his hand over the pictures. "An accident here, a senseless crime there. There's really no trick to it at all."

"You're a monster."

He gave her a lopsided grin. "Dermot has told you how he was injured when he was in the army." Something in her face must have told him that she knew what he was talking about. "Then you should have no doubt that there is nowhere I can't reach. If you want to keep these people safe, then you will have to work with us."

"You can't do this." Sarah hissed.

He chuckled low and smug stepping back from the desk. "I'll leave these with you so you can think about it."

He walked to the door and stopped before opening it. "And one more thing. Don't try telling James or anyone else about this conversation. It will not go well for your people if you do."

Sarah watched him slink from the room and close the door behind himself. She looked back at the photos. The threats to Dermot and Seonag were nothing new, but this was the first time that she had worried about her family's safety. She touched the photo of Duff, who had urged her to run far and fast from the Stuarts. She should have listened. They would have all been better off if she had given up on Dermot all those months ago. But she had thought she couldn't live without him. Now, he and everyone she cared about were in Walter Stuart's crosshairs. Sarah looked back at the bowl to find her mother looking up at her. Her face reflected Sarah's own pain. "You tried to tell me, Mama. I'm sorry I didn't understand."

***

Dermot was right back where he'd been the afternoon before, pacing across the stone floor of Lyall Green's front hall waiting for the verdict. He'd planted himself there after picking at his breakfast. Sarah hadn't shown her face in the breakfast room. She hadn't even looked at him as The Nine had filed into the library, none of them had except for Ruaraidh who had given him a terse nod as he walked by.

He turned back to the hallway that led to the dining room to find James standing there watching him. He looked like his night hadn't been much easier than Dermot's. "I need to talk to you."

"I dinna think that's a good idea." Dermot really didn't want to come to blows with James, and he was wound so tight at the moment that he wouldn't need much provocation to do just that.

"Hear me out, please." James came toward him. "I think we might be able to solve at least one mystery."

"And which one is that?" Dermot turned away from him to look out the window.

"I think I have a way to find out who your father is."

He turned back to his one-time friend who looked to be in earnest. "We'd need my father's blood for a paternity test."

James looked over his shoulder to where his parents and uncle waited in the drawing room. He lowered his voice. "Not for DNA testing."

"Actual DNA testing, not magical?" Dermot was skeptical. DNA testing was still relatively new, and as far as he knew that was only used for research and criminal investigations.

"Exactly. I might be able to get us tested. It could tell us why the pool didn't see a difference between us."

"I'm not sure there's much point in that." Dermot wished James could have come up with this idea months ago. But then they hadn't known they would need it months ago. "If The Nine choose one of us, there's not much the other can say. I dinna think identifying my father will matter."

James's face fell. "Wouldn't it matter to you? I know you've always wondered."

Dermot shook his head. James didn't get it. He looked into the prince's blue eyes, eyes that he should have noticed were like his long ago. "If I dinna have her, nothing matters."

James looked crestfallen. He leaned against the back of the front door beside where Dermot stood. "Well, the option is there. I know a research scientist who could test us. It might take weeks, but we could get some answers. Will you think about it?"

Dermot shook his head and sighed. "Aye. I'll think about it."

"I hate being at odds with you." James kept his eyes on the tops of his shoes.

Dermot didn't have an answer for that. This wasn't the time for a heart-to-heart chat about where and how their friendship had gone awry.

The library door opened and every muscle in his body tensed. James came to stand beside him vibrating with a similar tension. Jujhar stepped out into the hallway looking grim. "We have an answer. If you'll gather everyone in the drawing room, we'll come join you to explain."

CHAPTER TWENTY-EIGHT

The Nine entered the drawing room together led by Lyall Green. They carefully didn't look at Dermot or James where they each stood behind the couches. Dermot's stomach went sour. He felt like he'd touched a live wire. One look at Sarah's stooped shoulders told him all he needed to know.

Lyall Green looked around the room verifying that he had everyone's attention. Dermot kept his eyes on Sarah. Her eyes never left the floor. He fought the urge to scream, 'Look at me!'

Through the roaring in his ears, he heard Green say, "We have narrowly agreed that James Stuart is the better match."

Dermot closed his eyes as if he could block out what was happening. When he opened them again the room and all the people were still there, all looking at anyone but him. His jaw clenched and he gripped the back of the couch in front of him. Walter Stuart watched the proceedings with all the smugness of a man who always got his way. Dermot wanted to tear the man's head from his shoulders.

On the opposite couch Anne and Henry sagged with relief. James watched Sarah trying to see her reaction to this vote. Her eyes were trained on the floor, but Dermot saw one tear fall to the carpet in front of her. It reminded him of the time after they'd argued in Chapel Hill and she had told him to stay out of her life. She had been miserable and alone then, and she looked miserable and alone now. He wished he could just grab her and take her away from here. But they would only be stopped by the security team, just as they had been in April.

"Before you start celebrating." Green shot a look of censure at the Stuarts. "We want you to always remember, that there is an alternative." He shifted a hard look to Walter. "If she is not treated with the respect, and reverence due to one of the Sisters, this result can always be changed."

'Not bloody likely.' Dermot thought. Once the Stuarts had their hooks in her there would be no getting away from them. It was a lesson they all should have learned by now. He more than anyone else should have understood that there was no breaking free of them.

Dermot's breath came short, and he fought to stand there and listen to Green. He wanted out of that room, out of that bloody house and out of this web of secrets and ambitious maneuvering that he now knew had started before he was even born. As soon as Green stopped talking, he was gone. Dermot strode out of the room without a backward glance leaving the Stuarts to celebrate as they wished. He wouldn't be a part of this scheme anymore. He took the nearest way out, by the front door.

The sun was high and hit his eyes hard. He blinked and held up a hand as if he could block it out. He wanted to block everything out. So many thoughts raced through his mind at once, that he couldn't latch on to any one thing. All he knew was that he had to get away from the house before he did something that he would regret.

He broke into a run past the guards, and down the drive to the road. He didn't stop running until he reached the river. Water babbled over the rocks on its way to Loch Assynt. Dermot knelt on a rock and splashed some water on his face.

Even in summer it was cold and helped to arrest the panic and fury that had been building since he'd heard those words. "James Stuart is the better match."

He should have known. Didn't James always get everything he wanted? Walter had told him it was his job to protect and defend James. Here he was again, taking second place just as he'd done all his life. Everything in his life was for James. He was always meant to be second. Bitterness flooded his senses, and he spat on the riverbank as if he could clear it out. He sat back on his heels watching the water rush by.

He should have tried to get her out of there before the ceremony. They should have run, should have risked it with or without a passport. He had thought of little else since their first attempt. He couldn't think of a way to do it without hurting a guard or two, but now that it had come to this...

He looked back up the road. Green's house was around the ridge. Maybe they still could get away. They could leave tonight after everyone was in bed. He could borrow one of Ruaraidh's maps and they could make their way through the hills like they did before. He'd figure out some way to get them away from Scotland, and to stay under the Stuarts' radar.

First, he needed to do some recon.

***

Sarah heard the front door close behind Dermot. He was gone, and a very large, very important piece of her heart went with him. She fought to keep from crumbling into a sobbing heap right there in front of everyone. Her hands shook with the effort. She reminded herself that Maggie MacAlpin's granddaughter was made of sterner stuff than that. She had faced down her mother in the worst of her meltdowns when she was just a little girl. She could face these people, even without the man she loved.

While the Stuarts congratulated each other, Sarah took in a deep breath and firmed her jaw. She lifted her eyes and found Walter Stuart watching her. He inclined his head slightly as if to say, 'I'm glad we're on the same page.' His eyes were like icy pools, and Sarah wanted to scratch them right out of his skull. She settled for staring him down. She'd beaten bullies before. She just had to figure this one out, hopefully before the damage was permanent.

"Welcome to the family, my dear." Henry stepped in front of her and took her hand. His tone was kind and his look told her that he knew this wasn't her choice. "I hope you and James will be very happy."

"Of course, they will." Anne took Henry's arm. She smiled at Sarah in a proprietary way, as if she were assessing a horse she'd just bought. With her other hand she gave Sarah's arm a squeeze. "We're going to have to get straight to work when we get back to Edinburgh. We have a wedding to plan."

"Let's give Sarah a few minutes to breathe before we start pressuring her about that sort of thing, mother." James subtly inserted himself between Sarah and his parents. With a hand on his mother's elbow, he steered them from the room. "I'd like some time alone with Sarah now."

Sarah looked behind her to see that The Nine had cleared out while she was talking with the Stuarts. Walter followed Henry and Anne out, James closed the door behind them.

She couldn't read his expression. He was always so careful when others were around, so polished. She was sure it served him well in boardrooms, but it also made it hard to tell what he was thinking. Sarah looked out the window at the hills beyond. There were deer grazing on the plateau on the other side of the river. She wished she could be out there with nothing to worry about but finding the best grass. The stag raised his head showing a rack of antlers to rival Edwin Landseer's "Monarch of the Glen", and she remembered that deer had the same wrangling over mating rights and leadership that they had just had. It seemed there was no escaping it.

James slowly came to stand next to her. He followed her gaze out to the deer across the glen. Sarah didn't say anything. What was there to say? At least he wasn't celebrating, or gloating. He seemed subdued, even unhappy.

It was James that broke the silence, after a few minutes. He didn't take his eyes off the deer. "I know that this is not the result that you wanted. I am sorry that we find ourselves in this position."

Sarah remained silent. There was no point in raging at James. She was sure that he knew nothing of his uncle's threat. She was tempted to tell him, tempted to see what he would do. He had told Walter before that those tactics were forbidden, but that hadn't stopped his uncle from threatening everyone she loved. James was just a figurehead when it came to the Stuart's cause. He wasn't in control.

"I think we should try to make the best of this situation. We can do a lot of good together, even if we're not happy about being together."

"What, no professions of love, no rejoicing at the happy union?" She couldn't keep the bitterness from her tone.

"My feelings for you haven't changed." James paused and took a deep breath. "But I think it's clear that you don't love me and probably never will. I lost hope on that front when you cut yourself that second time at the pool. Your aversion to me was apparent."

"I'm sorry. It's not about you."

"You're right. It's not about me. It's about Scotland. I don't relish forcing you into something that you don't want. I wanted to call it off, to let you choose." He cleared his throat. "But I was reminded that giving you up meant giving up everything that we've been working for, independence, the crown, Scotland for Scots. There is so much potential in this country, and it is being sucked out of us by a government that sees Scotland and its people as inferior. We are trying to remedy that. I won't give up. I can't. To achieve that, I need you, Scotland needs you. That's more important than my happiness. And I know it hurts now, but it's more important than yours too."

She looked at him for the first time. His eyes so like Dermot's were trained on the window, but he was no longer seeing the deer across the way. He was seeing an independent Scotland, with him on the throne. Sarah had hoped there was a chance that she and James could come to some kind of understanding, but she couldn't compete with that. There were plenty of arguments to make about democracy, and monarchy, and self-determination, not to mention her doubts that one American woman could make the difference in his quest for independence, but she didn't feel up to them now.

She felt wrung out. Wrung out and heartbroken. The controlled shell that she had built around herself since her talk with Walter Stuart that morning cracked. The tears started slowly; the dam that was holding her emotions in had sprung a leak. A sob escaped her, and the dam broke. She couldn't do anything to stop it.

James caught her when she started to collapse and pulled her into his arms. He didn't try anything. He just wrapped his arms around her and held on while everything that she'd been holding inside came rushing out in heaving sobs.

CHAPTER TWENTY-NINE

Mark Shaw would be livid if he heard the way that his security staff was talking about their shift changes and procedures in a pub, even a small one that was only populated with A. P. Security staff. Dermot had planted himself at the bar and ordered a pint. With his back to the room, he could listen to all of their conversations. He learned the time that the outside guards changed over, where they were patrolling around Taigh na Damh, and even what sort of alarm equipment the house had. The fact that they still talked about it around him, meant that they had no idea what had gone on at the house that morning.

A plan was starting to take shape in his mind. He and Sarah could get out of the house via the back door around three A. M. without being detected. Then they would have to make their way through the hills and around the mountains. They could go northeast to Kinlochbervie or west to Ullapool and get on a fishing boat. Lochinver was too close, it would be the first place they would look.

From there, he didn't quite know what to do. Some of the boats docked as far south as Portugal, maybe they could sneak into those countries and start fresh even without documents. It had been the plan before. They could do it again. He just had to get her away from the Stuarts.

"Ye never struck me as the type to drown his sorrows." A familiar voice sounded beside him. He turned to see Ruaraidh and Jujhar standing at the bar. Their faces were full of compassion.

Dermot lifted his pint with a wry smirk. "I'm not. Spent a while by the river contemplating drowning someone else."

"Not surprising." Ruaraidh took the stool next to Dermot at the bar. Jujhar went to his other side. Ruaraidh lifted his chin at the innkeeper. "Can I have a pint of Innis & Gunn, Andy?"

"How is she?" Dermot asked when the innkeeper had walked away.

"That's a difficult question." Ruaraidh answered. The innkeeper slid a pint of beer in front of Ruaraidh and took Jujhar's order for a cup of tea. Ruaraidh waited until the man was out of earshot before speaking again. "The right words are coming out of her mouth, but her face says she's just made a deal with auld Clootie himself."

"She made that deal a while ago when she agreed to this test. But then we didna have many options. Now we have even less." Dermot took a sip of his beer.

Ruaraidh looked around the room. There were a couple of A. P. Security guards eating lunch in the corner, and another at the other end of the bar chatting with Andy the innkeeper. When he spoke, it was in Gaelic. "I hope these lowlanders don't have the Gaelic."

Dermot lifted an eyebrow at him. He responded in Gaelic but kept his voice low. "I doubt it."

"What are you going to do?" Ruaraidh shifted closer to him until their shoulders almost touched.

"I had hoped you might help with that. Do you have a map of the area ye can spare?" Dermot leaned closer to him keeping his voice low.

"Of course." Ruaraidh set his keys on the bar between them. "Take anything you need."

"Cheers, mate." Dermot took another sip of his beer. "To the heather again."

Jujhar who had been quietly drinking his tea on the other side of Dermot cleared his throat. When the other two looked his way, he asked in Gaelic. "Are you sure she'll go?"

Dermot sighed. "I know she gave her word, but I think I can convince her that this is the best way."

"I would not be so sure." Jujhar's dark brows drew together, and he chose his words carefully. "It was Sarah who broke the tie."

For a second Dermot thought he heard the man wrong. That was not possible. He was too stunned to speak. She had not chosen James.

Ruaraidh broke the suddenly tense silence. "That vote was secret. How do you know it was Sarah?"

Jujhar looked truly sorry to be delivering that news. "I have been working side by side with her for months. I know her handwriting. Sarah's was the only vote that changed."

"No." Dermot shook his head in a short sharp motion. "I won't believe it. She wouldna do that."

At the same time Ruaraidh said. "Why would she do that?"

"Your guess is as good as mine." Jujhar responded to Ruaraidh's question before addressing Dermot, his voice full of regret. "But it's true. I'm sorry."

Sorry didn't come close to covering how Dermot felt. However bitter and angry he'd felt before, it was nothing compared to what he was feeling now. It was the culmination of nearly thirty years of subjugation to James Stuart and his family's ambitions. It seemed like every person in his life had groomed him for this. And now, the woman he loved had thrown him over for James. He could barely wrap his mind around it. He grabbed Ruaraidh's keys off the bar and stalked out.

CHAPTER THIRTY

When Sarah had exhausted herself crying, James had dried her eyes with a monogrammed handkerchief, and walked her back to her room. He hadn't tried to cheer her up, or flirt, or even kiss her. He had been a perfect gentleman, which Sarah supposed he was. He left her at her door with advice to, "Get some rest."

Sarah went to the bathroom to get a cold washcloth for her eyes. As soon as she turned on the tap, the door leading to Oona's room opened. Her sister examined her from the doorway before saying, "How are ye?"

Sarah had thought there were no more tears left, but Oona's concerned look had them welling up again. All Sarah could do was shake her head and try not to completely break down.

"Right." Oona took the still dry washcloth from Sarah's hand and held it under the water. Then she rang out the water and folded the cloth into a long pad. She nodded at the stool that was under part of the counter. "Sit and put this over yer eyes."

Sarah sat on the stool and leaned back against the counter laying the cold cloth over her eyes. Oona started water running in the bath, and Sarah heard her opening and closing drawers and cabinets. Oona muttered. "There's got to be something here for a hot bath."

"Oh, I don't take baths." Sarah didn't take the cloth off her eyes. "But thanks."

"It'll help ye relax."

"I almost drowned in a bathtub once. I've stuck to showers ever since." Sarah reminded herself that Oona was trying to help.

Oona stopped hunting for bubbles or bath oil and was quiet for a moment. Then Sarah heard her utter a soft. "Shit."

Sarah lifted the cloth to see her sister sitting on the edge of the bathtub staring at her wide-eyed. "Used your gift, huh?"

"How old were ye?" Oona's voice was soft, as if in awe.

"I was six. She died a few months later." She didn't need to give Oona the details, her gift meant that Oona could see or feel whatever Sarah's truth was. "How does your gift work? Do you see a vision, like scrying?"

Oona appeared to think about it for a few seconds. "It's more like a feeling, like for a time, I'm in yer head feeling what ye feel."

Oh, that wouldn't do. She couldn't have Oona feeling her way into what Sarah had done today. For that matter it was probably not great for her to be feeling around in Sarah's emotional memory at all. It wasn't the most pleasant place. "I'm sorry you had to feel that."

"Ye're a lot stronger than ye let on." Oona studied her closely.

Sarah decided that that needed to stop. Walter's admonishment not to tell anyone about his threats came to mind. For Oona's own protection, Sarah needed to distance herself. She dropped the washcloth onto the counter and stood up. "You know I think a shower sounds like a great plan. If you'll excuse me, I'll take one now."

Sarah pulled up on the hem of her shirt, hoping that Oona would take the hint and leave the room. But her little sister was like a dog with a bone now. She was looking closely at Sarah, and she started shaking her head. Sarah was afraid of what she might see. "Okay, now you're just being rude."

"Christ! You changed yer vote. Ye did it for him, for all of us." Oona breathed; astonishment written on her face. "I was so selfish, voting against ye…"

"You didn't know." Sarah gripped Oona's arm determined to keep her from feeling guilty about her choice. She had considered Oona when she changed her vote, but Walter's threats had been a primary factor. "You couldn't have known, and you can't tell anyone, not even Ruaraidh."

"Especially not Ruaraidh." Oona agreed. "Ye havena seen it, but he got his temper from Gran. And he canna abide a bully."

"Well, we have that in common." Sarah sat down next to Oona on the edge of the tub. "Please don't tell anyone else. I know it's a big secret to keep, but people's lives depend on it."

Oona looked at their reflection in the mirror. Sarah was struck once again by how similar they were. Oona had her mother's freckles, and her hair was auburn under the black dye, but they both had their father's eyes, and his cheekbones. "I wasna sure what to think of ye. Ye've been like a ghost in our family all my life, Da's other child hovering in the back of his mind all the time. His guilt over ye caused so much heartache. Now, here ye are. Ruaraidh raves about ye. Mum is ready to adopt ye. But I didna think I could get past the baggage." Her green eyes met Sarah's in the mirror. "I'm sorry. I'm sorry for all of it."

"You have absolutely nothing to be sorry about. None of what's happened to me is your fault, or even your mother's fault, or Da's. There's no point in assigning blame or living with guilt. The best we can do is move forward." Sarah put an arm around her little sister, hoping to convince Oona and herself that moving forward was the only way. She had to let go of the past, and of her hopes for herself and for Dermot. The only way to protect the people she loved was to move forward and make the best of things. Keep eating, keep breathing, keep sleeping one day after the next until it doesn't hurt anymore. She had done it before. She could do it again. She hoped.

***

Sarah sat up suddenly in the dark room. It had been so long since she'd had the bathtub dream, she had almost forgotten how bad it could be. She shouldn't be surprised that she was having it now. Suddenly Molly's mutterings all those years ago made sense. 'They can't have you. They're not going to get their hooks in you.' Molly hadn't known about the Stuarts, but she had known about the people of Làrachd an Fhamhair and their plans for her child. She had tried to keep this very thing from happening to Sarah.

"I tried, Mama." Sarah whispered into the darkness. It had been early evening when she had fallen asleep, and the sun had still been out. She had taken a long hot shower after her talk with Oona, then laid down with a cold cloth over her eyes. She must have slept through dinner, not that she regretted missing the opportunity to sit across a table from everyone. Eventually, she would have to face them, but not now, not tonight.

"Is it true?" Dermot's voice was a low growl in the dark room.

Sarah closed her eyes to block out the sense of dread his question had sparked. "Is what true?"

"Ye changed yer vote." He spat the words out like venom surprising her. He came out of the shadowy corner into the soft moonlight. The planes of his face were stark in the low light making him look harder, all angles and sharp edges. "Ye chose James."

She had known this conversation was coming. Although she had hoped it could wait until she felt stronger, until she had her story straight. There was only one lie that he might believe. "I chose security."

He drew in a sharp breath. She had confirmed his suspicion. His tone dripped bitterness as he stalked closer to the bed. "I've killed for ye." He spoke slowly, clearly, emphasizing the word killed. "Ye still doubt that I can keep ye safe."

In her head she was screaming, 'Never!' but she said, "You're only one man. He practically has an army."

He stood beside the bed looking down at her, seething. "No doubt the money doesna hurt either."

She closed her eyes again trying to keep him from seeing the truth in them, and to keep the tears from starting again. Her voice cracked. "Everything hurts."

"Och, poor Sarah. Tell me again how much it hurts when ye're dressed in silk and dripping with diamonds." He bent down placing a hand on either side of her hips. She leaned away from him. "Every day of my life, I have played second fiddle to James bloody Stuart. The one person!" His hands gripped her arms tight and shook her. "One person I thought he couldna buy. And he bought ye."

She felt his breath on her lips coming out in angry huffs. His eyes burned with fury as they held hers. She couldn't look away. She wanted so badly to tell him the real reason, that she'd struck a devil's bargain with Walter Stuart, that she had done it for him. But she couldn't. Even without Walter's threat, she feared what Dermot would do with that knowledge and the fierce grip he had on her told her that she was right to be afraid of how he might unleash his temper on Walter. If he did anything foolish, she couldn't protect him from himself. She could only meet his anger with tears and compassion. "If hating me helps you feel better, then hate me."

His eyes widened. For several fraught seconds they stared at each other his anger finding no good counter in her resignation.

With a groan he released her and spun around taking several steps away from the bed. He ran his fingers through his hair in agitation. Sarah just waited, not knowing what else there was to say.

She wasn't prepared for when he whirled around to her again. This time he fell to his knees beside the bed and took her hands. "Come with me now." His voice was full of urgency, pleading with her. "I know ye didna mean it. Come with me. Ruaraidh gave me a map and some gear. I know when the guard changes. We can take to the hills like we did before."

Sarah's breath hitched, and tears stung her eyes. She laid her hand against his cheek. It hurt physically to push the words from her chest. They scraped her throat like broken glass. "I can't. I'm sorry."

He went still, a mask of steel coming over his eyes. "Can't or won't?"

"It doesn't matter." She cried. "The result is the same."

"It matters to me." The muscles in his jaw flexed with tension.

She lied. It was the only thing she could do. If she told him the truth, he would know that it hadn't been her choice and he would do something stupid that would probably get him killed. She lied to protect him, and Duff, Seonag, Oona, Amy, and Barrett. She made her expression as flat as she could. She had to sell it. "Won't."

He exhaled like he'd taken a soft hit to the gut. His head dropped onto their joined hands. Sarah fought to keep from sobbing. After a moment, he turned his head away from her. He didn't look at her as he returned to the corner where he'd been sitting when she woke up. He picked up a bag from the shadows and slung it over one shoulder.

Every muscle in his body seemed to ring with defeat and disappointment. Without looking back at her, he silently let himself out and closed the door behind him.

CHAPTER THIRTY-ONE

Dermot took a couple of steps back and sat down on the end of the bed, his eyes fixed on the empty closet. He'd known it would be empty when he'd let himself into Sarah's eerily silent flat. When the heavy front door to the building had slammed shut behind him, he'd heard the echo reverberate through three floors that should have had at least some security staff in it. But there was no one.

That was fitting. He'd been alone for days, walking about in a bubble of pain and rage since he left Taigh na Damh. He'd hiked away from Sarah and James and all of it with no plan and no idea where he was going. He had thought that he would never come back, thought that he would just hop on a boat and leave it all.

Who would miss him? Not his mother. God knows, Sarah's life would be easier without him around now that she'd made her choice. His academic work had fallen down his list of priorities since he and Sarah had planned to leave it all. There was no one who would care. Maybe that was best. After days of walking and sleeping under the stars, he'd wandered into the caravan park at Clachtoll Beach. He'd met up with a group of middle-aged men on a fishing holiday who offered him a ride south, and for lack of any other ideas, he'd taken it.

They'd dropped him off in Stirling and he'd taken the train back to Edinburgh. Even that morning in the crowded train station, he'd considered leaving. In the end, he'd decided that if he was going to leave, he would need more than a backpack full of empty granola bar wrappers, bottled water and a map of the Highlands. So, he'd come back to Bernard Terrace. He didn't know what he'd been expecting. Maybe there was some tiny scrap inside him that had hoped she'd be there, that she'd say she'd changed her mind and they could leave together. But staring at the empty closet, he knew that there had been only one likely result. He'd lost her. He'd lost everything.

He was jolted out of feeling sorry for himself when the door downstairs slammed again. Thinking it might be her, he went for the hallway. It wasn't. It was the last person on earth that he wanted to see. James stood in front of the door to Dermot's flat.

James heard him and looked up the staircase. "Finally, you're back."

"Miss me, did ye?" Dermot arched an eyebrow at him. What more could James possibly want to take from him? "Come to gloat?"

James wasn't having it. "Have you ever known me to gloat?"

Dermot huffed. "Nah. That would be far too plebian."

"Sarah is worried sick about you." His tone suggested that Dermot should feel guilty for having worried her.

Dermot sauntered down the last few steps. "Well, ye've seen me. I'm alive and I am no longer her concern."

James pressed his lips together. "You know that's not true."

"I know she's your fiancé." Dermot snapped. "Dinna think the rest of it matters."

"Then you're a fool." James snapped back. Irritation showed in every line of his face. "Anyway, I've come to offer you a job."

Dermot's laugh was bitter and fatalistic. "No."

"Please hear me out." James held up a pleading hand.

"What more can I offer ye, James?" Dermot didn't have the energy for this. "Ye've taken everything that I had of worth. Ye have exactly what ye wanted."

James seemed to deflate in front of him. "Not even close."

"Boohoo. Poor wee prince." Dermot poured thirty years of pent-up bitterness into his tone. "Got his princess and still not satisfied."

James shook his head and ran an irritated hand through his too perfect hair. "I know this is hard for you to believe, but I do care about Sarah as a person."

Dermot rolled his eyes and took out his keys to let himself into his own flat. At least he might get the satisfaction of slamming the door in James's face.

"She's miserable." James's voice had lost its commanding tone. He wasn't prince or billionaire CEO now. He was truly worried about her.

"It's only been a week. She'll get used to it." He had to admit that part of him thought it served her right.

"I'm not so sure." James leaned a shoulder against the wall beside the door. "She's heartbroken. She's given up so much. I don't think she's sleeping. She barely eats."

"I dinna think seeing me is going to help that." Dermot ground out. "She chose you. She'll have to learn to live with that."

James looked out toward the street, but his gaze was unfocused. He was clearly thinking about Sarah. "But you know her. You can help me find ways to pull her out of this."

Dermot looked at his old friend in disbelief. "Let me get this straight. Ye want me to help you romance the woman that I love."

James looked at a loss. He blew out an exasperated breath. "I want you to help me help her. Or are you so bitter that you don't want her to be happy if it's not with you?"

Dermot exploded. Partly because he was angry at James and partly because he was angry at the part of himself that was that bitter. The miserable, weak little boy inside him that wanted her to hurt as much as he did. Before James took another breath, Dermot had him pinned to the wall with a forearm across his throat. His eyes blazed as he leaned in close. "How DARE ye! We'd be happy now if ye'd held yerself to that same standard months ago. Dinna come here with yer shite about selfless love. Ye could have stepped aside. Ye could have let her be happy. Ye could have let me have the one person in this world who loved me. And ye took that from both of us."

James's face turned red, but his too blue eyes stayed focused on Dermot's. He choked. "I tried."

"Bollocks!" Dermot spat.

James drew in the shallow breath that Dermot would allow and rasped. "Wish I could…too much at stake…Scotland."

"Still." Dermot growled. "Ye still think that Scotland canna be independent without yer guidance. That's bloody insulting to the people, not to mention delusional." He pushed away from James who bent over coughing and rubbing his throat.

Dermot paced down the hall trying to prevent himself from beating James to a bloody pulp.

Between coughs, James managed to say. "It's a shared delusion, and I can't control everyone who shares it. But I can keep her safe, and we can try to help her make the best of it."

"Ye're assuming that I want to help." Dermot stopped looking out the front window at the limousine waiting at the curb. "I have no interest in yer great royal delusion anymore."

"That's a lie." James stated baldly. "Even if you won't concern yourself with Sarah's welfare, there is still the question of your father. I know you. That's going to nag you until you have an answer. And we both know that answer is probably in my house."

"Aye well. I've gone this long without a father. I can live the rest of my days not knowing how I'm connected to you lot."

"Another lie." Dermot turned back toward him, on the verge of using his fists to end this conversation. James backed away holding up a hand. "I'll leave."

"About bloody time." Dermot muttered.

Still rubbing his throat. "You know Sarah said something to me a few weeks ago about the kinds of love, grasping and possessive versus giving and uplifting. She told me yours was the uplifting kind, the kind that makes you strong and wise." His gaze ran up and down Dermot who stood tense, fists clenched. "Maybe she was wrong about that."

Dermot shook his head turning away from James fighting the desire to pummel him. The front door clanging back into place told him when James had gone. Dermot finally went into his own flat and shut the door. He pulled his shirt over his head and went for a cold shower trying to tamp down his temper. How dare James Stuart come here and lecture him on love. Sarah had made her choice. His father whoever that was had made his choice. What did he need from them? What did he need from any of them?

It was after the shower, his first in days that he got a good look at himself. He seemed winnowed down. His eyes were red above dark circles and his beard was grown out and scruffy. He hadn't been drinking, but the face in the mirror reminded him more than a little of Sarah's father. Rab Ballantyne had let her mother down when she needed him most and had spent the next twenty-six years being eaten away by shame and regret. He was only now getting his life together. Bloody James was right. He couldn't leave the Stuarts behind without answers about his father. And maybe Sarah had chosen James, but he had pledged himself to her. He'd made a vow, and he couldn't break that. Not until he knew she'd be alright.

He closed his eyes, blotting out his own image and that of Rab Ballantyne. "Damn."

***

"The word is out." Felicia Banks came into Sarah's room without knocking. "The press release went out this morning and the barbarians are gathering at the gate."

"Do you hear that?" Tony, Felicia's chosen hair and makeup guru, cocked his head to the side as if listening for some far-off sound. A wide grin spread across his face. "That's the sound of thousands of models, actresses, and heiresses crying out in disappointment."

"Does that make me the Death Star?" Sarah asked as Tony went back to putting just the right amount of blush on her cheeks. This time he'd been instructed to make her look somewhere between librarian and ingenue. Felicia had decided to play up Sarah's academic credentials, and humble background. She had declared Sarah would be like 'Cinderella with a degree'.

Accordingly, Felicia had instructed her stylist, Gillian, to stick to classic conservative clothes. Sarah was preparing to be introduced to the world in a very modest soft yellow and pink flower print dress with a tailored navy-blue jacket. Tony had swept her hair into a loose bun leaving curling tendrils around her face. When he finished her makeup, he stepped back so that she could see herself in the mirror.

Sarah took in the image she was presenting. She had to admit, they had taken her from looking utterly miserable to presentable in record time. She'd spent much of the last few days getting used to her new surroundings and trying not to look completely devastated. Felicia and her crew were a welcome change from Anne who seemed to view Sarah as her own personal Eliza Doolittle. She'd had her accent corrected countless times and been told that 'y'all' isn't something people in her position say.

Anne would no doubt be pleased with what Sarah was looking at in the mirror. "I look like a kindergarten teacher."

"Darling, a kindergarten teacher could never afford those shoes let alone that frock." Tony chuckled while putting his various pots and brushes back into their proper places in his makeup case.

He wasn't wrong about the shoes, although Sarah would have preferred flats or clogs, Gillian had equipped her with a pair of navy wedge heels. At least they weren't too high. Sarah was sure she would have tripped on anything higher. It wouldn't do to fall flat on her face at the exact moment when they were announcing their engagement.

Oh Lord, her engagement. James had been nothing but understanding and thoughtful since she'd been moved from Bernard Terrace into his house. She'd been given a separate room that was next to his. He'd made sure she had coffee in the mornings and had managed to slow down his mother's near-obsessive wedding planning. He had even suggested that his parents spend a couple of days at Tweedholm to give Sarah some space. Of course, they had arrived back the night before and Anne was chomping at the bit for Sarah to meet with her wedding planner.

Sarah was grateful for the few days that James had bought her. He had given her space to grieve and try to wrap her head around the idea of becoming Lady Caledon. She had only seen him for dinner in the evenings, which had been awkward but not unpleasant. The trouble was that no amount of space or time was going to fix her heart. She had to get used to walking about with a broken one. Hopefully, this morning, she could at least see her way to faking happiness long enough to get through this appearance.

Felicia grabbed the door handle and looked at Sarah. "You look perfect. We should go wait in the study for James."

With one last glance at the stranger in the mirror, Sarah blew out a breath. "Might as well get this over with."

As they made their way downstairs Felicia gave Sarah instructions. "I know you're nervous. Don't worry about hiding that. It can work in your favor. You're miles above the kind of woman they've seen James with in the tabloids. You have substance. You don't need to be showy."

"Well, that's a relief, because I don't think I can fake confidence right now." Sarah muttered.

"I don't know why not. You're a star." Felicia assured her as they rounded the corner toward James's study.

Sarah allowed herself one last uncooperative moment. "I don't want to be a star."

Felicia grabbed the doorknob to open the study door. "What is it you Americans say? That horse has already left the barn."

Felicia swung the door open to reveal James already there waiting. He had been leaning against the desk talking with Miss Lennox, but he stood when he saw her. His face lit up, and Sarah felt her tension ease slightly. After all his thoughtfulness over the last few days, she was coming to rely on him to get her through the requirements of this new role. She forced a relieved smile, as he came forward to take her hands. "You look beautiful."

"I feel like a fraud." Sarah whispered, just for his ears.

"Nonsense. You're the most genuine person I know." James whispered his lips brushing her ear.

"Mind the hair and makeup." Felicia called from the window where she was watching the crowd gather.

James pulled back with a smile. "Wouldn't dream of undoing Tony's handiwork."

The door opened behind them and Henry and Anne came in. When Anne saw Sarah she grinned, "Oh yes, Miss Banks. That is exactly right."

Felicia nodded at the compliment. She and Anne had disagreed on the clothes. Anne had been for a more stayed and sedate Chanel suit, but Felicia had pointed out that it fit neither Sarah's style nor her age. Sarah hadn't bothered to express an opinion. She'd been drifting along in a fog of misery and worry letting everyone else decide where she should go and what she should wear. What did any of it matter anymore?

Still, she was glad that Felicia had won that argument. She imagined she would have been twice as uncomfortable in the pale pink designer suit that Anne had favored.

Henry came to Sarah giving her a kind smile. "Ready to brave the vultures, my dear?"

"No." Sarah tried to sound cheerful. "But I doubt I ever will be, so we might as well get it done."

"That's the spirit." He beamed at her.

Felicia answered a knock at the door. She leaned out and spoke a few quiet words to someone in the hall. Then she turned back to them, her face was bright with excitement. "It's time."

James's hand at the small of her back propelled Sarah forward through the hall and to the front door of the house. Sarah kept her focus on the door telling herself 'Just get through it. You can handle this.'

Felicia stopped in front of the door and addressed the group. "Smiles, everyone. It's a happy day."

Sarah took a breath and tried to put on a mask of happiness. She hoped the world wouldn't see through the lie of her smile.

When Felicia was satisfied with the group, she nodded to the security guard at the door. He opened it and the flashbulbs started. It was all Sarah could do not to recoil. James put his hand at the small of her back again and whispered. "Brave face. It'll be over soon."

He was right. All that fuss for less than five minutes of standing and smiling. James, Anne, Henry and even Sarah had answered a few of the shouted questions. She hoped with the correct amount of cheer. When James thought the questions started getting too personal, he had held up his hand. "I think that's enough for today. Thank you all for coming and for your good wishes."

Sarah gave him a grateful look as they turned their backs on the flashes and continued questions. He looked down at her with that dazzling smile of his.

When they came inside Felicia grinned. "Pitch perfect! Well done, all."

Sarah sagged with relief, and James's arm tightened around her. He leaned close and kissed her temple. "You were brilliant."

"Thanks for keeping it short. That was about all I can take of questions right now." She turned so that he could hear her in the busy hallway. That was when she saw the man behind him. Dermot stood there with his back to the just closed front door. He wore a black suit and an earpiece. Sarah pushed past James. "What are you doing?"

Dermot looked down at her, his face impassive. "Keeping the mob out."

"You know what I mean." She snapped in Gaelic lowering her voice. She was conscious of the staff and James's parents behind her.

"I offered Dermot a job in my security detail." James stepped close beside her. "I thought you would be glad to know that he's safe. I know you've been worried about him."

"And you think he's safeguarding you?" Sarah asked James. Without waiting for an answer, she turned back to Dermot. Her breath came short and tears pricked her eyes. Her voice quavered as she spoke to him in Gaelic. "First, you take off without a word. Now you reappear while I'm trying to pick up the pieces."

Dermot leaned in, bringing his face close to hers. "What pieces? This was your choice, remember?"

As if she could forget. She wished she could tell him, but Walter had been clear what would happen if she did. She had to keep him safe. Her voice sounded so small. "Are you trying to punish me?"

He shifted his gaze straight ahead, pointedly looking away from her. Still his expression didn't change, but she saw the muscle in his jaw jump.

"That's it, isn't it?" Her voice grew thick with unshed tears. She'd told him to hate her if it made things easier. She didn't expect him to do it in her presence.

"This is my fault." James interrupted before she could say anything else. He ran what he no doubt intended to be a comforting hand down her back. "I offered him the job."

Sarah was afraid to say anything else. Her carefully crafted facade was cracking, and she didn't want to lose control in the middle of all these people. She sent James and Dermot both baleful looks before turning to the stairs. She fought against the tears that threatened with every step until she reached her room. Thankfully, it was empty.

Sarah closed the door, collapsing against it. Her chest ached and she felt like she couldn't breathe. She tore off the jacket and dress, and kicked off the shoes, running for the bathroom. She turned on the shower to mask the sound of her sobs. She stepped in meaning to scrub off Tony's war paint and the false persona that she was forced to wear, but she wound up curled into a ball in the bottom of the shower tears blending with the water running down her face.

CHAPTER THIRTY-TWO

"Hillbilly Heartbreaker, Gold-Digging Grifter?" Walter Stuart came into the conference room and angrily slammed the newspapers onto the table in front of Felicia. "This is your purview, Miss Banks, and I'd like to know what you plan to do about it."

Felicia sat forward and opened her mouth to speak, but James beat her to it. "Uncle, the stories will all die down. In another day or two they'll have found someone else to fling mud at."

"In another day or two, they'll dig up some boy she dated when she was a teenager and have another salacious story." Walter whirled on his nephew. "And if it's not that, another of your trust fund trollops is going to crawl out of the woodwork."

"Beatrice Harcourt is a hanger-on." He turned to face Sarah who had been silently watching this interchange. "I was never interested in her. It was always one-sided."

Sarah shrugged. "I honestly don't care who you dated or didn't date."

"But the point is that they do." Walter picked up one of the tabloids again and waved it at them in irritation. "She told them you were on the verge of proposing."

James sent an annoyed look in his uncle's direction. "That's a lie."

"You know what Churchill said about lies." Felicia seemed unperturbed by Walter's anger. "The problem now is that this lie is already halfway around the world, and we've made no attempt to correct it."

"Again, Miss Banks, I would like to know your plan." Walter demanded.

Felicia looked at Sarah. "I know that you value your privacy, and you're not a fan of the media. But the best way to combat this is to give an interview."

Sarah had been afraid she was going to say that. It had been two weeks since announcing their engagement. The pain of losing Dermot, and her career had dulled enough that Sarah could function and be polite. She had endured more shopping trips and dress fittings than she thought any one person should have to in the space of that time. She had even tolerated Anne's back-handed way of making her over into something resembling her ladyship's idea of what a royal Stuart bride should be. But she wasn't sure that she was up to answering questions about her feelings for James or her background in an interview.

As she had learned when she was being hounded by paparazzi, the press could be merciless. The headlines started out embracing Felicia's narrative about James and Sarah's unlikely romance. "From Fellowship Flowers Romance", and "Real-life Cinderella Story" were headlines after the initial announcement. They were usually accompanied by photo of James looking adoringly at Sarah and her looking back up at him as they walked back inside his house after making their big announcement. Her relieved smile had been easily mistaken for affection. The belief that they were in love took hold.

But since then, the tide had turned. Starting with complaints about her American-ness and her background. Before Sarah had a chance to push back, Felicia held up a hand. "I know that you don't want to, and I don't blame you. But they're hungry for stories about you and if you won't give them access, they will find a way to get the information they're looking for. With an interview, we can control the narrative. It's a delicate balance between access and privacy, but a little sharing will go a long way."

Sarah studied Felicia for a moment before looking at James. He was watching her, but she couldn't tell what his preference was. It would certainly help him. His political ambitions could be hurt if the public thought he was being manipulated by a gold-digger. She appreciated that he wasn't making that case or pushing her to do something she wasn't comfortable doing. She turned back to Felicia. "What do you have in mind?"

Felicia smiled her approval. "We can choose someone sympathetic. There are a few television journalists that I can think of who would love to interview you."

"Television?" Sarah asked nervously.

"She's not ready for that." Anne put in from her place further down the table. "She'll sound exactly like what they're accusing her of being."

"A hillbilly?" Sarah sent an irritated look her way. "Sorry, the accent is not going away. I can only be myself."

"That's what we're worried about." Anne muttered almost too softly to hear.

"Mother." James hissed in a warning tone.

"We can approve the questions ahead of time." Felicia went on addressing Sarah and ignoring the by-play among the others. "We won't let them ask you any questions that you aren't comfortable answering."

"That's going to be a very short interview." Sarah half-joked shifting in her seat.

"See what I mean." She heard Anne whisper to Henry.

This time even Felicia gave Anne a warning look. "It can all be carefully controlled to present the narrative we want to portray."

"And you're sure you can find someone who will stick to the questions we approve?" James seemed skeptical.

"We still have the upper hand. There are plenty of journalists who would like to build a relationship to get access for more important stories down the line. They offer a softball interview now, and then when there is a bigger story, like independence or a political campaign they will already have a good relationship with us. Access is a powerful drug for reporters. Some of them will do anything to maintain it."

"Okay." Sarah settled into the idea. "I knew I would have to do something like that eventually."

"We're going to have a lot of prep work to do." Anne added.

"My staff and I can take care of that." Felicia told her looking annoyed. Sarah was surprised. She would have expected Felicia and Anne to be on the same page as far as making Sarah a princess went.

"Right." Walter seemed to have heard enough to be satisfied that the issue was being addressed. He stood and cast an imperious look around the table before settling his gaze on Felicia. "I'll expect a progress report on my desk by Friday with a list of prospective interviewers and questions."

"I'd like to see those questions as well." James added.

"Of course." Felicia agreed following Walter out of the room.

The rest of them stood and Anne approached Sarah. "We'd better get started. You're going to need some lessons in comportment before you go in front of cameras again."

"I'd like a few minutes to talk with Sarah, Mother." James's tone warned Anne that he wasn't going to take no for an answer.

"Certainly, darling." Anne gave him a pinched smile before kissing his cheek and leaving. Henry gave his son a nod as he followed Anne out.

"Are you sure you're alright with this?" James turned back to Sarah once the door closed behind his parents and took her hand.

She wasn't okay with any of this, but she didn't have much choice. "In for a penny, in for a pound, right?"

He chuckled and even she had to admit the sound was sexy. "We'll make a Scot out of you yet."

"I knew this was part of the package." She shrugged.

"You seem to be doing better." He observed. While they had seen each other over the last two weeks, they were rarely alone together. Sarah assumed that James had been giving her space after she'd seen Dermot on his detail.

She pressed her lips together and looked at their joined hands. "I'm keeping it together. I'm not sure I'd call that better so much as numb."

"I'm sorry that you're unhappy." He brought his other hand up to cradle hers. "I appreciate that you are honoring our agreement in spite of your feelings."

He had her at a loss. He had been nothing but kind and accommodating, and she didn't want to seem ungrateful. And yet, she also didn't want to give him false hope that she was going to return his feelings. "James, I…"

"I know." He stopped her before she could say anything he didn't want to hear. He smiled, not the dazzling smile that he often employed, but a soft hopeful smile. "I'm not foolish enough to think that your feelings could change in so short a time. I just want you to know that I see how hard this is for you. I understand. I hope that at the very least we can be friends."

He was making it hard to see him as the enemy. Besides, Sarah was well and truly stuck in this relationship. "Friends."

James pulled her into a hug, and she let him. It was nice for once to feel like she could lean on someone, even if that someone was James. She'd been feeling so alone in this new world she'd been plunged into.

He walked her to the elevator. Fleming fell into step behind them as they walked out of the conference room and got on the elevator with Sarah.

"I'll see you this evening." James told her pleasantly before the elevator doors slid shut. Sarah barely heard him. Over his shoulder beside the door of the conference room where they had just been stood Dermot, looking the part of bodyguard with his dark suit, earpiece, blank look. She wished she could be so stoic. She still couldn't for the life of her understand why he had taken the job with James. Was he trying to torture her or himself?

***

This was bloody torture. Dermot stood at the ready outside the conference room door while James was inside talking with

Sarah. Fleming stood waiting on the other side of the doorway while Miss Lennox was nearby at her desk in front of James's office. He'd waited through the meeting trying not to obviously listen through the door to the murmurs going on inside. He had heard precious little after Walter's loud demand that Felicia do something about the press coverage. Then everyone else had left and here he was trying not to be sick with jealousy that James was on the other side of the door alone with her.

"She's miserable, ye know." Fleming's voice was soft.

"No doubt." He tried not to betray his feelings. He shouldn't feel bad that she was miserable. She'd chosen this. But it had been a couple of weeks and he'd thought she would be settled in by now. He thought he'd feel less raw about it. He and James had decided that he should stay out of her way after the announcement. He hadn't caught more than a distant glimpse of her before today. Didn't mean he hadn't been thinking of her.

"I'm sorry, mate." Fleming continued.

"Aye, me too." He cleared his throat trying not to show that he was bothered by her presence.

Fleming looked like he wanted to say more but bit it back. "Look, if it's possible, can ye stay out of her sight. I know ye're working with James, but...She's just getting herself back together. If she sees ye, it's only going to make things worse."

Dermot narrowed his eyes at Fleming. He was glad that Sarah had a bodyguard who was so observant and protective but being told to stay away rankled even if that was what he'd already been doing. "Anne isna pestering her too much, is she?"

Fleming blew out a breath. "She's keeping her busy, fitting her out with a new wardrobe and turning her into an aristocrat. Sarah hates every minute of it."

The door opened and James ushered Sarah out of the conference room, with his hand at her back. Dermot ground his teeth at the possessive gesture before schooling his features into the on-duty blankness that was customary.

Fleming followed them to the elevator, getting in just ahead of Sarah. She turned back to James who told her he'd see her that evening. But Sarah's eyes caught sight of him. She blinked as if surprised to see him there. As angry as he still was about the choice she'd made, she pulled at him like gravity. He gritted his teeth and fought the urge to run forward and push James out of the way, joining her on the elevator, and taking her out of there. The doors slid shut blocking her from his view.

Dermot took his new position next to James who said, "She's just agreed to do a television interview. I'm worried she's too fragile."

"She's not as fragile as ye think. She's survived more in twenty-six years than most people have to in a lifetime. Remind her of that, and she'll eat reporters for breakfast."

James clapped him on the shoulder, before walking back to his office. "Thank you. I'll do that. I know this is difficult for you. I couldn't do this without your help."

James had no idea how difficult this was, but Dermot couldn't begin to tell him. It wouldn't change anything if he did. Sarah had made her choice he told himself again.

"Have you thought any more about the DNA test that I mentioned before?" James shifted topics.

"If we're related, my father has had ample time to step forward. And he hasn't. Does it really matter who he is anymore?"

James cocked his head to the side, as if considering. "I think it does. I would want to know."

Dermot wanted to know, and he didn't. Maybe knowing and confronting the man would help him feel less angry. Maybe he could finally understand why. "Aye, alright."

"You'll do it?" James looked surprised and even excited.

"It's not as if I'm going to find answers any other way." His mother wasn't likely to tell him. And even if Sarah had made her choice, knowing might give him some leverage over Walter. Leverage was never a bad thing where that man was concerned.

CHAPTER THIRTY-THREE

July

"Oh good. You're awake." Anne chirped as Sarah walked into the dining room for breakfast the next morning.

Sarah sat down and laid her napkin across her lap. "I usually am at this time."

"We just don't always see you this early.' Anne's bright tone masked the low-key censure in the comment.

'That's because I can't stand the sight of you until I've had half a pot of coffee.' Sarah thought. "Well, I'm here now."

"I'm glad." Anne picked up her teacup and took a careful sip. "We have engagement photos in a week and the television interview coming up. We have a lot of work to do to prepare for them. Not to mention wedding planning."

"I'm happy to leave the wedding planning up to you. I'm sure you already have more ideas and preferences than I do on that front." Sarah buttered a piece of toast.

Anne's head bobbed and she smiled at Sarah's deference. "Naturally, I have some ideas. But I'm sure you do as well."

Sarah took a sip of her coffee and shook her head. "No, not really."

"Every girl dreams of her wedding. And you're marrying…"

"Prince Charming?" Sarah supplied. "Not this girl. I honestly never even considered getting married. I've been so focused on my career."

"Well, this is your career now." Her tone suggested she viewed this change as some sort of step up from Sarah's chosen career.

Sarah had so many responses to that bleak statement, but none of them would change Anne's view or her position. Sarah just blinked at her and took a bite of toast.

Anne leaned forward looking excited. "Come on. You didn't clip pictures of wedding dresses from magazines when you were a girl."

Sarah cocked her head to the side and studied Anne for a moment. "Lady Anne, my grandmother was a moonshiner and a subsistence farmer. We could barely afford to buy shoes. There wasn't money for bridal magazines. And my belief in fairy tales like Prince Charming died about the same time my mother did."

Anne's face fell and she sighed as if bored. "And yet, here you are."

"Mmm." Sarah gave her a withering look. "Which is why I am happy to leave the wedding planning to you. I have no ideas and even if I did, I don't know the country that well. I wouldn't know where to start."

"Then you truly won't mind if I take things in hand?" Her future mother-in-law asked her. Sarah got the impression that the question was less out of concern for Sarah's feelings and more a voucher that Anne would use later if Sarah raised any objections to her plans.

Sarah wondered what minefield she would be walking into if she gave Anne carte blanche, but she honestly didn't care about the wedding details. What did they matter when you were forced into it anyway? "I mean, I suppose I would want to have a say in my dress."

"Of course. We'll get Gillian to line up some designers for you to look at." Anne looked pleased. "Just leave everything else to me. Now, we have an appointment with a hairdresser at ten o'clock, your personal shopper at eleven thirty, and a dialect coach at two."

Sarah's eyebrows flew up as Anne rattled off the day's schedule. "That sounds like a full day."

"As I said, we have a lot of work to do." Anne gave her an assessing look as if she were checking to make sure she had lined up all the professionals she would need to turn Sarah into a proper princess/executive's wife. Sarah must have used the wrong knife to butter her toast or held her cup wrong, because Anne added. "We may want someone to instruct you on etiquette and comportment as well."

Sarah was tempted to lean back in her chair and put her feet up on the table while gesturing with a half-eaten piece of toast. That seemed to be what Anne expected from her. "What's the dialect coach for?"

Anne looked at her with pity. "Your accent, my dear. We can't shed the Hillbilly Heartbreaker moniker if you sound like exactly what they think you are."

Sarah leaned forward and looked directly at Anne laying her accent on thick. "I am a hillbilly. I grew up fishing in the crick and foraging for mushrooms, ramps, and huckleberries in the holler. I went barefoot in the summer and learned to cook on a wood burning stove. I don't think putting on another accent is going to change that."

Anne's eyebrow shot up. Disdain hardened her already sharp features. "No, I don't suppose we can make a silk purse out of a sow's ear. But we are going to do our best."

Again, Sarah had the urge to act like an absolute cretin just to get under Anne's skin. But she supposed if she wanted to maintain a harmonious relationship with James, she would have to appease his mother. She finished off her coffee and stood up.

"Right. Then I'll go get ready."

***

"You have a very unusual accent." Phylida Lippincot, Anne's dialect coach looked over the top of her glasses after listening to Sarah read a paragraph from a magazine. Her helmet of silvery blond hair bobbed back and forth as she looked down at the sheet of information about Sarah that she held on a clipboard in her lap. "Where in North Carolina did you say you are from?"

Sarah had already suffered through the pain of getting highlights put in newly cut hair and trying on at least a dozen outfits and getting poked with pins while they were being marked for alterations. Now she was sitting in the too hot parlor of the cozy apartment in Haymarket. "A little place called Kettle Holler. It's outside of Boone."

Mrs. Lippincot tilted her head to the side and looked at Sarah as if she were speaking another language entirely.

"I'm guessing you don't get a lot of clients from western, North Carolina." Sarah stifled a laugh.

"I will admit I was expecting longer more rounded vowels. Yours are thinner, almost nasal. But your R's are quite clipped." She eyed Sarah like a puzzle with the wrong number of pieces.

Sarah gave her an indulgent smile. "You might be thinking of a South Carolina low country accent. They tend to have rounder vowels and softer consonants. As for my R's, they are probably clipped because my grandmother was Scottish, and we spoke Gaelic at home."

The woman's eyebrows lifted in surprise. "You seem to know a bit about dialect yourself."

"Professional hazard. I'm a folklorist, I have to be able to understand a lot of dialects and accents." Sarah shrugged. "You develop an ear."

"Do you hear your own accent? Some people don't." Mrs. Lippincot asked.

"I do. It's hard not to go so far from home without noticing how you sound." Sarah got used to people reacting to her accent as soon as she left the mountains. Chapel Hill was hours away from Kettle Holler and the accent in the Piedmont was decidedly different.

"Have you ever tried to fix it before?"

Sarah gave her a bless-your-heart smile and deepened her accent. "Well, as we say in the States, 'If it ain't broke, don't fix it.' Seriously though, in my line of work it can be an asset. I tend to talk with people who are older and from more rural places. Those folks have top notch bullshit detectors." She slid a sour look at Anne. "Having an authentic rather than an adopted accent goes a long way toward getting people to trust you."

Anne scoffed from across the room. She had taken a seat some distance away so as not to interrupt the session. Clearly, she wasn't out of earshot. Sarah looked at her, one eyebrow raised as if to say, 'I'm here aren't I?' Anne sighed and returned to flipping through her copy of Vogue.

"Mmm..." Mrs. Lippincot tapped her clipboard, deep in thought. Sarah could almost see her running through a list of ideas for how to make this American with the unusual accent sound like someone who should be marrying a prince. "Well, I'm not sure we'll ever be rid of it completely. But I think we should be able to soften it so that people can understand you more easily. I have an exercise that I would like you to try."

She set the clipboard aside and sat up straighter in her chair prompting Sarah to do the same. "We're going to practice opening up your jaw. You tend to keep it closed when you're speaking. If we want to broaden some of those vowels, we need to practice relaxing it. Relax your jaw and hold your fingers against your cheeks like this." She held her arms up like wings and placed her hands on either side of her face with the backs of her fingers against her cheeks. "Now, try to make an O sound without moving your jaw."

Sarah copied her posture and made an O sound with her fingers against her cheeks. It reminded her of some of the singing exercises she had done in choirs she'd sung in as an undergrad.

"Very good." Mrs. Lippincot gave a quick nod of approval. "Now, make a long U sound the same way. Don't move your jaw." Sarah did as instructed. "Good, now I want you to go back and forth between those two O and U sounds for a minute without moving your jaw."

Sarah started alternating the sounds. It was a challenge keeping her jaw relaxed when switching from the O and U. Whenever she closed her lips to make the U, her jaw wanted to close a little.

They went through a few more exercises with various sounds that were designed to open Sarah's jaw. There were also some breathing exercises that were familiar from her singing days. When the hour was over, Mrs. Lippincot gave her a list of exercises to continue doing before their next session in a week.

Sarah added the homework to the ever-increasing list of things she needed to learn; learn how to not sound like a hick, learn how to walk in spindly heels, put on makeup, style her new haircut. Tomorrow, they were supposed to tackle table settings and comportment. Sarah sincerely hoped that this crash course at Lady Anne's Very Private Finishing School would be brief, but she was afraid that Anne would be constantly reminding her of her perceived inferiority for the foreseeable future.

She sat next to Anne in tired and uncomfortable silence as they drove back to the house. They were a few blocks from Mrs. Lippincott's apartment when Sarah spotted a familiar building outside the car window. It was the care home where Seonag Sinclair lived. She wondered if Dermot was still visiting his mother every week, and how she was doing. She doubted asking him was a good idea. Surely, he wanted to talk to her even less than she wanted to talk to him.

***

By the time they reached home, Sarah felt like a southern fried Eliza Doolittle about to break into a round of 'Just You Wait, Lady Stuart'. She claimed a headache when they arrived home and decided to hide in her rooms for the rest of the evening. It wasn't a lie. Her head did hurt, but mainly she just didn't think she could be in Lady Anne's company for much longer without unleashing her temper.

Once she got to her sitting room, Sarah kicked off her kitten heels and unclipped her hair. She couldn't wait to get out of the conservative dress that Lady Anne had advised her to wear that morning and into something comfortable. She stripped off the dreaded pantyhose and gratefully unhooked her bra. She had to dig in her wardrobe to find some clothes from her previous life, clothes that hadn't been picked for the person they wanted her to be, clothes that she had chosen. She settled on a pair of gray sweatpants and a worn Squirrel Nut Zippers T-shirt. When she threw the shirt over her head she felt infinitely better, almost like herself.

She went back into her sitting room and turned on the television needing to do something normal, needing a break from the Stuarts. She was just settling in to watch a cozy mystery when there was a knock at the door. Sarah opened it to find the butler, Conley standing in the hall. He took in Sarah's extremely casual clothes and raised an eyebrow. "There's a phone call for you, miss."

"Who on earth would be calling me here?" Sarah asked.

"I'm afraid I do not know. It is a gentleman." Conley's tone was carefully neutral. "There is a phone at the top of the stairs."

Sarah glanced back into her room. She hadn't noticed before that there was no phone in her room. She knew there were phones in other rooms in the house, the study, the drawing room. She felt sure there must be a phone in James's bedroom, but not hers. Sarah wondered if that was an oversight, or if they were afraid, she might call the American embassy, or home, or Dermot. She pursed her lips. "Well, I guess the hallway it is."

"Right this way." Conley swept his arm toward the landing where a small table beside a chair waited. Sarah went to the table and picked up the phone. Conley showed her which button to press to answer the call that was on hold.

Sarah held the phone to her ear and waited for Conley to descend the stairs before saying, "Hello."

"Och! I'm that glad to hear your voice." A man's voice came over the line. It took Sarah a few seconds to recognize it. The last time she'd heard that voice it was thready and still a little slurred.

"Rab?" Sarah's mood lifted. She was excited to hear from her father. "How are you?"

He laughed. "Well, I've had better days, but I've had much much worse. Are they treating ye alright?"

It was Sarah's turn to laugh nervously. She'd only met her biological father a few months ago, but after reading her mother's account of their time together, she felt like she knew him. He had taken to her immediately. But after decades of drowning his guilt over abandoning Sarah and her mother, he had finally gone to rehab. Sarah didn't want to tell him anything that would jeopardize his sobriety. "Yeah. Of course, they are. Only the best."

"I'm glad to hear it." He gave a relieved sigh. "After I talked with yer brother I wasna so sure."

"Well, I wasn't very happy the last time he saw me. I'm doing better now. Settling in." That was a lie, but Rab didn't need to know how unhappy she was. "I was so glad when they told me what you're doing. I know it's hard, but it'll be worth it."

"Aye. I just wish I had done it ages ago." Regret soured his tone. "I know yer brother and sister wish it too. I have so many regrets."

"It's never too late. I know they'll appreciate it." Sarah assured him.

Rab cleared his throat and paused. "I ken what ye did for my lass, Oona."

Sarah didn't know who was listening, and really didn't want to talk about it. Oona had only been a part of her decision to choose James. "I don't know what you're talking about."

"I think ye do." Rab's tone was firm. "Ye've no reason to be kind to any of us. We've…I've caused ye so much pain without even knowing ye. Ye've the best of yer mother in ye. Of that I'm sure."

Tears pooled in her eyes. "I only did what was right."

"Aye well, I needed to tell ye how much it means to us." She heard the flick of a cigarette lighter followed by an inhale.

"How are things going there?" She changed the subject.

Rab took another drag on his cigarette and exhaled. "I'm getting to the part where I make amends for the things I've done wrong when I was drunk. It's one of the reasons they let me call."

"Except that you didn't do anything to me when you were drunk." Sarah pointed out.

"Ah, but what I did to ye was the wrong that started it all. I might have stopped before if I hadn't been so full of guilt over ye and yer mother. Can ye ever forgive me?"

"You know I already have." They had talked about this before. "I think you might want to talk to Ruaraidh and Oona.

Make sure they understand that it wasn't just me that got you to finally make this effort."

"Aye. Ye're right." He sighed. "I wasted so much time with them."

"They love you. I know they'll forgive you." She thought that was true. "I'm so proud of you for owning up to it and doing what you're doing."

He drew in a sharp breath and cleared his throat. When he spoke, his voice was thick with tears. "To think that ye could ever be proud of me after what I did."

"But I am." Her tone was unequivocal. "You need to forgive yourself."

"Aye." He sniffed. "Maybe one day."

"I'm so glad you called, Rab." She wrapped an arm around her waist as if she could hug him.

"Aye. Ye take care of yerself."

"I will. You too." She heard the line click. She was so relieved that Rab was doing something about his drinking problem. Maybe if he could stay sober, he could meet Oona's girlfriend. Maybe he could have a future where he could mend his relationships with his other children.

It had been good to hear his voice, but it also reminded Sarah of who she was protecting. Rab and Sheila and their children were four of the many reasons she was there. It was for them that she had to tolerate Lady Anne's snobbery and interfering. It was a reminder that she needed.

CHAPTER THIRTY-FOUR

"I'm told that all we have to do is swipe these swabs on the inside of our cheeks, and that should give us the answer." James explained pulling on a latex glove.

"What's the glove for?" Dermot eyed James's gloved hand with suspicion. James had called him into the study shortly after they arrived home that evening. Dermot would have preferred to wait in the staff lounge or near the front door to see if James was going out again. He had still tried to avoid being visible in the house when Sarah was home.

"Avoiding contamination. If some of my skin cells got on your swab, it would skew the results." James pulled a large cotton swab out of a plastic tube and held it up. "Open up."

Dermot opened his mouth wide and James swabbed the insides of both of his cheeks. Then he put the swab back into the tube and taped across the top to keep it sealed until it was opened for testing. "Do we need to label them with our names?"

"No names." James took another swab and rubbed it inside his own cheeks. "It doesn't matter whose swab is whose. We're only trying to determine our relationship, so our names don't matter. Besides, no one is likely to leak a nameless DNA test result, but one with my name on it…"

"Aye, right." Tabloids would be tripping over themselves to report about Lord Caledon's secret relative. "So how long is this likely to take."

"Two or three months, I'm afraid." James put the two tubes in a box inside a padded envelope. "I asked about rushing it, but he said they have a backlog of testing related to crimes. I can't ask to jump ahead of some poor murder victim. I'll have Miss Lennox send this by a secure courier in the morning."

James was still putting the address label on the envelope when a tentative knock sounded at the door. He quickly pressed the label on and shoved the envelope into a desk drawer. "Come in."

The door opened just enough for Sarah to lean in. She looked different. Her hair was less curly and lighter somehow. It was shorter too, coming just past her shoulders. He instantly missed the unruly cascade of honey-colored curls that he used to run his fingers through. She kept her eyes focused on James. "I was told you wanted to see me."

"Always." James smiled as if the sun had just come out from behind clouds. "Come in. We were just finishing up."

Sarah glanced at Dermot and stiffened slightly. When she stepped into the room, her back was ramrod straight, her chin high. It wasn't just her hair that was different. She wore a well-cut if stayed charcoal gray suit with a light pink blouse that had a bow tied at the neck. If it hadn't fit her so perfectly, he would have guessed she'd borrowed it from Anne. She walked forward on heels that he knew made her uncomfortable. "What's going on?"

James pushed away from the desk and met her as she crossed the room. "You look divine. My mother didn't wear you out, did she?"

"Why would you think that?" Sarah flashed a false smile. "Cinderella's fairy godmother has got nothing on your mom. I just wish there was more magic and fewer tweezers and blow dryers involved."

"Well, you look beautiful." James stepped back and held her arms out to survey the new and not so improved Sarah. "How do you like it?"

Sarah smiled. This time it seemed genuine. "Doesn't every girl dream of a makeover like this?"

Dermot wouldn't have thought she had. She'd never been impressed by that sort of thing when they were together. At least that was what she'd told him. But then he wouldn't have thought she would have thrown him over for James either. She'd done it for security. He could see that someone who had grown up the way she had would be attracted to the kind of financial safety that James's money would offer. He'd regretted his comment that night about her attitude when she was draped in diamonds and silks but looking at her today, he felt vindicated. Here she was, plucked and polished and smiling with his enormous diamond engagement ring weighing down her hand. "If there's nothing else then?"

"No, nothing else. I'll see you in the morning." James's eyes cut between Dermot and Sarah. He clearly felt the tension between them. "Thank you."

He crossed the study walking out of his way to avoid brushing past them. Stepping into the hallway, he pulled the door closed. He didn't look back, but as the door was almost closed, he heard her whisper. "I still don't understand."

He pulled the door to and stalked down the hall. He had to get out of there, out of that house. He'd accepted James's offer because he couldn't abandon her. But this new creature dressed like a politician's wife and bejeweled like a princess? This wasn't his Sarah. His Sarah wore jeans and flannel and pinned her curls up with a pencil. His Sarah drank beer and danced in her kitchen while cooking beans and rice for her friends. That Sarah was gone, and it was time he faced it.

***

"I dinna like unplanned stops. I'll have to report this to Mr. Shaw." Fleming groused as he and Sarah got out of the car. She had been on her way back from her second weekly session with Mrs. Lippincot when she had told the driver to stop in front of the Leith House Care Home. Thankfully, she had been able to convince Anne that she could manage going to the dialect coach on her own. Naturally, on her own meant without Anne, but still accompanied by her security detail.

"You can tell Shaw whatever you want," Sarah told him as she strode toward the front door. "But if you mention a word of this to Dermot, I will gut you like a fish."

"Dermot?" Fleming quickly stepped around her to open the door. "What's he got to do with this?"

"I'm visiting his mother." She made a beeline for the elevator and hit the button to go up to the floor where Seonag lived.

"Why?" Fleming's voice held a note of suspicion.

"Because she's sick and doesn't get a lot of visitors. I don't even know if he visits her anymore." Sarah told him stepping into the elevator. She turned away from Fleming not wanting him to see her as she got emotional. Whether it was about Seonag's situation or her own, she couldn't tell. "I don't want her to be alone."

He didn't complain again about their unexpected stop. They got off the elevator at the fourth floor and he followed

Sarah to Seonag's room. Dermot's mother was sitting in her chair facing the window as she had been when Dermot had brought her to meet Seonag. This time she was tapping her fingers on the arm of her chair and singing a Gaelic tune under her breath.

Sarah stepped up next to the chair and recognizing the tune sang along softly. Seonag's face lit up and they finished the song together. "Ah, A bhana phrionnsa! I had hoped to see you again."

"I'm flattered that you remembered me. It's been a while since I visited." Sarah told her.

Seonag went on in Gaelic. "My memory is not so good as it once was, but I remember seeing you. Will ye stay a while?"

"Of course." Sarah pulled a chair from the corner so she could sit next to Seonag. "How have you been?"

"I don't know. The days run together." Her voice was distracted as if she was trying to remember something.

"Are you not knitting today?" Sarah looked around for her knitting basket and spotted it under the night table.

"Och! I was knitting a scarf for my Dermot." Seonag looked around as if she was also looking for the basket. "But I ran out of yarn."

"Oh, well we'll have to get you some more then." Sarah reached into her purse for her agenda to make a note. "What colors do you like for the scarf?"

"I was using blue and brown. The blue brings out his eyes. He has such lovely blue eyes." Seonag rubbed her fingers softly on the arm of her chair.

"He does." Sarah agreed, seeing an opportunity. "I wonder where he got those blue eyes."

"Oh, from his father I expect." Seonag shrugged.

"He's never mentioned his father. Who was he?" Sarah hoped her question sounded innocent enough.

Seonag was quiet for a moment. Her fingers still rubbing the arm of the chair. Her breaths grew shorter, and her brows drew together. She turned to Sarah, tears pooling in her eyes. "I dinna remember. I should know that. A lad should know his father, but I..."

"It's alright." Sarah laid her hand on top of the older woman's "It's not important. You've done such a marvelous job with him."

"He's a good lad, my Dermot." Seonag relaxed back into her chair and returned her gaze to the window.

"Yes." Sarah felt tears clogging her throat. "Yes, he is."

She sat with Seonag for a while longer and they talked about knitting and the weather. When she left, Seonag walked her to the door. "Thank ye for the visit, lass. What's yer name again?"

"Sarah." She told her, understanding a little of what Dermot must go through every time his mother forgot who he was.

"Are ye one of my Dermot's teachers?" Seonag asked.

Sarah nodded hoping her voice wouldn't break. "That's right."

"I hope he's applying himself. He's very smart, but ye ken how boys are."

Sarah pressed her lips together and inhaled, trying to hold back the tears. "He's doing just fine. Top marks."

"Good, good." Seonag nodded, her eyes shifting back and forth as if she was trying to remember something. In the end she shrugged.

Sarah opened the door. Fleming was at his post right outside. She turned back to Seonag. "I'll come and see you again next week. And in the meantime, I'll try to have some yarn sent over."

"Och. Thanks for that. I miss my knitting." Seonag turned to shuffle back to her chair.

Sarah stepped into the hallway and closed the door behind her. She stood there for a moment looking into the narrow window in the door. Seonag sat down and returned to watching the city out the window, her fingers absently rubbing the arm of the chair.

With a nod to Fleming, she walked to the elevator without even looking to see if he followed. The tears that she'd been holding back spilled over. They got in and pushed the button for the ground floor. Sarah stood straight eyes focused on the elevator door as Fleming took his place in front of her, but there were tears running down her face. Without a word, Fleming offered her a handkerchief.

CHAPTER THIRTY-FIVE

"Ye do know this is madness, right?" Dermot muttered to James as they got into the car.

"I can see why you might think that, but I'm telling you these engagement photos will be brilliant." James grinned as he looked back toward the house to make sure Sarah and her entourage were getting into their car.

Dermot followed his gaze and only caught a glimpse of her back as she ducked into her limousine. She was taking the larger car because of the need for Felicia's make-up guru and stylist to ride with her. "Ye could take brilliant photos at the house, or Tweedholm, but a public park, James. It's too dangerous."

"Not just any public park, Princes Street Gardens and with the fountain and the castle behind us. It'll be worth it." He resettled himself in the seat adjusting his kilt as the car pulled away from the house. "And we're taking every precaution. Few people know we'll be there. They've cordoned off the area around the fountain and the lanes leading to it with construction barriers. No one is going to suspect what we're doing until it's too late."

"And ye're sure no one leaked it?" Dermot was skeptical.

"Felicia told the newspapers they could each send one photographer and if she caught them buying shots from free-lancers, she would cut their access. We've done everything we can."

"Mmph." Dermot still didn't like the idea. "I hope ye're right. Ye know things have a way of leaking, and ye canna stop everyone from being in the park."

"We have extra security and police presence." James elbowed him. "Mate, these photos are going to be historic."

"Aye, they'll be historic if Sarah gets killed while ye're taking them."

"Ah." James raised his chin. "I see what you're really worried about. You know I wouldn't do anything to put her at risk."

Dermot arched a doubtful eyebrow at him before turning back to the window. He shouldn't ask, shouldn't start down that road. She wasn't his anymore. She'd turned her back on him, but he couldn't stop himself. "How is she?"

James shrugged. "I wish I could tell. She says all the right things, does whatever is asked, tolerates my mother, but it's like…" He blew out a long, frustrated breath. "…a light has gone out."

"Well, she's been through a lot." Dermot watched the streets outside the window. Every conversation he and James had about Sarah was a tumbler of mixed emotions. He wanted things to get easier for her, but a small, venal part of him thought it served her right for picking James over him. Then he felt worse for feeling that way. He didn't want to help James. But he also couldn't stand to know that she was unhappy. "Is she eating?"

James thought for a moment. "I don't know. I haven't really noticed."

"How is she sleeping?"

"I don't know." James shook his head, pressing his lips together in frustration.

"Right." He felt a twinge of satisfaction that she and James didn't seem to be any closer, but it was mixed with frustration that James wasn't taking care of her. Dermot turned to face him. "She has nightmares and sometimes sleepwalks. Ye might want to watch out for that."

James listened attentively. "Good. Alright. And eating?"

Dermot debated for a second whether he should tell James about Sarah's trauma survival strategy. In the end his better angel won. "She's had a lot of bad things happen to her and she had to learn how to survive at a young age. After Cumberland tried to kill her, she told me how she got through. She just kept going through the motions of her life; eating, sleeping, going to school, until she got enough distance from the trauma that she could look back without so much pain."

"Except that everything has changed for her." James closed his eyes and leaned his head back against the seat. "There's no comfortable routine to keep up. There's nothing that interests her to distract from it. She's got nothing."

"Nothing but putting one foot in front of the other." Dermot confirmed, wondering how she was coping at all.

"Right. Well, that's given me something to think about. Thank you." James turned to him. "I know it's not easy for you to help me, but that does help."

"It helps her." Dermot cleared his throat. "Dinna ask me for tips romancing her."

"I think I know a thing or two about romance." He pointed to himself and smirked. "Prince Charming, remember?"

Dermot sighed turning back to the window. "Prince Something."

The car pulled into the lane that led to the famed Ross Fountain. Dermot slid on his sunglasses and opened the car door. He blocked James's exit until he had assessed the area. The element of surprise meant that there was a small amount of the public standing near the barrier that surrounded the fountain, but not a massive crowd. The newspapers seemed to have respected Felicia's threat of lost access. There were only a handful of photographers among the small crowd. Still, he didn't like the public nature of this excursion. If any of the various groups stalking Sarah or with a beef against James were in the small crowd watching, he would have no way of knowing. That made him nervous.

"Well?" James asked from behind him.

"Looks safe enough all things considered. Still, ye want to minimize yer time in the open. Give it a minute until Sarah's car gets here.

As if summoned, the limousine that carried Sarah's entourage pulled to a stop behind them followed by the photographer and his assistant in his car. The photographer got out and began walking around looking for the best angle and checking the light. Fleming got out of the front seat of Sarah's car and came around to the side near the fountain. He gave Dermot a nod, and they waited for a signal from the photographer.

In another minute, the photographer's assistant gave them the go-ahead. Dermot stepped aside to let James out of the car and Fleming opened the door to the limousine. Gasps could be heard from the spectators that had gathered at the barrier, and the paparazzi started clicking away with their cameras. In a Stewart dress kilt, even Dermot had to admit James cut a dashing figure.

Sarah wore a belted dress to match the blue in the tartan with a royal Stewart sash. He hadn't seen her since that afternoon in James's study. She did look thinner. He wondered if that was a loss of appetite or another thing that Lady Anne was trying to change about Sarah. James held out his hand to her as he walked toward the photographer who waited by the fountain. Sarah reached out and took James by the hand. They approached the fountain together looking to outsiders like any happy couple. Dermot shifted his gaze back to the crowd. He should focus on that, and not on James and Sarah smiling at each other and cuddling for the camera.

***

"You look amazing." The smile James gave her wasn't his usual megawatt smile. This one was intimate, and his compliment was spoken low enough that only she heard it.

"You're not too bad yourself." Sarah stood back to take in the sight of him in all his kilted finery. He was dazzling. She had gotten mostly used to James's good looks, but done up in fancy dress, he was something to behold. If Scotland wanted a prince, he certainly looked the part.

"Let's get started. The light is perfect at the moment, but I'm worried that some clouds might be rolling in." The photographer said. Anne had mentioned something about him being a famous fashion photographer, but Sarah had only been half listening. "I'd like you to stand next to the fountain."

He drew them to a spot near the rim of the pool. The enormous green and gold fountain towered above them on one side, and the castle loomed behind them. She could see why this spot was perfect for the Stuart's purposes. In the royal tartan, in front of the castle they would look propaganda poster perfect. It was chillingly calculated. And she was going to have to sell their fairytale love story with every smile. "James can you put your right arm around Sarah's waist?" The photographer asked after placing James behind Sarah and stepping back. "And Sarah, can you lean your head just slightly to the left? That's it. Perfect."

"I've barely seen you this week." James said to her quietly while they waited for the next direction.

"Let's turn toward each other. Sarah put your hand on his chest." The photographer told them. "And look at each other. Look of love."

Sarah looked up into James's blue eyes. He gave her a devilish grin and winked. She was struck by the ridiculousness of the situation and had to stifle a laugh. No doubt that picture would make them look giddily in love. "Your mother has kept me busy. It's a lot of work turning a hillbilly into a princess."

"Still, I think we should be making time to get more comfortable with each other." He told her.

"Let's get some casual action shots. Can the two of you just stroll around the fountain. I'll do the rest." The photographer directed them, oblivious to the conversation his subjects were having.

"What did you have in mind?" Sarah took his arm as they started to walk around the fountain.

James looked down at her. "You're not a runner, are you?"

"Not unless I'm being chased." She gave him a flirty look; sure the photographer would eat it up.

"I think we need to find something that we both enjoy that we can do regularly." James told her as they went around the back side of the fountain. "What are some things that you like to do, apart from your academic work."

"I enjoyed our hike up Arthur's Seat." She offered.

He laughed and shook his head. "No, you didn't."

Sarah giggled. "Well, I would have if I hadn't been hungover."

"That sounds right." He smiled remembering the time he forced her to climb Arthur's seat when she was barely able to hold her head up. He dropped his arm and took her hand instead, threading their fingers together. "But I'm afraid I haven't got time for a hike every day. Name something else."

They rounded the far side of the fountain, and the photographer started clicking away. Sarah thought for a second. "I like to cook."

"I don't know how to cook." James gave an embarrassed laugh. "Maybe you could teach me."

Sarah looked at him surprised. "Do you think your chef would allow that?"

"I think he could be convinced." James gave her a look that said his chef knew who the boss was.

"Sure, let's try that." Sarah nodded. "We can make that our evening appointment."

"I'll have Miss Lennox add it to my calendar." He gave her hand a squeeze, and they arrived back at the spot where they had started to stroll.

The photographer approached them. "Good. Let's try something else. Sarah, why don't you sit down on the edge of the fountain. James let's take a knee. Mind the kilt of course."

Sarah sat on the low rim of the fountain and arranged her legs and skirt in the way that Anne had showed her. James knelt beside her and took her hands as if proposing. "You know I never properly proposed."

"I'm not sure it's necessary." Sarah gave him a rueful smile.

"Don't most ladies want that sort of thing?" He looked serious and sincere.

Sarah leaned toward him. "If I were like most ladies, we wouldn't be here."

James lifted her left hand to his lips and kissed it beside the giant engagement ring which had been delivered to her without much ceremony the morning after she moved into Polwarth Terrace. His eyes were focused on hers. "You are truly remarkable."

Sarah gave him a soft smile. "Thank you. You have been nothing but kind and thoughtful to me."

"Brilliant!" The photographer raved. "Let's take a minute to just relax."

James stood and pulled Sarah up with him. He kept a hand on her elbow to steady her in her heels. While she busied herself straightening her skirt and sash, he told her. "We're in a difficult situation, but we should be able to make the best of it. We were friends once."

She looked up at him, caught by the note of yearning in his tone. She placed her hand on his lapel. "We're still friends."

His arm tightened around her waist and he drew her closer. He kissed her temple and whispered. "That means a lot to me."

And the camera shutters clicked like mad.

***

"Dermot!" The nurse smiled brightly as he passed her on his way to his mother's room. "It's good to see you. I think your mother is in the lounge."

No comment about how long it had been since he'd visited his mother. No guilt inducing looks. He was grateful for that. He'd been swamped with plenty of guilt on his own as soon as he walked into the building. There was no good explanation for why he'd stayed away for weeks. He couldn't exactly tell her that it was because he suspected his mother of…what, a conspiracy to restore the Stuarts to the throne? Or that he thought she's had him as an aide, servant, maybe spare to the Stuart heir? Anyone hearing him talk like that would think he was mad. And in her current state, he couldn't hold anything against his mother.

He turned the corner and made his way to the patient lounge. There were patients in various states of disability there. A couple were in wheelchairs. A pair of wizened men with oxygen tanks played chess in one corner. There was a row of armchairs that faced the wall of windows overlooking the courtyard garden. Dermot walked around one end of the row looking for his mother. She was in the far corner her unfocused gaze on the top of a tree in the courtyard.

"Hello, Mum."

She looked up and smiled. "Oh hello, young man."

"How are ye feeling today?" He asked, accepting that she didn't recognize him. He shouldn't be surprised.

"Alright." She shifted toward him in her chair. She leaned over the arm and crooked her finger at him smiling. "Look. There's a bird's nest in the top of this tree."

She pointed to a tree in the courtyard. Just as Dermot looked a robin with a bright red breast flew out of the leaves. His mother clapped her hands in delight. "There he is!"

"Look at that." Dermot laughed and marveled at her excitement. In spite of everything, she still found things to feel joy about. "I'm surprised he would build a nest inside the courtyard like that. Seems the people would scare him off."

"Och, nah." Seonag waved the idea away. "Robins will nest anywhere there are worms. They come up onto the sidewalk after a rain."

"Worms? In the city?"

She shrugged. "They dinna ken it's a city. I think the gardeners bring them in with the compost."

He chuckled shaking his head. She might not remember him today, but she was still able to think logically. It was bizarre how this disease worked. He pulled out the yarn that he'd picked up. He'd gotten a couple of colors feeling guilty that it had been a while since he'd brought any. "I've brought ye some yarn."

She took the skein that he held out to her. "Thank you. That's so soft."

"I'm sorry I havena brought any recently." He told her.

"That's alright." She slipped her fingers under a layer of yarn and rubbed it with her thumb. "I havena run out yet."

Dermot was surprised by that. He hadn't been here on over a month, and she knitted a lot. Maybe one of the nurses was bringing her yarn. He'd have to ask Liz about it. "What are ye knitting these days?"

She looked around the back of the chair before leaning toward him as if to tell him a secret. "It's for that nice nurse. The one with the braids. She helps me when I get upset."

She must mean Liz. The nurses tended to rotate in and out, but Liz had been a constant since Seonag had been moved there. "I'm sure she'll love it."

"I might knit one for the princess as well." She still fingered the yarn.

That caught him up. Of course, she didn't remember her own son, but she remembered meeting Sarah. Bitterness filled him. He knew it wasn't true, that it was the disease, but it felt as though she cared more about the prophecy than him. And wasn't that the point? Just like Sarah, his whole existence was to fulfill the prophecy. No, that was wrong. Sarah's parents had loved each other. He cleared his throat. "I'm sure she'll treasure it."

"She's so very lovely, the princess. Sweet lass." Seonag gushed her face lighting up.

"She made quite an impression on ye." His tone was sour.

She leaned toward him again. "Have ye seen my Dermot? He hasna visited in ever so long."

'I'm right here, mum.' He wanted to scream. "I believe he's guarding James."

"No," She scoffed. "He's too young to start that. He's just a boy, and James is at school in Switzerland."

In her mind they were still boys, but what did she mean. "Too young to start what?"

"Being a steward." She shook her head in frustration. "I told Walter he was too young to start training for that. He should let the boy be a boy for a while longer."

Dermot stilled. Was he on the verge of getting some answers to the questions he'd been asking himself? He couldn't resist pressing for more. "Did Walter listen when you told him Dermot was too young?"

She shook her head. "He'll always choose his own path. Even when we're all supposed to be working together. He went to Dermot's school on his own, never mind what I wanted."

"Did you not tell the school to turn him away?" Dermot asked remembering that first time that Walter had come to his school to talk about the skills he would need. He'd been interested in which classes Dermot was taking and in his physical fitness. He'd asked about Dermot's interests, which then had been typical for a twelve-year-old boy.

Seonag sighed. "There was no point. They'd have let him in anyway. He's a donor, a big one. I hope they havena let him take my Dermot out of school."

She had let it happen. She'd allowed Walter to groom him to be James's loyal retainer from the age of twelve even if it wasn't what she'd wanted. She'd set them all on this path, as if he wasn't a person. He was just a tool to them all. He shouldn't have said it. He wasn't sure why he did. There was no excuse for being short with her in her condition, but the words were out of his mouth before he could stop them. "Maybe Dermot is with his father."

She turned to him; her eyebrows drawn together in alarm. "How? I dinna even know who that is."

She didn't know? Now it was his turn to look at her alarmed. "How do ye not know who his father is?"

Her bottom lip quivered, and her breath came short. Her eyes darted back and forth blinking rapidly. "I don't know. I don't know!"

Guilt dropped on him like a weight. No matter how he felt about the decisions she'd made when he was young, she didn't deserve his derision. Now he'd upset her. He made his tone as soothing as he could. "It's alright, Seonag. It's okay if ye dinna remember. It was long ago."

"No, I..." She shook her head, and tears started falling. "...I don't know who his father is. I should know that. He should know that."

"Let's not worry about that now." He took her hands and tried to catch her eyes. "It's alright. Dermot is fine. He doesna need to know."

"Here now, Seonag. It's almost time for your lunch." Liz appeared at his elbow sounding cheerful and calm as always. To Dermot. "I'll take her from here."

"Thanks, Liz. I didna mean to upset her." He felt like a worm.

Liz smiled softly as she helped his mother out of her chair. "Don't worry about it. She's probably just realized something that she doesn't remember. It happens."

"Aye." He could only stand there impotent while Liz steered his mother away. "Cheers."

CHAPTER THIRTY-SIX

"I'm ready for my first cooking lesson." James, who was in the kitchen when Sarah arrived, turned around wearing an apron over his shirt and tie.

Sarah still wasn't sure she wanted to do this. It seemed more like a date than she was ready for, but she had to laugh. "You look like the guy on the cover of a romance novel where a lonely baker clashes with the real estate developer who wants to demolish her shop, but in the end, they fall in love."

James looked down at himself laughing, "I think you've missed your calling."

"I think novelist pays about as much as folklorist, which is precious little." She shook her head turning to the steel worktable. James's kitchen, or more accurately, Mr. Ratcliffe's, looked more like a commercial kitchen than one in a home. Ratcliffe had given Sarah a tour when she asked about cooking lessons with James. There was a double-sized refrigerator and a huge walk-in pantry, plus a six-burner gas stove and grill, three ovens and myriad other small appliances. It was a long way from Granny's ancient wood burning stove and farm sink. That night, Sarah only needed a few things. "We are going to make a southern American classic, deviled eggs."

"I think I've had these before." He took his place next to her at the table.

"You would be sorely deprived if you hadn't. They are a staple at any gathering of more than a four Southerners." She pulled a bowl next to the cutting board in front of them. "Fortunately, the tedious part has already been done. Mr. Ratcliffe boiled and peeled a dozen eggs for us."

"Isn't that the cooking part? I thought we were cooking." James investigated the bowl of peeled eggs.

"Baby steps. We're just going to work on seasoning and taste tonight." She picked up the paring knife that was laid out on the table with the rest of the ingredients and handed it to him. "Your first job is to cut each egg in half lengthwise."

"I can do that." He took an egg from the bowl and cut it in half as instructed.

Sarah took another bowl and spoon and scooped the yolks out of the eggs as James cut them. They worked side by side for a few minutes before he asked. "How was your day?"

"Well, I reviewed another designer for my dress, got drilled by your mother on etiquette and got makeup lessons from Tony." Sarah kept her focus on the egg yolks. "So, very busy doing nothing of value."

James cut through the last egg and set the knife down before saying. "I know it doesn't feel like it, but those things are valuable. Promoting a Scottish designer with your dress is important. Not offending dignitaries and potential political allies is important, as is looking your best. I know it doesn't seem like it, but those things open doors that we can use to accomplish things of value."

"I am perfectly capable of picking out a dress, being inoffensive and putting on eyeshadow without the guidance of your mother." She kept her tone relaxed. She wasn't trying to start an argument. She dropped the last of the egg yolks into the bowl and began vigorously mashing them with a fork. "And I am too educated to be merely ornamental, which seems to be your mother's ideal role for me."

"I would never consider you merely ornamental. Although, you are lovely." He rested a hip on the table beside her. "What's next?"

Sarah stopped mashing and looked down at the pulverized egg yolks. Talking about her situation had distracted her from their task. She had to think about the next step. She gave her head a quick shake "Mayonnaise and mustard."

James reached for two jars that were laid out on the table in front of them and handed them to Sarah. She opened the glass jar that didn't have a label but looked like mayo and sniffed. "At home we would use Duke's, but I guess Ratcliffe's will do."

"No store-bought mayonnaise and mustard in Ratcliffe's kitchen. He'd never allow it." James's smile was confident.

"Heaven forbid." Sarah spooned the mayonnaise into the bowl with the egg yolks. As she started to stir the yolks with the mayonnaise she explained. "We just want to cream these together into a sort of paste. Then we'll add the mustard and spices."

"You didn't measure the mayonnaise." James eyed her with suspicion.

"I put in just enough to get the consistency that we want. If it needs more, we can add more." She glanced up at him, still stirring. "Does it bother you that I didn't measure?"

He thought about it. "I don't suppose so. I'm just used to exact numbers."

"Here I thought you were the big picture guy. I figured you left the details to Miss Lennox and the people who work for you." She arched an eyebrow at him while reaching for the mustard jar.

He watched as she spooned some mustard into the bowl. "Miss Lennox is excellent with details, but I still read all the reports they give me. I prefer precision. In a company as big as A. P., small miscalculations can become big problems. If you put two percent more mustard than needed in that bowl, it wouldn't matter much. But if we were throwing a party, that two percent would be a much larger amount and could cause a lot of problems. Apart from matters of scale, when you are talking about supply chain a small miscalculation early can balloon into a major cock up down the line."

"I see how that could be an issue." Sarah sprinkled some salt and pepper into the bowl before stirring it together. "Just like one wrong choice in the matching ceremony twenty-seven years ago led to heartache, deaths and a lot of confusion."

"A butterfly flaps its wings…" James blew out a frustrated breath.

"And my life is no longer my own." Sarah kept her eyes focused on the bowl. She stopped stirring and laid her hands on either side of the bowl. She suddenly felt heavy with the weight of all the rapid changes in her life.

After a moment, James laid a hand on hers. His soft voice broke the silence. "My life hasn't been my own for years. I'm used to it now. It will get better."

Sarah drew in a sharp breath and shook off the self-pity. Granny always told her that would never get her anywhere. She took her hand from his and reached for a couple of tasting spoons. She held one out to James. He took it and together they dipped their spoons into the filling and tasted. 'What do you think?"

He accepted the change of subject and seemed to consider the taste for a second. "That's not bad."

"I think it needs a touch of paprika." She turned back to the ingredients grouped on the table to hunt for the spice. She found it and used a small measuring spoon to add some to the bowl. "So, you weren't in control of your life when you were jet-setting off to Ibiza with your latest arm candy? Must've been tough."

He folded his arms across his chest and leaned against the table with a sigh. "It might look like a lot of fun, but much of that is calculated to raise my profile. There is a certain caché to being a playboy that elevates my personal profile beyond that of just the CEO of A. P. You've never heard a story that one of those women complained about being treated badly. I don't supply them drugs. I don't tolerate that, or even drunkenness. I may have been photographed with a lot of women, but I don't subscribe to a hard partying life. And I have rarely been photographed with the same woman for more than a couple of weeks. Why, jealous?"

Sarah arched an eyebrow at him as she stirred in the paprika. "Hardly. I'm not saying this is a bad life. The cage might be gilded, but it is still a cage."

"And you're still beating your wings against the bars." It wasn't a question or a criticism, just a statement of fact.

Sarah's eyes met his and they stopped for a moment considering each other. Sarah wondered again if there was any chance of getting James to change his mind about the whole thing. But then she remembered his warning about not giving up on independence or on Scotland. Now wasn't the time to push. "Can you hand me that piping bag?"

He looked over the things on the table in confusion. "What is a piping bag?"

Sarah laughed. "Seriously? Have you ever been in a kitchen before?"

His eyebrow arched and amusement flashed in his eyes. "I warned you I didn't know how to cook."

Sarah picked up a plastic piping bag that Mr. Ratcliffe had thoughtfully included in the supplies. She held it up and pushed the sides down around the fingers of one hand. Then she began spooning the mixture into the bag. "This is a piping bag. We didn't have anything this fancy when I learned how to make deviled eggs. We just used a spoon. But this is much faster, and it looks prettier."

"Ah well, we have to make it look pretty." James joked.

Sarah finished loading the bag and snipped off the end. She moved to the plate of halved egg whites, bumping James out of the way with her hip. "Now watch closely. I'll fill a couple of these, then you can do the rest."

She squeezed the filling carefully, and neatly into a couple of egg halves. While she worked, she returned to their previous topic. "What did those models get out of that arrangement?"

"Hmm?" James was watching her fill the eggs and looked up in confusion. "Oh. They got the added prestige of being linked with me. Many of their careers were helped by the connection. I didn't leave any of them heartbroken."

"Some careers don't benefit from that kind of attention." Sarah straightened from bending over the plate. "And you left at least one heartbroken. What's her name?"

"Beatrice Harcourt?" His look said everything about his opinion of the woman in question. "She's not heartbroken. She's just skint. Beatrice's trust fund isn't up to the lifestyle that she wants. She wasn't trying to build a career, except perhaps as someone's mercenary wife. She wanted to raise her profile and meet people, but I think she decided that being with me was her most lucrative option."

"Ah." Sarah held the piping bag out to him. "Your turn."

James took the bag and looked at the plate of eggs before looking back at Sarah. "Are you sure you want me to do this?"

She grinned. "There's only one way to learn, and that's by doing. Use one hand to position the tip and remember to squeeze from the top of the bag. And go slow."

He set his jaw and bent over the plate of eggs concentrating. He positioned the bag over the first egg glancing at the two that Sarah had done. Despite her warning to go slow, he squeezed a little too hard and a stream of filling shot out missing the egg he was aiming at and landing on the rim of the plate. "Blast it!"

Sarah tried not to laugh and failed. "Didn't you?"

He laughed too. "I suppose this takes practice."

"And a soft touch. Let me show you." She put her hands over his on the bag. She guided it to the next egg and squeezed gently. When the space in the egg white was filled enough, Sarah stopped squeezing and pulled the tip up at an angle. "There."

That was when she noticed that James's eyes weren't on the eggs. They were on her. She met his stormy gaze and was struck once again by how compelling he was, and by how similar his eyes were to Dermot's. When he spoke, his voice was hushed and urgent. "None of those women meant anything close to what you mean to me."

Sarah really hoped he wasn't going to kiss her. She knew that she had agreed to that and more, but she wasn't ready for it. She wasn't ready to be romanced, even by Prince Charming. "You mean what I mean to your ambition."

"No, I don't." His frustrated breath blew across her face. "I love you. I know you don't want to hear that, but it's true. I wish you could believe it."

"I believe that you believe it." Her tone wasn't unkind, but she pulled back leaving him awkwardly holding the piping bag over the plate. Sarah busied herself straightening the ingredients on the table. "But your love is tangled up with your belief in this weird prophecy, and it's taken everything that I care most about from me."

James looked like he wanted to argue the point, to push her more but he must have decided that arguing further wasn't wise. He silently went back to filling the eggs. When he had done the rest of them straightened up. "There."

In the time it took him to fill the eggs, Sarah was able to collect herself and calm her nerves. Looking at the plate, some of the eggs were fuller than others. She could see moving across the plate where he had gotten the hang of it. "Not bad. Now a little sprinkle of paprika on top of these and we can taste."

"How are you sleeping?" He asked seemingly out of the blue.

She glanced at him. "Do I look tired?"

"You look beautiful." He brushed a stray curl out of her face. "I just worry about you."

'But not enough to let me go.' She couldn't help thinking. "I sleep...okay."

He watched her as if he were trying to decide whether he believed her or not. "I think perhaps you should take a break from the wedding preparations. Do something that's normal for you."

She turned away so that he couldn't see the effect those words had on her. She wanted so badly to do something normal but didn't dare. If she let in little bits of her old life, she was afraid that would make her new life even more intolerable. She set the paprika on the table. "Work was normal for me, my work."

"You had friends." James prodded. "You could invite them over here or to go to a friend's flat. Do something for yourself."

It sounded so good, so tempting. She missed Jujhar and Isla. Even more so her friends back home. But like work, she was afraid that if she spent time with them, it would make coming back to this world so much harder. "I'll think about it."

"Excellent. Now, let me taste one of these eggs."

She shouldn't have been surprised when Jujhar showed up the next day for tea. They had made pleasant conversation about his training with Lyall Green and the team's activities. Sarah had vented some of her frustration with Lady Anne, and her new life to him. Jujhar had as he often did, comforted her just by being near and given her encouragement to speak up for herself. It was good to have a friend, and when he left, she had made a note to invite him over again soon and to thank James for inviting him.

CHAPTER THIRTY-SEVEN

Sarah sat in the chair in front of Tony's portable makeup mirror in the dining room and tried to relax. She closed her eyes and took a deep breath. Her morning had been beyond trying. As if she wasn't anxious enough about the planned television interview, they were taping that day, Lady Anne had been worrying her about every little thing under the sun. In typical Lady Anne fashion, Sarah's breakfast had been ordered for her before she came into the room, tea not coffee, no sugar, no milk, half a grapefruit and a hardboiled egg. No toast, not even plain toast and definitely no bacon, sausage, black pudding or anything else remotely tasty.

Sarah had eaten the egg thanking her lucky starts she was at least allowed salt and pepper and picked at her grapefruit while Lady Anne briefed her for the hundredth time about how important this interview was and what she could and couldn't say about her relationship with James, her upbringing in North Carolina, and their future plans. Sarah had heard it all before ad nauseum.

Sarah thought that maybe it was a good thing she wasn't eating much. Her stomach was already in knots, and too much food would probably make her sick. She took some consolation in imagining a scenario where her nerves got the better of her and she vomited her meager breakfast right onto Lady Anne's Lagerfeld suit.

"That smile looks full of secrets." Tony held a makeup sponge loaded with foundation inches from her cheek. "Anything you want to share."

Sarah chuckled. "Not on your life."

"Alright." He tipped her face up with a finger under her chin and began applying the foundation. "But I'll just have to make up my own stories about what has you smiling like that."

"I can guarantee, you won't come anywhere close." Sarah told him.

Felicia Banks came bustling in followed by Lady Anne. "Good. You got the dress that Gillian sent over."

Sarah had put on the butter yellow knee length dress printed with tiny sprigs of lavender flowers that had arrived the day before. It had a high scoop neck and cap sleeves. It was paired with an amethyst pendant in the shape of a thistle on a silver chain. It looked elegant and conservative, very royal.

Lady Anne eyed the skirt that was visible under the small smock that Tony had put on Sarah to keep it clean while he worked. "I still think a suit would have been better. Make her look formidable."

Felicia shook her head. "No, ingenue is a much better fit for this situation. We want Sarah to appear approachable, and sweet. They'll stop calling her a heart breaker when we show them she has a heart of her own."

"Thank you, Felicia." Sarah exchanged a look of solidarity with the woman she had once thought her rival for Dermot's affections. She was glad that Felicia was there to help with the image management. She softened many of Lady Anne's dictatorial impulses.

Lady Anne seemed to resign herself to being overruled on the dress and moved on to reviewing Sarah's comportment lessons. "Yes, well at least we can fix that. The hillbilly part seems stuck in."

"Don't worry. I promise to wear shoes and not talk about raising chickens or making moonshine." Despite Mrs. Lippincott's best efforts and Sarah's occasional dialect practice, Sarah had decided that there was nothing wrong with her accent and refused to temper it. This seemed to bother Lady Anne to no end.

Lady Anne's only response to that comment was a raised eyebrow. "Remember to keep your shoulders back and still. You have a tendency to move them when you talk."

"Mmhmm." Sarah bit her tongue as Tony applied blush to her cheeks.

"Keep your knees together and only cross your ankles, never your legs." Lady Anne went on with her litany of admonishments. "This isn't the time for sitting cross legged as you often do."

Either Lady Anne's own nerves were prompting her to lash out or she thought Sarah was some kind of imbecile. Sarah hoped her tongue wouldn't be bloody from biting it by the time she got to the actual interview. She quietly seethed as Tony worked on her eyebrows.

"Don't cross your arms in front of yourself, but you can link your hands in your lap as long as you don't fidget..."

Sarah closed her eyes so that Tony could apply liner and tuned Anne out. When Tony tapped her cheek twice, his signal to open her eyes, she opened them to find him smiling with encouragement. He began applying liner under her eyes. Sarah gave him a crooked smile and drawing on all her hillbilly roots, she said, "Yes, ma'am," with a twang guaranteed to annoy her future mother-in-law.

Lady Anne's lip curled in disdain. "Have you learned nothing from your dialect lessons?"

"Oh, I learned plenty." Sarah kept her voice low, but her tone was biting. In truth, Sarah liked Mrs. Lippincott and didn't want her to get in trouble. But Sarah was also sick to death of Anne's constant efforts to improve her. "I think most of all, I learned that it doesn't matter a bit what the accent is if what I'm saying isn't genuine."

"What does that mean?" Lady Anne snapped.

Sarah looked around Tony who paused in applying her makeup. "It means that I'll be a lot more confident and convincing in this interview if I'm being myself."

"No!" Lady Anne looked horrified. "You will be the future Countess of Caledon. Sooner or later, you will have to start behaving like it."

Tony turned back to Sarah to resume his task, but she stopped him with an up-raised hand. She slowly rose out of her chair. "You know, you and your people have gone to great lengths to convince me that only I would do for your son. You've sent emissaries and thrown parties. We've..." She cast a glance at Felicia, Tony and Gillian and thought better about detailing some of the more esoteric methods that had gotten them to this point. "...done tests and consulted spiritual advisers, all to determine that James and I would be best for each other. And don't even get me started on your brother-in-law. Even after all that, I'm not good enough for you."

Felicia made frantic hand motions to her team and began to hustle them out of the room before the argument went further. Sarah went on ticking things off on her finger, "I'm too American, too casual, too bookish, too country when the real problem is that I'm NOT too impressed with you."

"Em. Not to interrupt," Felicia stood in the doorway. "But I do want to remind you that a camera crew and journalist are down the hall."

"Yes, this is not the time." Lady Anne looked down her nose imperiously.

"Oh, no." Sarah snapped, keeping her volume low. Felicia backed out the door softly. "This is the perfect time. Because, I've had it up to my eyeballs with your attempts to fit me into your mold."

***

"I have four men making sure the television crew doesn't stray from their designated area in the drawing room." Dermot told James as the latter descended the stairs.

"Well done." James gave him a megawatt smile. "How do I look?"

Dermot scanned him up and down. His clothes were casual, but there wasn't a wrinkle in sight or a hair out of place. "Ye'll do."

"I'll take that as approval." James gave him a friendly clap on the shoulder as if they were a couple of mates meeting up for a pint not Lord Caledon and employee. "Where is Sarah?"

"Still in makeup in the dining room. She should be done in a minute." Dermot had checked in with Fleming a moment ago. He was supposed to escort Sarah to the drawing room when the time was right. "Which means I should make myself scarce."

James pressed his lips together, frustration apparent. "You two will have to get used to being around each other eventually."

Dermot muttered. "We're exes. It's been a couple of months, but it's still fresh enough to hurt for both of us."

James didn't say anything to that. He simply shook his head and sighed. A small commotion from the direction of the dining room caught their attention. James looked down the hallway first. Dermot prepared to get out of the way fast in case Sarah came down the hall. But James signaled for him to follow. Dermot tentatively fell into step behind James who was already halfway to the dining room.

They found Felicia standing in front of the closed dining room door, her head was turned to the side and she was obviously listening. Her stylist and makeup artist leaned toward the door also listening. They straightened and backed away as soon as they caught sight of James coming toward them.

"What's going on?" He demanded.

Felicia kept her voice low. "Sarah and Lady Anne are having words."

For the first time, Dermot noted a Southern accented voice coming from the other side of the door. He and James exchanged a look of blended curiosity and dread as they leaned closer to listen.

***

"I have tolerated you telling me what to wear, how to sit and stand, what to eat. I went to your dialect coach and practiced softening my R's and sharpening my T's and enunciating every consonant." Sarah rounded the end of the table approaching Lady Anne. "But the thing is, I knew how to do that stuff before. I learned it singing in choirs in college. There's nothing wrong with my accent. Just like there's nothing wrong with my education, or my figure, or my attitude."

"There are ways these things are done." Lady Anne seethed. "There are standards."

"And there is a reason why you need me." Sarah pointed to herself. "Not one of his boarding school classmates, not some socialite who already knows the standards, not even my sister. Me. You seem to forget that I'm the one your ridiculous prophecy foretold. I'm the one your son has fallen in love with. And I'm the one who is going to be Lady Caledon in a couple of weeks. You, Lady Anne, are inconsequential."

"So, you can clutch your pearls and look down your man-made nose at me, but I suggest you do it from over there." Sarah jerked her chin toward the far corner of the room. "I'm going to do this interview as myself, not some dressed up fairy princess doll you ordered from Harrods. And if you don't like that, you are welcome to retire back to Spain, or Tweedholm or whatever dusty cupboard you crawled out of."

"Are you finished?" Anne seethed.

"No, mother. I think you are. At least for now." James's voice interrupted them. Both women turned to see him standing in the doorway. Never had Sarah imagined that a polo shirt and khakis could have looked like a suit of armor, but at that moment he seemed like a knight come to rescue her from their resident dragon.

He closed the door behind him shutting out the image team who were still huddled wide-eyed in the hallway waiting to get back to work. As soon as the latch clicked Anne started, "Darling, you would not believe the way this…" She waved a hand at Sarah.

James didn't let her finish. "I heard every word. And I have to agree with Sarah. While you are right that there are standards and conventions, she was chosen for a reason." He glanced at Sarah and took her hand. "What you see as informal and provincial about Sarah can be a great asset to us. People love her because she listens to them. It's what her previous career was all about and it can work to our advantage now that she is on our team. We are going to need the public on our side, and she can get us that. They just need to see the real Sarah."

"I am only looking out for your interests." Anne pleaded.

"Now that we are engaged, Sarah's wellbeing is one of my interests. If she's unhappy, then that needs to be remedied." His tone was patient, but it was clear he would brook no dissent. "Perhaps after the television crew leaves today, you and father should spend the rest of the week at Tweedholm. The peace and quiet of the country might do you some good."

Anne inhaled nostrils flaring, and Sarah thought for a second that she would push back on his suggestion. She must have decided that discretion was the better part of valor. "If you think that's best, son."

"I do." He gave Sarah's hand a secret squeeze. "Now, Felicia and her team need to finish their work so that we can get on with this interview. Can you send them in?"

Dismissed, Lady Anne walked silent and stiff-backed to the door.

Tony, Gillian, and Felicia came back in. Sarah tried to return to Tony's chair, but James didn't let go of her hand.

She turned back to him not sure what to expect. He wouldn't scold her for talking to his mother that way in front of the staff, but she also wasn't sure that his show of support was genuine.

He took a step closer to her. His eyes were shining with something that looked a lot like admiration. "I'd better get this in before they put your lipstick on." He nudged her face up with a knuckle under her chin and kissed her. Since their engagement had been announced he hadn't pushed her into any sort of physical relationship, for which Sarah was grateful. Even though she knew she should prepare herself for that, she wasn't sure she was ready for it yet. He pulled back with a crooked smile that reminded her entirely too much of Dermot before saying. "Welcome back."

***

Part of Dermot wanted to crow at Sarah's set-down of Anne Stuart. That was a confrontation that was long overdue. Maybe the Stuarts hadn't bought Sarah off entirely. That flash of temper showed that there was something left of the woman he'd fallen in love with, even if she wasn't his. On the other hand, Sarah standing up to claim her role in the Stuart plans was a step further away from him. James standing up for her only strengthened them as a team. He wasn't sure how he felt about that.

Dermot's initial fury at Sarah's choice of James had mellowed into a mix of disappointment, worry and yearning over the weeks since she'd made her choice. He couldn't be angry with her anymore. She had done what she thought she had to do. Since then, he had only caught glimpses of her, usually at a distance. She seemed to have transformed into Lady Anne's paper doll idea of a princess. The last time he'd seen her, he hadn't recognized the woman that he thought he knew. Today's outburst showed him she was still there, and he couldn't help the hope that bloomed in his chest as he heard the twang of her true accent, and the flash of her temper.

He couldn't seem to make himself move from that spot. He wanted to see her. A few moments later, Fleming arrived. He gave Dermot a nod and a smile before going into the dining room to tell them it was time.

Dermot quickly positioned himself against the wall as the door swung open. Fleming emerged blocking the hallway between Dermot and the couple with his body and ushering James and Sarah out. Sarah stepped into the hallway looking fresh as a summer wind. Her dress was the color of soft sunlight. Her curls were tamed, but not too tamed. Luckily, she didn't turn his way. He didn't want her to see him there, to see the longing he was sure was written on his face.

Placing a hand at the small of her back, James led her down the hall. Fleming followed and they were joined in the foyer by another bodyguard. Dermot let out the breath that he'd been holding. They turned toward the drawing room and he watched as Sarah and James shook hands with the interviewer, Miranda Taylor. Then the drawing room door was closed, and he was left standing there in the shadows.

CHAPTER THIRTY-EIGHT

"He took over his father's title and the family business at the tender age of twenty-six. That might not be unheard of in many families, but this title is Lord Caledon, and the family business is the UK's largest oil company. A vast fortune combined with matinee idol looks have made James Stuart a tabloid darling. His exploits and rumored romances have been fodder for the gossip pages since he was a university student." Images of James partying on a yacht in the Mediterranean, or Ibiza, or London clubs were interspersed with those of him beside half a dozen different women.

Dermot seethed.

Miranda Taylor's voice went on as the photos of James changed to those of James and Sarah from March that had sparked the countrywide hunt for the mystery woman. "All of that changed this past winter when James Stuart's much talked about social life ground to a halt. It seemed that a mystery woman had tamed Scotland's favorite playboy."

A groan escaped Dermot as he turned toward his kitchen. "Do we have to watch this?"

"Well, it is part of my job." Felicia told him as she carried two plates of takeaway pad thai to his small living room from the kitchen. "I have to know how they edited it all together."

Dermot took the plate she offered him and settled onto the couch to watch. He wasn't sure he should, but Felicia was right. It was part of their job to know in real time how the interview appeared to the public. He didn't think it would cause any additional security concerns for James, but it might for Sarah. It was the most public thing she had done since announcing their engagement and had the potential to draw out anyone who meant her ill.

"She did incredibly well, in the room. I think that row with Lady Anne beforehand gave her a confidence boost." Felicia lowered herself to sit beside him on the couch.

"Let's begin at the beginning. How did the two of you meet?" Miranda's voice was morning show cheerful as they shifted from a montage of tabloid photos and video clips to a footage of James and Sarah seated in the drawing room at his home.

Sarah and James shared a look as if deciding which one of them should tell the story. James started it. "I was in the States on business last fall and thought to swing down to North Carolina to drop in on an old friend. We were catching up when his colleague, Sarah, knocked on his door asking him when he was going to come out and enjoy the good weather. I was immediately smitten. She was like no one else I'd ever met."

"And you, Sarah. Were you smitten?"

The camera shifted to Sarah who regarded James with a playful smile before responding. "I can't say that I was. I mean, sure I thought he was good looking. Who wouldn't?" She held a hand out toward James as if he were exhibit A. "But I had no idea who he was."

Miranda leaned forward, her voice going up in surprise. "You didn't know?"

Sarah shrugged. "Well, James isn't as much of a target for tabloids in America, and I don't read them anyway. I'm a bit of a workaholic. I don't pay attention to celebrity gossip. My roommate had to tell me who he was."

"I actually found it quite refreshing." James put in. "I don't often get the chance to be anonymous. It let me get to know her in a way that would have been very difficult here, as later events proved."

"Mmm," Miranda made a noise of agreement. "That was less than a year ago. Things seem to have progressed quickly."

James smiled at Sarah, his eyes full of affection. "Well, it did for me. She took some convincing."

Sarah looked sheepish. "That had nothing to do with James. I was applying for the fellowship with Scots Preservation and I didn't want it said that I got it because I was seeing James. I prefer to earn things on my own merits. At the time I was only worried about the gossip in academic circles. Little did I know that just knowing James would generate so much attention."

Miranda nodded knowingly. "It has that. Is that why you chose to keep the relationship secret?"

James laid his hand over Sarah's where it rested on her knee and gave it a squeeze. "That was one reason, yes. It's difficult to romance a woman when you're constantly worried about photographers and gossip columns. I knew, I still know that people will love her as much as I do once they know her. But I wanted to protect her from that kind of scrutiny for as long as I could. And she had professional concerns. She knew that it would be hard for her to do the work that she has dedicated her life to if she was being followed around by paparazzi."

Sarah tensed slightly when Miranda turned to her. No one who didn't know her would have noticed it, but Dermot could tell by the set of her jaw that she was expecting to be grilled about the disastrous end of their research trip. He wondered how much she would reveal.

"And that proved to be the case when you were on your research trip through the Highlands. That's where you disappeared for three days."

"Yes." Sarah nodded stiffly. "I knew as soon as I saw that first photo that our trip was going to have to end. I tried to disguise myself in various ways to look different so people wouldn't recognize me, but eventually someone did."

"I don't think Lochinver has seen that much excitement in some time." Miranda joked.

"I feel terrible about the furor that created. I had never experienced that kind of attention. I'm from a small town and have kept a relatively low profile. That was unreal. The photographers started showing up in the village and within a few hours it was overrun. We sent part of our team out as a decoy, and then Dermot, Jujhar, and I left by another route." She cleared her throat nervously and turned the hand under James's over and laced their fingers together. *"Still, they found us. One car in particular chased us at high speed and bumped into us causing us to run off the road and flip the car that we were in. Fortunately, there were only minor injuries."*

"What about the other car? Did they not stop?" Miranda's face was full of concern.

"They did." Sarah looked up, blinking rapidly. "A man got out and came up to the car, and took pictures of it, of us."

"She's brilliant." Felicia's voice was full of admiration. "We didn't spend much time rehearsing answers on the accident, but she'll gain some sympathy there."

Dermot's brows drew together. He knew PR was Felicia's job, but there was more to Sarah's recounting of the story than gaining sympathy. It had been terrifying to see her hiding in the brush at the roadside while he was trapped in the car unable to defend her. "Ye do know I was in that car, right?"

"Of course." She tapped his knee with the back of the hand that held her fork and gave him a sweet smile. "I'm so glad you're alright."

Of course, he didn't tell Felicia that the man had intentionally run them off the road or that it had been a gun and not a camera that he had pointed at them. He certainly wouldn't tell her that he'd left the man's bloody corpse in a cave a few miles from the crash site.

"How did you get out?" Miranda asked breathlessly.

Sarah smiled remembering. "A good Samaritan who luckily is involved with Mountain Rescue was driving by and stopped to help. It's amazing that he saw the car. It was on its side and down an embankment. We were incredibly lucky."

"Does this good Samaritan have a name?" The reporter asked.

Sarah smiled and shook her head. "He would prefer to remain anonymous. I wouldn't want to repay his kindness by drawing unwanted attention."

"I did try to reward him." James added. "But he refused. He said it was what any good citizen would have done."

Sarah spoke up. "Which, I should add, has been my experience since coming to Scotland. With the obvious exception of the photographers who chased us, everyone that I've met has been so helpful. There is a real community spirit here that I very much value. I've fallen in love with the country as much as I have with James."

"Oh, that's good." Felicia nodded her approval.

Dermot thought he was going to be sick. He put his plate down.

"Of course, I made a sizable donation to Highland Mountain Rescue in response to his kindness." James added before turning an adoring look on Sarah. "I don't know what I would have done if Sarah hadn't come back to me."

Sarah met his look with one of her own and for a moment they just regarded each other.

"That's the look." Felicia pointed a fork toward the screen with enthusiasm. "There's a whole romance novel in that look. The public is going to eat that up."

A romance novel was not what Dermot was seeing in that look. From James, he saw gratitude for Sarah choosing him. From Sarah he saw something much harder to explain. She looked at James as if he were her lifeline in a storm-tossed sea. She was trapped and she knew it, but James was stuck too, and if they were stuck together maybe it wouldn't be so bad.

Miranda interrupted their silent exchange, her voice soft. "And now you've had to take a step back from your work haven't you, Sarah?"

Sarah cleared her throat and looked at their joined hands in her lap for a second. "Yes, I have. As I mentioned before, it's difficult to interview people about old stories and songs when most of the attention is on you. It's not conducive to getting people to share their own stories. But the Scots Preservation team is still hard at work. This summer, they'll be touring through the northern Highlands. I believe they are planning to renew their efforts next spring in Argyle. They've been busy."

"You've been working on your doctoral thesis. Is that something that you expect to continue?"

"I don't know." Sarah looked regretful. "I am focused on preserving and protecting Gaelic culture, and Scots culture. I definitely see myself being active in support of that. Whether that includes finishing my degree still remains to be seen. I would certainly like to, but as we've seen fieldwork is difficult at the moment."

"I understand you speak Gaelic fluently." Miranda looked impressed.

"Tha. Gu dearbh." Sarah brightened. "My grandmother was from Assynt. She called it the 'language of her heart'. We always spoke it at home, which I can tell you in our little town in North Carolina was very unusual."

"It's not the only thing that's unusual about your upbringing." Miranda leaned back into her chair seeming to

settle into the topic. "Can you tell us more about where you grew up and what life was like?"

Sarah took a deep breath and looked somewhere off camera. "It may seem unusual to a lot of people, but apart from speaking a different language, it wasn't that strange for where we lived. I grew up on a farm in the mountains. We were poor, but there was a lot that we managed to get from the land. We foraged and fished and hunted."

"Goodness! Yours sounds like a literal Cinderella story." Miranda enthused.

Sarah gave a little half-nod in agreement, her lips curled into a secret smile. "There is a certain fairy tale aspect to it."

Miranda cocked her head to the side. "Is it true that your grandmother supplemented her income by distilling liquor?"

Sarah raised an eyebrow at that and bristled a little. "You must have a source in Kettle Holler." She smiled showing that she wasn't embarrassed by that information. "Yes, my grandmother distilled illegal whisky. In the States, we would call her a moonshiner. And that didn't supplement our income. It was our main income. My grandmother was very resourceful and did the best she could with the skills she brought with her when she left Scotland. She was well known in the mountains for her whisky and her home remedies."

"And it was your grandmother who raised you. Your mother died when you were a young girl."

"I was six years old."

'That must have been difficult for you."

Sarah blinked rapidly and cleared her throat. James squeezed her hand, and she laid her other hand on top of his. "It was. Yes, I was old enough to have memories of her, of us together. But young enough for her to have missed a lot of *milestones in my life where a girl might look to her mother for guidance. My grandmother did the best that she could, but I still missed my mother."*

"My family has made her very welcome." James put in giving Sarah's hand a squeeze. "My parents adore Sarah."

Felicia almost choked on a mouthful of noodles. "You didn't see Lady Anne when Sarah started in on her this morning."

"I can imagine." Dermot had caught the sharp side of both Lady Anne and Sarah's tempers.

"Don't get me wrong. Lady Anne deserved every bit of that and more. She's been hounding Sarah about every little thing since the engagement was announced. I'm glad our girl finally woke up. And just in time too."

Just in time. Dermot's stomach sank. Sarah 'waking up' as Felicia put it was a sign. She was settling into her new role with James. She was getting her fight back, the fight that had kept her going through her mother's illness and death, the fight that had led her to build a life when everyone she loved was gone, the fight she'd shown after Ryan Cumberland had tried to kill her. He should be relieved. She was coming back to herself, but she was sitting next to James. And he was watching from across town.

"Does it bother you when the papers call you the Hillbilly Heartbreaker?" Miranda asked tentatively.

Sarah laughed softly shaking her head. "It's a pretty ridiculous name for someone like me. I am the most boring so-called heartbreaker ever. When I'm not doing fieldwork, I spend most of my time in the library. I'm not sure who could imagine that I would set out to snare anyone, much less someone like James." She smirked. "I guess they got the hillbilly part right, but not much else."

"If anything, she almost broke my heart." James added with a longing look at Sarah who cocked her head at him in question. "After the incident with the photographers in the Highlands, I almost lost her. She didn't want a life in the spotlight, and who can blame her with all that's been made up about her over the last couple of months. Between that and her career, she's giving up a lot to be with me." James looked at Sarah, their eyes holding. "I can only hope to be worthy of the sacrifice she's made."

CHAPTER THIRTY-NINE

August

"Good afternoon, Seonag." Sarah sat down next to Seonag Sinclair in the lounge area on her floor of the care home.

"Good afternoon, lass." Seonag smiled brightly at her as she usually did. Whether Seonag remembered her from one visit to the next, Sarah didn't know. But Dermot's mother always seemed happy to have a visitor.

"I've brought you some yarn." Sarah handed the small bag that Jujhar had brought her. Sarah had been ordering yarn for Seonag for weeks now but hadn't been able to shop for the yarn herself. This time she had gotten Jujhar to do the shopping for her. The result was a merino and cashmere blend that was soft enough for a baby. Sarah couldn't wait to give it to Seonag.

The older woman reached into the bag, her face lighting up in surprise as she pulled out the skein of blue yarn. "Oh! That is soft."

"I thought you would like it." Sarah patted Seonag's knee. "It'll make a nice scarf."

"And a wonderful color." Seonag rubbed the yarn with her thumb as Sarah had seen her do many times before. "Thank ye so much, lass."

"You're very welcome. I can't wait to see what you make with it." Sarah told her. "How have you been this week?"

"Not bad. It's been warm. We've been outside to the courtyard when the weather is fine. I thought to read one of my books, but I keep losing my page."

"Have you tried dog-earing the page?" Sarah asked.

"I did, but then when I go back it doesn't seem like the right page." Seonag made a frustrated face.

They'd had this conversation a couple of times before with varying results. At least today, Seonag didn't seem upset by her inability to remember her place in a book. Sarah thought short stories that she could read in one sitting might be better and made a note to look for a collection. "Shall I read to you? Where is your book?"

"I think it's in my room. Dinna leave, though." Seonag reached for Sarah's hand. "Tell me a story."

Sarah gave Seonag's hand a squeeze to show her she wasn't leaving. "You asked the right girl. I know a lot of stories. What sort of story are you in the mood for; funny, sad, epic?"

"A love story." Seonag turned her face to the window.

"A love story…" Of course, she would ask for the one kind of story that Sarah didn't want to think about. She tried to think of a love story that ended happily, one that wasn't full of tragedy, but that's just not how most legends work. In the end she lit on one that Seonag would be familiar with hoping that that familiarity might bring some comfort. She relaxed against the back of the chair, keeping Seonag's hand in hers.

"Iseult was a princess of Ireland. She was young and fair. Her beauty was spoken of far and wide."

Seonag leaned her head against the back of her chair settling in to listen, a soft smile on her face.

Sarah watched her, her heart both full and breaking. In the weeks she'd been visiting Seonag, she had gotten to know Dermot's mother more. On her good days, Seonag was sharp-witted and fiercely intelligent. Sarah saw where Dermot had gotten his sense of humor. And on her bad days, she had seen where his quick temper and dogged tenacity came from. She had started visiting Seonag out of concern, but her visits had become a much-needed respite from the wedding buzz. She watched Seonag as she went on telling the story, her voice smooth and rhythmic. "Because her father was a powerful king, he was owed tribute by a number of lesser kings, including King Mark of Kernow. King Mark's father before him had pledged tribute, but Mark had refused to pay for years. So, her father sent her uncle to collect three hundred young men and three hundred young women from Mark to bring back to Ireland. King Mark refused to provide the tribute. Her uncle, Morholt, decided to allow Mark to choose a champion. If this champion could defeat him in single combat, then Kernow would not have to pay.

"The lords and knights of Kernow were very much afraid to challenge Morholt because his skill in combat was well known. But there was one, Mark's nephew Tristan volunteered to be their champion. The battle took place and was hard fought on both sides. In the end Morholt's body was returned to Ireland with a piece of Tristan's sword still embedded in his skull. Their sorrow was great. Not only had they lost her uncle, but they had also lost the tribute.

"One day weeks later, Iseult was walking along the coast and she came upon a boat that had washed up on the tide.

There was nothing in the boat but a man with a festering wound in his hip. He was unconscious and she thought that surely, he would die. She called her mother the queen who knew something about healing. They took the man into their castle and treated his wound."

"When the man recovered, he told them his name was Tantris and that he was a minstrel. To thank them for their care, Tantris entertained them with songs and stories. He taught many of these songs, and how to play them on the harp to Iseult." Sarah couldn't help recalling the times that she had worked with Dermot transcribing and recording old songs and stories. She swallowed past a lump in her throat.

"In time," She had to pause, breathe, and try not to betray the memories that were blending with the story. "The two fell in love. But because he was a minstrel and she was a princess, they could not marry. So Tantris told Iseult that he would have to leave, because eventually she would marry, and he didn't want to have to see her married to another man. Iseult was heartbroken," Sarah hated that her voice was cracking. Why did she pick this story? "But she resigned herself to her future."

"Some time later a dragon began plaguing Ireland. It ate their livestock and destroyed their crops. Most of their efforts to kill or drive off the dragon were frustrated. In desperation, Iseult's father declared that he would give her in marriage to whoever could kill it. Many tried and failed in pursuit of the dragon, and of Iseult's hand. Word traveled across the sea of the King's challenge. Then the king's steward appeared at court carrying the head of the dragon, and the King betrothed Iseult to the steward.

"But Iseult doubted the man, because he was not known for his prowess in battle, nor at hunting. She and her mother examined the head of the dragon and realized that it was missing its tongue. They went in search of the beast's tongue and found Tantris unconscious with the dragon's tongue tucked into his clothes. Iseult was overjoyed that her love had defeated the dragon and earned her hand." Sarah felt a tear slip down her cheek.

"But her joy didn't last long, because as they were carrying Tantris back to the castle to heal his wounds, she discovered that his sword was missing a piece, a piece that matched the piece that was found in her uncle Morholt's head. That was when she realized that Tantris was actually Tristan, the champion of Kernow who had slain her uncle. Iseult was furious and she tried to strike Tristan with his own sword but found that she couldn't do it. He awoke and convinced her to spare him.

"When it was revealed to the king that Tristan and not his steward had slain the dragon, he announced that Tristan had won the hand of Iseult. But Tristan had not come on his own behalf. He'd been sent by King Mark to gain the hand of Iseult as Queen of Kernow. Again, Iseult was robbed of being with her love, and again she felt deceived that Tristan had claimed her not for himself but for Mark. Still, it was Iseult's duty to abide by her father's decree. King Mark was growing more powerful and if they didn't honor the agreement, he might invade." Sarah cleared her throat, trying to stave off the tears. "Her people could be slaughtered."

***

"Her people could be slaughtered." The words hit Dermot like bullets. The crack in her voice showing how keenly she'd felt them. He should have known. She wouldn't have thrown him over so easily, not for money, not for security. She had been ready to give all of that up before. How had he let himself be convinced that she'd given up on him?

He sank into a chair behind where Sarah and his mother sat. He had suspected when James told him about Sarah's Wednesday afternoon activities that this would be where he would find her. She was the one who had been bringing his mother yarn, and visiting with her, not one of his old teachers as his mother had told him one day. He had to remind himself that Sarah wasn't his anymore.

She sniffed and went on with the story. "Tristan and an angry heartbroken Iseult set sail for Kernow. Before they left, Iseult's mother in sympathy for her daughter's plight gave her maid a love potion to give to Iseult and Mark on their wedding night so that they would love each other and be happy. But on the journey, the maid accidentally gave the potion to Iseult and Tristan. Their love for each other was renewed, and consummated. But when they landed in Kernow, they were still bound by their positions and Iseult was forced to marry King Mark."

She closed her eyes and wiped a tear off her cheek. His gut twisted. He'd been so caught up in wondering who he was and who his father was that he'd forgotten who she was. He'd let his jealousy of James blind him to what was happening to her. He leaned forward in his seat and listened closely as she went on.

"Iseult couldn't bring herself to stay away from Tristan, and they continued to meet in secret in an orchard near

Mark's castle. One day, they fell asleep in the orchard with Tristan's sword between them. Mark came upon them while they slept. Because he loved them both, he could not strike either of them down. So, he replaced Tristan's sword with his own. When the lovers woke and discovered Mark's sword between them, they knew that they had been caught and that they'd been offered amnesty."

"Upon returning to the castle, they reconciled with Mark. However, Tristan agreed that he could not stay at court and stay away from Iseult. So, he decided to make his own home in Brittany."

"And they both died broken hearted." His mother murmured. It was a story Seonag knew well.

Sarah cleared her throat. "Yes, after some treachery on the part of Tristan's eventual wife. I knew you would know that story."

Seonag laughed. "There are very few from that time that I don't know. You don't often hear it from Iseult's perspective."

"Well, they were all written down by monks when that one was committed to paper. I can't imagine they cared much about the woman's perspective." Sarah's tone was wry.

"Mmm…" Seonag leaned back in her chair as if deep in thought. "Perhaps we should rewrite them."

"Maybe we should." Sarah gave Seonag's hand a squeeze. "I'm afraid I have to go now. I'll want to see what you do with that yarn next time."

"It's been lovely, lass. Thank you again." Seonag grinned at her.

Sarah kissed his mother's cheek and stood to go. When she stepped around the chair and lifted her head, she saw him.

Sarah froze muscles tense, and the color drained from her face.

She took a couple of steps in his direction. When he realized that she was planning to walk by him, he gripped her upper arm and pulled her out of the lounge and into the hall right past Fleming, who conveniently looked the other way.

"How long were you listening?" She asked as he searched for a private place where they could talk.

"Long enough." Dermot hustled her into his mother's room. He released her arm and closed the door behind them. "Who was it?"

"Who was what?" She asked not meeting his eyes.

"Come on, Sarah. Who threatened ye?" He watched her closely.

"Do you want a list?" She snapped.

"I want ye to look at me.'" He softened his voice. When she finally lifted her eyes to meet his. "Who threatened ye to choose James?"

She shook her head. "Not me. You, and her." She looked back in the direction of the lounge where his mother sat. "And Duff, and Amy, Barrett, Rab and Ruaraidh…anyone that I care about."

"Walter." He spat. It shouldn't have been a surprise. "God damnit!"

Sarah pressed her lips together and waited for him to rein in his temper.

"I should have known. I should have known it was something like that." He looked up to find her sagging against the wall. She looked deflated, as if the secret she'd been keeping inside was all that had been holding her up. "Oh God! What have I done to ye?"

He took her face in his hands, his eyes searching hers. "I should have had more faith in you." He told her before taking her mouth, tasting the tears that were streaming down her face. "I've been so caught up in my own head about James and my mother and how we're related that I didna look deep enough at what was happening to you. Ye should have told me."

"I was trying to protect you." She sobbed.

"I'm sorry. I'm so sorry, love. I should have known." He said between kisses.

Sarah's lips met his eagerly. Her hands caressed his face. They devoured each other. Minutes later, she pulled away, pressing her forehead into his chest. "It doesn't matter."

"Why didn't ye tell me?"

Sarah started to speak, and thought better, then finally. "He would have killed you if I had or you would have killed him and damn the consequences. I was protecting you. But it doesn't matter why."

"It matters to me." He tilted her face up until she met his eyes. "I thought ye chose him. Like everyone else in my life has chosen James, has put him above me for as long as I can remember. Hell, I'm starting to think the whole reason I was born was to play second to James."

She threw her arms around his waist resting her ear over his heart. "I'm so sorry. I thought it would be easier for you if you blamed me." He pulled back from her and gave her a half-grin. "That didna work when I tried it on you, did it?"

She rolled her eyes before her brows knit together. "What did you mean about the reason you were born?"

"Something Green told me." Dermot looked past her to where a picture of him as a little boy stood on his mother's bureau. "He's my grandfather."

"Lyall Green is your grandfather?" He could see the puzzle pieces shifting in her mind.

"Aye, that was my reaction too. She was his apprentice, until she started researching the Stuarts and your people in his library. Then she left him and went to Henry. They'd been friends at university. She offered to help him."

"So is Henry your father?"

He shook his head. "He says not, but James and I took DNA tests to find out our relationship. We're waiting for results."

"Have you tried asking your mother?" Her tone suggested she knew that was a long shot.

"She says she doesna know. Whether that's because of her memory or she never knew, I canna tell. How could she not know though?"

Sarah raised her eyebrows and tilted her head. "I can think of a few ways."

He looked surprised at her for a second, then his mind flicked through a number of scenarios where a woman might not know, drunken hook-up, multiple partners in a short time, assault. "Right. In any case we're not likely to know. It could still be weeks for the test results."

"That'll be interesting." Sarah tilted her head in thought. "But that's actually not what I meant about it not mattering. I meant that it doesn't change anything. It doesn't make Walter any less of a threat or me less engaged to James."

"We can figure something out. I know we can." He gripped her shoulders. "Give me a chance."

"Dermot, the wedding is less than two weeks away."

"Then I need to get to work." His mind was already spinning with possibilities.

Sarah shook her head. "There is no way that we can protect everyone from Walter in that time and get away. I love you, but there is too much at stake."

"I'm going to figure something out." He would not allow doubt.

"I have to get back. Fleming is probably losing it in the lounge." She laid a hand over his heart. "I love you. Please be careful."

He gave her one brief, fierce kiss before she slipped out the door.

***

"Speak of the devil." Sarah muttered as they pulled up to the house to find Walter Stuart's car in the drive. She was still reeling from the conversation with Dermot and wondering if it could still be possible to get away.

"Sorry?" Fleming asked from the front seat.

"Nothing. Don't mind me." Sarah waved off his concern.

As was their routine. She waited for Fleming to get out and open the door. He helped her from the car and walked her to the door. As they approached, the door swung open to reveal James waiting in the front hall. His smile was dazzling, and he opened his arms to her. "There you are."

Sarah glanced at her watch before stepping close for an embrace. "You're home early."

"My uncle has brought you the most wonderful wedding surprise and I wanted to be here when you see it." He greeted her with a kiss on each cheek.

"I can't imagine he would have—"

"Sweetmeat!" A familiar voice practically screamed from the direction of the drawing room behind her. Sarah froze in horror trying not to show just how disastrous this surprise was.

She whirled around to see not only her friend Barrett Markham, but also Amy Monroe rushing out into the hall. She quickly tried to paste on a smile for them. "Oh my gosh! I thought y'all couldn't come to the wedding."

"Are you kidding? We wouldn't miss it." Amy threw her arms around Sarah hugging her tightly.

"I mean, we weren't going to be able to because of the cost, but James's uncle fixed that little problem." Barrett hugged her, and Sarah had to fight back tears. She was so torn between joy at seeing her friends again, and horror at seeing them unwittingly in the clutches of Walter Stuart. She was also sure her friends would take one good look at her face and know that she was miserable.

Over Barrett's shoulder, she spotted a very smug-looking Walter standing in the drawing room doorway his bespoke suit showing nary a wrinkle. "I thought you would appreciate having your friends with you on your wedding day."

"How very thoughtful of you." Smiling, her eyes shot daggers in his direction. She wanted to scream, to tell her friends to run far and fast away from this nightmare. When Amy released her, she turned back to James and Barrett. "I hope y'all haven't been waiting for me long."

"Nah." Amy hooked an arm around Sarah's and started pulling her toward the drawing room. "Our flight just got in an hour ago." She leaned closer and whispered casting a glance over Sarah's shoulder toward the security guards by the front door, "Is Fleming your bodyguard now?"

Sarah knew that look. There was more to Amy's question than idle curiosity. "Mmhmm."

Amy hmm'd trying to look innocent.

"So, I guess you've both met James by now." Sarah settled onto the couch.

Barrett waved a hand toward James who sat next to him. Amy sat next to Sarah on the opposite side of the coffee table. "Oh yeah. We're like old friends now."

"Well, I hope you haven't told him too many embarrassing stories." Sarah looked around to find Walter Stuart taking his own seat in a wing-back chair off to the side. "So, Uncle Walter just came to Chapel Hill and picked you up?"

Amy and Barrett exchanged a look before Amy explained. "Well. He did call us a few days ago. He said he was going to be in the Research Triangle and offered to bring us back with him for the wedding.

"I was worried about missing work, but managed to get the time off, and thanks to Mr. Stuart we don't have to worry about rent this month." Barrett added.

Sarah blinked in surprise before looking over at Walter. "Wow. That really is generous."

"It's nothing compared to yours and my nephew's happiness." The smile he gave her looked predatory.

James shook his head, smiling. "I honestly don't know why I didn't think of it."

"So," Amy gave her an eager look. "Let's hear about these wedding plans."

They talked for the rest of the afternoon about everything from wedding plans to weather. Walter Stuart left them just before dinner saying he would leave the young people to their fun. No doubt, he felt thoroughly satisfied with the implied threat he'd made by bringing them here.

The four of them chatted their way through dinner with Amy peppering James unabashedly with questions about places he'd been and people he knew. James seemed eager to get to know her friends, which Sarah had to give him credit for. Their relationship certainly didn't depend on whether her friends who lived an ocean away liked him. But he seemed to be doing his best to charm them, or maybe he just charmed everyone out of habit.

By midnight, they'd gone through several bottles of wine. Barrett was regaling James with a story about a production of Jesus Christ Superstar that he'd been in, which Sarah thought was a little ironic given James's supposed lineage.

Amy flopped down beside Sarah on the couch. Sarah threw an arm around her friend and Amy snuggled into her side. "Are you sure you've forgiven me?"

"Of course," She tightened her arm around her friend. "Are you sure you've forgiven me?"

"You shouldn't even have to ask. I was one hundred percent in the wrong." Amy put the emphasis on the percentage.

"I went too far snooping on Ryan."

"If he was a normal guy, maybe. But he was stalking you and I refused to see it." Amy admitted before nodding toward James. "This guy on the other hand…"

"He's alright." Sarah watched James lean his head back laughing in genuine amusement at something Barrett said.

"I'm still not clear on what happened with Dermot." Amy's voice took on a note of concern.

Sarah shifted settling further into the couch. Part of her wondered if she could just melt into the furniture to avoid talking with Amy or Barrett about her seemingly inexplicable relationship whiplash. "It just…wasn't working. You know we both have quick tempers, and it ended up being an unhealthy combination."

Amy lifted her head and looked at Sarah, who held her breath waiting for her friend to call her on that bit of bullshit. "I guess it's lucky you had Hottie MacMoneybags waiting in the wings, huh?"

"I don't know if I would call it lucky." Sarah muttered "I probably would have given James a pass too if it hadn't been for the tabloids. Once they started chasing me, it didn't matter if I wasn't in a relationship with James. That was the story they had. So, I came to James for help dealing with them."

"And that's when the spark happened?" Amy looked back at James and Barrett who now bent their heads close together as if sharing a secret.

Sarah watched them too trying to think of how to answer Amy's question. Was there a spark between her and James? She liked James. He was certainly sexy enough, but he wasn't Dermot. "Yeah."

"How about his folks? I thought they would be here." Amy's voice was getting softer as she spoke.

"They're at Tweedholm, their country house."

Amy put on an exaggerated accent. "Tweedholm. Eh?"

"Yes, James suggested they go there to give us some space before the wedding."

Amy nodded slowly showing that she understood. "So, not great with the parents?"

"His father is easy enough to get along with." Sarah brushed Amy's hair back where it had fallen in front of her eyes. "His mother and I are coming to an understanding."

"Oh," Amy yawned expansively. She pushed herself away from Sarah. "I am wiped out. Jet lag is no joke. I think I'm going to hit the hay and sleep for a week."

Sarah chuckled. "Okay, I'll wake you up when it's time for the wedding."

"Bear, come on. Let's give the lovebirds time to say goodnight." Amy stood and waved Barrett in the direction of the door.

Barrett came to stand in front of Sarah and leaned down close to her and whispered. "He's okay. I expected him to be a spoiled douche, but he's not bad."

"Well, that's a ringing endorsement." Sarah grinned at him.

Barrett kissed her on the forehead and rested his forehead against hers. Sarah could feel him swaying from the wine and jet lag. "Night, baby girl."

"Night, honey."

He stood and threw his arm around Amy's shoulder. The two of them made their way carefully out of the room.

"I like your friends." James sat on the coffee table in front of her. Sarah was surprised at how relaxed he seemed. Maybe it was the wine, maybe the company, maybe the lack of pressure from his family for the evening. "I don't think I've ever met two more unpretentious people."

Sarah had no doubt that Walter had brought Amy and Barrett there to prevent her from getting cold feet. If she had needed a reminder of the threats that had made her choose James, this was an effective one. She only hoped that he wouldn't find it necessary to use any more of her people to remind her. "I think you've been hanging out with the wrong people."

He looked over her shoulder where they could still hear Amy and Barrett talking as they made their way upstairs. "Maybe you're right."

CHAPTER FORTY

"There you are." Jujhar approached Dermot on the darkened street.

"Good. Ye're here." Dermot turned toward the warehouse where Des had moved his workshop. "It's this way."

Jujhar glanced over his shoulder behind them before falling into step with Dermot. "Why are we here? I was sure those blokes on the corner were going to assault me."

Dermot shrugged. "It's just as likely they'll be in our meeting."

"Meeting with who?" His voice betrayed his nerves. "You said this was about Sarah."

"It is. The people we're meeting are going to help us get her out of here." He kept his voice low, although the street was deserted.

"How do you know these people?" Jujhar's brows knit in doubt. "And do you trust them?"

"One of them is an old friend, and yes. I trust him."

Dermot stopped at a recessed door in the middle of a long and high brick wall. He rapped his knuckles on the door twice paused and then three times just as Des had told him to. He'd half expected his old mate to give him a password, or to outright refuse to help. Especially as this time he didn't have the money to pay for Desmond's services.

The door opened. Dermot saw nothing but darkness beyond it. He thought about calling out but didn't want to draw any more attention.

"Are you sure about this?" Jujhar whispered from behind him.

"Dinna have much choice." He stepped into the darkness. Jujhar followed, and as soon as they cleared the door, a small flame flared to life. Its faint glow revealed just enough of the face of the person holding it for Dermot to make him out. "Is all this necessary."

"It's been rough going since the last time I saw ye, mate. I had to move my whole operation, and this is the result." Des cocked his head to the side. "It seems the authorities got a hold of my handiwork and have been looking for a master forger."

Dermot had been afraid that would happen when A. P. Security confiscated the passport Des had made for him. "Sorry."

Des shrugged. "Nae bother. It would be flattering if it weren't so bloody inconvenient." He tilted his head to the right. "It's this way."

They followed Des lit by the tiny flame of his Zippo lighter further into the warehouse. They'd gone about twenty steps when Des asked. "Who's yer friend?"

"Ah, sorry." Dermot glanced back at Jujhar. "This is Jujhar. We can trust him."

Des stopped and turned bringing the light closer to Jujhar so that he could get a look at him. His tone went serious. "Ye canna tell anyone about this. I might have a soft spot for Dermot over there, but I'm not a man ye want to cross."

Jujhar surprised Dermot by arching one black eyebrow and smirking. But then Jujhar had spent the last few months studying with Lyall Green. It seemed that studying under the old wise man had lent his friend some extra confidence. "You would be mistaken to think I scare easily. I've kept bigger secrets than yours."

Des's eyes went wide in surprise and he grinned. He looked at Dermot. "I think I like this one."

Des led them to an alcove at the far end of the building, which contained an iron staircase that went down into a huge basement that was nearly as dark as the floor above. Tucked into a corner and lit by bare bulbs and computer screens was Des's workshop and three people Dermot didn't know. They were talking amongst themselves, but went silent when Des, Dermot and Jujhar approached.

"Feet off the table, Miles." Des groused swatting a rough looking man's feet off of a worktable. A disgruntled look crossed the man's long pockmarked face as he shifted on his stool. "Right, lads, this is my mate Dermot, and his pal Jujhar. We're going to be helping them out. Nothing we say in here goes further than these walls. Ye got that?"

The three grunted or nodded their agreement before Des went on. "That's Miles." Des tilted his chin toward the man who had his feet on the table. "He's going to help with coms. Ye'd never ken it to look at him, but he's the best radio man I know."

Dermot and Jujhar nodded greetings at Miles, who gave them a once over and seemed to find them wanting.

"That clarty bastard over there is Brody, jack-of-all-trades." Despite the late hour, Brody appeared to have just rolled out of bed. His brown hair showed a couple of cowlicks and what looked like an HP sauce stain on the overstretched collar of his gray sweatshirt. Patchy stubble showed on his round face.

"And Black Douglas over there is our muscle." Dermot looked up expecting to see a club bouncer-sized man. Instead, a petite woman stepped out of the shadows. Her loose-fitting black clothes made her look like a teenage boy, but her jet black hair was pulled back severely into a ponytail at the nape of her neck. The only thing that hinted at her role was a small scar that cut through one eyebrow. Her only acknowledgment of the introduction was to meet Dermot's eyes, her mouth pressed into a firm line.

Dermot recognized the coiled power in her stance. He also couldn't miss the nickname Des gave her. The Black Douglas was a famously ruthless warrior in the wars of independence. He was said to have beheaded and burned the entire English garrison who had captured his family home at Douglas Castle. Before being driven from the castle again, he had destroyed all the provisions and poisoned the well. "Black Douglas, eh?"

Des spoke up. "Dinna let her size fool ye. She's like us but tougher."

Dermot took 'like us' to mean former Army, which made her stance seem more appropriate. "What did ye do in the Army?"

"Personnel extraction." She deadpanned.

Dermot pulled back in surprise. Black Douglas might have exactly the skill set they needed. "Right then. Shall we?"

"These three are my need-to-know crew. If we need any other support, we'll keep them in the dark. Ye can trust them. The floor is yours, mate." Des waved toward a couple of folding chairs. Jujhar pulled one closer to the table where Miles and Brody were sitting.

Dermot stayed on his feet. "Is everyone familiar with Alba Petroleum?"

The team looked bored. Dermot went on. "Well, we're going to liberate the CEO's fiancée."

Miles choked off a laugh, while the other two raised their eyebrows in interest. Dermot went on. "Her name is Sarah MacAlpin. She's basically a prisoner in James Stuart's house. The challenge is that she's surrounded by A. P. Security staff most of the time."

"So, we're extracting the princess from the tower." Douglas spoke up. "How do you know she doesn't want to marry Prince Charming?"

"Because until a couple of months ago, she wanted to marry me." Dermot gritted his teeth. "And because I've just discovered that the Stuarts gained her agreement to marry James by threatening people that she cares about, me included."

Des shook his head. "Wait, aren't you working for A. P. Security now?"

"I am on James's personal security detail." Dermot stepped closer to the table. Which means that I know their procedures and I can get inside information on Sarah's movements."

Miles leaned forward looking confused. "Wait. He steals yer lass and then hires ye to protect him?"

"We're old friends." Dermot explained, but when that answer didn't seem to satisfy, "It's complicated."

"Yer right about that, mate." Miles leaned back in his stool again and went to prop his feet on the table, but Des stopped him with a look.

"Let's focus on what we're working with rather than the why of it, eh?" Dermot sent them all a quelling look. "Des, do ye have something we can draw this out on?"

Des got up and walked toward the shadows behind a rack of shelves that held various kinds of paper and printers. He returned sliding a large whiteboard on a stand in front of him. He positioned it near Dermot.

"Cheers." Dermot picked up a marker and started to draw out all the people they needed to warn, protect or move. The group set about gaming out ideas.

After about an hour Jujhar stood back looking at the board. "Well, that solves the question of everyone else, but all of this is moot if we can't get Sarah away from the Stuarts."

"He's right." Douglas leaned a hip on the worktable and looked around at the group. "If we can't get her out of the house, it would take a small army to extract her. Even outside the house with the bodyguards, it's going to take careful planning and a team."

"You're forgetting something." The voice came from the dark beyond Des's work area. Dermot's shoulders sank as he realized who it was.

Miles and Brody leapt from their chairs as the whole group turned to see who had managed to find them in the warehouse basement. Dermot shot a questioning look at Jujhar who shook his head, as if to say, 'I didn't tell him.'

Lyall Green stepped out of the dark into the pool of light where they were all standing. As usual, he looked serenely confident and polished, as if he'd walked out of his tailor's straight into Des's workshop. "You are talking about transporting one of the most recognizable faces in the country just now. Everyone saw Sarah MacAlpin's interview, and there was already one reward offered for her safe return. Surely the reward for a fiancée will be even higher than the reward for a friend."

"That's why we have to get her out of the country before anyone has a chance to look for her." Dermot gave Des a sour look.

"My card Mr. Thomson." Green extended his arm, a business card held between two fingers like a magician performing a trick.

Des took the card and read it. Snapping his fingers, he looked back up at Green. "Ye handled my cousin Art's estate."

"Yes, I did." Green nodded at the board. "I might be representing yours as well if you persist with this plan."

"Well, we're certainly open to suggestions." Des waved at the board in invitation.

Green stepped in front of the board and turned to address the group. "I suggest you stop. Go back to your lives and forget everything you've heard here today."

Dermot felt his temper start to boil. "Ye know good and well that Sarah doesn't want this. Ye know Walter is holding her hostage."

"I do. And I also know that Walter Stuart is a powerful enemy with resources that you cannot compete with and no compunction about using them in ways that aren't entirely legal. You know that, or does your knee not still hurt when it rains?" His grandfather's eyes went to his knee and Dermot felt a twinge, just a hint of the old injury.

"My knee is healed." Dermot took a step toward Green. "And ye know just how that happened."

Green raised an eyebrow in warning, as if reminding Dermot not to talk about the cauldron among the uninitiated. "I do know that. But you know what Walter Stuart can do. I worry for you, and your..." He cast a look around the group his eyes settled on Jujhar. "...friends. I am especially disappointed in you, Mr. Gurudat. I thought you understood our role."

Jujhar looked down at his hands, obviously affected by Green's words. "I do understand. But when the end result is the same, why should the players be unhappy. Sarah would not be in her position if she hadn't been coerced. She is sacrificing her career, her independence, and her happiness for the safety of her family. You know it doesn't have to be that way."

"That is what leaders do." Green's tone was patient. "Her sacrifice only demonstrates that she is worthy of the role she's been given."

Jujhar shook his head. His usually placid brown eyes sparked. "Her willingness to sacrifice makes her worthy. But the actuality of it will mean that the end will not be. A child raised in misery, surrounded only by ambition and privilege, in a home without love will not become the leader you are looking for."

"I have seen it." Green hissed, stepping closer to Jujhar. "The outcome is the same."

Jujhar met Green and lowered his voice so that Dermot barely heard him. "Perhaps your solitary existence has blinded you to the importance of familial love. But I come from a large family full of women and I know that when they are not happy, it makes a difference. The material facts may be the same with either path, but there is more to making a leader than that."

Green's eyes went to Dermot, who wondered if Green was thinking about his own child, and the difference a happy home had made for her, or for her son. Dermot still wasn't sure about his mother's motives or choices, but he knew she loved him. After a moment studying his grandson, Green addressed Dermot. "I will not stop you. I owe you that. But you must think long and hard about what you are proposing. All of you should. You're on a dangerous path."

With that Green turned and walked off into the dark. He seemed to melt into the blackness. Des snapped his fingers at Miles and Douglas. The three of them went off into the dark in different directions. Jujhar came closer to Dermot and whispered. "I did not say a word to him."

"I'm sure you didn't." Dermot let his shoulders sag. "He has his ways."

"I wish he would help us." Jujhar looked in disappointment in the direction where his mentor had disappeared.

"He's watched me my whole life and never helped me before." Dermot muttered bitterly. "I dinna know why he would start now."

"I canna figure out where he went." Des came striding back into the lighted area.

"It's like he disappeared." Douglas came into the light from the other direction. Miles soon returned as well, but just shook his head confounded.

Dermot sighed. "Now that ye've had a warning from the ever-helpful Lyall Green, ye're welcome to back out, but I will expect discretion. If a word of this meeting gets back to the Stuarts, I promise ye, Walter Stuart isna the only one ye'll have to worry about."

Brody was the first to speak up, which surprised Dermot as he'd been quiet up until then. "If I'm honest, I was feeling a bit meh on the whole thing. But now that I've been told not to do it, I'm definitely in."

"Aye, I quite like the idea of getting one over on Prince Charming." Miles grinned, his eyes sparkling with mischief. "We only have to worry about our safety if we're caught. I havena been nicked yet."

"I'm in." Was all Douglas said.

"There ye have it!" Des threw an arm around Dermot's shoulders. "The old Double-D ride again. I'll get to work on identities for everyone who needs them. You need to find a way to get her out of the house."

***

Sarah, Amy, and Barrett sank into comfortable chairs for tea. They had been making a day of shopping for wedding outfits for Amy and Barrett with the help of Sarah's personal shopper. The benefit of letting Lady Anne handle most of the wedding preparations was that Sarah could sit back and enjoy having her friends around. As long as she could keep them distracted with a private tour of the city and visits to the few sites, she could go without attracting too much attention, she could avoid talking about anything too serious or letting them examine her relationship with James too closely.

Amy reached for one of Ratcliffe's delectable cream scones. "I could get used to this."

"The personal shopping or the baked goodies?" Barrett relaxed into his chair after taking a couple of finger sandwiches from the tray.

"Both." Amy broke off a bite-sized corner of her scone and popped it into her mouth, closing her eyes to savor it. "James doesn't have a brother hidden around here somewhere does he?"

Sarah nearly choked on her Darjeeling. She sat forward coughing into her napkin.

Barrett patted her on the back, and Amy looked concerned. "What did I say?"

"Nothing." Sarah struggled to get the coughing under control. "Anyway, what do you think we should do tomorrow?"

"Bachelorette party?" Barrett arched an eyebrow.

"They call them hen parties here, and I'm sure there would be endless logistics and security concerns involved with that." Sarah explained. "Also, paparazzi. Since I've just managed to get them to stop calling me the Hillbilly Heartbreaker. I don't think that's a good idea."

Barrett giggled. "I know you hate it, but I love that nickname."

Sarah nudged his foot with hers. "You would."

Amy glanced toward the edge of the patio where Fleming Sinclair stood keeping an eye on the canal and the side entrance to the garden. "I don't know that I would mind taking the security team along."

"Stop harassing my security team." Sarah teased.

"It's not the whole security team," Barrett cut his eyes to where Fleming stood. "Just that one. They had a moment in Chapel Hill after you skipped town."

Sarah arched an eyebrow at Amy. "That explains so much."

"I just want a code name like yours." Amy joked. "Thistle."

"What would your security code name be?" Barrett asked around a bite of sandwich.

Amy looked off into the distance in thought. "Honeysuckle?"

"Too long." Sarah quipped.

"Fine. Barrett, what's yours?" Amy tossed a grape in his direction.

Barrett caught the grape and popped it in his mouth. "Adonis."

Both girls snorted with laughter. Sarah shook her head. "More like Jester."

Barrett laughed with them. "I'll take it."

Sarah hadn't laughed this much in months. She might hate Walter Stuart and his machinations, but it was good to have her friends around. She felt more like herself than she had in too long.

A throat cleared between their table and the door. "Miss MacAlpin."

Sarah turned to see Mr. Conley, the butler standing near the door. At first, Conley had looked down his nose at Sarah, much the way that Lady Anne did. But with some well-placed kindness and empathy, Sarah had started to win him over. "Yes, Mr. Conley."

He smiled a little. "There is a rather large delivery for you. I believe it is a wedding gift. I've had security open it and told them to place it in your sitting room."

Sarah hoped this wasn't another of Walter's reminders. "Is it a person?"

Conley looked confused but glanced at Amy and Barrett before saying. "No."

"Thank you, Mr. Conley. I'll see to it in a moment."

"Very well, ma'am." He nodded and retreated into the house.

"Wonder what it could be." Barrett's eyes went wide over the rim of his teacup.

"Knowing these people, it could be anything from a pony to a Porsche."

"Well, now I can't wait." Amy put her cup and saucer on the table.

Sarah rolled her eyes. "Okay. Let's find out."

In Sarah's sitting room, they found an enormous, framed painting leaning against the wall. Amy went in first. Her jaw dropped. "Holy cow!"

Barrett stood at a distance studying the painting. "Is this an Oona Ballantyne portrait?"

Sarah looked sharply at him. "How do you know Oona Ballantyne?"

"Y'all might be into folk art, but I like to keep up with the finer things." Barrett dismissed her curiosity with a wave, though he didn't take his eyes off the painting. "This chick is an up-and-comer. I read about her in a magazine. She had a show in London a few months ago of portraits of just random people she met, from street people to businessmen. But her portraits go deep. She shows how someone looks on the outside and their inner selves. He placed a hand over his heart. "There was one of a homeless man, but in these warm colors and hinted at his longing for his family, I couldn't stop looking at it. Her portraits are starting to be in high demand, although she interviews subjects and refuses more clients than she takes."

"That doesn't surprise me." Sarah stood back to take in the whole image. It was a portrait of her with the matching pool. She was dressed in a saffron yellow sheath dress, like the one she'd worn for the matching ceremony. Unlike that day, this Sarah looked like a warrior. Muscle and sinew were defined in her arms, her features were sharp, and her gaze fierce and challenging. She held a large book in one hand like a shield and in the other hand she held a knife. She looked directly at the viewer, green eyes peering into anyone who dared to look.

Her hair was a riot of golden curls blown up by wind to blend and tangle with the branches of a huge tree that loomed over the pool. The trunk of the tree forked above Sarah's head, the branches on one side were covered with green and blue leaves, while the other side was in flames, the charred black branches looking skeletal in contrast. On closer inspection, there were faces hidden in the flames and in the leaves. They were only a shade or two off from the color around them, so they were faint, but there were dozens of them crowded together, some overlapping. Sarah recognized some of them including that of Rachel, Oona's girlfriend. On a hillside in the background, a stag stood, his antlers spearing the sky in front of a rising sun.

"Hey, Bear. This one looks like you." Amy pointed to a face hidden in the leaves of the live side of the tree.

Barrett leaned closer and whispered. "How is that even possible?"

At Sarah's feet in the painting was the pool, and there were faces in that too. They were upside down, as if reflecting the world above the surface of the water. These, Sarah recognized easily including the one of Oona herself, and Maili, Rab and the rest of their unusual family. There was even one that looked like her grandmother. Sarah was speechless, and tears welled in her eyes. Oona had used her gift to create this. It was a testament to the power that they both had within them.

"Did you sit for this?" Barrett asked breathlessly.

"No." Sarah didn't take her eyes off the painting. "I met Oona a couple of months ago."

"This is amazing." Amy's tone was hushed. "Everywhere I look there's some new piece of the story."

Amy was right. The painting was so full of subtle images that Sarah struggled to take it all in. The more she looked at it, the more faces emerged. Hours later, when everyone had gone, Sarah found herself still staring at the painting.

The next morning, when she walked out of her bedroom with her hair still damp from the shower, it was the first thing she saw. The sun was streaming through the window and struck the painting from a different angle, and Sarah noticed something she hadn't before. Hidden in the patterns of the bark of the tree behind her was the figure of a man. It was so subtle that Sarah hadn't noticed it in all the time she'd studied the painting the day before. She drew closer, her eyes scanning the faint shapes over her shoulder until she found the face.

She should have noticed before. She'd looked at those lines so many times, the sharp line of his nose the cut of his jaw, and deep-set eyes. Oona had painted Dermot in the bark of the tree, like a bulwark at her back, her champion. Oona had seen Sarah's truth, and maybe Dermot's too.

CHAPTER FORTY-ONE

Still shaken by the by the discovery of Dermot in the painting, Sarah entered the breakfast room to find Barrett buttering a piece of toast. She poured herself a cup of coffee, and toast took a seat.

Barrett picked up his own coffee. "You just missed James." Sarah glanced at the clock. "He hasn't left for the office yet, has he. That seems early."

"I think he went upstairs."

"Did I just see Dermot waiting in the front hall?" Amy came in wearing a confused look.

"Probably." Sarah tried not to look interested. A couple of days ago she would have felt miserable that he was so nearby and yet inaccessible. But now her heart leapt with excitement. "He's James's bodyguard."

Both of her friends stopped what they were doing and stared at her slack jawed. Amy managed to ask. "Are you serious?"

Sarah shrugged. "He was James's bodyguard before he went back to school, and he's gone back to it. They grew up together and James trusts him."

Barrett blinked in astonishment. "You people are weird."

'You have no idea.' Sarah thought to herself remembering the three sisters who led her people. She pushed back from the table. "Excuse me, I want to say goodbye to James before he leaves for work."

***

He had a feeling that Sarah would come out of the dining room when he'd seen Amy pass by. He was glad James had told him that Amy and Barrett were here otherwise he might have betrayed his surprise and frankly terror at seeing them. The Machiavelli of the Mound had struck again with that threat disguised as kindness.

He'd thought about nothing but her since he saw her at the care home with his mother. He'd spent the last few days conferring with Des and some of his less than savory friends gaming out possibilities for an escape that would get them and their families away from the Stuarts. Walter's gesture of bringing Sarah's friends to Scotland threw a wrench into their plans. Not that their plans would amount to anything. Sarah had been clear the other day that she didn't want to put any of the people they cared about at risk. He doubted her mind would have changed now. If anything, she would be more afraid of Walter than before.

He glanced at his watch wondering how long he had before they left for the office. Conley had told him that James had gone upstairs for something.

Sarah emerged from the dining room and closed the door behind her. She came straight to where he was standing by the front door. Her body language was stiff and formal as if she didn't want to hint that they had reconciled. She cut a look at him and tilted her head toward the hallway that led to James's study.

He waited a good thirty seconds before he followed her. A few feet into the hallway, he heard her clear her throat. He found her in the powder room. As soon as he closed the door, she turned on the tap before whispering. "Still think you can get me out of here?"

"We've been working on a plan." He whispered back.

"Who's we?"

"Des and his crew, and Jujhar."

"Jujhar?" She seemed surprised.

"He agrees that yer happiness is more important than James's position. He's willing to help us."

"Does Green know?"

"He's not happy about it, but I dinna think he'll talk. He has no more love for Walter than we do."

"And do you trust Des and his people?" She looked doubtful.

"I trust Des," He wasn't sure about the rest, but didn't need to tell her that. "He didn't sell us out when there was a reward and the whole country was looking for us."

"And you think that will hold true this time?" She hissed.

"I've been to war with Des. I trust him." He hoped she understood. He took her hand. "Does that mean ye're thinking about it?"

Sarah looked down at their joined hands before her eyes came back to his. She squared her shoulders, and he recognized the fire he'd seen in her before. She'd been missing that spark for a while. "If you have a plan, I'm in."

"We should be able to get you away, if we can get ye past the security detail." Dermot had been wracking his brain trying to figure that out. "We need a distraction, preferably out of this house."

She paused tapping his arm absently. "I might have just the thing. Amy and Barrett were asking about a hen night."

"And ye think Mark Shaw will agree to that?" He had his doubts.

"He will if the order comes from the boss." She nodded with confidence.

"Ye think ye can get James to let ye out on the town?" He stifled a laugh.

Sarah cocked an eyebrow at him. "We've been getting closer."

Dermot couldn't help the low growl that came from his throat. "Aye, I heard all about yer cooking lessons."

Sarah raised an eyebrow at him. "And by closer, I mean I think he's starting to trust me more. He definitely seems interested in making me happy, and we might be able to use that."

He wasn't sure he liked the sound of that. "What d'ye have in mind?"

"If I can convince James to allow a hen night, then that would be a good time to get away." Her eyes were intense with calculation. "What about Walter's hostages?"

"We've already made a plan to move my mother to another facility under a different name." He told her. "We can do it the same night."

"If someone can get a warning to Duff, he'll be in the wind before Walter even knows. I've been keeping my distance from the Ballantynes ever since the Highlands, trying to make Walter believe that they're not the leverage he thought they'd be."

"Probably wise." He conceded. "What about Amy and Barrett?"

"I can work on that. I'll figure something out." She looked unsure, but he could tell she was already thinking of ideas.

They heard voices coming from the front hall. "That's probably James."

She turned toward the door, but he stopped her putting his hand on it. "Are ye sure ye want to do this?"

"No," She shook her head and sighed. She leaned closer lowering her voice even further. "But if I don't, Walter Stuart will own me, own all of us. I don't know a lot about my gift or this prophecy, but I'm reasonably sure that my people didn't spend all this effort and time to become a wholly owned subsidiary of Alba Petroleum."

He pulled her to him for a quick and intense kiss. "I love you."

She closed her eyes and smiled savoring the moment. "I love you too."

He turned off the tap and mouthed. "You go. I'll be there in a tic."

She straightened her shoulders before slipping out the door. Dermot counted to sixty before following her. In the front hall, Sarah was making a show of seeing James off to work. James was eating it up.

Dermot took a position by the door to wait for James who cast a glance his way before turning back to Sarah and saying. "I'm not sure a hen party is a good idea."

Sarah straightened his tie letting her hands linger on his chest. "I understand your concern. It's just," She sighed and looked up at James shyly from under her lashes. He was glad she'd never tried those flirty tricks on him. He wouldn't have been able to deny her anything. "You encouraged me once to enjoy the city. I haven't really had a chance to do that, and now my friends are here. I want to show them something besides your garden and the back entrance to Harvey Nichols."

James looked at her for a moment, his brows drawn together in thought. "I'll have to think about that, and I'll ask Shaw if it's feasible."

Sarah beamed at him and leaned closer. "That's all I ask."

"I'll see you this afternoon."

A week ago, he would have been eaten up with jealousy, but knowing that she was willing to leave with him made seeing them together much easier. Now, when James pulled her in for a kiss, Dermot didn't grind his teeth and fight the urge to tear them apart. Now, he had hope.

***

"Have you thought about what you want to do for your hen night?" Amy's eyes met Sarah's in the mirror of her walk-in closet which was big enough for all of them to work and relax. Per Lady Anne's wishes, the designer of the dress was a big secret to be revealed on the wedding day. Of course, he was Scottish, and the dress was created just for Sarah. It was a strapless confection of multi-layered sheer fabric in white, silver and the palest blue with a riot of silver thistles and white Scots roses appliqued on the top.

Sarah fingered the sheer silver fringe of a thistle at her waist. The designer's assistant who had brought the dress for fitting tugged at a loose sweep of white tulle over Sarah's hip and pinned it under the edge of the bodice. Sarah glanced up at Amy's reflection. "I wouldn't get too excited. James hasn't agreed to it yet. He only said he would ask his security chief."

"Don't you feel like a prisoner with all this security?" Barrett muttered as he lounged on a nearby ottoman. He leaned his head back against the edge of a rack of ridiculously expensive shoes that Sarah hated wearing. "I mean this seems like overkill."

Sarah winced as the seamstress, Gina stuck her hip with a pin. Gina apologized nervously. Sarah waved her apology off saying, "It happens. No big deal." Before answering Barrett. "Well, if we were just worried about photographers it might be overkill, but there have been some threats."

"What kind of threats?" Amy stopped flipping through a magazine and looked at Sarah in the mirror concerned.

Sarah had to tread carefully. Amy didn't need to be reminded of Ryan Cumberland who had duped her into letting him get close to Sarah before he tried to kill her. It still amazed Sarah that it had only been eight months ago. She also didn't want to reveal about the Invigilare, or the Circle. That would be a much longer conversation. Amy and Barrett would never believe her if she told them all about her people and the prophecy or worse, they would and they would get themselves killed trying to get her away from there. She hated lying to them, but it was for their protection. "Just some obsessed fans of James."

"Do oil executives have fans?" Barrett looked both affronted and doubtful.

"They do when they look like James and have royal connections." Amy answered. "I showed you those tabloids. James is the most eligible bachelor in the UK. No doubt some folks are jealous."

"I'm not going to get my hopes up about a hen night." Sarah watched Gina adjust another layer of tulle. "But if we are able to do it, I'll have to call my friend Isla. She's a musician so she's usually plugged in to the nightlife scene. She could tell us the best place to go."

"Is this the one that was on the research team?" Amy asked.

"Yep. Y'all are going to love her." Sarah remembered what a welcome companion Isla had been when she and Amy hadn't been speaking.

Gina stood back examining the overall look of the dress. She took a few steps around Sarah making sure the dress looked right from every angle. Eventually, she nodded. "That should do it. You can take it off now."

"I'm relieved to see that you've been keeping up with the wedding preparations." Lady Anne's voice came from the doorway making Sarah tense immediately. She heard the in-drawn breaths of her friends and Gina.

"Of course. I think you'll find that once certain pressures are relieved, I'm more than capable." Sarah eyed Lady Anne in the mirror. There was no mistaking the tension, but her tone was friendly. She went to greet Lady Anne with air kisses near her cheeks. "I hope you had a nice relaxing time in the country."

Sarah could tell Anne was seething at the subtle reminder that she'd been sent to Tweedholm by her own son. Anne's red lips parted in a smile that was all teeth and no mirth. "It was lovely. The gardens are always so beautiful this time of year. Very restful. I'm more than ready for the final wedding push."

That last sentence came with a smile but sounded like a threat to Sarah. Fortunately, Sarah's recent successes had her feeling more confident, and thanks to Walter she had reinforcements. "Let me introduce you to my friends. Amy Monroe, Barrett Markham, this is James's mother, Lady Anne Sinclair. Countess of Caledon."

Lady Anne pasted a welcoming smile on her face, but Sarah could see the muscles in her neck twitching with the effort not to stick her nose in the air. Amy did her mother's etiquette lessons proud with a carefully polite greeting. Barrett's greeting was polite enough, but he took the opportunity to step closer to Sarah. The protective gesture was clear.

Anne studied the three of them together. She seemed to decide they had everything in hand. "Well, I believe I'll go and help Henry get settled before tea. You seem to have this in order."

Anne cast one more look around the room before leaving. When she was out of earshot, Barrett meowed like an angry cat, and Amy turned to Sarah. "You might be born for this aristocrat thing after all. Butter would not melt in your mouth."

Gina who was putting away her pins behind them stifled a laugh. Sarah glance back at her and they shared a smile before Gina offered. "Let me help you get that off."

Barrett turned his back to the ladies so that Sarah could change out of her dress. "Are we in a cold war with that gorgon or is it a hot one?"

Sarah chuckled. "Oh, I'm not worried about her." Sarah scoffed. "Eventually, she'll go back to Spain or Tweedholm. James has already made it clear what he and I are willing to tolerate. Lady Anne will just have to get used to it."

"Bless her heart." Amy muttered in a tone that was far from kind.

An hour later, they were sitting in the parlor with Lady Anne and Henry who was doing his best to be charming. He asked Amy and Barret all the appropriate questions to show mild interest in Sarah's friends. They had commented on how much they were enjoying Scotland. An open-ended invitation was made for them to visit the country house some time in the future. They were descending into stilted silence when James arrived looking dashing and excited.

He made a beeline for Sarah taking a seat next to her on the couch. "Good news. Shaw thinks we can manage a hen night. Would Thursday night work?"

"Thursday sounds fine." Sarah was drowned out by an exclamation from Lady Anne.

"A hen night?" Anne looked horrified.

"Hello, mother." James spared her a nod before turning back to Sarah. "Of course, wherever you choose will have to be reviewed for security, but he thinks it can be managed as long as you stay in one place. He can't manage a pub crawl."

"I'm sure we can find a place." Sarah assured him. "I'll check with some friends to see what's going on this week. I would love for Amy and Barrett to see some local musicians."

"James, are you sure that's wise?" Lady Anne interrupted. Sarah thought that was progress. A few weeks ago, Anne would have thought that she could lay down the law.

James turned to his mother. "If the security can be managed, I'm not concerned about anything else."

"We'll discuss it." Anne cast a look at Amy and Barrett as if to say, 'not in front of the guests'.

James cocked his head and gave his mother a level look. "I don't feel the need for that."

Lady Anne leaned back in her seat clearly put in her place. She looked off toward the window and took a tense sip of tea to cover her feelings.

Sarah caught Barrett and Amy's eyes before turning back to James, "We'll pick a place this evening and then we can tell Shaw to start his review." She gave his hand a squeeze. "I really appreciate this."

James grinned at her. "I told you before, I will dedicate myself to your happiness."

CHAPTER FORTY-TWO

Dermot watched Anne and Henry leave the parlor and go upstairs. Anne looked fit to burst, and Dermot had no doubt that she was holding in a tirade that poor Henry would have to listen to as soon as they were behind closed doors. Dermot kept to his position by the door. He was waiting for confirmation from James that the hen night was on for Thursday, and he was hoping to get a moment with Sarah.

He had called Des the night before telling him about Sarah's idea. Des had known exactly where they should go. In the course of his business, Des had experience smuggling items into almost every pub in town. They had formulated a plan in the hopes that Shaw would allow the hen night. Dermot had offered his own encouragement when James had mentioned it to him. Now he needed to tell Sarah the plan.

They'd already gotten Douglas hired by A. P. Security. Her military experience had made her attractive to the managers at A. P. Security. She was currently guarding the corporate offices. But Dermot would put in a word that there should be a woman on the hen night team so that Sarah would be able to go to the ladies' toilets without having a man follow her.

After a few minutes, Sarah came out into the hall. Dermot only had time to catch her eye and nod before James followed her. Sarah looked at him and gave her head an almost imperceptible tilt toward the garden as James wrapped an arm around her waist and steered her toward the stairs that descended to the ballroom and out to the garden.

Before they left the ballroom, James turned back his way. "Oh, Dermot. I won't be going out again this evening. You're free to go."

Dismissed. "Cheers."

He watched them walk away, each playing their parts. If Sarah didn't look like a completely enamored fiancée, she at least appeared to be content with her situation. James looked pleased as punch. He'd told Dermot in the car home that he thought the hen night would go a long way toward winning Sarah's heart. Dermot had let James think what he liked.

Dermot let himself out the front door and made his way to the A. P. Security car that was parked in its usual place on the street in front of the house. Sitting in the driver's seat supervising the team for the evening was Archie Sinclair. Archie still wasn't sure Dermot could be trusted after their confrontation at Waverley Station and Dermot was always wary of the man. "Evening, Arch."

"Dermot." They were distant relations through his mother's stepfather, but it was clear that Archie wasn't a fan.

"The boss says he's in for the night. Told me I should take off." Dermot told Archie, who as team lead would be keeping a record of the team's comings and goings.

"Aye, right." The older man pulled a clipboard from an organizer on the passenger's seat and write down the time before holding it out to Dermot to sign. "Need a car to take ye home."

Dermot took the clipboard and signed. "Nah. It's still early. I think I'll head over to visit Mum. I'll take the bus."

"Right then." Archie replaced the clipboard before picking up his radio to inform the rest of the Polwarth Terrace team. "Lion is in for the night."

"Cheers, Arch." Dermot caught the man's eye before walking toward the bus, knowing full well that Archie would be checking. When the bus came, he waved it on and ducked down the opposite side of the church. There was a narrow footpath along the canal that ran under the bridge and would take him back to the Stuart house. Dermot clung to the garden walls to avoid being seen by anyone along the way as he made his way back to the house. He had to crouch low to stay below the top of the garden wall.

As he approached, he heard Sarah and James talking. "I hope you won't let my mother get to you. Now that she's cooled off, I'm going to have a talk with her about trusting you."

"I appreciate that." Sarah sounded sincere. "I don't want to cause a rift between you two. I really would prefer to get along with her, but I won't be pushed around."

"Of course." James agreed. "And your friends are having a good time? I'm sorry you can't take them sightseeing."

"Me too, but I think they understand. Even in the States they had heard about the accident and me going missing. They're not interested in taking any unnecessary risks."

"I'm glad." He kissed her cheek and turned back toward the house. "I'm going to go have that chat with my mother before dinner. Hopefully, that will make things a little easier."

"I think I'll stay here for a few minutes. It's very peaceful with the canal flowing by." Good. She knew he would be coming to talk to her.

"Alright. Don't be too long." James told her.

"Oh, one more thing about the hen night." Sarah paused ready to broach an awkward subject. "Can we make sure that Fleming Sinclair is not on the team that night?"

"I thought you liked Fleming. Is he not working out?" James sounded confused.

"No, no. He's great, I have no complaints." She lowered her voice. 'It's Amy. Apparently, she's developed a bit of a crush. I'm worried that after she's had a couple of drinks, she might lose her inhibitions and it could get a bit awkward for him. I don't want to put him in a position where he gets distracted or has a hard time doing his job."

"Ah," He chuckled. "I see. I'll make sure Shaw gives him something else to do that night."

"Thank you." Her gratitude was genuine. Of course, Dermot knew the real reason she wanted Fleming out of the way. She didn't want to get him in trouble by slipping away on his watch again the way she had done in North Carolina.

Dermot heard a brief kiss, and then footsteps on the stone path back to the house. He peeked over the fence to find Sarah edging her way toward the shed that was near his spot outside the wall. Dermot glanced over the wall to make sure the way was clear and vaulted over.

***

The garden shed was dark when Sarah snuck in trying not to swing the door too wide. She closed her eyes to let them adjust. When she opened them, he was there. She could barely make out the shape of him by the little bit of light that came in through the small windows. They stood there for several heartbeats just breathing the same air. Like a spell had been cast that held them there in between the world they wanted and the one they lived in.

Slowly, not wanting to break the spell, Sarah lifted a hand and laid it over his heart. He placed his hand over hers and reached to pull her closer. His mouth found hers and his lips and tongue obliterated all other thought. His fingers slid into her hair tightening to tug deliciously at her scalp. But that tug reminded her of the danger. She pulled her lips away and he kissed his way down her neck letting out a soft growl just over her pulse.

"Dermot." She whispered as he nuzzled her neck to kiss the soft spot just below her ear. She whisper-yelled. "Dermot!"

He froze with his nose brushing her ear lobe, his breath hot on her skin.

"I can't risk getting messed up." She leaned away from him slowly lifting a hand to smooth her hair. It would be just my luck to run into Anne looking like I've just tumbled in the bushes."

He groaned in frustration and turned aside to catch his breath. After a minute he looked at her from the corner of his eyes. "Soon."

Her eyelids felt heavy, and her resolve weakened a little at the tone in his voice. "Soon."

"Sleekit Beastie." He growled.

She huffed a short laugh. "There's a Burns quote for every occasion, but I don't think I would have picked 'Tae a Mouse' for this one."

He chuckled low. "No, the Sleekit Beastie is the pub where ye'll have yer hen night."

"The Sleekit Beastie." She repeated to make sure she would remember. "That's in the Old Town, right?"

"Aye. Just off the High Street. Isla will know it. She's probably played there a few times." He studied her lips, disappointment that they didn't have more time written across his face. "And there will be a woman on yer security team. Listen to her. She's with us."

She studied him. He really had been planning. She just hoped Des's team was as trustworthy as Dermot thought they were. "Does she have a name?"

"Douglas." He craned his neck to glance out the window back toward the house. "She's a wee thing, with dark hair she keeps pulled back tight."

"Okay." She took a breath trying to tamp down the anxiety that surged at the idea that this was really happening. "Anything else?"

"Just that I love you."

She leaned into him for a brief but passionate kiss then sighed. "I love you too. I'd better get back."

"Aye." He stepped back from her. "I'll see ye Thursday."

"Thursday." She looked at him one last time before slipping out of the door.

After feeling around her hair to make sure it was still in place, Sarah strolled through the garden giving off all appearances that she was just enjoying the warm evening.

***

"First let's account for the people who are not in Edinburgh." Dermot addressed the team as they met for the last time before Sarah's extraction.

Miles looked at a pad of paper in front of him. "I have gotten warnings to Ruaraidh Ballantyne, Sheila MacLeod-Coulson, and Oona Ballantyne in London. They've all been warned to be on their guard and offered assistance if they would like to disappear. To which Oona Ballantyne said, 'Not bloody likely.'"

"Aye, that sounds like Oona." Dermot muttered.

"I was not able to get a message to Robert Ballantyne." Miles warned. "The rehab facility that he's in doesna allow calls, except from family. His son assured me that he would deliver a warning, although I think he's fairly well pinned down. I still have not been able to reach Grant MacDuff. The number that you gave me was disconnected and the police department said that he resigned, and they did not know where he went after that. He apparently left no forwarding address."

"Then he's in the wind." Dermot assured. "MacDuff has flown under the radar for a long time. He knows how to stay safe."

"Then that's all we've got for Sarah's people outside the city.' Miles concluded.

"Des?" Dermot nodded to his friend.

"Right." Des stood poised in front of the whiteboard to review the plan. There was a map of the Old Town taped next to the list of people to be moved. "Late Thursday afternoon, Dermot and Brody will check his mother out of the care home and deliver her to her new location. Douglas will be meeting with Sarah's security team to prep for the hen night, which Jujhar will also be attending."

Dermot picked up. "Once my mum is deposited at the new care home. I will rendezvous with Des to go through the vault route and meet up with Douglas in the vault under the club."

"I still think it's safer for ye to wait in the van, especially if ye get delayed with yer mother." Des cut in.

"That's not on, mate. Bad things happen when Sarah and I are apart. Plus, she doesna know ye or Douglas. She'll want someone she knows with her." Dermot told him for the fifth time. "Miles ye'll be waiting at the exit point of the vaults keeping the engine running in the van and a lookout for trouble."

"Wait." Jujhar spoke up. "I thought the vaults had been filled in with rubble."

Des grinned. "Not all of them. About ten years ago they smuggled a defecting Russian Rugby player through them. They're even talking about giving tours."

"At twenty-three seventeen, I will take Sarah to the ladies toilet. Except we'll really be going to the storeroom where Des and Dermot will be waiting to escort us through the vaults via the secret entrance." Douglas added.

"I had a chance to walk the route and it looks clear. The only place we need to be careful is near the loading dock of this hotel." He pointed to the spot on Niddry Street where the service entrance was for the hotel. Shouldn't be too busy that time of night, but there's a manhole with access to the vaults here." He drew an X on the spot near the loading dock. "Which is why, Brody, I want yer eyes on that manhole as soon as ye're able and radio if there's a problem."

"Will the radios get reception in the vaults?" Jujhar looked doubtful.

"Aye, ours will." Des held up a large black hand radio. "Police surplus."

"Surplus?" Dermot raised a skeptical eyebrow.

Des's head wobbled in equivocation. "Well, they didn't need this set."

"And they're not on a frequency that the police or A. P. Security will hear?" Dermot asked.

"I've made sure that we're using a different channel." Miles chimed in. "We'll be fine."

"Now that's covered." Des continued. "Once we've got Sarah, we'll make our way through the Southbridge vaults. We will emerge here where Niddry Street crosses Cowgate where Miles will be waiting with the van."

"Meanwhile," Jujhar added his part. "As A. P. Security are distracted by Sarah's disappearance, I will deliver the passports and plane tickets to her American friends and see them safely into a taxi to the airport."

"And Sarah and I drive off into the sunset." Dermot was satisfied with their plan. Des had also helped with papers and a plan on where they would go once they got out of Edinburgh, but the rest of the team didn't need to hear the details. The fewer people knew about that, the better. "Do we have contingencies?"

"I have a mild sedative for yer mother in case she gives ye any trouble while ye're moving her." Dermot almost objected, but Des cut him off. "I asked my chemist, and she assures me that it doesna have negative interactions with any common Alzheimer's medications."

"And what are her qualifications?" Dermot pressed.

"Relax, mate. She's an actual chemist at the hospital."

Dermot hoped he wouldn't have to use that sedative. "Cheers, mate."

"If we have trouble getting away at the exact time, or if someone wants to come to the ladies with us, there might be a few minutes delay." Douglas warned. "But I don't think that will be a problem. Des will be in communication with you all."

Des nodded his agreement. "Exactly. They are still excavating the vaults, but I dinna think there will be anyone down there that late at night. If someone else is in the vaults at the time, we can detour to avoid them and come out here on Blair Street." Des marked another spot on the map. "I'll let you know by radio if that becomes necessary."

"And if we have a problem with the van or get stopped by anyone curious, we'll be two working men taking a break after dropping off several beer kegs at the hotel." Miles added.

Dermot surveyed the whiteboard and the group. "Looks like we've thought of everything we can."

"It's going to work, mate." Des slapped him on the shoulder. Dermot wished he had a bit of Des's confidence.

CHAPTER FORTY-THREE

Sarah was surprised how quickly it all came together. A couple of phone calls to Isla and Jujhar and a word to the security staff about where they wanted to go, and everything was taken care of. Caught up in the whirlwind of final wedding preparations, it felt like nothing more than the blink of an eye before Sarah found herself sitting in a corner booth watching Amy and Isla laughing and dancing to the band that was playing on stage. She'd been right about her friends liking each other. Amy and Barrett had taken to Isla the minute she'd showed up with the requisite headband for Sarah that came complete with a tulle veil and silver letters spelling BRIDE across the top. Even Jujhar had joined in on the good-natured teasing. They had joked and laughed their way through a light supper at the Stuart house before a limousine took them and the security team to The Sleekit Beastie.

In fact, the most difficult thing about the evening so far had been faking excitement when there was a storm of anxiety raging just below the surface. She had gone into this evening blind. There had been no chance for Dermot or the quietly intimidating Douglas to explain the plan to her beforehand. She'd been introduced to Douglas the day before by Archie Sinclair who had seemed more than a little pleased that now Sarah wouldn't even be able to go to the ladies' room without supervision. She couldn't blame Archie, he was only trying to protect his son, which made her even more glad that she'd gotten Fleming the night off. Now Douglas stood about ten feet away keeping a weather eye on their table and anyone who approached it. There were also guards posted at the exits to make sure no one carrying a camera made it inside, and of course to make sure Sarah didn't leave without A. P. Security knowing.

With the other ladies dancing, Barrett had gone to the bar for another pint of cider. Jujhar was seated next to Sarah on the long bench against the back wall. He seemed to be enjoying the music, although Sarah could tell that he was anxious too. "I usually feel calmer when I'm around you, but you are not helping me tonight."

"Sorry." He gave her a sheepish look. "I'm helping in other ways."

She rested a hand on his arm. "I know. I can't thank you enough."

He turned his dark brown eyes from the crowd to her giving her an intense look. "Just be safe and be happy. I'm sure you'll see me again. That is if Green doesn't dismiss me after tonight."

"He wouldn't."

"He might." He huffed nervously. "He thinks I'm taking too active a role."

"Well, it's not like candidates are lining up for the job."

"True, but it's not like he has an expiration date either. He'll just keep going until he finds the right replacement. Nicholas Flamel and the Comte de St. Germain both lived longer than Green has."

Sarah's eyebrows drew together. "You can't be serious. Those are just legends."

He arched a dark eyebrow at her as if to say, 'You still don't believe in magic?'

Sarah shook her head in exasperation. "Fine, but the number of people who believe that stuff is dwindling by the day."

Jujhar leaned back against the cushion behind him. "That's where I think you're wrong. I think there are people out there who are hungry to believe these sorts of things. I think the Internet is going to connect them. And once the curious find each other, they'll start connecting the dots and spreading their theories. Between those theories and simple math. It's only a matter of time before someone puts two and two together and figures out that our friend is far older than he looks."

"All the more reason for him to retire soon." Sarah leaned in closer so that she wouldn't have to shout. "I saw him without his glamour. He's tired."

"Tired and a bit stuck in the past." Jujhar shrugged. "Helping you is the right thing to do, even if he would rather do nothing. I just don't want him to shut me out for it."

Sarah leaned her head on his shoulder. She'd much rather have a trusted friend in that position than the mysterious Mr. Green. "Me too."

"What is this? You can't be tired already." Barrett arrived back at the table.

"Not tired. Just having a moment." Sarah lifted her head and tried to look cheerful.

"Well, come have a moment with me, I'm going to miss you when we have to go home." He put his cider on the table and held out a hand in invitation. "Let's dance."

***

Dermot's heart was in his throat as he knocked on the window of the van that was parked off Richmond Place.

The van door slid open. "It's about time. Where've ye been."

"My mother had a bit of a panic when she realized she wasna going back to the care home she knew." Dermot climbed in and made room for Brody to follow him.

"Didn't ye give her the stuff?" Des asked from the passenger's seat as Miles pulled into traffic.

"Didn't need to when we were moving her, only when we tried to leave, and the care home had stuff of their own. Here." Dermot handed him a capped syringe.

"Cheers." Des took the syringe and stuck it in the inside pocket of his jacket.

They drove the few blocks to Niddry Street. Miles pulled to the side near the exit point and Des and Dermot got out. Before sliding the door closed Des reminded them. "Brody, keep yer eyes on that manhole. And Miles, watch this door. No distractions."

The two nodded, and Miles drove up the street to the hotel.

"Ye do trust them, right?" Dermot muttered when they were far enough from the van.

"I wouldna have asked their help if I didn't." Des assured him. "D'ye trust me?"

"I wouldna have asked for yer help if I didn't."

***

"To Sarah!" Jujhar exclaimed lifting his glass of water.

"To Sarah!" The others echoed only to find that half of them were out of drink.

"Oh! We need another round." Amy looked down into her empty glass.

"I'll get it." Isla jumped up and started for the bar.

"I'll help." Amy followed her, leaving Sarah at the table with the guys. She almost missed Jujhar's subtle head tilt toward the spot where Douglas was looking at her. When Sarah's eyes met the other woman's, her adrenaline surged. Douglas gave her head a jerk toward the ladies' room. It was time. "If you'll excuse me, gents. I'm going to run to the ladies' room while they're gone."

"We'll be right here." Barrett drained the little bit of stout left in his glass.

Sarah tried not to look nervous or rushed as she approached Douglas who was waiting for her in front of the hallway that led to the restrooms. "I do actually need to use the ladies' room first."

"Right." Douglas verified that it was safe.

Sarah tried to breathe deeply to calm herself as she went about her business. She washed her hands and gave herself one last look in the mirror. "Here we go."

When she stepped out into the hallway. Douglas grabbed her by the arm and pulled her further back into the hallway where the lights from the barroom didn't reach. She was hustled through a door into a dark room. Douglas closed the door before switching the light on. Sarah blinked against the sudden brightness. Looking around all she saw were shelves of supplies. "This was the big escape plan?"

"Patience." Douglas told her pushing aside a rolling mop bucket to reveal what looked like a trap door in the floor. She knelt and knocked twice on the door.

A scraping sound was followed by the door being pushed up a few inches. Douglas gripped the edge of the heavy door and pulled it back on silent hinges. In short order Dermot appeared through the opening and waved her toward him. Sarah almost melted with relief. She rushed to the trap door ready to descend.

Dermot moved down the ladder giving her space. "Mind the ladder. It's old."

She climbed down carefully, trying not to imagine what beyond Dermot might be waiting below. She stumbled at the bottom, but Dermot caught her his lips finding hers in a fierce and exhilarating kiss.

"Shift, mate. Give Douglas a chance to climb down." A voice came from behind them. Dermot and Sarah shuffled back from the ladder. She glanced in the direction of the voice to see a man about Dermot's age with a mop of dark brown curls. He wore a dark hoodie and pants as did Dermot.

Douglas was working her way down the ladder grunting with the weight of the trap door. She had one hand on the ladder and one supporting the door above her head to keep it from slamming back into place. When the door quietly met the frame, she slid down the rest of the ladder.

Safely out of the club, Sarah looked around. By the light of the flashlight the other man was holding, she could see that they were in a small chamber surrounded by stone walls. The Sleekit Beastie was already in a basement, this was even lower. "Where are we?"

"There's a network of vaults that were created when they built the Southbridge. They link up with a lot of the buildings on the neighboring streets." The man waggled his eyebrows. "They're sometimes used to move contraband."

"You must be Des." Sarah smiled at him.

He bowed his head with a rakish grin. "At yer service."

"Here." Dermot pulled two dark hoodies from a black bag and handed them to Sarah and Douglas. Sarah pulled hers over her clothes. Douglas stripped out of the suit jacket and white shirt that were her A. P. Security uniform.

After pulling the hoodie over her head, Douglas touched her earpiece listening. She filled them in on the A. P. Security chatter. "The lads just told them we were in the ladies' toilet. They haven't raised the alarm yet."

"Good." Des grabbed the duffel bag and turned to torch toward an arched doorway in the far corner of the room. "With any luck, we'll be halfway to the rendezvous before they know she's gone."

They followed Des's lead, but Sarah stopped after a couple of steps. "What about Amy and Barrett?"

Dermot put his hand in the small of her back urging her forward. "Jujhar has documents and plane tickets for them."

"Sounds like you've thought of everything." They made their way through the next room. It was much like the first, but there were some piles of stone and brick rubble in the corners.

"Tried to." Dermot spoke quietly. He filled her in on the rest of their precautions and arrangements as they made their way through the vaults. Sarah was glad of the distraction. The vaults felt odd. They were empty of life, just rubble and trash from who knew how long ago, but there was a lived-in feeling all around as if someone had been there but just left.

"Shh!" Des waved a hand back at them. He held a large black hand radio to his ear. They all stopped, and Sarah could hear a voice coming from the radio, but the volume was turned down low, so she couldn't make out what was said. After the radio hissed again, Des turned back. "Miles says we've got company. We're going to have to make a detour."

Douglas glanced around at the dark stone walls. "To where?"

"Plan B?" Dermot asked.

"Aye" Des agreed.

"What's plan B?" Sarah's pulse started to race, as if fumbling through dark sub-basements wasn't unnerving enough.

Des turned away from the arched doorway they had been about to enter and made his way down the wall to another smaller doorway with an iron gate in a dark corner of the vault.

"Des and I mapped out an alternate route just in case we were tracked to the vaults." Dermot explained as they followed Des.

"Do the others know about this route?" Douglas asked crouching beside Des as he pulled on the iron gate which didn't seem to want to open.

Des looked back at her significantly. "No. Just in case one of ye turned."

"So much for a team you can trust." Sarah muttered.

Des glanced over his shoulder at her. "The Stuart's resources can turn even the most loyal."

The stubborn gate finally gave way scraping the stone floor and the accompanying echo sounded deafening in the otherwise silent vault. They all froze for a minute listening for any other movement. When there was no further sound, they slipped through the gate into the dark chamber beyond. Des scanned the room with his flashlight. This room hadn't been cleared as much as the others they had been in before. There was only a narrow path dug out amid the rubble and debris. The group picked their way along the path as silently as they could with Des in the lead.

The next chamber was not quite as crowded, but it was damp. Sarah could hear water dripping somewhere off their path. The next found them climbing over piles of stones and nineteenth century rubbish. Sarah thought she even spotted some bones. They made their way silently through a series of chambers. Some were full of rubble, some empty. All were dark as pitch except for the flashlight beams.

It was a flashlight beam that tipped them off that they weren't alone, a faint spot of light that appeared on the ceiling of a chamber when the one Des had was pointing at the floor. Des turned his off and they all held their breath for a few seconds in the dark. The light bobbed and flickered across the ceiling. It must have been coming through the doorway behind them. Before Sarah could ask what to do, Dermot gripped her hand and drew her into a corner behind some rubble. "Stay here."

He disappeared into the dark. A body pushed Sarah's down into a crouch and huddled over her. Douglas whispered in her ear. "It's me."

Sarah could hear a scuffle going on but couldn't tell where it was. There were so many hard surfaces in the vault for sound to bounce off, every shuffle, and grunt seemed amplified. Sarah lifted her head but couldn't see anything. She could only feel the pile of jumbled stones in front of her and Douglas's body close behind and above her.

Someone cried out as if they'd been hurt. Sarah thought maybe it sounded like Des, but it was hard to tell. She got quickly frustrated with the darkness and feeling powerless. There was a menacing click above her head, and light filled the vault.

Sarah blinked through the brightness to look up to see Douglas's eyes cold, almost black. Sarah looked down at Douglas's hand to see the gun that was pointed right at her. "Up ye get."

Douglas backed away from Sarah so that she could come out of the corner she'd been sheltering in. When she rounded the pile of rubble, she saw two men holding Dermot and Des's arms behind their backs. The light came from the torch in Douglas's other hand.

Sarah turned to face Douglas. "Well, you haven't shot me, so I'm guessing you work for Walter Stuart."

"You might say that." Douglas clearly felt in control of the situation.

"If you shoot me, he won't pay you anything." Sarah warned. "He needs me."

"He doesn't need them." Douglas shifted the gun to point it at Dermot.

"Bitch!" Des spat. "I trusted ye."

"You've only yourselves to blame. After yer man got caught with that forged passport, A. P. Security instituted additional document checks on all applicants. They caught me right away." She motioned with the gun for Sarah to join

Dermot and Des on the other side of the vault. "Then they made me a better offer."

Des shook his head. "I picked ye up after the Army spat ye out. I gave ye a job. Ye said I gave ye a purpose. And this is how ye repay me."

Douglas cocked her head to the side, and tsk'd. "And now, they've given me a better one." She shifted her gaze to the man holding Des. "Do you have the zip cuffs?"

"Aye, in my back pocket." The man's hands were full holding Des.

"Princess, if you'll oblige." Douglas looked at Sarah and jerked her head toward the man.

"You want me to cuff them?" Sarah couldn't believe it.

"I do." Douglas lifted the gun that was pointing toward Dermot. "I know you will."

Sarah stared daggers at her, but she didn't have much choice. She went to the man holding Des and pulled two sets of flex cuffs that stuck out of his back pocket. She slid one set over Des's wrists, and pulled them tight, but not so tight that Des couldn't get out.

"Make sure they're nice and tight." Douglas warned. The man holding Des used one hand to push Sarah's hands out of the way and pull the cuffs tighter.

"Now, Dermot." Douglas directed.

Sarah went to Dermot and slid the other set of cuffs onto his wrists. His fingers brushed the inside of her wrist as she pulled the cuffs tight. She gave his fingers a squeeze. She didn't know how they were going to get out of this, but they were certainly going to try.

CHAPTER FORTY-FOUR

They were pushed and shoved through several vaults. All the while Des was spewing his fury on Douglas for her betrayal. Apparently, their history wasn't' limited to skills she'd learned in the army.

Dermot used the distraction, Des's diatribe offered to talk to Sarah. He spoke just loud enough for her to hear without being audible over Des's litany of complaints. *"Nuiar as urrainn dhut, ruith."* (When you can, run.)

"Chan ann ás aonais thusa." (Not without you.) Was her only reply.

"Feumaidh tu." (You must.) He hissed.

Douglas who had been leading the way, turned back at something Des said that was especially vitriolic. When she turned back around, she tripped on a brick and dropped the flashlight.

Dermot seized on the opportunity and dove into the back of the man who held Des. Turned and kicked out at the man who had been holding Dermot while falling toward Douglas who went down like a bowling pin.

***

Sarah immediately took off into the darkness. She hated the idea of leaving Dermot, but if the hard-headed idiot was going to get himself shot, she wasn't going to let it be for nothing. She had no idea how she might make it out of the vaults with no light and a bunch of Walter Stuart's lackeys on the hunt for her. But maybe, just maybe if they were busy chasing her, then Dermot could get away.

Stretching her arms in front of her to avoid running into walls, Sarah went as fast as she could to get away from the sounds of scuffling behind her. She had run through maybe two chambers before the shot rang out. Sarah froze. She turned back toward the sound and considered running back. Until she heard Dermot shout. "Damn it, Des!"

"Hold him! She's getting away." Douglas barked.

Sarah closed her eyes and inhaled. Then she ran. She took every twist and turn she could to get as far away from the group as possible. When she couldn't hear them anymore, she slowed down enough to search for some crevice to hide in. Tripping over the outer edge, she landed hard on her knees on the stone. When she reached out to steady herself, her knuckles caught on the corner of an arch. Feeling her way around in the dark, she discovered it was one the shallow alcoves that she had seen in some of the other chambers. The rubble in front of the alcove should shield her from searching flashlights. With a steadying breath, she sat down behind the pile and scooted back into the alcove until her back hit the wall. She tried not to think about what might be on that floor, or what else might be taking refuge in her dark corner. It seemed a safe enough place to wait out Walter's goons. If she could manage to stay quiet and hidden, she could find her way back to the street level when the coast was clear.

She didn't know how long she sat there in the dark. Long enough for her breath to slow. Long enough for her to notice the regular drip of water somewhere in the chamber, and the dank smell of wet stone and earth. It reminded her more than a little of the dark cave they'd taken refuge in in the Highlands. Only this time, there was no Ruaraidh to guide her and no Green waiting with a warm fire and a cup of tea at the end.

"C'mon out, Sarah." Douglas's voice came from a short distance away. "You'll never find your way out of here. It's a maze. We can help you."

Sarah silently inched back further, trying to make herself as small as possible.

"No one wants to hurt you." The voice came closer. "Dermot is fine now, but that may not be the case if you don't cooperate with us."

She debated giving herself up for Dermot's sake. She knew what he would say to that.

"I can't say the same for Desmond. It really is a shame. I liked him." Her voice was louder now. If Douglas wasn't in the same chamber as Sarah, she wasn't far off.

Tiny feet scurried over the back of Sarah's hand. She gasped and slapped a hand over her mouth, terrified that Douglas had heard her. Shit, shit, shit! She waited listening for footsteps or any sign that she was coming closer. Nothing. Not a sound. After almost a minute, Sarah slowly let out the breath she'd been holding.

Like lightning, or a snake striking, a hand grasped her ankle. Fingers wrapped around and yanked. Sarah kicked at Douglas's hand hoping to dislodge it but got nothing more than a grunt in response. In the dark she couldn't see the other woman who was dragging her out of her hiding place. Taking a different tack, Sarah reached for the pile of rubble she'd been hiding behind and grabbed the biggest rock she could get her hands on and threw it at where she thought Douglas's head must be.

That got her a grunt, and the grip on her ankle loosened. Sarah twisted her ankle away and prepared to get up and run past Douglas.

"So you aren't just a helpless princess" Douglas lurched forward and wrapped her arms around Sarah's torso almost knocking them both to the ground. Sarah wriggled against her hold as she slowly got her feet under her. Douglas took a couple of steps backward to get out of the alcove. Not ready to give up, Sarah used Douglas's grip on her upper body to lever her feet up. She found purchase on the edge of the stone arch and shoved with her legs. Douglas went down flat on her back with Sarah on top of her. Sarah scrambled to her feet and prepared to run in the direction she hoped led to the door. She didn't get more than a couple of steps before she ran into something solid. Hands grasped her upper arms in a tight grip. "Alright there, Douglas?"

"Knocked the wind out o' me." The other woman gasped. "She's a fighter."

"Let's get her to the boss."

***

Dermot twisted his wrist hoping to weaken the zip ties that held them behind his back. Des had been left where he fell, bleeding out on the stone floor a few vaults back. Dermot didn't have time to mourn his friend right now. He needed to get through this. At least Sarah had gotten away. He prayed they wouldn't find her. He hoped she would be able to find her way out of the vaults.

"James is going to be so disappointed in the two of you." Walter sauntered in from the next room looking perfectly put together and satisfied with himself. "He does so want to believe the best of you."

Dermot had nothing to say to the old man. No amount of persuasion was going to change whatever Walter's plans were. Once Walter Stuart set his mind to something, he went after it with a disturbing single mindedness.

Walter leaned against a wooden crate that sat on the opposite side of the vault. A lantern sat on the crate beside him. "I'm sure we won't be waiting long for Miss MacAlpin. Miss Douglas is proving to be quite capable."

Dermot sat there stone-faced on the cold floor.

"Get your damned hands off of me!" Dermot's heart sank as Sarah's voice cut through the silence. He closed his eyes cursing quietly that she hadn't escaped. From the scuffling sounds he thought she must be giving Douglas a difficult time. Good.

Walter sighed whether with relief or resignation. "It seems none of Anne's comportment lessons took."

A male voice grunted in what sounded like pain. Sarah's voice sounded closer. "Serves you right."

Dermot turned to see the man who had been holding Des and Douglas half-pushing half-dragging Sarah into the lit room. One of her sleeves was torn at the shoulder, but other than that she looked unhurt. He couldn't say that for Douglas who was limping slightly.

"I'm glad you could join us, Miss MacAlpin." Walter spread his arms to encompass the large vault.

Sarah squirmed against the grip on her upper arms. She looked at Dermot, giving him a quick once over as if checking for injuries. With one last long look, she turned her attention to Walter. "Bite me."

"Really, there is no need to be uncouth." Walter examined her from a short distance away. "We wouldn't be here if you had paid attention to my earlier warning."

Sarah narrowed her eyes at him. "Your earlier warning is exactly why we did this. Fortunately, my friends are on their way to the airport by now."

Walter laughed. "Your friends are in the drawing room at Stuart House worried sick and wondering if you've been kidnapped."

"No." Sarah shook her head.

"Yes. We intercepted Mr. Gurudat's message to them. We were well prepared for your little escape attempt." Walter leaned closer to her, showing her a smug grin.

Sarah glared at him. For a moment Dermot thought she might spit in his face. Instead, she gritted her teeth. "Well, I supposed you win this round."

"Oh, my dear." Walter tilted his head to the side in a condescending look. "It's not going to be that simple. This sort of breach requires some assurance that you will go through with this wedding.'

"I don't have any more options now. Do I?" Sarah's tone was testy.

"Still, I don't want to risk another incident like this." He walked a few steps back to the crate before turning to face her again. "And there is the need for your continued compliance after the wedding." He raised his haughty chin in the air. "Gentlemen."

Dermot got to his feet preparing to hurl himself at the people holding Sarah. He wasn't sure what Walter had in mind, but it didn't sound good. What he didn't expect was another pair of armed henchmen to appear through the doorway to the vault that Walter had come from moments before. Each man led a gagged and bound man in front of them. Dermot's blood ran cold when he realized who they were, Rab Ballantyne and Grant MacDuff, the only two on their list that he hadn't been able to talk to. Each of her fathers looked at Sarah. Rab's eyes were full of terror, but Duff looked fiercely stoic, as if he was willing her not to listen to Walter.

Sarah cried out and struggled harder. "No!"

A sick smile flitted across Walter's face at the sight of her distress. "One of these men is going to walk you down the aisle on Saturday. You just have to choose."

Dermot held his breath. Sarah must have sensed that Walter meant more than just wedding logistics. She turned to look at the two men who had loved her mother. Duff who had helped raise her and Rab who had pined for her for decades. Sarah shook her head again, tears filling her eyes. "I'm not going to play your sadistic game. Let them go. I'll walk myself down the aisle, or they can both do it. I don't care, but you're not going to make me choose."

Walter walked closer to the men holding Rab. He took a handgun from the holster at the man's belt. The man still kept a grip on Rab's arm. Walter raised the gun and waved it in the direction of the men. "You are going to choose, or I'll choose for you."

Sarah's eyes went back and forth between Duff and Rab. Duff gave his head a brief shake. Sarah returned her gaze to Walter's Rather than say anything, she stuck out her chin in a show of defiance.

Sarah and Walter stood there; eyes locked on each other for several heartbeats. Dermot thought everyone in the vault must be holding their breath. Eventually, Walter shrugged. "Very well."

He raised the gun, taking aim at Duff's chest and pulled the trigger.

CHAPTER FORTY-FIVE

Kettle Hollow
Late June 1976

"Stupid shoes." Sarah dropped down so she could hang her feet off the edge of the porch. The short skirt of her best blue dress rode up and the boards felt hot on the backs of her thighs. But that was nothing compared to the pain in her feet. "Stupid, stupid shoes."

It was late June, and she hadn't gotten a pair of new shoes since the fall. When Granny had dressed her that morning for her mother's funeral, she'd had to wear the shoes they bought last fall for the start of the school year. Now, she felt like one of Cinderella's stepsisters trying to cram her feet into shoes that were too short for them. She wasn't too happy about the dress either. She would much rather have spent the day fishing in cutoffs. But here she was in her good dress, and her too small shoes waiting to go to the graveyard.

The graveyard. What was the point of burying Mama in the graveyard with all the people who used to whisper about her behind their hands and no doubt still would? Why were they having a funeral at all? The only people who cared anything about Mama were her, Granny, and Duff. Now she had to go out there in front of those people and act like she was sad about her Mama accidentally falling off a cliff when she knew the truth. Mama didn't fall off a cliff, and it surely wasn't an accident. Somehow Sarah was supposed to pretend to be sad for all these lookie loos in town when what she really was mad. And her feet hurt.

She kicked them back and forth off the edge of the porch thinking it might feel nice to kick something more than the hot summer air. She hopped off the porch wincing when her feet hit the ground. She stalked over to the driveway and found a big clump of red clay that had been left on the edge after the spring rains. She hauled her right foot up behind her and kicked it. The clay exploded into orange dust that flew up in the air. It felt so satisfying that she found another bit of clay and did it again. It didn't make her feet feel any better, in fact it made her toes feel worse, but it felt so good to let out some to the anger that had been brewing inside her since she'd found her mama dead in a pool of her own blood that she didn't care if she broke toes.

She kicked at some more clay until her feet were screaming and she was surrounded by a cloud of orange dust. She didn't hear the screen door slam, or the footsteps coming up behind her. She didn't hear anything but the blood roaring in her ears until Duff picked her up off the ground and started carrying her back to the porch.

"Hey now, hey." His gravelly voice would have been soothing any other time, but then it just made her more mad. She balled up her little fist and swung it at him just as he sat on the edge of the porch with her in his lap. She caught him in the shoulder, and it felt good, like kicking the dirt without the pain. So, she did it again. It didn't matter that Duff was her friend. She just had to let it out. He didn't stop her. He could have. He was three times her size. He just let her swing her little fists at him as long as she wanted, as long as she had fight left in her. "That's it. Get it all out."

When the fight ran out of her, she collapsed against him, and he wrapped his arms around her and held her. He murmured reassurances while her little body was wracked with sobs, shaking with the release of days of pain and fury she'd been holding in. When she tired herself out, he just held on humming a soft tune.

At some point she heard the screen door open and felt him shake his head. The door thwacked back into place, and everything was quiet. Sarah heard the hum of the bugs in the woods nearby, a rustle in the dry leaves, and Duff humming. When she lifted her head, Duff gave her a soft smile. "I had a feeling something like that was going to happen. I've been waiting for it."

"Waiting for what?" Sarah swiped the back of her hand across her cheek and it came away wet and dirty.

"For the explosion." Duff took a bandanna out of his pocket and started wiping the tears, and snot and clay dust off her cheeks. "You haven't said a word since you found your mama. I knew there was a lot of hurt bottled up in there." He tapped a finger in the center of her chest. "It had to come out sometime."

Sarah sniffed and leaned into him. "I'm sorry I hit you."

Duff laughed. "It's not the first time a MacAlpin girl has taken her frustration out on me. I dare say it won't be the last." He continued wiping her face until it was mostly clean. "You want to tell me what set you off?"

"My shoes are too small." She held up a foot. "Makes my feet hurt."

"Well, you can't go where we're going with no shoes. Let me see what I can do." He shifted her from his lap and set her beside him on the porch. He lifted each of her feet and pulled off the worn brown leather shoes. Her feet tingled with the new freedom, and she wiggled her toes to relieve the sensation. Duff pulled out the pocketknife that was always on him. He grabbed her ankle and held a shoe up against the bottom of her foot. "I think I see what the problem is. Your feet are too long. We're going to have to cut off your toes to fit them in here."

He lifted her foot into his lap and acted like he was opening the knife. Sarah giggled and gave his thigh a soft kick. "Silly."

Duff tickled her foot and Sarah pulled it back out of his lap. He picked up one of the shoes and opened his pocketknife. "I'll have you fixed up in no time. Then we'll have to get Granny to fix your pigtails. Can't have you showing up looking like you just wrestled a bear."

Sarah put a hand up to her hair and felt where some of her curls had escaped the braids that Granny had put in them that morning. "Why do I have to show up anyway?"

Duff stopped; his knife poised beside the seam in the heel of one shoe. He let out a sigh. "Because she was your mama, and she loved you."

"No, she didn't." Her mother had tried to drown her in the bathtub. She had attacked her over the dinner table, and who knew what else. Living with her mother the last few months had been hell. She hated that her voice cracked. "I don't know what I did to make her so mad at me."

"Oh, honey." Duff put the knife down and wrapped an arm around her hugging her to his side. "Your mama…" He seemed to search for words. "Well, she had a sickness in her head and in her heart. There wasn't anything you did. There wasn't anything that your Granny did. I don't think there was anything that I did to make it worse or better. It just was."

Sarah thought about that for a minute while Duff picked up the knife again and started cutting through the stitches on the back of her shoe. "But if she wasn't mad at us, then why did she leave us?"

After cutting through the stitches, Duff used his thumbs to separate the two sides of the heel and worked it with his hands until it was flexible. "I wish I knew. Maybe she thought we'd be better off without her. Maybe she just couldn't take being sad for one more day. Sometimes people do things that we just can't explain."

He picked up the other shoe and cut the stitches on that one too. Sarah turned his words over in her mind. It was hard to imagine. Mama must have had a reason for what she did. It wasn't fair to make them all wonder about it. Sarah didn't like not knowing the answers to things. "What are we going to do now?"

"Well first, you're going to try on these shoes." He handed her one of the now loosened shoes. And Sarah slid her foot inside. With the heel seam cut, her foot had the extra room it needed for her foot. "Then we're going to fix your hair. And then we're going to the graveyard to show all those Kettle Holler gossips that we're stronger than they think we are."

"What if I'm not?" Sarah slipped on the other shoe.

"I know you are. I know your Granny is." Duff pressed his lips together and took a breath. "I think y'all are going have to help me be strong."

For the first time, Sarah noticed the redness around his eyes, and the tears threatening to spill over. She realized that Duff had lost Mama too. She put her hand on his where it rested on his knee and leaned against him looking out at the trees swaying in the summer wind. "I'll help you if you help me."

Duff drew in a sharp breath and cleared his throat. "You got a deal."

***

Edinburgh
August 1996

It all happened so fast that Sarah didn't see it coming. Walter just casually aimed at Duff and shot. Rab must have seen his intent. He had to have made his move an instant before Walter pulled the trigger or he would never have made it in time. The man holding him must have been stunned by the whole proceeding for Rab to twist out of his grip so fast. Duff had always told her, that in a fight surprise could make up for other disadvantages. She had used it herself a time or two. But not the way Rab did.

In that instant Rab threw himself at Duff, and right into the path of the bullet. Both men went down. The man holding Duff let go and backed away, no doubt wanting to avoid getting hit himself. Her fathers fell to the stone floor in a heap.

"No!" Sarah wrenched free from her captors and rushed to where they lay tangled together on the floor, blood spattering them both.

She was vaguely aware of a struggle going on to her right, but she couldn't focus on that. Her hands fluttered over the men in front of her searching for the source of the bleeding. "Whose blood is this?"

Duff wriggled out from under Rab and sat up, his hands still bound behind him. He shook his head at Sarah, unable to talk through the gag. Rab grunted when he sank to the floor but didn't move. His back was to Sarah and she looked for the source of the blood. "Hold on, Rab."

Angry shouting and more scuffling went on behind her as she searched her father for a wound. Her heart sank when she found a small round hole seeping blood near the center of his back. She cried out looking around the vault. "Help! Somebody!"

The only people on her side literally had their hands tied. Everyone else worked for Walter. The men looked at each other, but none of them moved to help. Dermot shouted. "Are ye just going to let him die?"

Walter who was now pushing himself up from the floor and clinging to the wall grunted. "That's precisely what they're going to do. I pay them well enough."

Sarah looked at each of Walter's henchmen and Douglas. They all looked uncomfortable, but none of them moved to help her, not even the ones who had been holding Duff and Rab. Cursing under her breath, Sarah pulled her shirts off. She pressed the lighter blouse that she'd been wearing at the club to the wound in Rab's back. "Hang in there, Rab."

"You sick bastard!" Dermot bit out.

Sarah tuned out their argument. Focusing her attention on Rab. She looked up at Duff, who now knelt beside her trying desperately to free his hands. When she caught his eye, he paused. "Can you help me turn him over?"

Duff looked down at himself and nodded. Sarah reached for the shoulder that was closest to Duff and gently pulled. Rab groaned and Duff scooted forward on his knees supporting Rab as she slowly carefully turned him over. Sarah fought back tears when she saw where the bullet had exited. The flesh near his shoulder was a mess of blood and muscle. Broken fragments of bones peeked out. Sarah gave her head quick shake as if shooing away her worry for him. She pressed her lips together and folded the sweatshirt to cover the wound. Trying not to think about the track the bullet must have taken inside him from the middle of his back almost to his collar bone.

Duff grunted for her attention, and when she looked up, he jerked his head up calling attention to the gag in his mouth. Sarah lay the folded fabric over Rab's wound and straightened to pull Duff's gag out of his mouth.

Duff stretched his jaw. He jerked his chin toward Rab's head. "His."

Sarah pulled Rab's gag out, and he started working his mouth like Duff had, but his movements were much weaker.

"Don't try to talk." Sarah told him returning to his wound to apply pressure. She looked up to find Rab's green eyes so much like hers beneath drooping lids. "We're going to get you out of here. Even if I have to drag you out myself."

"Sarah." Duff's tone was kind, but she could hear the resignation in his voice.

"No. I just found him." She bit out at him. "You were getting sober. You can't leave us now. Your children need you. We all need you."

Rab shook his head. His words were barely a breath. "Never have."

Sarah choked back a sob. "Yes, we have. Don't leave us."

Rab lifted his eyes to Duff who leaned over him at Sarah's shoulder. "Couldn't take ye." His breath came shorter, and he grunted with pain. "Ye're the father she deserved...the man Molly deserved."

Duff couldn't speak. Sarah heard his breath hitch and wondered about the memories of all the years that Duff stood by her mother while all the time Molly was pining for Rab.

Rab's breath slowed like his body was running out of steam. He coughed and a bloody froth escaped his lips. "My...children..."

"Are mine now." Duff assured him fiercely.

Rab's eyes drifted back to Sarah. "Tell...them..." He struggled for breath, in the end he mouthed, 'I'm sorry' before closing his eyes. His head fell to the side. He only took a few more breaths before his chest stopped rising and every muscle sagged.

A raw gut-wrenching sound exploded from Sarah's chest. Her eyes were so flooded with tears she couldn't see. As she bent over the body of her father, she was swamped by the decades of regret and missed connections that had marked her life before she was even born. The only thing that kept her from dissolving and seeping between the stones in the vault floor was the solid presence of Duff, who leaned into her shoulder offering what comfort he could with his hands still bound.

CHAPTER FORTY-SIX

"How touching." Walter Stuart's voice cut through the silence when Sarah's sobbing ebbed. Dermot fought the bruising hold Walter's henchmen had on his arms. They'd better hold him, or he'd show Walter again just how much damage he could do with his hands tied behind his back.

He had wrenched away from them and dove for Walter when he'd raised the gun, but he'd been too late. He hoped he'd given the old man a concussion when he'd driven him into the wall. Maybe he'd broken some ribs when he'd kicked him. He only regretted that Walter's goons had pulled him off before he could do any lasting damage.

The monster smoothed the hair away from his forehead as if to show that he wasn't at all bothered by watching a man die, nor by getting tackled and kicked soundly. Dermot noted though that Walter had yet to stand up straight, his shoulders curled slightly in as if protecting those ribs. Dermot seethed. "James isna going to like it when he hears about this."

Walter pulled his eyes away from Sarah and Duff to give Dermot a fierce look. "James will not hear about this. I think I've proven to you all that I'm not above punitive action. The next time you think to break our agreement, it may be Mr. MacDuff or that brother Sarah is so fond of."

"You stay away from them!" Sarah exclaimed.

"That, my dear, will be up to you." Walter spat holding his ribs with one hand. "Now, this is what's going to happen.

We are going to take Miss MacAlpin somewhere where she can get cleaned up, and then back to Stuart House. Mr. MacDuff will be taken to a location where I will hold him until the wedding has taken place."

"No!" Sarah gripped Duff by the arm. "I'm not letting him out of my sight. I'm sure as hell not trusting you."

Walter walked closer to her and bent down to get on her eye level. His gaze cut to her father lying dead on the floor before coming back to meet her eyes. "You. Have. No. Choice."

Dermot watched a thousand thoughts flick through her brain: rebellions, retorts, plans, and contingencies. In the end her eyes turned to steel. "One day."

A laugh was trapped in Walter's throat and his hand rubbed his side as he straightened up. To the men who had captured them earlier. "You three, clean up this vault and dump the body where he'll be found but not traced back to us."

"What about him?" The man closest to Walter asked jerking his chin toward Dermot and then toward the vault behind them. "And we left another body back that way."

Walter turned to look at them. His eyes found Dermot's, who was surprised by what he saw. After attacking him, Dermot would have expected fury, or indignation, but what he saw was disappointment. "Drop him off near the University, and I don't care what you do about the body, just make sure it doesn't come back to us."

"I'll take care of that body." Douglas volunteered. Dermot glared at her.

"One of you help her with that." Walter nodded toward Sarah. "Get her out of here."

"No!" Sarah dodged the man who went to grab her and ran around to wrap her arms around MacDuff. "I'm not leaving without Duff."

"No such concern for your lover, I see." Walter smirked cutting a side-eye at Dermot.

"James doesn't know about Duff." Sarah bit out. "But you'd have a hard time explaining to him how you killed his best friend."

Walter sneered. "Fine. Take them both."

Two of the men grabbed Sarah and Duff by the arms and pulled them through the archway to the next vault. Sarah's eyes met his just before they shuffled out of view. They were bright green and full of tears. He felt like his heart was being torn from his chest as he watched her go.

"I am going to tell James the good news that our security team removed Sarah from the pub quickly after spotting a suspicious person, but she's fine now and will be home soon." Walter straightened his clothes and stepped over Rab Ballantyne's body. He came close to Dermot. "I strongly suggest that you adopt the same story. It's only a matter of time before I find where you've stashed your mother. If James hears the truth about tonight's events, there will be no helping her."

***

Sarah turned off the shower in the bathroom of the house that they were taken to. A nondescript brick bungalow on a street like dozens of others. Some sort of safe house for Walter and his goons. Sarah got the impression that Walter's men didn't work for A. P. Security. She was willing to bet that James had no idea that his uncle kept his own mercenary force that was off the Alba Petroleum radar. The two men that had escorted her and Duff to the house, had quietly shown her to the bathroom and provided her with soap and a washcloth and towel as well as a pair of sweats to change into complete with the A. P. Security logo on them. All outward appearances would support Walter's story that everything had been under control the whole time. Considering that Walter had gone to the trouble of bringing Duff and Rab there, it seemed everything had been under his control despite Dermot's planning.

Sarah turned the water in the shower to scalding as she stripped off her bloody clothes. She dropped the blood-soaked designer jeans she'd worn to the pub into the garbage, catching herself in the mirror. She looked wrung out, exhausted. Her eyes were red from crying and tears diluted a smear of Rab's blood on her cheek. She felt sick. Sick and hopeless because it was all so familiar.

Twenty years ago, she had walked through the door to find her mother's body in its own pool of blood on her bed. Just like tonight, she had rushed in, In the hopes of stopping the inevitable. She had tried to shake her mother awake like she would from a nap, because at six years old what did she know of checking for vital signs. When she hadn't been able to wake Molly, she had hugged her, and lain her head on Molly's chest and cried. And she had ended up covered in her mother's blood. For a frozen moment in that mirror, her reflection blended with that of little six-year-old Sarah, the one who still believed in princes and fairy tales, the one her mother had died to protect. *"Dh'fheuch mi, a' Mhami."* (I tried, Mama.)

She was tired; tired of trying, tired of pretending, tired of fighting, tired of losing. She had nothing left; no weapons, and after tonight it seemed no allies strong enough to help her out of this blood-soaked misery that her life had become. Sarah didn't think she had ever felt so hopeless and for just a moment she understood what her mother must have felt that day in 1976. Broken.

But little Sarah hadn't given up back then. She had kept going. She hadn't given up when her mother left her. She had faced down all the whispers and taunts. She had grown up and survived losing her grandmother. She had made a life. She had survived Ryan Cumberland and every other assassin they had sent after her so far.

Sarah pulled back the shower curtain and stepped into the steaming shower and began scrubbing the blood and dust off of her skin and out of her hair. She knew that nothing was going to remove the stain on her psyche. Nothing was going to stop the recriminations. If she hadn't tried to escape, Rab would still be alive. If she hadn't agreed to marry James, it might have happened even sooner. If she had run in North Carolina when she'd had the chance, if she had never come to Scotland. If she had given up Dermot as a lost cause half a dozen different times, then Rab would still be alive. Ruaraidh and Oona would still have a father.

As the hot water pelted her, she found that it washed away the sharp edges of hurt and shock along with the blood. By the time she had scrubbed herself nearly raw, she regained her resolve. No one, no matter how much they wanted to was going to rescue her from this. There was no one apart from Dermot that she could trust, and unfortunately Dermot alone couldn't fix this. It was a painful lesson, but she had definitely learned it.

She turned off the water and dried off. After putting on the sweats they had given her, she tied her -wet hair into a bun. Her red-rimmed eyes still made her look tired, but now the fight was back in them. She was going to have to push through. She would persevere, or she would take Walter Stuart down with her. She glanced at the tiny window above the shower to see the first hint of dawn filtering into the room.

Opening the door, she traced her steps back to the front room of the safe house. The curtains were pulled tight. Duff sat on the couch, elbows resting on his knees and his head in his hands. Sarah felt a moment of surprise that they had untied him. Then she saw the man she'd call henchman number one sitting on a desk on the other side of the room, his gun hand resting on his knee. Duff lifted his head as she came into the room. The henchman stood up and eyed her warily.

Sarah cleared her throat. "I need to use the phone."

"Not likely, dearie." Henchman number two strolled into the room carrying four mugs and an electric tea kettle. He seemed to think that he was in charge.

Sarah waited for him to put the mugs down and look at her. "I need to call my brother and tell him that our father is dead." Her tone brooked no argument, it was one that she had heard Lady Anne use with anyone who didn't hop to do her bidding. "Now, unless you want me to scream bloody murder until the neighbors call the police down on us, I suggest you bring me the god damned phone."

CHAPTER FORTY-SEVEN

Dermot knocked on the study door and waited. He hadn't been surprised when he was summoned to the Stuart house mid-morning the next day. He fully expected to be sacked or worse disappeared like some Invigilare henchmen. After last night's failure, he wasn't sure he didn't deserve it. Walter Stuart had said that James wouldn't hear of their escape attempt, mainly to cover up his murder of Rab Ballantyne. But Dermot wouldn't put it past the old man to manufacture some other reason why James should be rid of Dermot.

A subdued and pensive James opened the study door and stepped back so that Dermot could enter. "Thank you for coming. I know you were supposed to have the day off." James waved at the tray on his way back to the desk. "Help yourself to some tea."

Dermot remained standing near the center of the room. If he was going to be banished, he might as well get it over with. "What's this about?"

James picked up his own teacup and leaned back against the desk. He didn't look angry, but he didn't look like a man who was about to be married either. "Sarah's father has died."

It seemed Walter had kept to that part of his cover story. Dermot put on his sternly surprised face. "What happened?"

"A fall." James pressed his lips together as if suppressing something else he might have said. "He left the rehab facility where he'd been staying. I assume his plan was to attend the wedding. Apparently, he celebrated a bit too much in advance last night. He fell down The News Steps and cracked his skull."

Dermot hid his relief by turning to sit on the couch. He ran a hand through his hair. It seemed Walter had not told James about Dermot's attempt to rescue Sarah. "Have ye told her?"

James nodded; the memory of that conversation was written in the weary lines of his face. "She's taking it in stride. Between that and last night's scare at the pub she's exhausted. I asked if she wanted to postpone the wedding, but she says she only met him a few months ago, and there was no need. I can't imagine she doesn't feel it though. I saw how close she is with her brother."

Dermot expected she would feel differently if Walter weren't still holding Grant MacDuff. Sarah wasn't going to let anything happen to him if she could help it. "Aye. She'll grieve for his sake if not for her own. I've told ye before, she's tough."

"You did." James came closer and sat in the wingback chair next to the sofa. "But I'm worried about her. She's willing to press on, but she seems...brittle. We've just reached a point where we feel almost like friends. I'm afraid she's going to retreat into her shell again."

Dermot didn't know how Sarah would react to these events either. She had been through so much in the last few months alone. She was capable of putting on a brave face when needed, but he couldn't predict her reaction when the world wasn't watching. "There are a lot of mixed emotions around her father. He abandoned Sarah's mother when she needed him, but he lived most of his life regretting it. Sarah forgave him, but she's also been clear that she doesn't want to bring the media and attention that comes with a public life to her family's doorstep. She'll have to grieve him on her own in her way."

James leaned back in his chair and sighed heavily. "I wish she'd been more prepared for all of this. I feel like we've stolen everything from her."

"You have." He said bluntly. James sent him a sharp look. Dermot held up a hand to stop James's retort. "I'm not trying to start a row, just telling the truth. We both know that if she had her way, she would finish her degree and live the rest of her life teaching somewhere and collecting songs. It may take her a while to recover from this, but she's a fighter. You just have to give her time."

"I can be patient, but I don't know how long I can hold off my uncle. He's already pressuring me about an heir." James rolled his eyes.

Dermot's teeth ground together keeping his thoughts about Walter Stuart from spilling out. "Ye'll have to find yer own way of dealing with Walter, but ye canna let him push ye around. If ye're to be king, ye have to lead."

James hmphed and took a sip of his tea. "Sarah said the same thing."

"I'm not surprised." As much as Dermot didn't want to believe in the prophecy, Dermot had to admit that Sarah might provide the counterweight to the more Machiavellian people in James's circle. She could make him a better king if that was what he was going to be.

James leaned forward holding his teacup and resting his elbows on his knees. "I'm going to need your help. Now, more than ever."

"I'm here to help her." Dermot's voice was firm. "That's the offer ye made me after The Nine chose you."

"The Nine did choose me. So, helping me helps her." James warned. They studied each other for several seconds. Walter may not have told James about their escape attempt the night before, but it was clear that James didn't entirely trust Dermot either.

"Ye've had me on your personal security detail for weeks. Do ye still not trust me?" Dermot tried to sound incredulous.

"I do, but an occasional reminder of what we're facing can't hurt. I need you to remember that I am the one protecting her from the forces that would harm us. Her safety is tied to mine, and to my success. You and Sarah may not like that. I'll admit I don't enjoy feeling like her jailer, but that is the world we live in. I need to know that we can count on your support."

Dermot took a slow breath. His eyes never left James. "I will always support what is best for Sarah."

A muscle jumped in James's jaw, but his voice didn't betray any tension when he said. "Are we agreed that going through with tomorrow's ceremony is the best thing for Sarah?"

Dermot saw what James was driving at. The wedding was going to happen. Thanks to Walter's hostage taking, that much was no longer up for debate. Now, Dermot would have to choose to support it and James, or he could break his vow to Sarah and walk away from them all. The Stuarts had invaded every corner of his life from his schooling to his career, to his mother's care. James was offering him a way out. He'd be a liar if he said the idea of finally being free of them wasn't tempting. But Sarah needed him. He'd made a vow to her. The words tasted bitter, but he said them. "We're agreed."

"Good." James took a deep breath but didn't seem to relax much. Dermot knew there was something more he wanted. He'd seen the same look enough times on Walter Stuart's face. He waited for the other shoe to drop. "I would like for you to escort Sarah to the chapel tomorrow."

Dermot's blood went cold. He straightened in his seat. "As what, some kind of sick test? Ye want to twist the knife one more time?"

"If you want to consider it a test, fine." James's irritation showed. "Or you can consider it a gesture of support for a grieving friend in a bad situation. She'll need a friendly face tomorrow."

"She has Amy and Barrett."

"But she has to hide from them." James pointed out. "You know the whole situation. She won't have to pretend with you the way she does with everyone else. She's going to need that." He set his teacup on the table and stood. Tension in every line of his body. "I know you still have feelings for each other. I know that you would change all of this if you could. I'm taking a big risk asking you to do this, but it's one I'm willing to take to help make this easier for her."

Dermot could have been angry. He could have raged at James, but more than that he was tired. Bone-deep tired from being out all night, from walking this tightrope between James and Sarah for months, from constant vigilance to protect her from threats, and machinations, and heartbreak. And he was tired of failing at it. His voice when he spoke was hoarse as if the internal screaming he'd been doing for months had roughened it. "Ye're right. I would change all of this if I could. It's not fair to any of us. Ye deserve to be loved. She deserves to be happy. We all deserve better."

"I'm sorry." James turned back to face him. He actually appeared to regret the situation. "I know it's hard for you to believe, but I am trying to find a balance between Scotland and Sarah's happiness. We do deserve better, but we may have to settle for the best we can get. Help her get through tomorrow. She's going to need it."

"And after that?" Dermot asked.

"After that, we're both going to need you. But I think we'll both understand if you decide to choose your own path." James looked resigned.

Dermot gritted his teeth. "I made a vow to her, one that is just as binding to me as any ye'll take in that church tomorrow. Aye, I'll get her there, and I'll protect ye both after. I'm not going anywhere."

CHAPTER FORTY-EIGHT

'This is not your fault.' Those had been her brother's words spoken with passion after she had tearfully explained to him how their father had died. Nothing that she had to do on her wedding day would be as hard as that conversation. Or as hard as pretending when she got back to the house that everything was fine. Nothing to see here.

James, Amy, and Barrett had been waiting in the drawing room when she returned early Friday morning. Sarah had slipped in the door hoping to get to her room unnoticed, but they had come rushing out into the hall to hug her and exclaim themselves 'so relieved' to see her. Sarah numbly accepted their hugs and answered their questions. She felt like she was walking around in a fog. Faces would loom out of a mist and say things that she was expected to respond to. She hoped she responded correctly.

Everyone seemed to accept the prescribed story. She supposed if she had to lie, sticking close to the truth made it easier. James had watched her carefully whether that was from suspicion or concern, Sarah couldn't tell. She had talked with him privately a couple of times since then, including when he had told her that her father's body had been found on Market Street at the bottom of The News Steps. His skull had been broken. No word about the bullet wound. It seemed there was little the Stuart money couldn't cover up. Of course, Sarah had done her best to seem appropriately shocked.

She hadn't mentioned anything when she saw in the newspaper on the Friday morning breakfast table that the body of Desmond Thomson had been discovered in a warehouse riddled with bullets. Thomson, nephew of a well-known gangster was likely the target in a turf war for drug trafficking. And another death was easily explained away.

If James suspected that she was anything other than surprised and grief-stricken about her father's death, he didn't say anything. Through the wedding rehearsal and elaborate dinner, the night before, he hadn't indicated that he didn't believe the story.

Now, as she sat at the foot of her bed the morning of her wedding staring across the room to where her dress was hanging on the door of the armoire, she tried to calm her nerves so that she could use her gift to check on Duff. She had done it almost every time she'd been alone since Thursday night. Of course, the day before her wedding, she had rarely been alone. There was always someone there to measure this, pluck that, or powder something else. Fortunately, Lady Anne was rarely among them. She had been surprisingly circumspect in her dealings with Sarah. But then Sarah imagined that Lady Anne was the first person Walter had told about her escape attempt, and about Rab's murder. She hadn't gloated. She had actually looked at Sarah with sympathy and offered to help where she could.

"I know what it is to lose a parent suddenly, even one that you barely knew." Lady Anne had poured Sarah a cup of coffee in the dining room the morning after. "I am sorry for your loss."

Sarah had been too numb to argue that it wouldn't have happened without the Stuarts' intervention. She simply nodded and accepted Anne's quiet offer of help.

Amy and Barrett had been harder to fool about her mood. They knew something was wrong, but what could she tell them. They had each asked her if she was getting cold feet if she was scared off by the need for security and getting whisked away with no notice. In the end she had had to tell them that she had gotten some bad news about her biological father and hope they would leave it at that. So far, it had worked.

She pulled her feet up to sit cross-legged on the bed and turned herself to face Oona's painting. Even at her darkest moments, her sister's vision of her helped give her confidence. She worked to slow her breathing. Inhale...exhale...in...out...

As it usually did, her mind's eye envisioned her sitting on the bed, then the roof of the house expanding out to show Polwarth Terrace and the Union Canal. Then higher above the neighborhood, and over the Old Town to the imposing Georgian buildings of the New Town and the grand circle of Moray Place. 'Of course,' Sarah thought. 'Walter would keep him close.' She found Duff in a bedroom on the third floor. He stood arms folded in front of a window with a view of the park and the Water of Leith. Sarah could see his mind working through ways that he could sabotage Walter Stuart's plans. She hoped he didn't try anything. She didn't want to lose him too.

A knock at his door had him turning around. The door was opened by a man in the typical dark suit of A. P. Security. A uniformed maid wheeled in a cart with what looked like breakfast. Duff thanked her and she bobbed her head before leaving. The security guard followed her out and closed the door again. When they were gone, Duff went to the cart and inspected the food. There was a full Scottish breakfast complete with black pudding, beans, and eggs. Suspicious of everything, Duff took a glass to the bathroom and filled it from the tap rather than the pitcher on the cart before returning and selecting a slice of plain toast. He carried his toast back to the window to resume his vigil.

Sarah pulled her co-walker back to herself opening her eyes in her bedroom. Soon enough she would move from this bedroom to James's. It had been too much to hope that they wouldn't have to share a room. She understood that some couples of the Stuart's class didn't. But when she had asked James about that, he wouldn't hear of it. It was one of the rare conversations where he had put his foot down. He planned to make their marriage 'a true one', not a sham of convenience with nothing more in common than producing an heir.

Looking up again at Oona's portrait. Sarah saw all the people who had made her, her mother, Duff, Granny, Amy, Barrett. She had their strength to carry with her. Then there were all those who were depending on her; Oona and Ruaraidh, now more than ever, as well as Dermot, Seonag, and Oona's girlfriend, Rachel. She didn't want to compete with Walter Stuart, but to protect those people she would. And it would start today.

There was a knock at her door. She was sure it would be Tony coming to do her hair and makeup, and probably Amy who wouldn't want to miss any of the prep. With a deep breath, Sarah rose from her seat on the bed and tightened the belt on her robe preparing for the onslaught.

***

There were only a couple of feet between them, but she might as well have been a thousand miles away. Sarah kept her face to turned to the window silently watching the city roll by. Although Dermot expected she wasn't actually seeing any of it, not with what she had seen in the last forty-eight hours, not with where they were going.

All he saw was her. She was all he'd seen since she had appeared at the top of the stairs in her wedding dress. Filmy layers of white and silver made it look like she was clothed in little more than Highland mist. His breath had caught in his chest and his heart ached.

She was impossibly beautiful in spite of the tension in her eyes. He had seen her briefly the day before. She had looked exhausted, her eyes almost vacant. Not anymore. He had no idea what had occurred to make the change, but she now seemed braced for a fight. Her eyes glowed with an icy green fire. She descended the stairs carefully and silently, as if speaking or stepping wrong might unleash a fury that burned just below the surface. For all the dress looked ethereal and serene, the woman inside it seemed strung tight as a bow string.

"Duff is already at the chapel." He'd told her as he stepped forward offering her his arm.

"I know. I had a few minutes to check before you got here." She muttered through clenched teeth as she took his arm. Her other hand swept down to lift the hem of her skirt before they stepped out the door.

Those were the last words she'd spoken. Since they'd gotten into the back of the limousine, she'd kept her gaze trained out the window. He had tried to look everywhere but at her. Looking at her hurt too much. They were nearly to the Old Town when he couldn't take the silence anymore. "Are ye sure, ye want to do this?"

She didn't turn his way, but he heard her draw in a shaky breath. "I don't see how we can do anything else."

He reached for her hand resting in her lap. *"Innis dhomh, thoir thusa air falbh.* (Tell me to take you away.) And I will."

"A bheil mise Grainne, a nis? (Am I Grainne, now?)" She asked taking him back to Donald Campbell's living room in Chapel Hill where she'd held a group of academics spellbound by telling the ancient Irish tale of Dermot and Grainne, who ran away from Fionn MacCumhail on her wedding day. Bitterness dripped from her lips. *"A Tormoid Mac na Cearda, an toit thu air falbh mi às an seo?* (Will you take me away from here?) Will all the bards sing of your bravery?"

The moment spoiled he turned to look out the window. The Royal Mile was lined with well-wishers and photographers hoping to catch a look at the soon to be Lady Caledon. Felicia had been right. Sarah had won a lot of hearts with that interview. The public was going to love her. "They'd sing of yours."

"I'm not brave." Her voice was almost a whisper. "I'm angry."

He leaned closer so that he could keep his voice low. "I know ye're angry now, and you have every right to be. But that anger is going to fade, and ye'll still be married to him."

"And you'll be safe, or at least safer." She kept her voice low, but firm. "And everyone else that I care about. Losing Rab was a wakeup call. You lost a good friend too. There's no getting out of this. So, I'm going to have to find ways to get through with as much of myself intact as I can."

What could he say to that? He could tell her that he didn't care what happened to himself, but there were all the others. And now they knew that Walter wasn't bluffing.

The car left the Royal Mile and drove through the Esplanade in front of the castle. They stopped briefly at the gatehouse, then ascended the winding cobbled drive. Just before the car pulled to a stop at the foot of Saint Margaret's Chapel Dermot gave her hand a squeeze. *"Tha gaol agam ort."*

For the first time since they'd gotten in the car, she looked at him directly. Her eyes were brimming with tears. She closed the space between them and pressed her lips to his in a fierce kiss. When she broke the kiss, she pressed her forehead to his. *"Tha gaol agam ort cuideachd. A nis agus gu siorraidh."* (I love you too. Now and forever.)

CHAPTER FORTY-NINE

The sun was bright, so bright that it was a shock to her eyes after the dim light inside the car. Despite everything, she felt lighter, at least able to face what was to come. Sarah thought about the last time she'd been to the castle. It had only been a few months ago that James had brought her there on their ill-fated date the night he'd shown her the Honours of Scotland, the night he'd kissed her, and she'd liked it. She had liked him. She still did, but he wasn't Dermot. That kiss had felt like a betrayal. If she thought a kiss was a betrayal, what was she about to do?

And yet he was right there beside her, literally. Dermot climbed out of the car. Together they turned to face the path ahead. Sarah looked up at the stone wall of the chapel rising to their left, blinking back tears and hoping that Tony had used waterproof mascara. She took a deep breath. In through her nose, out through her mouth trying to marshal the emotion that threatened to surge up from her chest. She couldn't crack, not yet.

"Alright, then?" He asked, his voice a gentle rumble.

"Not really." She'd much rather climb back into the car and ride off with him.

He wrapped her in his arms not caring who saw them. His hand was a solid calming weight on the back of her neck. His broad chest was the framework that kept her from falling apart, like the scaffolding of a building under construction.

His lips next to her ear whispered. "Ye're the strongest person I've ever met. Ye've been through tougher things than this. I know it feels like there is no other option, and maybe there isn't, but we'll get through this."

"I can't lose you." Tears clogged her throat.

"Ye never will." His arms tightened around her. "As long as my body is able, I will serve ye. My hands and my heart are yers. I pledge my life to the protection of you and the lives of yer children. Ye're not alone."

He released her and offered her his arm. Sarah kept her eyes on his as she took it. He laid his hand on top of hers and gave that half-smile that she loved so much. "Come on. MacDuff is waiting."

They walked up the path to the landing. Where the path widened there was a smattering of guests who stood outside to see the bride arrive. Duff was waiting for them at the bottom of the steps. Sarah sagged against Dermot's arm in relief at the sight of him. He looked fine, dashing even in his tuxedo. Dermot gave her hand a squeeze.

Duff opened his arms when she came near, and Sarah let go of Dermot to hug him. For a few seconds she laid her head over his heart and listened. Alive. Duff was still alive and if she did this right, he would stay that way. When he let her go, she looked into his eyes. "Are you okay?"

He studied her for a moment, as if taking an inventory. He cleared his throat and gave her a crooked smile, his eyes crinkling at the corners. "I'm better now that I've seen you."

"That's not what I asked." She said without heat.

"I'm alright. I haven't been treated badly."

"Good. Did he tell you when he's going to release you?" They turned toward the steps. She took Duff's arm.

He shook his head. "Not exactly, but I'm not sure I want to leave with you in their control."

"No, you need to get out of here as soon as you can." They walked up the steps to the courtyard outside of the chapel. Dermot followed behind them at a respectful distance giving them time to talk.

"Then I'll be gone as soon as I can shake these two." He tilted his head slightly to the two suited security guards who flanked them. Sarah had been so happy to see him that she hadn't noticed them.

"So as soon as they blink, huh?" She gave his arm an affectionate squeeze.

He chuckled. "That's about right. I figure I need to pay visits to your brother and sister now."

"That's not exactly away from the Stuarts." Sarah cautioned.

"I know." His tone gave no leeway. "But I promised your father."

"You did." They reached the top of the steps to find Felicia, a photographer, and more guests and security. As the highest ground in the castle complex, there was an expansive view of the city, which was why there was also an enormous cannon placed there. For the first time in days laughter bubbled up inside her.

When Duff shot her a confused look she waved at the cannon, Mons Meg as she had learned before. Her shoulders shook. "I've heard of shotgun weddings, but this is taking it a bit far."

Duff snorted a laugh, and for a second Sarah could see the bearded drifter who had been a lonely little girl's friend, who had carved her wooden animals, and taught her to defend herself. After they shared a laugh, she told him. "I love you so much, Duff."

"I love you, Sarah-girl." Tears pooled in his eyes. He cleared his throat again and walked on. "This is not what your mama wanted for you."

"I know."

Before they got to the ramp that led into the chapel he stopped and took both her hands in his. "Promise me..." He paused searching for the words. "Promise me, that no matter how bad it gets, you won't..." he shook his head unable to finish his thought, but Sarah knew what he meant. Promise that she wouldn't take her mother's way out.

"I won't." She squeezed his hands. "There's not a lot I can control these days, but I can promise you that."

His shoulders sank in relief. He nodded silently, and he pulled her hand into the crook of his arm. "Alright then. Let's get this over with."

"Right." That summed up her feeling accurately. Still, she pasted on a smile like war paint.

Built in the twelfth century, Saint Margaret's Chapel was a small stone building on the top of the crag on which the castle was built. It was an intimate setting for a wedding, housing only about thirty people. Although the reception would be a much larger affair, they had decided to keep the ceremony small. When Sarah and Duff entered the chapel, all eyes turned to the back. Amy and Barrett sat in the front row on the bride's side. There was just enough room for Duff to join them on the bench that served as a pew. Everyone else was a Stuart friend including Walter who sat closest to the wall on the groom's side next to Henry and Anne.

James stood at the altar looking like a prince in his dress kilt. The light from the altar window was like a halo behind him. Though all eyes were on her, Sarah only had eyes for James. It wasn't out of a sense of love or even fascination, but because he was the friendliest face she saw. Her ability to keep her emotions in check depended on her keeping her focus on the task at hand. She wouldn't be able to do that if she saw Henry or Anne looking satisfied, or her friends smiling believing in the fairy tale. She would want to shout the eight-hundred-year-old walls down around them if she saw Walter Stuart's smug grin.

James for his part looked like he understood that all of this was overwhelming. His eyes were full of kindness and admiration as Duff walked her up the short aisle. His smile was genuine, that totally focused beaming smile that could make a person feel like the most important person in the world. It only made Sarah feel bad for them both. James truly cared for her and he deserved a wife who loved him.

Duff stopped just in front of the altar. He kissed her cheek and squeezed her hand before taking his seat in the first pew. James held out his hand to her, and Sarah reached for it stepping up to the altar.

"You take my breath away." He whispered.

Sarah's own breath caught in her throat.

***

Dermot stood there in the back of the chapel itching to stop it. The room was small. It wouldn't take much. Four strides and he'd be standing between them. He stood on the balls of his feet, ready to spring to action. But then what?

He'd be tackled by security, probably arrested, definitely sacked, and that was just for starters. Walter Stuart would make sure to ruin him. He would probably punish Sarah's family even further. Dermot looked at Duff, Amy, and Barrett's backs where they sat in the front row behind Sarah like honored guests, not hostages.

They took their seats on a bench in front of the altar, and the minister from the Polwarth parish church began his remarks. Dermot kept telling himself that it didn't matter. Her heart was his. Then the minister said something that caught his attention.

"James said something to me when we were discussing marriage, something that Sarah told him about the nature of love." The minister looked around the small congregation making eye contact with several people. "It was a fitting message from the American writer John Steinbeck. He wrote there are two kinds of love; the kind that lifts you up, makes you better, and the kind that clings and drains you and drags you down."

Dermot recalled Sarah telling him about the conversation she'd had with James about love. Clearly that conversation had stuck with him. The trouble is that those whose love is destructive, usually think it's the giving kind. They see what they gain from the love, but not what it takes from the object of their affection. The minister went on. "It reminded me of chapter thirteen in 1 Corinthians with which you are probably all familiar. It's one that often comes up at weddings." Again, the minister scanned the room making eye contact with people. "Love is patient, love is kind. It does not envy, it does not boast, it is not proud."

Dermot knew that they were meant for James and Sarah, but he felt each verse, and with each verse the frustration and fear that had been choking him was distilled into something finer, purer.

"It does not dishonor others, it is not self-seeking, it is not easily angered." All his fury at Walter's actions fell away. "It keeps no record of wrongs." His litany of hurts at James always being put first by their families became unimportant.

"Love does not delight in evil but rejoices with the truth. It always protects, always trusts, always hopes, always preserves." He could not let the corner that they had been backed into, the trauma of their separation dim his resolve. He had promised her that he would be her champion, her bulwark. He couldn't allow their situation to change that. He was hers. Always.

The minister raised his voice slightly for the last verse. This one seemed written just for them, and it added a spark of hope to Dermot's newfound determination. "Love never fails. But where there are prophecies, they will cease; where there are tongues, they will be stilled; where there is knowledge, it will pass away."

***

The ceremony went by in a blur. Sarah couldn't remember anything that was said by the minister, although he had talked for some time. Everything seemed distant from her in both sound and perception, like she was underwater. It reminded her of the bathtub, when her mother held her under, all the while talking, muttering, telling her how she wouldn't let them have her. But here she was, standing beside the prince, the kind that little girls are told of in fairy tales, the one that her mother had tried to warn her about.

Her breath came short, and for a moment she thought she might panic. Then James gave her hand a squeeze. She looked up into his eyes. He smiled at her, so open and caring, so hopeful and reassuring. She started to calm, still detached, still feeling somehow set apart, but her nerves eased.

They spoke the appropriate words at the expected times. All the while James's hand in hers was like a tether that kept her from slipping away. He was a solid, dependable presence holding her to the Earth. Their eyes met again when he slipped a ring on her finger. His eyes were full of love, tentative and unsure of their bond, but love, nonetheless. It reminded her that however unfair this was to her; it was unfair to James too. He was trapped as she was, and he deserved better. They both did.

When the minister grinned and told James he could kiss his bride, the barrier seemed to break. Suddenly everything around them came into high focus; the scratch of a seam in her bodice, the pinch of her toes in her shoes, the new solid platinum ring pressing against her finger.

James brushed his lips against hers, and Sarah heard the sighs of the congregation. James pulled back and grinned. Well, it was done. They were married, at least in the eyes of the law.

They turned to face the gathered people. Everyone stood and applauded. James led her down the aisle, and she found Dermot standing at the back of the chapel. He smiled the same encouraging smile that he had given her over a year ago the morning after he had rescued her from being lost in the forest. He'd saved her from herself that night, and from embarrassment the next morning. And she knew that he was there for her still.

He took a step back as they neared the end of the aisle, and James led her to the doors. The chapel doors were opened, and Dermot fell into step behind them. With James beside her and Dermot behind, Sarah felt calm. For the first time, she felt like she might be able to get through this.

CHAPTER FIFTY

After emerging from the chapel, the real wedding whirlwind began. Sarah and James were shuffled from one place to another without much of a chance to say two words to each other. They were posed and photographed, feted and fawned over, toasted and cheered. Through it all, James was solicitous of her comfort and anything she might need. He held back everyone for a few minutes after the photos so that she could catch her breath and wiggle her numb toes. He ran interference in the receiving line whenever one of Edinburgh's elite said something snooty. She did the same when anyone tried to press him about politics. He had mentioned that he wanted the day to be about the two of them, not about where they or the country were going. They each helped the other get through the day.

"Are you sure you don't want to go to the memorial?" James whispered as they swayed on the dance floor. He held her close bending his head to hers. In spite of all of the eyes that were on them, he somehow managed to make her feel as if it were just the two of them.

She didn't have to ask which memorial he meant. He had been nothing but supportive after telling her about Rab's death even suggesting that they postpone their honeymoon so that she could attend the funeral and be with her family. Sarah wasn't even sure they would want to see her. For all Ruaraidh had insisted it wasn't her fault, she couldn't help feeling responsible. "We come with a circus attached and I won't inflict that on his family at a time like this. Having to explain how I'm related would be an awkward distraction that they don't need."

"If you feel that's what is right." He rested his cheek on the top of her head. After a few beats, he bent to her ear again. This time his tone was more contemplative. "I know that this isn't what you wanted or saw for yourself. I know that I'm not him. I hope that we can make the best of things."

She couldn't look at him. If she did, she would cry. Instead, she looked out at the people scattered around the reception. Half of them were dreamily watching the bride and groom dance as if they were the fairy tale couple that the public thought they were. That was her job, her mission. She was supposed to help him sell the image. "I think we can. I'm certainly going to try."

Sarah felt his muscles relax just a fraction. "I can't tell you how relieved I am to hear you say that. I know it will take time, and I'm willing to give you time to adjust. I really do believe that we can be happy."

He sounded so hopeful, that Sarah had to look up at him. His blue eyes captured hers and for a moment she almost believed it. "I want to believe that too. If this is going to work, we have to be united, not subject to outside influences. I think together we can do great things. But not if we allow others to pull us apart."

He lifted a hand to cup her cheek, his face glowing. "Then we won't. We'll be a united front."

He bent down and kissed her. When he released her, she laid her head on his shoulder.

Across the room, through one of the double doors that led out to the hall, Sarah caught sight of Duff. He stood watching her, his hand on the handle of the outer door. His bow tie was undone and hung from his open collar. Their eyes met and held for a few heartbeats. She knew it would be some time before she saw him again. She gave him a teary smile. At last, he would be free, if only until the next time Walter needed leverage.

Another couple danced past in front of Sarah, blocking her view for only a second. But when they had moved on, Duff was gone. The fist that had been clenched around her heart since Walter had begun parading his hostages in front of her eased just a fraction. 'Please, let him be safe, at least for now.'

Given the lead-up to the wedding, Sarah was amazed that the day itself went as well as it did. There were no confrontations, no press sneaking into the reception hall, no threats from outside groups. Despite Sarah's dislike of the incredibly tight security, they had ensured that none of James's or her enemies could disrupt the big day. Even Amy hadn't been able to distract Fleming Sinclair from his post by the wedding party's table at dinner.

The reception was winding down when Henry asked Sarah to dance. "How are you doing, my dear?"

"That is a very loaded question, and this song isn't long enough for an honest answer." Sarah's tone was not unkind. "So, I'll just say that my feet hurt and I'm exhausted."

"Yes, as I recall our wedding day was a whirlwind. I think we both fell asleep as soon as we left." Henry carefully didn't acknowledge the undercurrents of coercion, death, and hostage taking. Sarah wondered if he even knew what his brother got up to in the name of their cause, or if he was as clueless as James.

"Yes, I suspect that's what I'll be doing this evening." Sarah looked over his shoulder to where Amy and Barrett were resting. They'd been having the time of their lives dancing and watching the cream of Scottish society. "Maybe after I soak my feet."

A tap on Henry's shoulder signaled that someone was cutting in. Henry moved aside to reveal Walter Stuart. If Sarah's feet didn't hurt so much, she might have kicked him, or at least stepped on his toes. Surrounded by guests, there was nothing she could do but pretend to be civil. He wrapped an arm around her waist and held her as if they danced together all the time. A smug light shone in his dark blue eyes. "You've done well today. I would never have known how supremely unhappy you are."

Sarah took in a breath and pulled her shoulders back a fraction more. She hated bullies. For a second she fantasized about smashing her fist into his face as she'd done to Ronnie Sue Corbett when she was twelve. That would make for a great tabloid headline, 'Society Wedding Ends in Bridal Beating'. They could replace 'Hillbilly Heartbreaker' with 'Brawling Bride'. The thought almost put a smile on her face.

"MacDuff has left, but don't think we can't touch him." Walter went on not waiting for a response from her. "None of your people are safe."

Sarah's gaze sharpened as their eyes met. "Seonag Sinclair is. If you've let MacDuff go, you're not likely to find him again. The U.S. government looked for him for years and didn't find him. Your threats may have gotten me to the altar, but you don't own me."

He laughed deep in his throat and executed a turn that shifted their focus so that Sarah could see where James stood near a table talking with one of the A. P. executives that she'd been introduced to earlier. "I beg to differ. I can keep you dancing to my tune for a long time to come. I've found your Achilles heel."

Sarah tilted her chin up in a show of defiance. "And what do you think that is?"

"Your heart." He smirked and tightened his arm around her waist. "You care too much for your people. They're a drag on you, and they will always be good leverage."

Sarah peeked over Walter's shoulder and caught James's eye. She lowered her gaze before swinging it back up to James in a come-hither look. Sarah shifted her focus back to Walter and smiled. "You're wrong. Caring for people is never a weakness. You wouldn't know it. You've probably never had a relationship like that. I love the family of people that I've gathered around me and they love me too. That kind of loyalty can't be bought. You might have won this battle, but you've made a tactical error. Because now, James is one of those people. I promised to care for him, and cherish him, and he promised the same for me. He loves me. And now I have all the time in the world to strengthen that bond." She slid her hand behind his collar and leaned close to his ear. With all the menace and determination of six-year-old Sarah facing down her mother's attempt to kill her, twelve-year-old Sarah swinging a fist, or even the Sarah of less than a year ago arguing with a murderer, she whispered in his ear. "I have your king in check."

Walter pulled back in surprise at the same moment that James tapped his shoulder. He spoke to Walter, but his eyes were all for Sarah. "Pardon me, Uncle. I couldn't spend one more minute away from my bride."

ACKNOWLEDGMENTS

What a journey writing this book has been. I took a break and wrote a non-series book between Thrice to Thine and this one, but it felt so good to return to Sarah and Dermot. These characters are so dear to me. Fortunately, they're dear to a lot of you as well. I can't tell you all how much it means to me to hear from readers. That is what has kept me going this year throughout all of the stress and anxiety and remote school. Every communication with a reader means the world to me.

As always, I have to thank my supportive tribe starting with the Kettle Holler Literary Society and the ladies of the Fill the Page Writers Group. My beta readers this round; Ashley, Carol, Leigh, Diane. Valerie, Jen and Dina gave me some great and useful feedback that contributed to making this book the best one I can give you.

Last but never least, I couldn't do any of this if it weren't for the unflagging support of my husband, Eric and our wonderful kids. Also, my extended family for their lifelong support.

ONCE & FUTURE SERIES

The River Maiden

Sarah MacAlpin has plenty of ghosts. Her mother mental illness plagued her early years, and her grandmother who raised her died when she was just eighteen. In spite of her difficult upbringing she's built a life for herself. One of the things that still haunts her is a song that her grandmother taught her. Growing up in the Blue Ridge mountains there were plenty of folk songs to learn, but the one Granny taught her was from her home in Scotland, in Gaelic, and unlike any other Sarah has heard.

Cauldron

Sarah's life is in shambles. Her best friend won't talk to her. The man she loves says they can't be together. She's just discovered something that destroys the main thesis of her dissertation. To top it off, she's learned that her dream fellowship in Scotland was given to her with ulterior motives by her billionaire benefactor. Sarah has to choose whether to accept the fellowship anyway and get caught up in James Stuart's web, or try to find a different path.

Thrice to Thine

After the revelations of her mother's memoir, Sarah is determined to learn everything she can about the mysterious tribe that her mother called the Auld Folk and the three "sisters" who rule them. She wants to uncover the secret that they are guarding and why it threatened her mother's happiness and her life. But their village was hidden for hundreds of years and may prove just as elusive for her. Working side by side with Dermot Sinclair, Sarah embarks on a search across the Highlands and Islands to find her people.

ABOUT THE AUTHOR

Meredith R. Stoddard writes folklore-inspired fiction from her writing shed in Virginia. She studied literature and folklore at the University of North Carolina at Chapel Hill before working as a corporate trainer and instructional designer. Her love of storytelling is inspired by years spent listening to stories at her grandmother's kitchen table. She also advocates for the preservation of traditional fiber arts and the Scottish Gaelic language.

You can also follow @M_R_Stoddard on Twitter.